Praise for Lexi
M

"I can always trust Lexi Blake's Dominants to leave me breathless...and in love. If you want sensual, exciting BDSM wrapped in an awesome love story, then look for a Lexi Blake book."
~Cherise Sinclair USA Today Bestselling author

"Lexi Blake's MASTERS AND MERCENARIES series is beautifully written and deliciously hot. She's got a real way with both action and sex. I also love the way Blake writes her gorgeous Dom heroes--they make me want to do bad, bad things. Her heroines are intelligent and gutsy ladies whose taste for submission definitely does not make them dish rags. Can't wait for the next book!"
~Angela Knight, New York Times bestselling author

"A Dom is Forever is action packed, both in the bedroom and out. Expect agents, spies, guns, killing and lots of kink as Liam goes after the mysterious Mr. Black and finds his past and his future... The action and espionage keep this story moving along quickly while the sex and kink provides a totally different type of interest. Everything is very well balanced and flows together wonderfully."
~A Night Owl "Top Pick", Terri, Night Owl Erotica

"A Dom Is Forever is everything that is good in erotic romance. The story was fast-paced and suspenseful, the characters were flawed but made me root for them every step of the way, and the hotness factor was off the charts mostly due to a bad boy Dom with a penchant for dirty talk."
~Rho, The Romance Reviews

"A good read that kept me on my toes, guessing until the big reveal, and thinking survival skills should be a must for all men."
~Chris, Night Owl Reviews

Master No

OTHER BOOKS BY LEXI BLAKE

EROTIC ROMANCE

Masters and Mercenaries
The Dom Who Loved Me
The Men With The Golden Cuffs
A Dom Is Forever
On Her Master's Secret Service
Sanctum: A Masters and Mercenaries Novella
Love and Let Die
Unconditional: A Masters and Mercenaries Novella
Dungeon Royale
Dungeon Games: A Masters and Mercenaries Novella
A View to a Thrill
Cherished: A Masters and Mercenaries Novella
You Only Love Twice
Luscious: Masters and Mercenaries~Topped
Adored: A Masters and Mercenaries Novella
Master No, *Coming August 4, 2015*
Just One Taste: Masters and Mercenaries~Topped 2, *Coming Fall 2015*
From Sanctum with Love, *Coming February 23, 2016*

Masters Of Ménage (by Shayla Black and Lexi Blake)
Their Virgin Captive
Their Virgin's Secret
Their Virgin Concubine
Their Virgin Princess
Their Virgin Hostage
Their Virgin Secretary
Their Virgin Mistress

The Perfect Gentlemen (by Shayla Black and Lexi Blake)
Scandal Never Sleeps, *Coming August 18, 2015*
Seduction in Session, *Coming January 5, 2016*

URBAN FANTASY

Thieves
Steal the Light
Steal the Day
Steal the Moon
Steal the Sun
Steal the Night
Ripper
Addict, *Coming September 22, 2015*

Master No

Masters and Mercenaries, Book 9

Lexi Blake

Master No
Masters and Mercenaries, Book 9
Lexi Blake

Published by DLZ Entertainment LLC

Copyright 2015 DLZ Entertainment LLC
Edited by Chloe Vale
ISBN: 978-1-937608-43-9

McKay-Taggart logo design by Charity Hendry

Sign up for Lexi Blake's newsletter
and be entered to win a $25 gift certificate
to the bookseller of your choice.

Join us for news, fun, and exclusive content
including free short stories.

There's a new contest every month!

Go to www.LexiBlake.net to subscribe.

ACKNOWLEDGMENTS

All books are difficult to write. Don't let anyone tell you the act of creating a story is a breeze. Putting your heart and soul on the page is always hard, but some books are more difficult than others. Master No was one of those books. Tennessee Smith was a hard nut to crack and I sometimes get cranky when I have to deal with those characters. My husband likes to call me a "method" writer. I often carry the character's emotions and moods home with me and Ten wasn't fun to live with through much of this novel. So I would like to thank my family and friends who got through my "Ten period" with tolerance and love and likely a bunch of liquor.

Thanks to my editor and all around sister from another mister— Chloe Vale and to my beta team. Riane Holt and Stormy Pate, you're the best!

And I would like to thank you, dear reader. This is summer marks my fifth year in publishing and I'm still floored every single time you pick up a book and follow me down the rabbit hole. I'm going to warn you, this particular hole is deep and sometimes a bit dark. But it you follow me to the end, I promise there will always be light.

PROLOGUE

Saudi Arabia
Eight Years Before

Tennessee Smith took a deep breath, his body aching. At least his lungs still worked. God knew his nerves were still functioning in places. They were firing off like a machine gun, shooting never-ending pain through much of his system. Not his arms though. No, his arms had gone numb long hours before, and he was fairly certain there would be some damage there. Twenty-four hours hanging from a fucking meat hook would do that to a guy. Twenty-four hours of blood and pain and torture. Twenty-four hours of hell.

"You're awake," a familiar voice said. "I told them you had the constitution of a rutting bull. They didn't believe me. They think you'll be out for another few hours, but I knew you wouldn't let me down."

Oh, but she'd let him down. Months they'd spent working together. She'd been his cover, his "wife" as he traveled through the Middle East. They'd been paired together, and though he'd hated the idea of having a partner, he'd settled into it. Hell, after a couple of times in Dawn's bed, he'd started to like having regular sex, and then he'd just plain liked her. She was sweet, treated him like he could do no wrong, always listened to his advice. He'd been the senior partner and she the helpmate. It was like the Agency had sent him a sexual partner and backup all in one super-hot, blonde package.

Over the months they'd worked together, he'd fallen into a relaxing pattern. They would move to a new city and slowly he would work his way into a position where he could start to gather the information he needed. She would talk to the wives, but beyond that, she would turn whatever place they were staying at into a home—into a place where he could relax. She would cook his favorite foods, somehow find his favorite bourbon even in Muslim countries. And she would fuck him every night.

Somewhere along the way, he'd stopped thinking about her as cover and he'd started thinking of her as his girlfriend.

He'd even bought her a ring. He'd known he would never find another woman who suited him, who understood his needs. Dawn had been the perfect wife for him.

She'd also been a double agent, and now he was in the hands of a terrorist group who wanted to know drone locations and the identity of agents in the area.

Nice.

"Go to hell, bitch."

"Oh, there's the Tennessee I knew was always hiding under the surface," Dawn said with a smirk. "I always knew there was a nasty bastard brewing there."

"And I should have known there was a traitorous bitch under your fifties housewife exterior."

Dawn simply laughed. "It worked pretty well on you. You think you're so deep, but you were probably the easiest agent I've ever worked over. You were a breeze, Smith. All you needed was a dose of constancy and you gave it all up."

She was wrong. He'd given absolutely nothing up. His trust, perhaps that had been given too quickly, but he hadn't told her anything the reports wouldn't have told her. And this torture scene wasn't going to play out the way she hoped. He'd already been worked over for hours, and he'd found a place where the pain couldn't touch him. Now it was all coming back, but he'd survived the torture. He hadn't broken and he wouldn't. He would let them cut pieces off him before he gave up his secrets.

Secrets were all he had now.

For a brief moment he'd thought he had something more. He'd actually called Jamie and talked about how to ask Dawn to marry him.

He should have asked Jamie how to get his damn hands off a meat hook. The trouble was he could barely touch the ground. His toes wouldn't quite meet the concrete. He needed something to push off of.

Or something to change the game map.

He let his head hang low as though he simply couldn't hold it up a second longer. His shoulders ached. Not more than the holes in his abdomen. Oh, these guys were smart. They cauterized the wounds. Hell, one of them had shoved an actual hot poker through his left side. Minimal bleeding, maximum pain. They'd burned the bottoms of his feet and sent electrical charges through his system that made his whole body twist and turn abnormally. He'd been sure his bones would break, but he hadn't made a sound.

He'd been well trained.

If only he'd listened to his handler about women.

"You know you're going to break, Ten," she said in a low, seductive voice.

He kept his head down. He didn't need to see her to know what she would do. She enjoyed his vulnerability. She liked being the one in charge, got off on his pain when he'd never given her anything but his devotion.

Such a fucking idiot.

He saw her shoes come into view. Red heels. He'd bought them for her in Dubai. They'd spent a day in the world's largest mall, walking from store to store, and he'd enjoyed indulging her. He'd saved every dime he'd ever made. Dawn was the first woman he'd spent more than a few nights with.

How the boys at the Agency would laugh at him. Franklin Grant would be so disappointed. The men he recruited likely wouldn't ever respect him again. Ten Smith brought down by a woman.

It would never fucking happen again, he vowed. He'd been an idiot to think he could have what Jamie had. Dawn wasn't Phoebe. Not even close. Sometime during the night he'd been forced to acknowledge that he was so fucking envious of his brother. So envious that Jamie got the girl, that everyone loved Jamie, that Jamie somehow managed to see all the same darkness and maintain his light. It was exactly why Phoebe had taken one look at the two of them and promptly fallen head over heels with Jamie, never once giving Ten a single glance. No. Not even one.

Dawn had, but he'd been too stupid to see the predator behind those soft eyes.

"They're sleeping right now, but in an hour or two, they'll be ready for another round. You don't look like you're ready, lover," she said in a low voice.

He watched, those fuck-me shoes coming ever closer. Just a little bit more.

"Won't break," he said, slurring his words only a bit more than he actually needed to. He was kind of far-gone. The meditation techniques he used only kept the pain and suffering away for so long, and he needed to be in the moment now. She was overly confident that he couldn't do any damage.

He was going to prove her wrong.

"Damn, your body was already scarred. Now you're pretty much one massive scar. It's unattractive, you know. You're quite good in bed, but I had to close my eyes and pretend you're not a monster. You're ruined. I honestly don't know how anyone looks at you after this. At least they've left your face alone."

She wasn't telling him anything he didn't know. He was scarred, his body bearing the marks of long years of abuse, neglect, and accidents. Now he had burns from electricity torture and that damn poker they'd put through his side. That would be a beauty if he managed to survive it.

"All you have to do is give my group the information they need and this will all be over, Tennessee." She'd softened her voice, and he felt her hand on his back.

He tensed but didn't move. He couldn't do anything but hurt her in this position. He wouldn't mind hurting her, but breaking a couple of bones wouldn't solve his problem. Physics. He needed height and momentum to get out of this situation, and he couldn't get it where he was.

She needed to feel safe around him. Needed to forget that a wounded predator was often at his most dangerous right before death.

He let out a shuddering breath and allowed his head to fall back.

She chuckled and traced the new scars. "Poor Ten. All you needed was a little affection from a woman and you caved. I was told you were the hardass, the mighty Ten Smith, Agency golden boy. A few kind words, some regular sex, and you're a man like the rest of them. Tell me something. Where is your meet with Taggart scheduled for?"

Shit. She was after Ian Taggart. Well, naturally. Tag was one of his latest recruits, a man who was already a damn legend due to his years with the Green Berets. Tag was working another side of this operation and they were scheduled to meet...how long had he been here? God, he couldn't remember but it couldn't be more than a night. So he was supposed to meet Tag this morning in a teashop on the edge of Riyadh.

"I'm not meeting Tag for a few days," he managed.

He bit back a scream as she pushed a finger against one of the wounds on his back.

"That's a lie, Ten. I know you're supposed to meet him some time in the next few hours. We're not far from our apartment. You wouldn't have scheduled a meet more than thirty minutes away. I've learned all your habits."

He'd kept the meetings close because he hadn't wanted to leave her for long. They were in a dangerous situation and she was his partner, his lover. He wouldn't call it love. He didn't get that dumbass grin on his face the way Jamie did, but he was fairly certain he wasn't capable of the emotion. But Dawn had been his to take care of, and that meant something to him. Or rather it had. "Tag couldn't make it this morning. He's got a meeting with a man who can lead us to an arms dealer. I told him to take it."

How long would Tag wait before he called it in? Tag was smart. He was probably the best operative Ten had ever trained. He would still likely be too late. Even if Tag called Jamie and Jamie started looking for him, there was no way they found him. The first thing Dawn had done was to remove the subcutaneous tracking devices they had both accepted. A surgeon had removed hers. She'd simply torn his back open with a knife to get his. Another scar.

No. Taggart would be too late no matter how good he was. It would take him days to get the kind of crew they would need to track and find him.

If the Agency came after him at all. More than likely they would put his name on the wall and forget Tennessee Smith ever existed. He would be one more cautionary tale told to junior operatives. Jamie would take over Ten's post and the world would keep right on turning.

If he was going to live, it was up to him. He was alone, but then he'd always been alone.

"Should I tell you what they're planning for you today?" Dawn asked.

"Nope. I like surprises." She was moving behind him. He was hyperaware, as though time was slowing and he was waiting for that one perfect moment.

"Such a liar." Her shoes thudded against the concrete. She came into his peripheral vision. Thank god he still had that. At one point his vision had been so fuzzy he would have sworn it wasn't coming back. Now the adrenaline was pumping again and he was clear. "Let me make this plain to you. I don't get paid if you don't give these assholes something to work with. Give them Taggart. He's gotten too close to their base of operations. These are men who don't like their ties to terrorism to be published. They like the dark. If you give them Taggart, I think I might be able to save you."

He was the liar?

"How much?" He had to get her in the exact right position. Everything had to be perfect or he would miss the chance. God, could he even make his body move the way he needed it to?

She stopped in front of him. Not close enough. "How much? How much are they paying me? More than the Agency did. Way more. There's a whole world out there, Tennessee. Countries are so blasé. I like to consider myself an independent woman. You know, it wasn't so bad. Like I said, you're good in bed."

He'd spent more time in Dawn's bed than any other woman. He tended to keep his relationships shallow, sexual. He forced his head up and looked at her. Beautiful. She was a stunning woman with a slender figure and nice breasts. Platinum blonde hair curled around her jawline, and he'd never seen her without perfectly done makeup. He'd thought she did it all for him, but now he could easily see it was nothing but a mask. There was nothing underneath it but greed and vanity. He hadn't loved her. He'd simply wanted what Jamie and Phoebe had. He'd been willing to lie to himself to get it.

Her shoe tapped against the floor, an impatient sound. "Tennessee, they're going to start in on your teeth this morning. They'll pull them out one by one. You don't want that. Give me what I need to satisfy them. I can introduce you to people. A man like you can make a lot of money on the open market. Hey, we could actually be a force as independent contractors. There aren't a lot of couples working."

It was all a lie, but a useful one. She still thought she could get to him, still believed her feminine wiles would work on him. "Kiss me."

The thought made his stomach churn, but it would get her where he needed her.

"Kiss you?" Her dark eyes widened.

"Kiss me and I'll tell you where Tag is. I never liked that asshole anyway." Tag was likely gone. He would be smart. He would disappear, figuring the op was blown. Still, even knowing Tag was safe, he wasn't giving this bitch anything. Not a goddamn thing.

Well, except one final gift.

Her lips curled up in a satisfied smirk. He had her. She stepped forward. "I suppose I can do that."

The minute she was close, he swung his legs back and up. Pain screamed though his body, but he did what he needed to do. He forced his legs around her throat, the strength of his thighs drawing her in.

"What!" She screamed, but it was a muffled sound.

Ten couldn't help but laugh because that sound was totally muffled by his dick, which was happily covered with heavy denim. They hadn't gotten to the ball torture he was certain would have been on the menu today. Those jeans protected him from what he was sure was a sharp set of teeth.

"You never were any good at oral, babe."

She squirmed and tried to force him off, pushing up with her hands. Exactly what he needed. He jerked his cuffed hands up and over the hook and they went tumbling down. He groaned as his body hit the concrete, but he tightened his ankles. They were both down now. If he allowed her to get up, she would go for one of the guns. The only reason she hadn't been carrying was likely his seeming helplessness.

His arms would barely move, his body overtaken with pain, and she was fighting in earnest now. It was an instinct, really. His arms wouldn't work, but he could swing his torso. If he let her go, she would alert the others and then he was done. He would either get away or end this one way or another. He wasn't getting back on the hook. He tightened his thighs to hold her in place and threw his torso as far as he could to the left.

There was a horrible crunching sound and she went still.

So much for love and marriage.

Fuck. Fuck. Fuck. He couldn't think about this now. He couldn't look at her, couldn't do anything but survive this. His body shook as he tried to get up. Nope. Still wasn't working. He was a little afraid he was going into shock.

Couldn't wait. Had to move. There was at least one gun on the desk. He'd watched the last guy drop it there, as though teasing Ten with it. Just out of reach, too far away. No salvation for you, asshole.

He caught sight of Dawn, her eyes staring up. Not a hint of light behind them.

God, he was going to throw up.

The door opened and Ten groaned.

Too weak. Too fucking weak and he hadn't even gotten a weapon. He looked around. The concrete was stained with his blood, but there was absolutely nothing he could use to end his own misery. He had no way to eliminate the possibility that Dawn had been right and he would break. He couldn't break. If he did one decent thing in his miserable, pathetic life it would be to go out of it without giving up his operatives, his country.

He'd failed even at that.

"Thought I'd find you here," a familiar voice said. "Damn, I kind of hoped you'd both been taken. Guess the princess was a double."

With shaking hands, Ten forced himself up. His arms felt like noodles, but the fact that he was no longer alone gave him a weird strength. Ian Taggart was standing in the torture chamber, a P90 across his chest and blood on the T-shirt he was wearing. He was massive and solid, and none of that muscle would protect him.

"We have to go…" No. That was wrong. It was all fucking wrong and he had to do the honorable thing. "You have to go. Leave me a gun and get the fuck out of here, Tag. There are at least four men in this place and they don't play. I can't walk. You have to leave me."

Tag snorted, a thoroughly arrogant sound. "There were seven and now there are none. Nasty bastards. They were supposed to be all about religion and shit, but they had a ton of cheap-ass Scotch up there. I guess now they know about the evils of alcohol. You look like shit, Ten."

They were dead? Tag had killed them all? "I could kiss you, you know."

"That's what all the girls say," Tag replied. He sighed. "This is probably going to hurt, buddy, but we should really leave before reinforcements get here."

Tag leaned over and he was so fucking right. It hurt like hell to have a six and a half foot monster of a man throw him over his shoulder. Ten damn near blacked out. He forced himself to stay conscious. "How did you find me?"

"Didn't. Found her. I put a tracker on that bag you bought her. She was suspicious."

"Do I want to know what she did to make you suspicious?"

"You do not, brother. But let's talk about paying me back. How about an assignment that doesn't involve the shit end of the planet?"

So she'd probably come on to Tag, likely offered herself to him at some point. While he'd been planning a future, she'd been trying to fuck his friends. Still, the sight of her dead body sent him reeling. He had to force himself not to scream out. He hadn't loved her, but she'd represented a future—something he would never have.

"I promise." He forced the words out of his mouth as Tag walked through the house toward the door. "The next time something in Europe comes up, you're my man."

"Cool," Tag said. "Tell you what, how about you send me to Paris at some point and we'll call it even. I've heard good things about this club there."

Tag and his clubs. Tag still had some expectation of finding a woman. Oh, he wouldn't call her a wife. He would call her a sub, but it was all the same really. Tag thought there was a woman out there who could handle his darkness, who could bring him into the light.

Ten had finally let go of that daydream. It had never been for him and he would remember that fact from now on. All it got him was death and betrayal. Love was for the Jamies and Phoebes of the world.

As Tag carried him out into the light of day, he finally let go and unconsciousness claimed him.

CHAPTER ONE

Outside of Monrovia, Liberia
West Africa
Present Day

Faith McDonald turned her face up to the sun and breathed in long and deep. It felt like she hadn't taken a deep breath in the last six months, hadn't taken time to acknowledge something as small as the warmth of a lovely day because her world seemed so very filled with death.

"Hey, is that an actual smile I see on your face?" a familiar voice asked.

Faith opened her eyes and couldn't help but smile at her new friend. In the last several months she'd become close to her bodyguard. Erin Argent had a mass of unruly red hair and a sweet smile that belied her incredibly sarcastic nature. Faith appreciated both. "Togar's fever broke this morning."

Togar was a young Bassa boy. His mother had died in the first wave, when it had all seemed like another day in West Africa. Ebola had reared its ugly head, but in the beginning, none of the doctors in Faith's small charity hospital had truly understood what was coming for them. Togar had lost his mother, father, and three sisters in the months that followed before falling ill himself.

She hadn't been able to deal with it. She'd kept that toddler healthy all these months and his death right at the end of the horrible tide would have potentially broken her, but this morning—this beautiful and glorious morning—she'd won one. Togar had woken weak but asking to eat.

It was the classic doctor mistake. Don't get close. Don't let them in. Fix the ones you can and let go of the rest. Triage.

She hadn't been able to do it. There were times when what she did required more than mere logic and reason. There were times when it required a win to keep going. One life saved.

Erin joined her on the front porch of the small hut she lived in while she worked at the hospital. "I'm glad to hear that. I got fond of that kid. What happens to him now that we're going home?"

Home. God, she wasn't even sure where that was anymore. At least Togar had one. "I finally located his grandmother. She's in Sierra Leone. She and her husband will be here by the end of the week. He's going to be okay."

"Because you'll make sure of it. How much did you give the grandmother?" Erin asked, suspicion in her voice.

Faith sighed. "A couple hundred bucks, but she didn't ask for it. She really was happy to find out her grandson was alive. I won't miss it, but two hundred dollars can potentially change a life here."

Erin sat back. "I get it. I really do. Hey, babe."

Faith couldn't help but smile at the newcomer. Theo. That man was hot. With close-cropped blond hair, broad shoulders, and a body that didn't appear to contain a single ounce of fat, Theodore Taggart was simply divine. He was also taken by Erin. Like totally taken. She'd caught them kissing one night. Though she was ashamed to admit it, she'd hidden and watched. She'd watched as big, manly Theo had pressed Erin against the door of her hut and inhaled her like she was more necessary than his next breath. His hands had cupped her ass, hauling her close, and she'd heard him growling at her in a low, sexy, very dominant voice.

Yeah, she was getting hot thinking about it. If the bad news was Theo had a girl, the good news was he also apparently had a twin who looked an awful lot like him.

"Hey." Theo looked perfectly comfortable with the P90 strapped to his chest. His gaze warmed as he took in his girlfriend.

His sub. That had been a shock. Erin and Theo were involved in a D/s relationship. Not in a million years would she have expected to find another D/s couple out here in Africa.

Not another. She wasn't in a relationship anymore. Her "Master" had decided she wasn't worth the trouble and dumped her via text. It wasn't that she was horribly hurt. She hadn't been that invested, but now she was at loose ends and the prospect of trying to find a good play partner was daunting.

"So I hear you're coming home with us, Doc," Theo said, leaning against the railing.

"I don't know." When Erin had made the offer, she'd practically jumped at it. Not only were Theo and Erin in the lifestyle and really pleasant to be around, they had connections to a very swanky club in Dallas. Normally Faith played in her home city of Houston for a few months during her leave, but the breakup with her old Master might make things uncomfortable.

And wouldn't a new start be amazing? She only had a few precious months before she would be back here, fighting disease and poverty and increasingly dealing with radicals who would love to take out a Western doctor. Most of the year she had the weight of the world on her shoulders, and those sweet times when she could shrug off responsibility and indulge in her submissive side were like gold.

Did she really want to waste them on all the drama that would go with going home? Not only would she have to deal with her old Master and the nastiness of the mean girl club subs there, she would have to deal with her father and sister. She knew they loved her but they also judged her. With judgey eyes. Yeah, there was a reason they kept her far from the press. She used words like judgey.

"You don't know?" Erin asked with a frown. "I thought it was all settled. You can stay with me."

"With us," Theo corrected. "Faith, you are more than welcome to stay with me and Erin. We have a new house. It's not huge, but it's certainly got enough room for you."

"What?" Erin asked, her face flushing.

Theo's lips tugged up in a sexy grin. "Surprise, love. I asked my brothers to find us a place while we're here. I didn't want you to have to go back to your sad, nondescript apartment. You'll find Case and Ian have moved us totally into our new home."

"They moved me out of my apartment?" For a second Erin sounded shocked, almost angry, but then she took a deep breath. "That's a big surprise, Theo. Maybe we should have talked about that."

He shook his head. "You know that apartment was in a dangerous part of town, and I won't have you unprotected. You'll see. This is going to work out beautifully, and now we have a place for Faith. I would hate for her to have to sleep on your couch."

"Oh, no. I couldn't impose," Faith said quickly.

"Well, now you're not," Theo replied. "Now you're helping my lovely sub and I move on to the next phase of our lives. We'll be more than happy to have you with us, and I've already talked to my contacts at Sanctum. When we touch down in Dallas, there will be a contract waiting for you."

"Seriously?" She'd heard about Sanctum. It was kind of legendary in their circles. And incredibly exclusive. "I've got to ask. If you can afford a Sanctum membership, why are you here?"

"You can afford it. Why are you here?" Theo shot back.

He used that deep, dominant voice on her and she realized she was being incredibly rude. Even part-time Doms preferred politeness. It was one of the things she liked about the lifestyle. She would never be twenty-four seven, but she deeply enjoyed patches of time where she could sink into her submissive role. "I apologize. You're correct, of course."

Erin gave her a grin. "And he totally can't afford a membership. His brother runs the place. I'm surprised Theo could afford the house."

Theo shrugged. "I'm full of surprises, baby. And you know I always give you what you need." He winked. "I'm going to pack. Our flight leaves at 0900. If you're game, I'll set up a cyber meeting with a Dom from Sanctum. He can go over all the rules and your contract. If you decide to come with us."

Theo gave them a nod and started walking toward the security office.

"You've got some time, you know," Erin said. "Three glorious weeks where we check each other for fever twice a day. It's going to be a blast."

"My dad's place in Munich is beautiful." It was outside the city, actually. Out in the Bavarian countryside. She didn't go there often but her father and sister used the place for skiing holidays. Personally, she thought a three-week quarantine of perfectly healthy people was overdone, but her father had asked her to do it and offered up a really nice check for her clinic, so she would allow him to go all over the press stating his hero doctor daughter was observing the rules. Naturally they were rules set up by freaked-out politicians who knew nothing about medicine, but they were somehow "the rules."

That was the kind of crap one put up with when one's father was a senator. God, she prayed he never ran for president.

"Thanks for inviting us along." Erin sat back, crossing her legs at the ankles and leaning her back against the solid wood of the frame. "You know, I really admire you. I can joke about the rich girl stuff, but you do good work, Doc. I'm pretty cynical about the world myself, but you're the real deal."

"I don't know about that." Faith sometimes thought she was simply making up for all the crap her father pulled. Politics was a dirty business. "And it can be hard to stay naïve out here, but I try."

"Naïve? Why would you want to be naïve?"

That was an easy question and one she'd answered long ago. "Because cynics don't change the world. Naïve people do. Naïve people aren't smart enough to know that they can't beat a disease. When wave after wave of bodies start rolling in, the naïve idiot stands there and tries to hold the line."

She wasn't smart enough to cure the thing. Her sister was the research genius. Faith thought of herself as a private while Hope was a general.

Erin's lips turned up slightly. "It really is a war. I didn't get that until I saw it myself. You're a good soldier, Doc."

That was probably the highest compliment Erin could give. "Thanks, and please call me Faith."

"I will. Besides, it looks like we're going to be roomies for a while."

"You seemed a bit irritated with Theo."

"Only because he's a high-handed asshat who really should involve me in the decision-making process," Erin began.

"Is there trouble between the two of you?" She didn't like the thought. She kind of liked Erin and Theo being solid. She needed a couple to aspire to.

Erin turned thoughtful. "Always, but…let's just say I've learned a lot here."

Africa could do that to a person. It was why she kept coming back. She'd learned a lot about herself, about kindness in the face of adversity. About death and life. "Is it wrong that I really want to go to Sanctum?"

"Why would it be wrong?"

She was getting maudlin. "I don't know. I guess I'm going into it knowing it's only a short-term relationship. I want to relax."

"You want to have sex," Erin corrected. "And there's absolutely nothing wrong with that. Faith, there's not a thing wrong with asking for what you need. You're surrounded by death and misery nine months out of the year. Party the rest of the time. You deserve it. Anyone who says otherwise can bite my ass. You don't have a relationship right now so that frees you up to do as you please. If doing some super-hot Dom pleases you, then go for it."

She sighed. "Will he be super hot?"

"Oh, he'll be hot. I can promise you that."

"Might he look somewhat like your Dom?"

It seemed to take Erin a moment to understand, and then her eyes went wide. "Oh, no. No. You don't want Case. Jeez. Case acts like a five-year-old most of the time and I swear the dude needs a maid service. No. I've got the perfect Dom in mind. But you should know, he's definitely not a forever kind of guy."

She wasn't looking for that. She was looking for some fun, for some relaxation, and maybe an orgasm or two. "Do I get a choice?"

"Absolutely. Spend the next few weeks talking to Master T and we'll see how it goes from there. You're going to like it at Sanctum." Erin stood and brushed off her cargo pants. She always dressed in a utilitarian fashion. "And Faith, you should know that I'll make sure you're okay."

"What?"

"At Sanctum, I mean. Whatever happens, you're going to be okay. See you in the morning. I've got a few things to sort out with my Master." Erin strode off in the same direction Theo had walked.

And Faith made a decision. It didn't matter. Erin was right. Her life was her own and she wasn't going to let petty rules keep her from something she needed. Sanctum would be private. Her business wouldn't get out in the press and embarrass her father. She would be safe to indulge, and when the time came to head to her annual birthday party in the Caymans, maybe she would have a handsome Dom on her arm.

It was only for a while. She wouldn't get what Erin had obviously found, but that was all right, too. Not everyone found true love. She wasn't expecting that at all. She wanted a little companionship.

Some really good sex would be amazing, too.

Mostly she wanted some peace. That was really all she could ask for.

* * * *

Tennessee Smith sat in the cool conference room and stared at the file. Faith. What a fucking joke. Hank McDonald had named his daughters Faith and Hope. Very likely the bastard thought having daughters named after virtues helped him with the voting public. It certainly hadn't been because the man placed any value at all in either word.

Two sisters. One was polished and perfect looking. In the photo he held, Hope McDonald was dressed in a tailored Chanel suit. Everything from her hair to her manicured nails, right down to the heels she wore screamed money and power. In the shot he had of Faith, she looked weary. No makeup, scrubs, her hair frazzled like it hadn't seen conditioner in a few days. But the light hit her skin making it luminous. Her eyes seemed to stare out as though asking for something from him.

What did she need?

"So I dug up some interesting information on Hope McDonald." Michael Malone passed him a file folder from across the table.

"You dug it up?" Hutch huffed and rolled his eyes.

"Well, I compiled it and did the actual analysis. You just gave me a bunch of websites to click on, and I'm pretty sure one of them infected my laptop."

"Nah, that was from all the porn," Hutch shot back.

"Boys, do I look like I need to listen to this argument?" Ten gave

27

his men a stare guaranteed to have them falling in line.

He might not be a CIA agent anymore. He might have been disavowed. Hell, there was probably a price on his head, but he was still in charge of his damn team. Well, the ones who had been dumb enough to follow him.

At least he still had them. It was funny how knowing they'd been willing to give up their careers had made the whole "US government turning against him" thing easier to swallow. If he was half a man he would send them all away, but he'd proven time and time again what a ruthless son of a bitch he was. He needed them. And he needed Taggart.

The conference room door opened and Big Tag strode in followed by his half brother, Case. Any issues the two had in the beginning seemed to be resolved, and things had gone exactly the way Ten had always feared they would.

Case Taggart was Big Tag's man now, the way his twin Theo was. It was precisely the reason Ten hadn't mentioned them to Tag in the first place. He'd needed time to get two of the best soldiers he'd ever recruited loyal to him. He should have known in the end it wouldn't matter. Blood won out. It always did.

In the end though, he knew every man here would be Tag's, and that was all right.

After all, Tennessee Smith was fairly certain he wouldn't come out of this mission alive.

"Seriously? How am I supposed to take you seriously when you're wearing a baby?" Ten asked. The six and a half foot pain in Ten's ass was wearing something he'd only recently learned was called a sling. It was pink and covered Tag's chest in a large swath. There was also a tiny baby hand poking out of the top, as though the infant was reaching for her father.

Wanted. Kala or Kenzie…whichever kid it was…that baby was wanted. That child got carried around and cuddled close. No one had ever tossed her away like a piece of garbage.

Tag put a big hand on the sling as he lowered himself into the conference room chair. "She's fussy. When Kenzie's fussy, she likes to be in the sling. You're lucky because Kala's hanging off her mama's boob right now or I would likely have them both. What can I say? They like their dad."

Their dad had turned this whole office into a freaking day care center so he didn't have to place his precious babies out in the world. He could tell Big Tag was going to be a helicopter parent. An Apache attack helicopter parent.

"So are we a go? Did your girl do her job?" It was the question he'd wanted answered for weeks.

Erin Argent and Theo Taggart had been sent undercover months ago. Their mission—to get Faith McDonald to trust them. To bring her back to Sanctum. They'd been hired on as bodyguards for the small clinic Faith ran in Liberia. Now they were stuck in quarantine because they'd done their job in the middle of the worst urban Ebola outbreak in history.

Tag sat back in his chair. "Erin says we're a go. By the time they land in Munich, I'll have sent Faith a temporary contract and information about you. You're going to be her contact with Sanctum and you'll be her escort the first few nights here. I suggest you find some of that charm you used to have and get her interested before she steps foot in the club."

"Why not explain to her that I'm the only Dom available?"

"Because she understands the way things work and that would be highly suspicious. I don't want to scare her off. We need to figure out what her type is and go from there. All Erin will tell me is she doesn't like douchebags. Unfortunately for her, that's all I have here."

In the past such sarcasm from Tag would have gotten Ten's middle finger to make an appearance, but he couldn't work up the will to care anymore. He only cared about one thing now and that was bringing down Hank McDonald. With Phoebe safely and happily married to Jesse Murdoch, he could focus all of his attention on burning the man who'd burned him. More importantly, Hank McDonald was the man responsible for getting Jamie Grant killed.

James. His brother, not by blood but by choice. Jamie and Phoebe had been his only family in the world, and McDonald had sold out Jamie's unit, given them over to be tortured by the enemy.

McDonald was going to pay, and Ten didn't care how many virtuously named daughters he had to go through to do it.

"So what you're saying is if she comes to Sanctum and has zero interest in me, I have to let her find another Dom."

"Yeah," Tag replied. "I put in the no-caveman-calling-dibs rule years ago. I thought we'd spent months on training, man. What about safe, sane, and most importantly consensual do you not get?"

Case leaned forward. "Look, according to Erin, Faith is pretty attracted to Theo. Ian and I have been talking and I'll take a crash course in D/s over the next couple of weeks. If you can't get her to bite, maybe I'll be able to."

She was attracted to Theo? Well, it wasn't so surprising. Theo was young and strong and he didn't have a body covered in horrific scars. Theo was an open-hearted idiot who smiled for the sake of smiling. Naturally she would want Theo.

"This is my op." And he didn't want anyone else messing with it. If he couldn't get into Faith McDonald's bed, he couldn't get on to that island and into her daddy's house. All his intelligence pointed to the information he needed being in that house.

Faith McDonald spent her birthday at her father's vacation home in the Caymans. She'd always taken a boyfriend with her. He was going to be that boyfriend.

Not boyfriend. Dom. He was going to be her Dom.

He was also going to be the man who betrayed her because he would use her to bring her father's house of cards down all around her.

"It's always your op, Ten," Tag said in the most patient voice Ten had ever heard him use. "But if she doesn't want you, you're not going to force her."

He might. There were nights lately when he thought about simply putting a gun to Faith's head and seeing if Daddy loved his baby girl. The problem was Ten was fairly certain McDonald didn't really love anything beyond money and power. "I'll make her want me."

He could summon up some charm. It wasn't like it ever came easy to him in the first place. He'd learned it. If there was one thing he was good at doing, it was adapting. He'd figured it out at a tender age. When being rambunctious got his arm broken by a particularly brutal foster parent, he learned to be quiet and not make waves. When he found out shooting rifles was one of his kind guardian's obsessions, he'd become a marksman. As a teenager, he'd learned women were a damn good way to forget his troubles, so he studied and figured out how to please them.

He could wrap Faith around his little finger if he wanted to. After all, she identified as a submissive. She wanted to please the people around her according to Tag. The rich girl needed praise, it appeared.

She would get it. Eventually. The beautiful thing about D/s was it put him in charge. He would control Faith McDonald. He would train her to obey him. Oh, she would give him trouble in the end, but he would be ready for that, too. He stared down at her photograph. Unlike her sister, Hope, there were no press photos of Faith. Hope stood by her father in many of his publicity photos, but the shots they had of Faith were all casual, taken by Theo or Erin in Africa. Faith wore scrubs when she wasn't rocking a hazmat suit. Her dark hair was almost always back in a utilitarian ponytail, and if the woman knew what makeup was, he couldn't tell.

So why did she practically glow? She wasn't wearing a stitch of makeup and he was pretty sure he'd never seen a prettier woman. Not glamorous. There wasn't anything artificial about her. Or so she wanted people to think. He would withhold judgment. The good news was he likely wouldn't mind fucking her, which was good because fucking her was absolutely integral to the op. A woman who looked like that might show some loyalty to the man in her bed.

Until she realized the man in her bed was going to tear her world apart.

"What do we know about McDonald's movements?" He didn't like thinking about Faith. She was a tool, a means to an end. She wouldn't be the first woman he'd screwed to complete a mission, but she might be the most innocent looking.

Hutch had his ever-present laptop out. Ten could swear the machine was surgically attached to Hutch. "He's back in DC, but several members of his senior staff are currently in Pakistan. According to his office, they're gathering intelligence on the situation in the Middle East."

Ten didn't believe that for a second. Any intelligence McDonald gathered would be to enrich his own bank accounts. "My contacts say McDonald's looking for new clients. Since we took out Hani al Fareed, McDonald's money supply dried up. I've been talking to Ibrahim al Fareed."

"Any way we can convince Ibrahim to go undercover?" Tag asked.

Ten shook his head. The al Fareed brothers had gotten tangled in one of McDonald's plots. Hani had been working with radicals and experimenting on US servicemen in order to create sleepers to send back to the States. His brother, Ibrahim, had been horrified at Hani's activities. After Hani had been killed, it had been Ibrahim who took Ten in and allowed him to learn about the world Hani had chosen. It was a nasty underbelly filled with radicalized sons of Islam and money-hungry politicians who didn't mind blowing up parts of the world for fun and profit. And corporations. He'd been shocked at how many were thriving because the world was focused on groups like ISIS and Boko Haram. Terror was quite profitable, Ten had discovered.

"I won't bring Ibrahim into this any further than I already have. He's a moderate, and beyond that, he's not trained to handle this. He's an intellectual." With three happy wives and fourteen curious children. Every member of that family had accepted Ten into their home and made him feel welcome. He wouldn't bring them into danger now. "I've been talking to some of my contacts and also to Damon."

Damon Knight ran the European branch of McKay-Taggart Security Services. He was former MI6, and his contacts ran deep.

Tag nodded and the squirmy thing wrapped around his chest seemed to have gone to sleep. "Good. I talked to Damon about embedding a couple of his men on the island. He's sent the new guy and Brody in. They've taken jobs at a resort close to McDonald's compound."

"McDonald spends a ton of time at that resort. He plays golf there often and he uses them for catering." Case frowned. "I guess crime really pays. I want a personal chef."

"Yeah, you really need that, brother. You need gourmet chicken strips and hot wings." Tag liked to needle his siblings, but he was right on this one.

"You eat like a five-year-old." If Case knew how to do anything in a kitchen beyond warm up frozen food, Ten would happily eat his own shoe.

He, on the other hand, had learned to cook at a young age. Another way to please the people around him so they might keep him for a few months. Survival tactics. He was damn good at those.

32

He bet Faith hadn't had a decent meal in months. Unless her father provided them with a personal chef during their quarantine.

"So we're set in the Caymans. I wish we could have gotten someone in the actual house," Ten mused.

Case shook his head. "That's a no-go, boss. McDonald's very careful about employees. Everyone's local. I think he thinks he can buy their loyalty more easily. Guests are a different matter. Expect a few for the week you'll be there. Faith's sister will be invited. Likely a few of her friends."

"And the senator?"

Tag was rocking back and forth in his seat. "He'll show. He might not be there the entire time. Your best bet to get the data is before he shows. He'll have staff and security with him. Have we had any luck doing that computer thing to him?"

Hutch rolled his eyes. "Seriously? Does anyone know what I do?"

"You eat a lot of candy and make sarcastic remarks. You're a lot like all the other computer geeks," Tag replied.

"Yeah, but I'm cuter." Hutch grinned. "So I've been trying to infect the senator's computer with a virus that will allow me to control his system."

"Like Citadel?" Citadel was malicious software used by cyber criminals everywhere. Unlike Ian, Ten actually liked to try to keep up with his techs. They tended to speak a language he didn't understand most of the time. He hated to feel like he was behind, so he read all the reports the Agency sent out on the latest ways technology could fuck a person over. Well, he had before he'd gotten the boot.

"Citadel is child's play compared to what Chelsea and I came up with. If we put this sweet piece of malware out on the Dark Web, we could charge at least twice what Citadel goes for," Hutch bragged. "Not that we would because that would make us criminals. And I don't do that anymore."

Sure he didn't.

"Could someone explain what Citadel is to those of us who don't spend all our time in cyberspace?" Tag asked.

"Citadel is USDA prime malware," Hutch began. "It's basically a virus, but it doesn't shut your computer down. It's so much sweeter. It allows someone like me to take control of your system without you ever knowing I'm there. You move along like it's just another ordinary day, but your computer is now a zombie, controlled by me."

"Because you want to know what porn I watch?" Case looked at Hutch like what he was saying was no big deal.

"No, because he'll steal every password you have and drain your accounts. He can make it look like he's you," Ten pointed out. It was exactly what he needed.

"Dude, I'm not stupid enough to click on the places where I'll get infected," Case groused.

Hutch leaned over and started typing. "Give me a sec, Little Tag."

"Wait. When the hell did I become Little Tag?" There was the sound of a chime and Case pulled out his cell phone. His eyes widened as he looked at the screen. "What? What the fuck? This is a banking alert. It says I pulled five hundred dollars out of my account."

Hutch sat back, reaching for a licorice stick like a satisfied dude having a cigarette after sex. "You probably shouldn't have gone to that monster truck site."

"Son of a…" Case started to stand up.

"Sit down," Tag barked. "He's putting it back now. How many of us?"

Hutch was already playing on the keyboard again. "You'll find it all detailed in the report I sent. I thought it would be a good way to probe the team's weaknesses. Oddly enough, you and Charlie were among the ones I couldn't get to bite. You've got some serious protections on your systems. Chelsea?"

Tag nodded. "Yes. Please tell me you got Adam. Please. It will do my soul good."

"No can do, boss. Adam's system is secure, but I managed to get both Jake and Li with puppy videos. I'm not kidding you. I tried porn on them but nothing worked until I came up with videos of baby animals. Porn totally worked on Erin. That girl likes some seriously nasty shit, if you know what I mean."

If he allowed it, Hutch would go on all day. "Tell me you got Faith McDonald at least."

"There's your five hundred back. And you should really save more money than that. It's pathetic." He turned back to Ten. "Of course I got her. I've had her for days."

"And you didn't bother to mention this to me until now?" He was well aware he'd gone ice cold.

"She hasn't done anything interesting yet. And her Internet is spotty. I'll write a report when she does anything interesting." If Hutch was put off by the chill in his tone, he didn't show it.

Sometimes Ten thought he'd been too easy on his team. "I want to know everything. How did you get her?"

Hutch's eyes came up, looking thoughtfully at Ten. "Shopping for cheap medical supplies. I took her to an actual website I'd already infected and forced her to download an app to order. Once the app was active on her system, I was in and she got cheap latex gloves and surgical tape. I've got copies of her e-mails. It looks like her last Dom dumped her for a more submissive thing. I wouldn't ask Faith to mop your floors. I don't think she's that kind of sub."

"I thought you didn't know much about her." He found he didn't like the idea of Hutch getting such a personal look at Faith McDonald when all he had was a few reports from Erin and a folder detailing Faith's life.

Hutch shrugged in a way that let Ten know Hutch was more invested than he would like to be. "I find her interesting. I kind of wonder if it's right to use her like this."

Hutch was asking him that? Hutch, the former black hat hacker. Hutch, who had hacked literally thousands of people's lives? Hutch, who would likely be in jail if the Agency hadn't recruited him. "Do I need to remind you how many people died because of her father? They didn't simply die. They were tortured in horrific ways. Hank McDonald doesn't give a shit about the Geneva Conventions. He cares about money and if we don't shut him down, more of our servicemen and women are going to fall to his greed."

"We have no reason to believe she knows anything about her father's dealings," Hutch argued.

"We do know she's the only way in," Tag said, his voice deep with authority. "Do you think I didn't look at every angle? When Ten brought me this plan and asked to use my people, I analyzed it and found every single hole I could. This is the best plan of action, and Ten will ensure the girl doesn't get hurt. Well, physically hurt. It isn't our fault she was born the daughter of a monster."

"If we don't act, those deaths are on us." Case closed the file in front of him. "We'll all watch out for her. I know Theo really likes her."

It seemed Faith was good at finding friends. For Ten it was suspicious. No one was that good, that pure. Especially no little rich girl. He was already certain Hope McDonald was dirty. She was a doctor as well, though she hadn't gone the same route as her sister. Hope worked for a large pharmaceutical company. And there were hints she liked to test in non-FDA approved ways.

So why would Faith be different?

"I want everything you have on her. I want to read her e-mails. You said she recently broke up with her lover?" He needed to know everything about her. Not because he wanted to. No. His fascination with her was all about the op and nothing more.

"The dude was a dickwad who wanted a maid more than a lover," Malone said. "Faith knew him before he got into the lifestyle. He was a doctor she knew from her residency at a Houston hospital. They were lovers, though it seemed to be more of a thing of convenience than true love. After she started going to Africa on a regular basis, they got together when she was home. She's the one who got him into the lifestyle, though he seemed to take to it more fully than she did."

"How so?" From what he could tell, Faith was fairly into the lifestyle. She had a few months off every year and she spent them practicing D/s with her chosen Dom.

"Faith seems to use D/s almost as a relaxation tool." Once again it annoyed Ten that Hutch seemed to know more about her than he did. Hutch continued. "The way she describes it in her e-mails to friends is that she has to make so many decisions in her work, she prefers to leave it to someone else when she's home. But her ex took it further. He now has a twenty-four seven slave who lives with him and is dependent on him for her every decision. Faith wouldn't have been able to live like that."

Ten was used to Big Tag's version of D/s, which was really nothing more than a side dish while the relationship was the entrée. While Big Tag's wife submitted to him sexually, she would likely shoot his ass if he really ordered her around.

His life would be easier if he could have more control over Faith.

She wanted him to make the decisions about things like where they would eat and what they would do, but he wanted to ensure she obeyed him when the bullets started flying.

"Forward me everything you have on her including her e-mails, and watch her accounts. Now that she's out of Liberia, I want her watched constantly. If she's got any contact with her father, I want to know about it." Faith was the key. She was the one who would get him on the inside. Ten stood up. "We've got a couple of weeks. We'll watch her and continue to try to get some kind of line on McDonald. He seems to like the ladies. Let's see if we can find a pro who wouldn't mind planting a couple of bugs for us."

Case nodded. "I'll call some people I know in DC. That could work."

"Good. I'll be in my office if anyone needs me." He took his papers and stepped out.

McKay-Taggart made him nervous. The minute he stepped out of any room there was always someone waiting to wave at him. This time it was Grace, a lovely redhead who was married to Tag's younger brother, Sean. She was the receptionist and general office manager at McKay-Taggart. She held the keys to the kingdom. No client got through without being vetted by Grace Taggart.

"Hey, Ten. How are you today?"

"Good." He always kept his answers short and sweet with her. It was funny because he used to flirt with every woman at Langley, but the women of McKay-Taggart were different. If he showed any weakness at all to them, he would find himself at some family dinner or set up on a horrifying blind date because these were women who took an interest in a single man, and Ten wasn't talking about his penis. These women wanted every damn man alive to be some sort of family member, and he didn't play that way.

"Any chance you can join us at Top tomorrow night? Sean wants to experiment with lamb lollipops."

Actually that sounded delicious, but he knew if he went there wouldn't just be food. There would be bonding and family stuff. "Thanks but I have a lot of work to do, Grace."

"I'll work on him." His sister, Phoebe Murdoch, threaded an arm around his waist.

He couldn't hold back with her. Phoebe was the one person on earth who sort of belonged to him. Not really, because she was married now, but she was the only one who remembered Jamie the way he was when they were young—when it was just him and Jamie and Phoebe. God, he missed his brother.

His grief felt as sharp today as it had the day he'd found Jamie's body.

"How's accounting, sis?" He didn't need to bring Phoebe into his misery. She'd finally moved on. She was happy with Jesse and they were talking about babies. She teased him about being Uncle Ten.

He couldn't tell her that he would be long gone by then. If this mission didn't kill him, then he would disappear. He didn't belong in anyone's white picket fence happily ever after.

"It's good. I enjoy it, though I have been keeping up with your endeavor. You know I think I should be in on this."

No way. He'd already had a brother-to-husband talk with Jesse about this very thing. "You know you're no longer a field agent."

She walked with him toward his office, her easy affection one of the few comforts he could accept. "I know that. The crazy thing is I don't really miss it. I actually am perfectly happy with accounting and payroll. But that doesn't mean I'm not watching out for you. I want you to be careful."

"I always am." He was careful to get the job done. He wasn't always so careful with his life. The job was more important.

He started down the hall that led to the tiny thing Big Tag called an office. It was insulting, but then he wasn't here for long.

"I'm serious," Phoebe insisted. "McDonald is dangerous. Look, I get that everything is perfectly safe as long as you're at Sanctum, but once you hit the islands, you're on his terms. I would feel better if I went in with you instead of Erin."

"No." He didn't feel the need for any more explanation than that. "No" so perfectly summed up how he felt.

They stopped outside his office door. Phoebe gave him a frown that could freeze the balls off a man. "No? I think some form of debate is called for."

Fine. He could give it to her. "Are you and Jesse going to stop having unprotected sex any time soon?"

She sighed. "If it means making sure you're safe, then yes, Ten."

He stopped. "I don't like the sound of that."

She turned and faced him. His sister never backed down, and he should have remembered that. "I don't care what you like the sound of. You need to understand that I know what you're doing and I won't have it."

"What am I doing?"

"You're planning on doing anything you have to do to avenge Jamie, and I'm worried that if that includes sacrificing yourself, you'll do it. I can't let that happen. I owe to it our dad and to Jamie to make sure you're safe."

This was the last thing he wanted to talk about, but he couldn't fight Phoebe. He could ignore everyone in the whole damn world with the singular exception of her. The petite woman in front of him was his lone remaining link to the world. Sometimes—and he wasn't exactly proud of this fact—but sometimes he resented her for keeping him here. "I'll be careful, Phoebe. I promise. I'm going to be okay. Once I deal with McDonald, I'll handle my own situation. I'll find a way to make it right."

Meaning he would find a way to make it safe for him to live his life again. He was sure Phoebe thought after he handled this that there would be some way for him to come back and live in a world of backyard barbecues and football watching parties. A world where he was Uncle Ten and he went into some semi-safe job every day and got old and fat and happy.

Phoebe went up on her toes and kissed his cheek. "See that you do. I'll be back to pick at you until you agree to come to dinner."

She turned on her kitten heels and strode away. She'd made it halfway down the hall when a door came open and a muscular arm shot out, dragging her in. Ten could hear Jesse Murdoch's low laugh and knew that his sister was about to be taken care of.

The door to the conference room next to him opened. One of the daycare workers smiled as she walked out, a baby on her hip.

Yeah that never happened at the Agency either.

He ran into his office and closed the door behind him. He wasn't about to get attached to any of those kids no matter how cute they were. He wasn't getting involved with them any more than he wanted to get cozy with the women.

He wouldn't be here in a few months. It was best he left as little of himself behind here as possible. He'd learned early on to keep his suitcase packed because he never knew when he was going to be leaving. This time he did, and he wasn't going to hurt anyone when he went.

He sat down at his desk and the photo of Faith McDonald slipped from his grip and onto the tabletop.

Well, maybe one person. He'd hurt her, but there wasn't any help for it.

With a long sigh, he turned on his laptop and started writing an introductory letter to his first—and only—submissive.

CHAPTER TWO

*H*ello. *How was your flight?*

Faith couldn't help but get a thrill as she looked at the message. There were three messages waiting for her on her laptop. One from her dad, one from the clinic, but it was the one from Master T that made her heart speed up in her chest. She looked at the delivery time. It was only ten minutes before. He might still be at his computer.

She hesitated. This was crazy. She was starting a relationship with a man she knew next to nothing about except that he'd passed a background check and her friends liked him.

And he was gorgeous. That shouldn't matter. That didn't matter. Not really. But damn the man was hot in his pictures.

She could still get out of this. Was it a good idea to get close to a man the submissives at his home club called Master No? Erin had passed on that tidbit of information. Apparently Timothy Graham was a bit of a hardass when he wanted to be.

Still, she found herself typing.

It was nice, Sir. And hello to you. She winced as she pressed the return button. She didn't want to get out of this. This might be the first positive step she'd taken in forever. She'd taken back her professional life after what had happened in Ghana, but she'd allowed herself to stay stagnant in her personal life. Roger had been predictable and that was what she'd liked about him. He understood her. She understood him. Boring and yet comfortable. Like a pair of sweatpants.

She wanted her love life to be better than a pair of sweatpants.

I'm glad your flight made it in on time. I thought I would check on you. I sent you an e-mail. Did you get the contract?

The Sanctum contract. The one that basically gave large portions of her life over to this man. Of course, it was only a piece of paper. It was the symbol of it all that was making her stomach flutter with anticipation. Or anxiety. Maybe a bit of both. *I did. I've read it over. I would like to talk to you about some of the points of the contract when you have time.*

Of course, but for tonight, you get some sleep. You've had a long day. Write me when you wake up.

I don't want to disturb you if you're sleeping, Sir. Why don't you give me a good time to contact you?

I'm always awake. Contact me when you're ready. Good night, Faith.

Good night, Sir.

She sat back and read through the brief correspondence again. Master T. Her Sir. He'd known when she was scheduled to get in and he'd waited to welcome her back to the Western world.

"Hey, we're going to head to bed. I'm afraid I'm going to be horrifically jetlagged tomorrow. You need anything?" Erin asked as she poked her head through the open doorway.

She turned and smiled. "No, I'm good."

Erin frowned. "What happened? That's not a smile I've seen on you before."

She stopped herself from covering her face in a deeply girlish gesture. God, she needed to get a handle on this. Just because the man was hot—okay super hot, like Hollywood hot—and polite didn't mean she should lose IQ points when she thought about him. She was a doctor. She'd been to medical school and done her residency and ran a clinic. She was not a giggling schoolgirl. "I talked to Master T."

Erin grinned and walked through the door, setting herself on the bed across from Faith. "Seriously? He already called you. Eager beaver."

So she did kind of sound like a schoolgirl. She had to admit it was refreshing. It was far from the doom and gloom of the last few months. Months? She'd been doom and gloom for years now that she thought about it. It was kind of nice to have this bubbly feeling. She was thirty-two years old and it was fun to feel sixteen again. "He sent me an instant message. But I thought it was kind of sweet that he remembered when I was getting in. You know him, right?"

"Yeah. I work with him, though not specifically with him. Usually I work with a man named Liam. He's like my big brother. Well, if my brother was Irish and nice and had the coolest wife in the world."

"Don't you have a bunch of brothers?"

Her smile faded a bit. "Yeah, three. Trust me. Li is way cooler than my brothers. The place where I work…it's like a family. It's the best place I've ever been. I joke a lot. I know I have a dark sense of humor, but I really love where I work. I have to warn you though. Your man can be a dickwad. And he thinks he's the shit at covert ops, but we took his ass down."

"What?" Covert ops? He was supposed to work for a security firm not the freaking CIA. God, that was the last thing she wanted to get involved in.

Erin shook her head. "Sorry. Every now and then Master T and Big Tag play war games. A couple months back T decided to invade the office and dude got his ass kicked. Oh, he got some good licks in on Tag, but he lost and now Big Tag gets to punch him at random."

She felt her jaw drop. "What?"

"Sometimes I forget you're a civvie, Doc. It's all fun and games. Well, and broken noses. But hey, that's just cartilage and I personally think T was too pretty before Tag broke his nose." She leaned in. "I kind of wish someone would break Theo's nose. He's so fucking pretty I find it intimidating. He's even prettier without all those clothes. It's not fair."

Faith was getting into a world that she didn't understand. But maybe that was all right. She'd spent all her time around serious scholars and super-ambitious people. They never broke each other's

43

noses. Ever. Of course, most of the super-ambitious people she'd spent her life around hadn't looked like Master T or Theo. And most of them wouldn't have remembered when her flight was supposed to land and wouldn't have stayed by the computer to make sure she'd gotten in. They had important things to do.

Roger had only paid attention to her in clubs. He wouldn't have called or contacted her during this isolation period.

"I think a lot about what Master T will look like naked," she confessed. She'd seen pictures of him. After she'd agreed to the Sanctum membership and talked to a man named Kai, who apparently was the club psychologist, she'd been sent a couple of photos of Master T along with a very sweet letter about T's philosophy of D/s. There was no one way to practice and play, so it was important that their expectations be somewhat similar. T seemed pleasant. His philosophy centered on giving a submissive what she needed. He'd written that "while giving a submissive the support and discipline she requires to enjoy our time together, I receive the positive impact of aiding in a sub's journey."

She really liked that he'd thought about why he was attracted to the lifestyle. It made her realize she hadn't thought much about it beyond that she enjoyed the relaxing aspect of giving up control.

"I would bet Master T looks pretty good au naturel," Erin said. "He looks nice in a set of leathers. He's got a ton of scars though. Like a lot of us, he's taken some damage. Is that going to bother you?"

Scars merely proved the body and soul were stronger than they looked. Scars didn't bother her at all. "I think he'll be lovely."

Erin sighed and reached out, patting her hand. "He is and you're in trouble, girl. I know that look."

"Because you see it in the mirror?"

"I kind of wish I didn't."

"Why? You and Theo are so good together." Most of the time, Erin and Theo seemed in perfect synch. There had been a few instances when they hadn't known she was watching them when they'd seemed to fight. Erin would speak to him in low tones Faith couldn't quite hear, but it had been obvious the redhead was upset. And Theo would always soothe her. He would find a way to get his hands on her and those fights always seemed to end with Erin wrapped around his body and him maneuvering them somewhere private.

"It's hard for me," Erin replied. "I didn't expect to care about him. Honestly, I wish I didn't. I tried not to, but circumstances kind of forced us together and he's a sneaky bastard with ridiculously beautiful muscles. Dudes shouldn't be that pretty."

This was a side of Erin she hadn't seen. It was so fun to have a girlfriend again. Again? She wasn't sure she'd ever gossiped about men this way. Not since she was a kid. Hope was always so serious. She wanted to talk medicine and politics even when they were at a spa. "Circumstances? I thought you two met at work."

"We did, but I tried to stay away from him. He's not exactly my usual type."

"What's your type?" Theo Taggart was every woman's type. Of course, so was Master T.

Erin sat back. "I don't know. I've kept most of my relationships casual. I was in the Army for a long time. Not much chance at lasting relationships there. I've had a couple of boyfriends, but none like him. I've never dated anyone younger than me."

"He's not that much younger."

Erin shook her head. "Ten years. He's ten years younger than me. He's shiny. You know the type. Hell, you are the type. You see the world in a way I don't. Theo thinks people are good. He tries to see the good in them. I know they're likely to shoot me. The crazy thing is lately, I kind of like the world Theo sees."

"That's good. I think it's good for us to have partners who see the world in a way we don't. I think you and Theo are adorable."

Erin looked toward the door as though she thought he would show up at any moment. "I'm not a picket fence kind of girl. Theo's going to want marriage and babies, and I knew a long time ago that wasn't in the cards for me. I'm not built for it."

Faith knew that feeling. "Sometimes I don't think I am either."

"You? Nah. You're the kind of girl who ends up with a nice house and a nice husband and sweet kids. You deserve that."

But Erin didn't think she did? Some of her shiny mood faded. She was more like Erin than the other woman could know. She didn't foresee some peaceful suburban life for herself. She loved kids. God, she looked at babies like most women looked at hot guys. They were precious, and she wasn't sure she should bring one into this world around her. She'd been born to make it a better place for other people's kids. "I have high hopes for you two. And you know what? I kind of have high hopes for me. I think Master T and I are going to get along nicely, and I'm going to have a very good vacation."

She looked at Erin and realized something she hadn't before. They were going to fly home together. To Dallas. To the home Theo was surprising Erin with.

"You're not coming back to Liberia with me, are you?"

Erin's eyes seemed to get the tiniest bit misty. "No. It was a one-time thing. I'm going wherever Ian tells me to, but it won't be back to Africa."

So this was the end of their time together, too. Damn. She was going to miss Erin. It seemed like the life she'd chosen meant a constant flow of humanity. No one ever stayed. She'd learned to enjoy life where she could. "So let's have fun while we can. We're stuck here so my dad can play the righteous politician who ignores all solid scientific data. We should have fun. I'll call the liquor store tomorrow and find us the best tequila Germany can offer."

Erin stood up. "That's a deal, Doc." She winked and left, going off to find her too-pretty prince charming.

Faith had given them the master bedroom. She didn't need it. The smaller bedrooms in this place were more than enough for her. She hoped Erin and Theo brought some love to the place because she was fairly certain her father hadn't.

She quickly read and responded to her other messages, telling her father she'd made it to the house safely and no she didn't want to testify in front of congress on the impact of the West African Ebola outbreak and how it would impact the US. He wouldn't like her answer. She would push for funding for research and better hospitals in Third World countries, rather than his answer to fund pharmaceutical companies who would then take the money earmarked for a cure for hemorrhagic fevers and divert it into the next plastic surgery wonder drug that they would make billions from.

The second was from the doctor she'd left in charge of the clinic, asking about vaccines. She explained where they were stored and instructed him to put the protocols back in place with the singular exception of the flu vaccines from last season. She'd pulled those out of the rotation. She'd explained in the e-mail that those vaccines were not to be used under any circumstances until further notice. She had some questions about them and she would find the answers when she got to the States.

Now that the crisis was dying down, the clinic could get back to its primary focus of well care for locals.

She sighed and closed the lid of her laptop. She would do exactly as Master T had asked in the morning. She would wake up and prepare and then send him a message.

She had a few weeks to get to know this man, to talk to him and let him get to know her. It was good.

It was really good because she was pretty sure she was going to sleep with that man.

When she slept, she dreamed of a man with golden brown hair and a smile that made her heart pound.

* * * *

Ten's laptop chirped and he forced himself not to fall all over the place trying to answer it.

"Sounds like you have a message, boss." The reason for his stillness turned his way with a stupid grin on his face. Hutch had a bag of gummy bears in one hand as he looked over the top of his monitor.

Ten continued to his seat. He'd gotten up to grab a cup of that heated motor oil Tag called coffee. He slipped back into his chair.

Big Tag walked in, a cup of coffee in one hand and a thick stack of papers in the other. He looked over at Ten as Ten's computer chirped again. "You need to take that, lover boy?"

Ten glanced down and forced his face to remain perfectly blank.

Good morning, Sir. It's afternoon here, but I thought you should know we're enjoying our last day before coming back to the States.

Another ding and a picture came through. It was Faith wearing an oddly sedate bathing suit. Most women her age would be in a bikini, but Faith's suit was a one piece with a little skirt around the hips. Still, it couldn't hide her curves or the way the sun kissed her skin. Her face was up to the sun. He fought the instinct to reach out and brush his fingers over the picture.

He also fought his secondary instinct, which was to write her back, order her to go somewhere private and take that suit off for him.

Weeks of talking to her, flirting with her, were taking their toll. He wanted Faith McDonald. He wanted her underneath him, her legs spread, that warm smile of hers welcoming him deep inside her soft body.

"I think I can handle it, Tag. Why don't you get started?" He quickly typed back a message. *You look beautiful. I hope you'll enjoy the sun here, too. I've made reservations for the four of us at a friend's restaurant the night you come in. I'm counting the hours.*

He was disconcerted to discover he was actually counting the hours. Given the fact that Dallas was seven hours behind Munich, she would be going to bed soon to get ready for an early flight. He'd thought about picking them up at the airport, but decided to play it cool and simply meet her at Sean Taggart's restaurant later that night.

So Ian was picking them up. Ian would be taking them to Theo's new house. Ian would be hauling her suitcases around and it fucking rankled. Which was precisely why Ten wouldn't give and pick her up.

"All right then. Hutch has gathered some intel on the sister and Chelsea's been monitoring some activity from within the Agency," Tag explained as he played around with the computer that was stationed in the conference room. He seemed to be loading something he wanted projected on the back wall. McKay-Taggart was big on graphics. "She's trying to lay low for the moment so Simon's going to relay her report. And we might have to stop because we've got a couple of guests coming in. Grace is going to show them in when they get here."

Chelsea was laying low because Ten had been the one to hire Chelsea Weston. He was certain she was under a lot of scrutiny given her connections to McKay-Taggart. There was really only one question he wanted answered about the Agency. "Is there an active kill order on me?"

His laptop dinged again. *I'm looking forward to it, Sir. I'm very excited to finally meet you in person. I feel like I know you already.*

She knew absolutely nothing about him. Not even his real name. As far as she was concerned, he was Timothy Graham. He'd selected the last name with care. It had been Phoebe's alias for years. He was used to using it. Typically, he would have used his foster father's last name, but McDonald knew too much about Franklin Grant and his foster sons. So Graham had been a suitable replacement. It was best to go with something similar. Something easy for him to answer to.

Faith knew minor things. He'd purposefully kept his end of the conversation light. She knew he'd grown up in the south. She knew he liked barbecue and worked for a security firm.

Everything else he'd told her was lies.

Simon Weston sat forward, his face serious. He was dressed in a white dress shirt, slacks, and a tie. He'd hung up the suit coat, and that was about as casual as the Brit ever got. The only time Ten could remember seeing him without a tie around his neck was at Sanctum. "From what Chelsea's found, the Agency isn't actively looking for you."

Me, too, sweetheart. I'm eagerly awaiting your arrival. Get plenty of sleep tonight and let Theo carry your bags. That's my first command. Once you get here, there will likely be more.

Once she touched down in Texas, she was his sub. She was under his command. He'd spent most of his adult life with scores of assets under his command. He'd sent men and women into dangerous situations, some when he knew the likelihood was they wouldn't survive.

So why was this so different? Faith was another mission. Why did the idea of having her under his command, of being able to demand she undress for him, that she submit to him—why did that make his whole body tighten?

"Just because they're not actively searching for me doesn't mean there isn't a see/kill order." It was simple. He ran into an operative. The operative saw him. The operative killed him. The Agency was down one more problem.

"Chelsea doesn't think so," Simon replied. "She thinks you took care of the problem. She asked me to mention a certain e-mail you sent to the director during your time in Saudi."

Tag laughed. "The girl is good, Ten."

He should have known Chelsea would figure that out. Franklin Grant had taught him well. Franklin's final gift to his children had been a package of information he'd gathered over his thirty-year career with the Agency. Ten and Jamie and Phoebe had already received copies of the information after their foster father's funeral. They'd each added to it during their own careers. When Jamie had died, Ten had added his brother's information to his own before handing it over to Phoebe.

"Big Tag knows?" Simon asked. He sat back, watching Ten.

He knew Alex was Tag's best friend and that Tag's circle was pretty big, but Ten's wasn't. It was incredibly small. Hell, he trusted Tag more than he did anyone with the exception of Phoebe, and he hadn't wanted this burden on her. "He knows where the information is and he knows to get it out in the event of my death."

"An insurance policy," Simon murmured.

Hutch nodded Ten's way. "Boss practices what he preaches. When we joined up with his team, he told us it was important to keep track of things we'd learned. Especially the things that could damage the Agency."

He had enough on the higher-ups that they wouldn't want it to get out. He simply hadn't been sure they'd gotten the message. He'd passed on what he'd learned from his foster father to his own men. He'd always been an Agency man, but Franklin Grant had known things could turn.

Damn but he missed the old man.

"I watch out for my men. You have to have insurance. If you don't have leverage and the wrong people come into power, things can go bad quickly. As evidenced by me." One day he'd been a power player with his own operational team. He'd been given a fairly free hand to do whatever he needed to do.

And then he'd come up against Senator Hank McDonald and he'd been disavowed overnight.

He had to wonder if he didn't have a file documenting some of the Agency's worse secrets, if he wouldn't be dead already. If his men wouldn't have been taken out one by one. It was the one thing he wouldn't tell anyone. He hadn't simply bargained for his life. He'd let it be known that if his men suffered any sort of odd accidents he would release the information. If anyone from McKay-Taggart went missing, he would release the information.

He was going to protect his team and when he was gone, Taggart would do the job for him. Big Tag would use the insurance policy to protect the men who had been loyal to Ten. And Phoebe. They'd had the conversation about the fact that no one was more important to Ten than his sister. He could relax because Jesse Murdoch would lay down his life for her and Big Tag would watch over them both.

I eagerly await your commands, Sir. I'm kind of counting the hours until I get to meet you in person. It's been good that we spent time getting to know each other, right?

He'd gotten to know her. He'd gotten to know how sweet she was, how naïve and weirdly innocent. He wasn't sure what to do with a woman who played so innocent.

What if she really was innocent? He didn't mean that in a sexual fashion. Virginity meant less than nothing to him. But that lack of true cynicism was something he didn't understand. Who did what she did? She gave up her comfy life to help people she didn't know.

His eyes strayed back to that picture of her. He needed to understand her. "Tell me about the sister."

Send me another picture.

He was fairly certain either Theo or Erin had been on the other end of the camera, so he was likely going to get ribbed about that. He could handle it. He wanted another picture of her.

"Hope McDonald." Tag nodded toward the back wall where there was a monitor affixed.

A picture of a blonde came up. She was smiling but it didn't reach her eyes. He sat back and looked at her. Smart suit. Perfect makeup. Not a hair out of place. On the surface someone might think she was prettier than her younger sister.

Those people were dimwits.

His laptop dinged and a picture of Faith filled the screen. Fuck. His dick was hard. She was smiling without inhibition. She looked into the camera and radiated outward. Erin stood beside her, smiling with her friend. Damn. Even Erin looked happy next to Faith. The two women were holding glasses of wine. Erin was drinking red and Faith a white. A Pinot Grigio likely. She'd ordered several bottles of Noir and Grigio off the Internet along with a case of beer and a bottle of tequila from a local liquor store. She'd paid with her credit card and had it delivered with instructions to leave the boxes inside the courtyard of the chalet. He'd watched her every move, read her every e-mail for the last several weeks, watched every place she went to on the Internet.

She liked some fairly dirty porn. She was attracted to the fetish movies and she went there directly after their conversations. He could get her hot, give her what she needed. He'd done all the training he needed to be able to fit into his role, but he hadn't really gotten it until he'd started talking to Faith. It had been something to learn. He needed to dominate this woman. He needed to top her. Only her.

And that disturbed him.

"Hope graduated from Johns Hopkins, did her residency at Massachusetts General. She worked as a surgeon specializing in neurology until she quit seven years ago and joined Kronberg Pharmaceuticals." Tag clicked the remote in his hand and the picture changed. There was a list of the financials of Kronberg. Two billion a year in income. They were on the leading edge of medical technology. "She works in research, but she's got a ton of connections, and that's where Faith comes in."

Beautiful, sweetheart. Enjoy your evening. Tomorrow, you're mine. Let Theo take care of you in my absence.

"What do you mean that's where Faith comes in?" His eyes trailed back to the pictures. He would hoard all the ones she'd sent him, looking at them over and over again. She liked to send him pictures of her relaxing, a glass of wine in her hand, but he'd seen her be serious, too. They'd talked over FaceTime at least once a day and she'd talked to him about her job. She'd told him about the clinic she ran and what it meant to her.

She hadn't talked about Ghana. Even when he'd asked if there was anything about her job that scared her. She'd simply said losing children. Her mouth had turned down and she'd changed the subject.

Did she still dream about it?

Tag went on. "Kronberg has funded the majority of her vaccination campaign for the last few years. In exchange she gives them data on infection rates and vaccination protocols. She shares data so she can get drugs."

That didn't seem so bad to Ten. It seemed to him like she was working her connections to help people who couldn't help themselves. "Good for her."

Hutch huffed. "Good for The Collective."

Ten didn't want to hear that. The Collective was a group of

corporations that seemed to have banded together to practice some of the worst crimes against the public he'd ever seen. The Collective consisted of some of the world's biggest companies, and they maximized profits at the expense of anyone who got in their way. "Why do you think Kronberg is Collective?"

Hutch's shoulders moved up and down in a negligent movement that belied the fact that the man never accused without some solid evidence. "You know it's hard to tell. They don't publish their rolls or make public their meetings. So we have to look at patterns of behavior and rely on gossip. Damon Knight is the head of McKay-Taggart's London office."

"I'm well aware."

There was a knock on the door and then the man himself was stepping into the room. Damon Knight was a big bull of a man with pitch-black hair starting to gray at the temples. He was a broody son of a bitch. Well, he used to be. Now he was smiling and had a hand out as he stepped into the conference room followed by another man. This man wasn't smiling. He was leaner than Knight or Tag, built on predatory lines. A hungry wolf with dark hair and a close-cropped beard. He looked over at Ten with icy blue eyes.

"How was your flight?" Tag asked, shaking Damon's hand.

"It was commercial, you bastard," Damon shot back with a chuckle.

"Sorry, buddy, I'm not MI6. If you want a company jet, you're going to have to bring in some more cash," Tag joked. "How's Penny?"

Ten was fairly sure Knight was going to break his face if he kept smiling like that. "She's already found Charlotte. She's eager to meet your daughters. Especially now that she's about to become a mum."

Tag slapped Knight on the back. "Are you serious? You bastard, you didn't say a thing."

Knight waved a hand. "We wanted to wait a bit. She's only a few months along, but it appears everything is going brilliantly. Never thought it would happen. Imagine us. Two old dads."

They continued on as Hutch leaned in. "I do not get that. In my world, when a chick gets pregnant we all ask the dude how he managed to fuck up that badly. Wow. Erin looks hot. How is that possible? I finally see what Theo sees in her."

"They are both pretty girls," a low voice said behind him. A low, heavily accented voice. Ah, Knight had brought the Russian with him.

And the freaking Russian was staring at Ten's girl. He slammed his laptop closed. His target. Not his girl. Still. He didn't like the way the big bastard had stared at her.

"Are we breaking up?" Ten asked, well aware he sounded annoyed as hell. This wasn't a fucking backyard barbecue family reunion.

"Sorry, he's pissy since he lost his Agency spy decoder ring," Tag said, gesturing for Knight and the new guy to take seats. "Please join us. We'll catch up on the real life stuff after the people who don't actually have one are safely out of here."

Fuck Tag. Why the hell was he friends with that asshole anyway? Oh yeah, the loyalty stuff. Still sometimes he wished he'd won that fight between them and he still had several free punches left. He would appreciate Tag so much more if he could break the fucker's nose on a regular basis. "First introduce the Russian and then tell me what The Collective has to do with Faith's clinic."

When everyone was settled he flipped his laptop back open. She'd sent another pic, this one of her staring at the camera and blowing him a kiss.

Good night, Sir.

Good night, Faith.

He closed the laptop again, not trusting himself to not stare at her pictures.

Knight sat down beside the new guy. "This is my latest employee, Nikolai Markovic. He's former SVR."

"It all still KGB. Don't let new letters fool you." The Russian sat back with a long-suffering sigh. Ten put his age around thirty, young to already be out of the game.

The KGB had officially disbanded back in 1991 after a failed coup had been led by the former director. The government had split the KGB up and formed the Foreign Intelligence Service. SVR or *Sluzhba vneshney razvedki*, was the organization that handled Russian intelligence operating outside the federation.

But Markovic was right. It was all still KGB. Putin had taken Russia right back to playing the old games.

Damn, Ten really missed the Agency.

"I was recruited young. My father, he was a paper pusher in the SVR. Smart man, but without many physical skills. He offered up me and my sister to be operatives. My sister died during a mission to Ukraine and then the bastards tried to send me in to finish her job."

Ten could bet what that had been. "To stir up chaos in Crimea?"

Markovic nodded. "Yes, I am supposed to pose as Ukrainian soldier, to lead the revolution. My sister dies over gas pipelines. Putin is no leader. He is businessman. So now I am as well."

Not if he was working for McKay-Taggart. There was a bit of bluster in the Russian, but he'd chosen a company known for taking on the occasional case simply for the rightness of the cause. They were also known for sometimes turning in the companies that employed them if they discovered they were grossly violating the law. Tag did it quietly, but the man believed in justice.

At the end of the day though, he didn't really care why or how the Russian was here. It was a problem that he was here and not where he was supposed to be. "Shouldn't you be working?"

Markovic's lips curled up and suddenly his Russian accent completely disappeared. "You mean at the Jasper Bay Beach Club? I took some time off. I'm due back in three days. I'm in Florida checking on my elderly mother."

Damn. The man was good. His American accent was perfect and when he lost the broody ennui that he seemed to wear like a coat, he could absolutely pass for a guy from Florida, another dude trying to make his way in the world. "All right. Did you come in for anything in particular?"

His shoulders fell and he was right back to his former bleakness. "Besides wanting to wash sand out of ass? I don't understand the need to be at beach. Sand everywhere. I fuck one of McDonald's maids. She thinks doing it on the beach is sexy. I have sand coming out ass for weeks."

Tag laughed. "I take back what I said about his salary. He's worth every penny. Please tell me more about sand in your ass."

"Or you could tell us what you learned from screwing McDonald's maid." He really didn't want to listen to more.

"McDonald talk a lot about his daughters. He says they work well together. She says he is proud that they are working on projects

55

together. Also, I found out a bit about the layout of the house. McDonald's office is actually outside of the main house and there is much security around it. We'll have to have a hacker with us."

Oh, that was like putting a big old X marks the spot on his treasure map. "Then that's where he keeps the good stuff. Yes, I'm going to need to get into that building. Hutch, how do you like the beach?"

Hutch held up a hand. "Actually, I burn, boss."

"Excellent. Now do we have any connections between Kronberg and Faith's clinic? Because a donation of vaccinations only means Faith probably guilted her big sister into donating something she needed. And someone tell me why we believe The Collective is involved. I thought we'd cut the head off when the Brit offed the nerd."

Knight started passing out reports. "I've been working on Kronberg. This is the pharmaceutical company that I've verified once did business with Eli Nelson. Who is also dead."

"My pretty baby blew his ass up. It was her wedding present to me. She knows me well," Tag explained with a smile.

"According to Charlotte, Nelson told her he'd worked for a company who hired him to eliminate the competition, so to speak," Knight continued. "You'll see I've compiled a case against Kronberg. At the same time Nelson claimed he was working with the pharmaceutical company, their direct rival's over-the-counter pain reliever was caught in a criminal case involving cyanide-coated pills that had the Boston area and then the entire US in a complete panic. The rival's drug was pulled from the shelves and Kronberg's has enjoyed a swift bump in market share ever since. Nelson received a million dollars from an offshore account at roughly the same time. I've traced that account back to a subsidiary of Kronberg."

It was enough for Ten to believe. Still, it didn't mean Faith was involved. "Do you have direct proof that Hope McDonald is aware of The Collective? Ninety-nine point nine percent of all employees working for Collective companies have zero idea they're slaves to the bad guys. And what real proof do you have that McDonald is working with The Collective?"

"Beyond the fact that you're sitting here?" Tag shot back.

Big Tag was drawing lines without making real connections. He was letting his anger at The Collective and the way they'd targeted his family blind him to logic. "I will agree to the fact that McDonald has ties to the Agency and that he was obviously working with the bad guys. He made money off selling out troop movements to the enemy, which is exactly what I intend to prove by getting inside his hidey-hole. Everything else you've laid out is complete conjecture."

"His daughter works for a known Collective company," Knight explained.

Which proved nothing except that she had a job. "I need proof and not simply that she works somewhere. What's her job at Kronberg?"

Tag looked through his notes. "She's in research and development, but I don't think they've got a Criminal Department. Come on. You know there are very few coincidences in the world. McDonald is dirty. If he's in bed with one bad guy, he's probably up for an orgy."

"He likes the girl," Markovic said. "He thinks if one sister is bad, both are. He's probably right, but this is reason he requires more proof. He wants to believe pretty girl is good girl."

The Russian was making him sound like some kind of lovesick teen. "I simply need more than some poorly drawn lines. I haven't been in business for myself for years. I was trained to cross every *T* and dot every *I* before I brought justice down on someone because it was my butt on the line. I simply want the same level of confidence attached to this mission. I will have to present this to the Agency if I want my command back. I have to find out who McDonald's Agency mole is and I need proof. If I also find proof that the McDonald sisters are working for a criminal enterprise, then I will take the whole family down. I'll see them all in jail."

He stood up because it looked like the informative portion of the meeting was over. It was time for him to move on and let Tag and Knight talk about babies and puppies and shit. He needed to prep for tomorrow.

"If that's all you need me for, I could use the rest of the day to prep to meet with the target tomorrow," he said.

Tag frowned but sat back. "All right. We'll meet back here on Monday. Take tomorrow off if you need it. I'm going to debrief Markovic and I'll send you a report. You bringing her to Sanctum

Saturday?"

"That's my plan. I'd like for her to meet Charlotte and particularly Eve. I'm interested in her personal profile," Ten explained.

"You'll have it. She's ready. Are you?"

"To meet Faith? Of course. Thanks." He stepped out.

He was ready. It was time for him to put aside all doubt. This mission was about to begin.

CHAPTER THREE

"I'll be right there. I'm going to run and pick up some gloss," Faith said as they stood in front of the restaurant. She glanced up at the sign. It was pretty and looked like someone had spent a lot of time hand painting it. Top. According to Erin, Theo's brother owned the place. It was also where she was supposed to meet Master T in person for the first time.

So she needed some serious lip-gloss. She'd spied a Neiman Marcus half a block down the street, and they were a good twenty minutes early thanks to a shocking lack of traffic on the way from Erin and Theo's pretty ranch house to downtown.

"I should come with you." Erin looked back at the door where Theo had disappeared.

Faith shook her head. "No. I won't be more than ten minutes. I bet the makeup counter is on the first floor. Please stay. I swear I'll run in, use the mirror in the bathroom, and then I'll run right back out. Order me something sweet to drink."

For a second Erin looked like she would argue, but then she opened the door. "All right. But don't get lost. Master T was very excited about finally getting to meet you."

Which was precisely why she didn't want zombie lips. She'd bought some makeup at the duty free store in DFW, but she was woefully out of touch. It wasn't usually this hard. Her old Master was used to her being fairly low maintenance. He'd been a doctor, too.

The mysterious Master T worked in security, and by that she'd kind of figured out he was a bodyguard. It explained how he knew Theo and Theo's brothers. Faith walked down the street at a crisp pace. Germany had been nice, but isolated. It was good to be back in the States. It was particularly good to be back in Texas. As she passed people on the street, most sent her a smile or tipped their heads in acknowledgment. It was something unique about the Southern United States. She'd been all over the world, but she always missed this.

She strode up the steps that led her inside the cool environs of Neiman Marcus. Immediately the world seemed to slow, becoming a more luxurious place. She might work at a charity, but she couldn't help but enjoy the decadence of one of the world's premier department stores.

This was her indulgence time. She wasn't going to feel bad about anything for the next few weeks. She was going to use her credit cards and not worry about it.

She walked straight up to the makeup counter and started looking at colors.

"Can I help you?" A well-dressed clerk stepped up.

Faith smiled. "Can you make my lips look less tortured?"

Five minutes later, Faith was happy with the way the tinted gloss plumped her lips and made her look less like a woman who normally fought infectious tropical diseases for a living. She paid and was about to leave when her cell phone trilled. She pulled it out of her purse and checked the number. Her sister. Well, she knew she'd have to deal with her sometime. She slid her thumb across the screen, accepting the call.

"Hey, Hope."

"Well, if it isn't the warrior goddess." Her sister's rich laugh came over the line. "How does it feel to be home?"

"It's good. You would be proud of me. I'm in Neimans right now." It was actually good to hear her sister's voice. It reminded her that there had been a time when they were close, when she'd actually wanted to be exactly like Hope. She'd gone into medical school following in her big sister's footsteps.

"Seriously? Oh, we should go shopping while you're here. I was calling because I want to see you. I'm going to be in Houston next week and I thought we could do a girl's day. Spa, shopping, lunch, way too many cocktails."

That sounded great. There was only one problem. "I'm actually in Dallas for the next few weeks."

"Dallas? Why are you in Dallas?"

She was going totally casual with this answer. "I made a couple of friends while I was working. They live up here."

"What about Roger?"

She sighed. She hadn't wanted to get into her love life with her sister, but she supposed it was probably inevitable. "We broke up. I won't be seeing him anymore."

There was a pause on the line. "Well, that's for the best. He was kind of skeevy. I mean I liked the fact that he was a doctor but god, you can do much better than a general surgeon. Hello, general is for people who can't hack a specialty, if you know what I mean."

Yeah. She was considered a general surgeon. Now she remembered why she avoided her sister. "Look, I have to run, sis. I actually have a date tonight."

"Really? Well, it's good. Get right back on the horse, so to speak. What's his specialty? Tell me he's an orthopedist. My current research is heavily invested in ortho. I could use someone to talk to at your party."

"He's a bodyguard."

"I'm sorry. You're breaking up. What did you say?"

God, her sister was such a snob. If a man didn't have a doctorate, he wasn't dating material. For Hope it wasn't about money or society. It was all about skins on the wall. "He's not a doctor. He works security and he's very good at his job."

She thought he was probably good at his job. He sounded like he was good. They'd talked to each other over the Internet, and she'd realized the man didn't need to be good at anything. All he really needed to do was smile and women would fall all over him. Master T was a complete hottie.

Hence her need for properly glossed lips.

"A man working a fast food counter can be good at his job. That's not a reason to date him. God, please tell me he isn't into that stuff. The one good thing about you breaking it off with Roger is you can get away from all the nasty stuff."

Her sister wasn't with the sexually liberated age. And Faith kind of liked the nasty stuff. She'd spent weeks now thinking about doing nasty stuff with Master T. He'd agreed to her one real demand. He'd seemed perfectly happy to agree to monogamy while their contract lasted. He hadn't even hesitated. "I'm going to be late. I'll call you soon."

Hope tried to say something else, but Faith cut her off. She didn't need to explain this again. Hope didn't take anything but her work and their father's career seriously. She was never going to understand, but Faith couldn't help but remember it had been Hope who had taken over after their mother had been killed. Hope had to grow up quickly and she'd taken good care of Faith. It bought her some patience.

She took a look at herself in the mirror. Not bad. Not perfect but not atrocious. She had big green eyes and her hair was curling nicely. Now her lips didn't look so thin. She was...presentable.

Master T was a sun-kissed Greek god of a man. What was she doing? Was he going to take one look at her and run? Sure he'd seen her over the camera attached to her laptop, but he was probably thinking she would look better in person. She glanced down at her watch. He was going to see that she was late and start their relationship with a not erotic spanking if she didn't hurry up.

She gave herself one more look and saw a man in the mirror behind her. Close behind her. She gasped as he pressed her against the counter, and she could feel something hard against her spine.

"Hey." She tried to push back, but she was terrified of what that hard item was at the back of her spine.

His breath was hot against the shell of her ear. "Hello, sweetheart. I would suggest you don't move or yell out. Do you feel that?"

She thought about calling out, calculated the odds. Adrenaline started to pump through her body, heightening her senses and making her hyperaware. If that was really a gun, the movement required to force the man away could cause the trigger to move enough to fire. It would hit her at L2 and more than likely sever her spinal column, leaving her without the ability to walk. She decided to nod.

She could see him in the mirror. He was dark haired, with a close-cropped beard, his eyes clear and focused. He wasn't panicked and that was a good thing.

He smiled and she was sure to anyone glancing at them they looked affectionate. "If you say or do anything to alert these kind people, I'll shoot you and then I'll shoot them. Nod if you understand. And give me a nice smile."

There were five people within range. If he was a good shot, he could probably shoot her and at least two others. What did he want? Could she get him somewhere he couldn't hurt other people? She nodded and smiled, though she had to force it and wasn't sure she would fool anyone.

His smile was vibrant. He was a decent looking man for a total and utter criminal. He had a good half a foot on her. He was wearing all black and she couldn't see much of him, but she would bet there was a lot of muscle there. Bigger. Stronger. She couldn't see a single advantage she had over the man. Her heart was pounding so hard she was surprised no one could hear it.

"I want to take a little walk and we're going to talk. I need some information and you need to give it to me. When I'm satisfied that you understand, I'll let you go."

Sure he would. But maybe...maybe this was about her father. Maybe this was some move to scare her so she would talk to her father about legislation or something. She decided to go along at least until they were out on the street and she had a shot at not being in a wheelchair for the rest of her life. When they got out on the street, she could run. She could find something to use against him. There would be chaos on the streets the minute the gun came out, and she could use that to her advantage.

Also, Erin would come looking for her if she stalled long enough. Erin would know she wouldn't miss the meeting with Master T.

Keep your head. Don't risk the lives of everyone here.

"What do you want?" Faith kept her voice quiet.

"I want to talk. That's all."

The gun shifted to her side and an arm went around her waist as he pulled her back. She thought he would take her out the front, but they started toward a hall to her left. To her right was the rest of the store, with its designer bags and clothes she couldn't justify buying. It looked like she was going out an employees only door.

Panic threatened. Please let this be some nutbag who wanted to talk to her about her father's stance on fracking or taxes.

She looked around, praying someone was watching them. The clerks on the floor seemed involved with customers or preoccupied with product. No one was watching them. No one noticed when they slipped away.

Everything became quiet. The minute the door closed, it seemed like the world had been shut off from her. She was alone with him and the hallways seemed almost too bright. The fluorescent lighting made her blink. The walls were concrete, painted blocks. She got up close and personal with them when her attacker shoved her body against the wall and pressed in hard.

Pain flared. He hadn't held back. He'd used a great deal of force, and she felt it in her bones.

"You are awfully pretty."

She took a deep breath because she wasn't going to talk her way out of this. She would have to fight. His hands were on her. He'd holstered his gun, obviously comfortable with the fact that he could handle her now that they were alone.

He was wrong.

At least she hoped he was.

His hand moved down her torso. "So pretty. Maybe we could spend some time together before I do what I have to."

She didn't care anymore. She pulled her elbow forward as far as she could and brought it back on his ribs. A hard thud hit her ears and then she was free. She heard him curse, but didn't wait. She took off. Instinct led her away from the door he'd taken her through. He was in front of it and all she wanted was to get as far away from him as she could.

She ran down the long hallway, stumbling because she'd worn stupid shoes. Heels. She never wore heels but she'd put them on because she'd wanted Master T to think of her as sexy and sensual, and not practical the way all the other men in her life saw her. She never wore heels. She wore sneakers. God, she wished she was wearing sneakers now.

Up ahead she saw a door and didn't hesitate. She could hear him cursing. When she glanced back, he was getting up to his feet and she could see that shiny gun in his hand. It looked like he was no longer interested in feeling her up.

Pro. He was a pro. The idea whispered through her head. Someone had sent a professional after her.

She hit the door with force and immediately smacked into a mountain of muscle. She started to scream, but a hand came out and she found herself looking up into seriously blue eyes.

"Was there only the one? Did he mention whether or not he had a partner?" a deep voice asked.

Master T. He was here. He was standing right here dressed in a black Western shirt with pearl snaps and a Stetson sat on his head. She wanted to hug him, but they needed to get away.

Faith shook her head, trying to catch her breath. "There was only him. We need to go."

"Hush now, darlin'. You stay here while I take care of this," he said in a slow, Southern accent. He physically moved her to the side as the door was beginning to open.

"Now you've pissed me off," the man who had attacked her shouted through the door.

"Oh, son, you have no idea," Master T said as his booted foot came out and he kicked the door back in.

Faith heard the horrible sound of bones crunching as her attacker's hand got caught between the door and the jamb. The gun fell to the ground.

She stood and watched in complete horror as Master T opened the door again and then disappeared through it.

He didn't have a gun. At least not one she'd seen in his hands. Her hands. They were shaking. Her whole body seemed to be a live wire, every inch of her skin crackling with the fact that she'd almost been killed and now her new play partner was likely being murdered by a man who had been sent to kill her. What was she supposed to do?

Police. She should call the police. Yes. She opened her purse to look for her cell phone. Where was it? Why did she have so much crap in her purse? Panicking, she sifted through, trying to find her phone. Master T was likely dying and it was going to be her damn fault because she hadn't cleaned out her bag after the flight. She could find antibacterial soap and her passport but not her phone.

Finally. She grasped it and immediately dropped it. It clattered to the ground. It was twilight, but the outside lights hadn't come on yet. She started to reach for her phone when the door opened again.

Faith shrank back and was about to run when she saw Master T step out, hauling a body behind him.

"You all right?" he asked.

Nope. Not even close. She picked up the phone. "I'll get the police out here."

The words were shaky, forced from her mouth.

Before she could press the emergency button on her screen, the phone was in his hand.

"I need you to think about this for a moment. Do you recognize this man?"

She didn't want to look at him. "Is he alive?"

A big hand came up, cupping her cheek and gently bringing her gaze up to look into Master T's blue eyes. He was calm. Perfectly calm. "Stay with me, Doc. I know you don't want to look and if it's too much for you, then I can try to make an ID through pictures, but it would be very helpful if you could tell me if you've ever seen him before or not."

"Is he dead?" She knew the answer, but it made her sick to her stomach.

"Yes, he's dead. I snapped his neck during the fight. He's not going to try to hurt you again, but we need to figure out if this was a random pervert trying to get some or a professional sent specifically after you. That gun he was carrying makes me think pro. Most random rapists don't have that quality of suppressor on their weapons and they don't typically prowl the cosmetics counter at Neiman's."

Pro. It was what she'd first thought. "All right."

She started to move, but he stopped her. "Hey, it's all right now. You're fine."

She found herself wrapped up in his arms, his hands coming around to hold her tight. One big hand cupped the back of her head, sinking into her hair and gently guiding her against his really well-made chest. The other hand eased over her back.

"It's all right, Faith. He's not coming back for you."

His voice was deep and melodic and soothing, and before she could think about it, she was breathing in his scent. Sandalwood. There was a hint of it in his aftershave and his shirt smelled like fabric softener. She let the heat of his body sink into her own and listened to the beat of his heart. It was steady, as though what had happened was no big deal. She knew that should set off warning bells, but at that moment it was so good to have a stable sound. Master T was solid and she needed the comfort he was offering her. The world had gone crazy, but here was warmth and safety and protection all wrapped up in a gorgeous package of man.

"You're all right, darlin'." The hands on her body felt comforting, not sexual at all. He was a calming presence, but she was suddenly very aware she barely knew this man and he'd killed someone. He'd killed a man and his heartbeat hadn't ticked up at all.

She gently pushed away from him. "I'm good. It's just a lot of adrenaline. We should call the police now."

Master T stepped back, giving her space. The very act of disengaging from him made her wish she was back in his arms. "We can do that. You'll need to call your father and let him know what's coming his way."

"What do you mean?" Even before the question was out of her mouth, she knew what he meant. "The press. The minute they find out who I am, the press will be all over it."

No more anonymity. She'd likely be rushed into a safe house while her father took over the investigation and made her near murder a platform for a new law and order agenda. She wouldn't be able to walk outside, much less spend the next three months relaxing. She would have bodyguards. So many bodyguards.

"Faith, I need you to make a decision and quickly. We won't be alone out here for long and I suspect these security cameras picked up a lot we don't want them to see. If you're going to call the police in that's fine. If you're going to keep this quiet and allow my firm to handle it, then I need to get to work now."

She looked up at him. "Why were you here?"

"Because I saw you walking up the street and I followed you. I was curious. Was the lip-gloss for me?"

She nodded.

His hand came up, big thumb brushing across her bottom lip in a way that wasn't comforting at all. She felt that touch low in her abdomen. How could she get hot for a man when there was a dead body at her feet? "You look beautiful, Doc. I was going to approach you when I saw that man make his move. I realized where he was going and thought I'd surprise him. Make your decision. I'll back you either way."

"You killed him." She wasn't the only one her decision would affect.

"It was self-defense. I can handle the cops. I can also handle the investigation. I can protect you while we figure out what's going on, but I can't do both. If you bring the cops into this, your protection is going to fall to your father. So you need to choose."

She should bite the bullet and do the right thing. This wasn't Master T's problem. He'd already done enough. He'd saved her. She should call the cops and let him move on with his life.

"Call your firm. I've got money. I can hire them. Will you stay with me?"

One corner of his mouth tugged up and she saw the beginning of the sweetest dimples. When the man smiled, she didn't need sunlight. "Try to get rid of me, darlin'." His fingers tangled with hers while he pulled out a cell with his free hand. "Take a look at him and see if you know him. I'm going to call this in and we'll get you back down to the restaurant. You let me take care of everything from here on out."

She sighed and couldn't help but wonder if she was doing the right thing.

* * * *

"You couldn't leave him alive, could you?" Big Tag sat down with a frown on his face. His voice was low, his eyes trailing to where Faith McDonald stood in Top's small lounge area talking to Erin. "You know if he was alive he could do this thing. We call it talking. It's where we ask a few questions and he provides easy answers."

She had a glass of wine in her hand. Her second, he thought. Erin had been given explicit instructions on how to take care of her. Erin had also been given a serious lecture along with some threats he didn't normally pass on to ladies. She'd fucked up and she'd known it.

"Well, Tag, at the time he was trying to gut me," Ten replied before taking a short swig of Sean's first-class bourbon.

The battle had been short but nasty. Oh, he hadn't actually gotten his clothes messed up or anything, but the jerk had produced a wicked knife. Unfortunately, he'd also proven to have damn brittle bones. Or Ten had been a little pissed.

That fucker had walked right up to Faith and put his hands on her. He'd rubbed his body against her in that way a man did when he was proving to a woman he could have her and not because she'd said yes. He'd made her afraid. Ten had watched as Faith had gone from flushed with excitement about meeting her soon-to-be lover, straight to fear for her life. That motherfucker was lucky he hadn't had time to show the bastard how he really felt about the whole situation.

He took another swig. It wasn't about possessiveness. No. He'd been angry because that fucker had made his job ten times harder. He needed to get Faith into bed as soon as possible, and that asshole had practically raped her.

Yeah, that was why he was pissed off.

"You look awfully perfect for almost being gutted."

Ten gave him a devil-may-care smile. "Well, I do have a date tonight. Did the boys handle my mess?"

He'd left the body in a dumpster after calling it in. He'd needed to get Faith somewhere safe. He figured Top was a pretty good bet since most of the staff was ex-military and they worked with knives. Besides Top had a bar, and that girl needed a damn drink. He stared at her as she smiled wanly at something Erin said. Her eyes slid his way and he held her gaze. He winked her way to let her know everything was fine. She kept looking back at him as though to assure herself he was still here.

Maybe that old boy had done him a favor after all. She turned back to Erin, but he noticed she stood a little taller.

"Jesse's on it," Tag replied. "He's got the body and Hutch and Adam are making sure the cameras are suddenly and inexplicably out of order for the afternoon. Thank god everyone's gone digital. It makes my life so much easier. Unfortunately, I've got to figure out where to dump the body once we ID him. He's got some interesting tats on him."

"He was a pro. I've got no doubt. His weapon alone made me

realize that. The knife he had on him was military grade and the gun and suppressor were easily more than some street criminal could afford."

"Why not assassinate her from a distance? It's what I would do. I sure as hell wouldn't stride up to her in the middle of a store and take her out the back way. That was dangerous. How did you convince her not to call the cops? That was nice by the way. You lose her if the cops get involved."

He would have lost her on several levels. Her father likely would have ridden in to scoop his precious girl up and then the game would have been over. Ten had done his best to look different. Put on more muscle. Taken his hair down to a military cut. The senator wouldn't know him by looking at his identification photos. His cover had been expertly done by Chelsea. He wasn't worried about the cops making him, either. He would pass all the police tests, but the senator had contacts in places that would dig much deeper. They likely wouldn't go to too much trouble over Faith's date to the islands, but the minute the cops became involved, the game would change. There was no way the senator stayed out of that investigation, and he would want to know a lot more about Faith's hero. He would likely insist on meeting Ten, and Ten couldn't let that happen. The senator had friends in the Agency, and wouldn't they just love to know where Tennessee Smith was hanging his hat these days. No. If the cops had been called in, Ten would have been forced to pull back.

"I can't answer that question yet, Tag. Maybe it was a kidnapping," he replied as though it didn't matter. It was another intellectual puzzle to be solved and not something that kind of made his gut clench. "Her father's got a couple of important votes coming up. Hell, it might have been because she's a rich girl and Daddy would pay."

"She's pretty," Tag said before calling over a waitress.

"She's all right." She was fucking gorgeous. He'd watched her as she bought the lip-gloss and then answered her phone. He wasn't sure who she'd been talking to. He'd get the report on that later. Erin had bugged her phone a long while back. He could listen to the recording and hear her talk in that practical way of hers that seemed to do something to his dick. He'd hung back, pretending to be fascinated with scarves.

She was gorgeous and he'd been way too long without a woman.

"Hey, if this is going to be hard on you, let me send Case in. He's kind of got a thing for her. Case really wouldn't mind getting in bed with her. Ah, there it is." Tag turned to the brunette. "I'll take a Scotch. The one Sean keeps in his office."

The waitress nodded. "I'm supposed to tell you that you're a greedy son of a bitch and then get it for you anyway. Also Macon's got lemon madeleines in the back."

That seemed to make Big Tag incredibly happy. "Thanks, Ally. I have no idea what that is, but I'll look forward to it, and tell Sean that just for that, make it a double."

Ally smiled and walked off.

"There what is?" He had no illusions they wouldn't go right back to their increasingly uncomfortable conversation.

Tag sat back. "For a minute there, the mask fell away and you were ready to stab my brother through the heart."

"Don't." He wasn't falling for this shit. "Don't you play cupid here, Tag. You think I don't see through you. Everyone else here thinks you're the big bad, but I know what you are. You're a meek teddy bear dressed up like a grizzly. You've been declawed, brother, and you want the rest of us to be just as pussy whipped as you are so you manipulate and put people in positions where they have to couple up, and then you walk home and polish your fucking halo. You aren't doing it to me. I'm not falling into that trap."

"What would you like to bet on that? A thousand?"

"A thousand dollars?"

Tag nodded. "Yes. I have to go big. Have you seen what college costs these days? I have to make sure those girls get into Ivy League schools or they'll end up on the pole. I can't have my girls on the pole, man. Chris Rock was right. I got a mission in life now and it's keeping my baby girls away from skeevy dudes who go to strip clubs."

"You used to go to strip clubs."

"Exactly. No way I want my baby girls around any dude like me. Or you. Or Alex's kid. I see the way he looks at my girls." Tag eyed him as though sizing him up. It made Ten nervous. "When was the last time you were around a real woman? The last few months don't count because you distance from the women at the office. Don't think

I haven't noticed."

Tag seemed to notice everything. Didn't he have anything better to do? "Not that it's any of your business, but I met a woman in a bar last week."

He'd been out of sorts. Talking to Faith every day made him feel…weird. He'd needed to distance so he'd gone to a bar the previous Friday night, and within an hour he was back at some blonde's place. He couldn't remember her name. Wasn't sure he'd even asked. He'd steered her straight to the bedroom, ready to lose himself the way he always did. Sex had been his thing for most of his life. Since he'd been sixteen and figured out how good it made him feel, he turned to women when he got restless. He'd gotten the blonde out of her clothes, laid her back on the bed, and was going to get out of his own when he'd looked down at her and seen someone else.

He'd seen Faith.

Yeah, he wasn't about to tell Tag he'd made an excuse and walked out the door and spent the next week yanking his own dick.

Tag's eyes rolled. "I wasn't talking about getting your rocks off. I was talking about being with a woman. Talking to her. Having a relationship with her."

"You know how easy it is to have a relationship in my position? Yeah, working for the Agency, never knowing what continent I'll be on tomorrow, that's been a breeze for keeping a woman around." Had Tag lost his damn mind? "And hey, the Agency wanting me dead is another plus in my win column."

"Have they tried anything?"

Ten kept waiting. He'd been careful while he'd been out of the States. He'd spent time in Saudi, Iraq, and Pakistan while building his intelligence about the network Senator McDonald had put together. He'd been totally off the grid and constantly watching his back. It was easy in that part of the world.

It was harder here. He had a solid paper trail thanks to Chelsea. He had backup thanks to his old team and McKay-Taggart. He had babies in the room next to him. He had freaking two-hour Skype conversations with Faith McDonald where he told her lie after lie about his life and she talked about saving kids in Africa. The world was soft here. This was where they would get him.

"Again, I'm going to ask you to be reasonable," Tag insisted.

"What happened an hour ago changes everything. If she's got someone gunning for her, she needs protection. You can't watch her back and your own. Bow out gently tonight. Tell her you changed your mind and you think she needs a younger Master. I'll introduce her to Case and you can handle this whole situation the way you should—from the background."

"If you try to pawn my sub off on your fucking brother one more time I'm going to be the one throwing punches, Tag."

Tag slapped the table. "Two thousand. I will bet you two grand you're getting married at the end of this. Come on, man."

He wasn't ever getting married. He wasn't built for it. He'd known what he was born to do since the day he'd met Franklin Grant. He couldn't do that anymore. Not until he cleared his name and found out who'd burned him at the Agency. That man was the one working with McDonald. That name was why he was doing all of this. Yes, he wanted to take McDonald down. Yes, he wanted to stop the senator's network from ever making money off American lives again, but he wanted back in. He wanted his name back, his job back. He wanted to grind down the people who had sold him out.

No. He wasn't getting married and he wasn't getting close to Faith McDonald. Once he got her in bed, he would see that she was like all the rest. And then he could move on with his life.

CHAPTER FOUR

Faith poured a cup of chamomile tea and wondered if her hands were ever going to stop shaking. It had to be six or seven hours since it had happened. Now she was back at Theo and Erin's three-bedroom ranch house and she wondered if she should stay after all. Had she made the right choice? Should she call her dad and head down to the safety of his Houston mansion?

"Hey, you going to be all right?" Erin had changed into pajama bottoms and a tank top, her face scrubbed clean. She'd been hovering all night, and Faith was worried Erin had gotten into serious trouble over what had happened.

"I'm good." She put on a happy face. That was what she did. It was the same fake smile she used when her father forced her to go to campaign rallies. "I am sorry I seem to have gotten you into hot water with Theo's brother."

"Oh, she's not simply in trouble with Theo's brother. She's in trouble with Theo." Theo looked delicious in nothing but a pair of jeans. He strode into the kitchen and planted himself behind Erin, his hands finding her hips. The man couldn't seem to take his hands off his sub.

Which brought her to the other reason she was wondering if she shouldn't run to Houston.

"Erin's in trouble with everyone tonight." Master T stepped in after Theo. Unlike her friends, he was still completely dressed, with the exception of his Stetson. He'd taken that off and placed it on a table in the living room. "But I suspect she'll pay for it and be back in Theo's good graces in the morning."

Erin tried to move away from her Master, but he wasn't having that. She sighed and then relaxed back against him, his arms winding around her waist. "Theo often takes his job far too seriously and uses his position to his own advantage."

Theo's lips curled up in a secretive smile. "That's the thing, baby. Sometimes you think we're playing checkers when we're really playing chess, and that's about the time I take the queen. I'm going to spank the queen tonight because she was very naughty."

There was no way to miss how Erin's eyes softened at the thought. She wanted that discipline.

Faith wanted it too. It had been a stressful day and she wanted to feel a soft flogger on her back and let go of the tension. It was way too early for that. Wasn't it?

"I wasn't thinking," Erin admitted. "I've relaxed since we came home. When Faith said she needed a few minutes, I didn't think it was a big deal."

"You wanted to yell at me in private, Erin. That was why you let her go and that's why you'll be over my knee in a few minutes." Theo's tone held a bit of a bite, the Master coming out.

"Well, I'm back on the job now. Did Big Tag find out anything about our super-dead asshole?" Erin asked.

Master T leaned against the sink, his body all lean muscle and sharp lines. "We should have some kind of ID on him by tomorrow. He's got a tat that makes me think he spent some time in prison, so he'll likely be in AFIS."

"You get to use AFIS?" AFIS stood for Automated Fingerprint Identification System and was used by government law enforcement agencies. Not private investigators.

"The company I work for has some discreet contacts with law enforcement," he explained. "We took prints off your attacker and called in a friend with the DPD. He'll keep everything very quiet, but he'll get us a name by tomorrow, I suspect. We'll regroup and go from there."

She wasn't sure her father, with all his contacts, could work that quickly. He would also be hampered by the press. Maybe she was making the right call. "I'm sure this is about my dad."

"Are you? This couldn't have anything to do with what happened to you in Ghana?" Master T asked.

Just like that the world seemed to go cold. She had to force her hand to close around the mug or she would have dropped it. Ghana. She tried so hard not to think about Ghana. "No. That was an isolated incident. A crime of opportunity, in your vernacular."

Master T shrugged and then turned back to Erin. "And you're not her bodyguard anymore. I am. This is my op."

"I understand that, Sir. I do, but I've worked with her for months. I think I should..." Erin began.

"Stop." The order came out of Theo's mouth as a sharp bark. "Don't argue with our superior. I think it's time we had a talk. T, I've set the alarm and put out bedding for the couch. Is there anything else I can do for you?"

Wow. It was easy to see who was the boss here. Everyone deferred to Master T. She really had to have another name to call him by if she was going to see him in the vanilla world, which it looked like she would.

How had he known about Ghana?

"We'll be fine," Master T replied. "The security system seems up to date, but I'm not happy with all the windows. I'm going to have a discussion with my charge about moving this someplace more secure tomorrow. You're dismissed. And Theo, I expect you to talk to Erin or I'll have to. I know she's used to the way your brother runs an op, but I expect more. And I don't expect that your personal relationship is going to cause any more trouble."

"Of course not, Sir." Erin was practically standing at attention.

Theo nodded. "We'll take care of the situation."

He led her back to their bedroom, his hand finding hers.

"You didn't have to be so mean to her. She was trying to get some time alone with her boyfriend." Erin hadn't been alone with Theo very much because Faith was always around.

Master T stared at her. "She could have gotten you killed."

"She wasn't on duty. She's supposed to be my friend now. I told her to go with Theo."

"And she listened to you when she shouldn't have." He let that settle for a moment before he continued. "I wasn't being mean, Faith. I was being their boss. It doesn't matter that Erin's employment as your bodyguard ended when you left Africa. She should have been watching out for you until I could. And now they're back on the clock and they will answer to me."

"It all seems very military."

"And you have a problem with the military?"

Well, that answered one question she'd had. She'd wondered how he'd gotten into this particular career. She'd kind of been afraid to ask given the fact that she wasn't overly fond of military types. She knew it was all psychological. She really liked Erin. She told herself it was because Erin was the exception, but Faith knew that wasn't true. Erin still acted like she was in the Army half the time, and it didn't bother Faith at all.

Men. It was men in uniform that bothered her.

"Let's simply say I've run afoul of a couple of military men in my time."

There was a long pause. "That wasn't military that took you, Faith. It was a group of criminals."

"They called themselves an army." They'd worn camouflage. Of course, she also knew a real army didn't have little boys carrying weapons almost bigger than they were. Little boys who had pointed those guns at her, who had killed her staff without thought or remorse.

"They weren't," T said with authority. "The team that escorted you home after you were released, they were military. How did you feel about them?"

"Honestly, they scared me, too. I was grateful, but I think I'd seen far too much death by that point. If I never see another gun again, I could be happy." She took a deep breath, trying to banish the memories. "How do you know about this? I thought it was all classified."

"Nothing is truly classified. When Ian asked me to meet you, I looked you up. When I didn't find everything I wanted, I dug deeper."

"Why would you dig deeper?" Their relationship had an end date stamped plainly on it. Most men she knew would simply let it be since they wouldn't be around her for more than a few weeks, a month at most.

"Because I've learned that when something looks too good to be true, it usually is. I want to talk to you about our contract."

Her stomach clenched. She'd had a nice evening with him after her near murder and then him having to clean up after the attacker's actual murder. She'd already proven to be trouble. She'd told herself all night long that it was best to separate business from pleasure, but the idea of keeping a wall between herself and Master T didn't sit well. Still, she had to be practical. "I don't know that's such a good idea anymore, do you?"

"I think it's an excellent idea," he replied. "I think it's more important now than it was before. Are you afraid of me?"

She wanted to lie. She wanted to stand there and tell him yes because it would prove that she was halfway intelligent. She'd seen how deadly the man was. Within two minutes of being in his presence, there had been a dead body at her feet. "No. I know I should be. Why on earth would you think I'm too good to be true?"

He huffed and then turned and opened the fridge, coming back with a beer. "Let's see, you're from a wealthy family, but you're not pretentious or snobby. The fact that you're friends with Erin tells me that."

"I never really fit in with my peers." The kitchen suddenly seemed too small for the two of them. It hadn't been so intimate when Erin and Theo had been here, but she was very aware of how alone she was with Master T.

He stepped closer to her, his eyes on her face. Those blue orbs seemed to hold her so she couldn't look away from him. "You're stunningly beautiful, but you don't seem to know it."

"I definitely don't." She wasn't the beauty in the family. Hope was. Hope cared about things like makeup and hair. Faith's fingernails were cut to the nub and unpainted.

T's hand came out, brushing back a stray lock of hair. When his fingertips grazed her skin, she fought not to shiver. "You're smart and kind and surprise, you're also submissive when it comes to sex. You, Doc, are pretty much exactly what I would ask for if I was putting together the perfect female. So I'm not sure I trust that you're real."

How was she supposed to respond to that? "You're...incredibly attractive."

His lips curled up. "Not perfect for you though. Let's see if I can find my flaws. I'm not well educated. I work a job that most would consider dangerous. You prefer your danger to come in the form of germs and bacteria. And I'm ex-military and mean. That's strike three, Doc. Am I out?"

He was close. Really close. He hadn't been this close since that moment in the alley outside Neiman Marcus. Of course, they'd also been standing over a dead body, and there wasn't one of those here now. Just her and Master T. Standing really close together so that she could smell the sandalwood of his aftershave again.

All it would take would be to tilt her head up slightly and he could plant those lips on hers. Hadn't she been dreaming about it for weeks? She'd wanted nothing more but to know what it felt like to be in this man's arms. From the moment she'd turned on her computer and seen him on her screen, with his gorgeous face and quick mind, she'd dreamed about this moment.

"What do you want me to call you? Uhm, besides Master T. In the vanilla world, I mean. Should I call you Tim?" It came out all breathy when she'd meant it to be an intellectual question, not a "hey, I need something personal to call you in bed when you're taking me roughly" sort of question.

"Call me Ten, Faith."

"Ten? Like the number?"

"As in Tennessee. It's the nickname I grew up with. And yes, that's like the state." He took a step back, his jaw tightening as though he didn't like where the conversation was heading.

"It's an unusual nickname." She needed to know more. Now that she was here with him, she could see that they'd both kept their conversations to this point light and flirty. She knew he was a Cowboys fan. He knew she'd gone to the University of Texas at Austin and managed to never actually attend a football game. They'd talked about how they'd gotten into the lifestyle and told a few stories of some of the crazy things they'd seen.

She didn't know if he had a family. She didn't know where he'd gotten a name like Tennessee.

Ten's eyes focused, as though steeling himself to get through something unpleasant. "When they found me, they weren't sure what to name me so the social workers nicknamed me Tennessee. Later they changed it to Timothy on the registered birth certificate, but the nickname stuck. The bin they found me in was at a diner close to the state line. In a tiny town called Gayleburg. I was happy they chose to name me after the state and not the town."

"Bin? What are you talking about?"

He leaned back, taking a long sip of beer. "I suppose you should know what you're getting into. I don't have a family, Faith. I was raised by the state most of my life. I was found a few hours after I was born. My mother wasn't particularly interested in having a child so she dumped me in a trash bin outside a diner. A homeless man was dumpster diving and he found me. Got me to a hospital. I was there for a while. There's a lot of paperwork that goes along with adopting a kid. Most parents wouldn't touch me because of the legalities."

"Because if the father came forward, he would have the right to his child as long as he hadn't helped get rid of you." She was stunned. She saw horrible things happen all the time in Africa. It was hard to understand how they could happen here where there was so much wealth. Of course the wealth wasn't for everyone. "I'm so sorry to hear that."

"You're tenderhearted." He reached up again and brushed away a tear she hadn't realized she'd shed. "You shouldn't be. You should be hard after what happened to you. You should have screamed today, Faith."

And get more people killed? That was what haunted her about Ghana. The people who had died because she'd tried to run. It had been an instinct. Run. Hide. Live. How many people would have lived if she'd stood her ground? "He could have hurt other people."

He was back in her space again, looming over her. She could feel the heat from his body. If she took a step forward, her chest would touch his and he would likely know exactly how hard her nipples were. What kind of woman was she that she could hear his story and still be so aroused just being close to him? She should be feeling sympathy, not heat between her legs.

"You should understand that you're my first priority. Your safety is my job now. Until we figure out who's coming after you and why, I'm going to make the calls and the decisions and you're going to follow me."

80

"I thought we'd already agreed to that."

"We agreed I would entertain you for the next few weeks."

"Entertain?"

"Isn't that what submission is for you, Faith? You want me to make the decisions, but you want to be pleased with them. If we're going out to eat, you want me to pick the restaurant, but a good Master in your mind would select something that pleases you. I ordered wine for you tonight not because I wanted to force my will on you, but because I happen to know you like a white wine, not the red that would have gone with your filet. You're not really looking for a Dom. You're looking to role-play. Tell me something, have you ever truly submitted to a man?"

Wow. That was judgey. And might point out why her last Dom had left. "I can't help but be who I am, Sir. I suppose you're right. I do view it as a form of entertainment and relaxation and yes, I likely would have been disappointed if you had ordered red wine for me. It gives me reflux."

She tossed it out because she wasn't sure it mattered anymore that her digestive issues might make her seem less than sexy.

"You're used to being in charge," Ten explained. "I'm simply trying to understand you. I'm not saying it's a bad thing. People need different things to complete them. You want the fantasy Dom."

"If by saying fantasy Dom you mean I want a man who cares enough to know what I like and who wants me to have it, then yes. I want that fantasy."

"But you want it without having to ask for it," he accused.

"I didn't have to ask for the wine tonight. You'd already figured it out."

"Did you thank me for it?"

"Thank you. And yes, at the time I did say thank you. I also thanked you for saving me. I'm not sure what else you want." She was starting to get irritated. He was talking in circles around her. This was exactly what she didn't want from a man. She didn't want this horrible feeling in the pit of her stomach that she was missing something, that she wasn't good enough.

"And that's what I mean by role-play. You want your Dom to instinctively know what you need, but you don't want to give him the same courtesy. You want a man who seems to be dominant, but you're still completely in control. I'm having this conversation with you because while I might have been willing to play along in the beginning, everything changed this afternoon. You should understand that I won't allow you control in this aspect. I am in charge of the operation and of you. I will monitor you twenty-four seven. I will be informed of where you go and what you do, and I will select the guards to go with you when I can't. Every aspect of your life will come under my jurisdiction and with only one real goal in mind— you alive at the end of the mission. So I think we need to talk about our contract because it will have two parts. I'll be playing two parts, but understand the guard will always trump the lover."

"You make it sound like I'm hiring you to play both. I'm not hiring a lover." Was she? It had seemed like a fun thing to do. Find a Dom. Spend some time with him. Enjoy something with no strings for once in her life. Now it seemed cheap.

She had to decide between the guardian and the lover. Or she had to pack it up and go home and give herself over to her father and his brand of oppressive care.

"Faith, I'm trying to be honest with you."

She nodded. "And I thank you for it. I think I'll sleep on it. Do you have everything you need, Sir?"

He stared at her and for a moment she thought he was going to argue, but he finally nodded and finished off his beer. "Yes. I'll be on the couch if you need anything."

He nodded her way and walked out.

She needed to start the day over. She needed for things to not get so fucked up. She'd been happy thinking everything was fine. She'd been looking forward to weeks of not having to make decisions, of being taken care of.

Of pretending someone gave a damn.

Foolish. She was utterly and completely foolish and she needed to tell Master T…Ten in the morning that she was going home to Houston.

She was about to walk back to her room and pack her things when she heard it. The sound of a hand slapping flesh and a low, feminine groan.

"You know I'll give you what you need, baby. Always. I want to plan my fucking life around what you need. But give me something

82

back. I need a little something, Erin."

Another smack. Another low moan. "You wouldn't take a little, Theo. You would take everything."

"Only from you. I only want all of you," came the impassioned reply.

She moved away, the intimacy almost too much to bear. She stepped out into the hall and toward the guestroom.

Wasn't that what she was afraid of, too? That she would truly find herself giving everything to some man who wouldn't really care about the gift. Who wouldn't see it as a gift at all, but rather as his due? When she really looked at it from Ten's perspective, it did seem like she was hiring a lover.

Had she intended to take from Ten and give nothing real back? She supposed she thought their needs dovetailed neatly. She was submissive and he was Dominant, but it was so much more complex than that. She wanted to see him as a Dom, but he was a man and he had needs that went past sex.

She'd expected him to take care of her, never thinking that he might like a little care himself. Not simply sexual care or service. Maybe he wanted someone who saw him, too.

She stood there for a moment, her hand on the door, her mind on the man in the living room.

You want your Dom to instinctively know what you need, but you don't want to give him the same courtesy. Had he been right?

Did he want the same courtesy? A woman who gave him something he didn't have to ask for?

She wasn't good at this. She was good at treating patients. At connecting dots and coming up with a diagnosis, but sometimes even a diagnosis was more instinct than science. Every field doctor who had ever been forced to take on a patient knew that.

What did her instincts tell her about Ten?

He'd stepped back to tell her the story of his birth. He'd been close to her before, crowding her and pressing in on her space until she couldn't breathe without acknowledging him. He'd touched her hair, her face. He'd been tender until she'd asked about his name.

Nothing after. He'd expected rejection and she'd unwittingly given it to him.

He couldn't know she'd still found him attractive, still wanted him. He couldn't know she was simply afraid.

This was why she'd "hired" a Dom. So she didn't have to make herself vulnerable. So she didn't have to give him anything of true value.

So she didn't have to care.

Damn it. She already cared about Master T. He'd said she hadn't thanked him for saving her, for taking care of her. She'd given him words, but he wanted something else.

She had the feeling what Master T wanted wasn't sex, but rather affection, tenderness.

Did she really want to be cold? Did she want all the sweetness to flow to her without giving any back? Now that she thought about it, she could see why Roger had wanted more, but in the end, he hadn't been the man to draw it out of her.

Master T might be. She already felt far more for him than she wanted to admit.

The smart play would be to go to bed and head back to Houston in the morning.

So why did she turn? Why did her feet begin to move? Not toward her bed, but out to the living room.

She dropped the questions for the night. If she was ever going to find something real, maybe she should stop role-playing, and that began with giving her Dom what he needed.

* * * *

Ten wanted to punch his fist through the wall. What the fuck had that been? Did he have a goddamn brain in his head anymore? He was smooth. He knew how to handle a woman like Faith. They were all alike in the end. They wanted as much as they could take from a man without having to give anything back. Spoiled rich girls were all the same. They wanted a man to pay court to them. Faith wanted to pretend it was something different, that she was submitting when the truth was she was being cosseted and coddled without having to give anything back.

What would Old Ten have done?

Hell, girl, of course I'll be your Dom. Want me to anticipate your every need? I can do that. Want me to spank your pretty ass and give you an orgasm to make you scream, and pretend it was all because I couldn't keep my hands off you? I'm your man, darlin'.

New Ten had called her out. Something had happened to him since he'd been kicked to the curb by the Agency. He wasn't as smooth as he used to be. He was more irritable, more restless. He definitely felt a change in himself since he'd spent those weeks getting to know her. New Ten had pointed out that he wasn't willing to really do any of it. New Ten wanted more.

New Ten was a fucking idiot who was about to lose his only way onto that island.

He had to sleep on the damn couch to top it all off. He stared down at it. One would think given Theo Taggart's size that he would buy a large couch. Nope. Ten was going to have to cram his body on it.

Or not. It wasn't like he slept a lot anyway. He could sit up all night and try to figure out when he'd lost his edge.

"Ten? Master T?"

He turned and she was standing there. Great. He could probably head home now and save himself the crappy night's sleep since she was going to throw him out. "Yes, Faith?"

"I've thought about what you said and you're right. I am role-playing. It's a game, a way to relax and get something I need because most of the time I give over to what everyone else needs. I like to pretend that there's one person in the world who takes care of me. I guess at the end of the day, I'm willing to pay for the privilege."

"I don't recall sending you a bill." New Ten didn't seem to be able to shut the fuck up. New Ten didn't like the idea of Faith McDonald thinking he did this kind of thing for a living.

Her lips curled up in a self-deprecating smile. "Sanctum sure did. That's not a cheap club. I suppose I was looking at it like you were a package deal. I pay for a membership, they give me a Dom. Please understand, I didn't mean to hurt you."

"You didn't hurt me, Faith. But you have to know the rules of the game changed the minute that man tried to attack you."

"Kill me. I think he was going to kill me. At first I wondered if he wanted to kidnap me, but I saw the look in his eyes. He might have ransomed me back to my dad, but he would have sent back a corpse. You saved me."

That should have been enough to bond them. Weeks he'd worked at getting to know her, to anticipate her needs. He'd played it well in that moment. He'd held her, comforted her. Then he'd blown it and he knew why. He'd blown it because it felt different holding her. Just for a moment, he hadn't been thinking about anything but the fact that she could have died and he might never have held her.

"It's fine now, Faith. You're safe here. The alarm's on and I'm not letting anything get in."

"You're right. I didn't thank you properly."

He stopped. What exactly was she offering him? "If I'm your bodyguard, then I don't need to be thanked."

He should take whatever she offered and get them back on track. He could put on his pleasant mask, spread her legs and give her a great ride. In the morning, she would fall into her role and he would play his. He would let her use him for sex, for comfort, to build up her pride. He could do all of it. All he had to do was take what she was willing to give him.

She frowned. "I'm not good at this part. This is the part where the dominance stuff comes in and I really need an alpha partner to take over, but I'm going to try."

Her face had screwed up sweetly, as though she was determined to get this right. Her seduction techniques lacked subtlety. She walked straight into his arms and sighed as she held him tight. "I'm sorry, Sir. I think today was hard on you, too, and I didn't do a thing to make it better. I know we haven't known each other for long, but I think after three weeks of talking every day, well...I should have been better. A better sub. A better friend. I'm sorry and I'm truly sorry for how you began your life. No one should feel unwanted. I hope you know you're wanted now."

She didn't rub herself against him or start talking dirty. She held him, her hand stroking a line down his back. She placed her head against his chest and relaxed as though she could do it all night, just stand there and hold him.

What the fuck was he supposed to do with that?

Women didn't hug him. They fucked him. They got what they needed out of him. They didn't sigh and listen to his heartbeat and try to soothe him.

He waited for her to turn her face up, to offer him her lips, to rub her breasts against him. He understood sex. He knew what he was supposed to do. She did none of those things, simply stood there, holding him until he finally relaxed because there was nothing else to do. He sighed deeply because her warmth seemed to penetrate him and he could smell the lemongrass scent of her hair, feel his breathing synch to hers.

It had been a shitty day. A shitty month. A shitty year. Fuck, it had pretty much been a shitty life, and he couldn't remember a single time someone offered him comfort in the form of warmth and a heart beating against his. He'd held Phoebe when Jamie died, but he'd focused on her. His rage, his grief had been spent alone. His mourning had no partners.

It was right there. It was right on the tip of his tongue to tell her about his brother, to see what else she could give him.

He pulled away abruptly.

Faith took a step back. "I'm sorry. Was I wrong to do that?"

He forced a smooth smile on his face. "Not at all, darlin'. It's very sweet of you, but it's getting late. You should be in bed."

She grimaced as she looked down at the couch. "You're not going to fit on that."

"I've slept in worse places." It was true. He needed to buck up. He'd gotten soft in his old age.

"I could sleep on the couch. I would fit much better than you."

He wasn't sure he liked this side of Faith. He preferred the pampered princess. "Nah. I'm good."

She stood there for a moment, obviously trying to decide what to do next. "The guest bed is pretty big. I assume this is about the bodyguard part, right? You want to put yourself between me and the door. You could do that if we shared the bed. I'm not trying to…well, I'm not saying I wouldn't, but not tonight. I think I should probably know you better…I don't know what I'm saying. Tennessee, it's late and I would like to share my bed with you. Please come to bed."

He wasn't sure how it happened, but he found himself being led back to her room, his fingers tangled with hers. He watched her move in front of him. He took in how her luscious ass swayed as she walked, how her back was straight, her head held high. Her dark hair was up in a messy bun. It left the nape of her neck exposed and he couldn't help but wonder how soft the skin would be there. On all her questionnaires she'd said she liked a bite of pain. He wondered what she would do if he stopped her, pressed her against the wall, and set his tongue and teeth right where her neck met her shoulders. He would lick her, getting her taste on his tongue, and then bite down enough to make her shiver and moan in his arms. Barely enough to leave a mark so he could look at it the next day and remember the night before.

He was suddenly aware of how small she was compared to him. He had to have a half a foot on her and probably a hundred pounds. After what had happened in Ghana, what did it take for her to wrap herself around him like that?

He was fooling himself. She wasn't like the rest, and saying it over and over again in his head wasn't going to change the fact. He had to find a way to deal with her. He had to wake up in the morning and put them back on the proper footing.

But tonight, he was going to sleep with her.

She led him into the room she'd taken over. He wondered what her own rooms looked like. He would bet Charlotte had decorated this room. It was pretty and feminine. He'd heard some of the women talking about getting Theo's house ready. Theo had made the down payment on the house. It was in his name and he planned to live here. It was all supposed to be part of the setup for the op, but Theo was taking serious advantage of his situation.

Why shouldn't Ten? The girl wanted a Dom for a few weeks. She was obviously attracted to him. He was more attracted to her than he would like to be. What would it really hurt to fuck her long and hard? Hell, it was almost a requirement.

His cock lengthened in his jeans. He would get her in bed and by morning, everything would be back to normal. He would have them on the proper setting and he could get on with his mission.

The bed wasn't big. Barely a double. He would have to sleep on top of her, but that was all right with him.

She dragged the covers down and looked over at him. "Which side do you prefer, Sir? I can take either. Honestly, I'm still getting used to a proper bed. I mostly sleep on cots with lots of mosquito netting."

Because she spent most of her time trying to do good in some of the world's hellholes. "I'll take the side closest to the door."

It wouldn't really matter because he intended to roll her all over that bed. He'd sleep wherever the hell he ended up afterward.

Condoms. He'd forgotten the condoms. "Hey, I've got to grab my bag. I'll be right back."

She was getting under the covers. "No problem. Good night."

He was out the door and practically running down the hall. He forced himself to slow down. Eager. He didn't want to look too eager. He had a chance to right the boat, but he wouldn't do that by jumping up and down like a preteen at a boy-band concert. She needed to understand he was in control of everything and that included his dick. He would go slow and steady and swamp her senses with pleasure before he let himself take his own. She would understand their dynamic then.

He grabbed his bag, which included his SIG, two backups, extra ammo, and a couple of knives in addition to his clothes and laptop. And condoms. They were a weapon, too.

He stepped back into the room, pretending his cock wasn't jumping in his jeans at the thought of finally getting inside her. Weeks of talk had led to this.

She was asleep, her eyes closed and her breathing already steady. She'd curled on her side away from him. Her arms had come up as though protecting her chest.

How much had been left out of that report on Ghana? The "general" she'd been taken by was known for being brutal, but he also had his own code. He would brutalize anyone he couldn't make money off of. Faith would have been a prisoner, but she likely hadn't been beaten or raped because the "general" had been waiting on payment and believed in his business reputation. As long as payment was made in a timely manner, the prisoner was released whole and unharmed physically.

Her ransom had been paid and she'd been released. All the reports claimed she'd been in good physical health, though dehydrated.

She likely hadn't known she was safe. She'd likely seen her colleagues die and wondered if she was next. She'd been held in a prison, wondering if every day would be her last.

He'd had the same thing done to him, though his captors hadn't been so kind and there had been no talk of a ransom. He'd known he would die in that dank prison. He'd practically accepted it, but Faith hadn't been trained. Faith hadn't viewed the world the way Ten did.

What had it taken for her to go back?

He turned off the light and shrugged out of his shirt. It was dark, but he could make out her form in the bed. He set his bag down because it didn't look like he was going to need those condoms tonight.

Most women in her situation—most people—would have hightailed it home and never left the safety of the States again. Faith had simply moved from Ghana to Liberia and set up shop again. She'd been back to vaccinating babies and treating people who couldn't afford medical care. And then she'd been on the front lines of the Ebola outbreak.

She was tough, but she didn't look that way now. He shoved out of his jeans and got down to his boxers and thought about what he would tell her about his scars. His body was covered in them. They were ugly, but there was no way to hide them. He damn straight wasn't going to fuck her with his clothes on, though he'd done that before.

Somehow he thought Faith wouldn't mind his scars. She wouldn't turn away in disgust and she wouldn't be one of those women who was fascinated by them either. Faith would likely simply accept them.

He got into bed, knowing damn well he wasn't going to sleep. He rarely did for more than a few hours at a time. He never slept with someone. Never. He might take a woman, but he left her before he fell asleep. He'd made that mistake exactly once and he had the scar from the knife wound to prove it.

So he wouldn't sleep.

He stared at the ceiling, listening to the sounds of her breathing, and then she turned. She sort of sighed and cuddled up to him. Before he knew what he was doing, his arm had curled around her like it knew where to go. Her head found his chest and one leg curved over his, her arm draping over him.

"Warm," she whispered. "You're so warm."

Then her breathing was back to that even gait.

He wasn't warm. He was cold on the inside, despite the heat his body gave off. He had nothing to give her but dominance and pleasure, and the pain that would come after. Still, his body seemed to mold to hers and somehow between the even sound of her breathing and the hum of the ceiling fan, his eyes closed and for once, Tennessee Smith found some peace.

CHAPTER FIVE

She came awake slowly, well aware she'd slept better than she had in forever. Maybe she'd made a horrible mistake by sleeping alone all this time. Even with Roger, they went their separate ways after sex. It had been years since she'd actually slept beside another human being.

She cuddled close because she wasn't exactly beside the man. She was mostly on him. One leg had gotten thrown over his and her arm was wrapped around his muscular chest.

"You're a cuddly thing, aren't you?"

God, that Southern accent sounded good. Deep and rich. Master T's voice rumbled from his chest.

"You're warm, Sir. Apparently Theo and Erin like to keep their house subarctic, but it's all right because you're so warm." He was like a furnace. She'd gotten used to sleeping in the heat. The air conditioner at the clinic and in the small houses for the doctors only worked sporadically.

He shifted slightly, though not away from her. His arm curled around her shoulders, drawing her near. "I'm glad I could help. I suppose I should be happy you're so cuddly. Otherwise one of us would have ended up on the floor. This bed was not made for a man my size."

It worked because they'd been plastered together all night. When she'd woken from a bad dream, she hadn't been alone. The minute she'd startled awake, she'd felt his skin under hers and known she was safe. It made it harder to do the right thing.

"I don't want to call my dad," she admitted, her cheek against his chest.

"There's no reason to," he replied.

"I don't want you to get hurt." There it was. Her deepest fear. That she would make the wrong call and he would pay for it. That she would panic and more lives would be lost. Every one of their faces haunted her, their names stamped on her brain so she never made the same mistake again.

He moved, rolling over so he was on his side, staring her in the eyes. "This is my job, Faith. I'm not some nurse who wants to vaccinate babies and help the helpless."

"I didn't say you were." It was unnerving that he saw so much of her.

"But they're the ones you're thinking about. You're thinking about those nurses and patients who died during your kidnapping. You're blaming yourself. First of all, it was the kidnapper's fault. Second, this is a completely different situation."

"You could still get hurt." She couldn't stand the thought. It had been so much easier when he'd simply been a name on a piece of paper.

"You're not dragging me into something. I'm telling you that I will protect you. I will figure out who's trying to hurt you and I'll stop them. I'll do it without completely disrupting your life."

His hand came out and ran along her arm, making her shiver. It had been so long since someone touched her in anything but a friendly way. There was intent in Master T's touch.

"I think attempts on my life are pretty disruptive," she replied.

"I was talking about your daily life, darlin'. You had plans to spend time with me, to play with me for the next several weeks. That hasn't changed. We can still do that, but my orders have to do with your safety as well as your pleasure. Don't call your father in. Everything changes the minute he gets involved. Let me take care of you."

"Maybe it was a one-time thing. Maybe it won't happen again." She was trying to be an optimist.

His hand moved, running down her arm. "Maybe."

He was looking at her lips. Staring in fact. She couldn't help but stare back. She'd spent weeks dreaming about him. Those three weeks where they'd talked and flirted and gotten to know each other made it so much easier for her. Despite the fact that she'd basically picked up a man to have an affair with, now it seemed like their relationship was real.

Which it wasn't.

"Hey, what went through your head right then?" His hand came back, brushing her hair out of the way. "Are you still afraid?"

After the way he'd easily taken down the first guy? Yes. She was, but not for herself. She was afraid for him. And a little afraid of him, but not in a physical way. "This feels different than I thought it would."

"How so?" His thumb ran across her lower lip.

"I didn't expect to like you so much. I thought it would be…less personal."

One side of his mouth curved up in the most arrogant, sexy smirk. "There's nothing impersonal about this. This feels really personal to me."

So much of him didn't add up. She was trying to merge the cold Dom Erin had described with the warm man in front of her, and she had to add in the cool professional who had killed a man and never broken a sweat.

"Do they really call you Master No?"

He chuckled. "Apparently. But you're not going to call me that. Are you?"

He was right back to staring at her lips. Actually, it was nice to see the horny side of Tennessee. She loved his name. It fit the man. Enigmatic. "Why do they call you that?"

He scooted closer to her, so close their chests almost touched. "Because I don't play around. Not with women who don't mean something to me. I have my duties at Sanctum and I fulfill them, but I'm not indulgent with women who don't belong to me. I tend to be very much the opposite."

Another thing she didn't understand. Even in their texts and Internet conversations, he'd been indulgent with her. He seemed to want to see her do things that pleased her. He'd ordered her to eat chocolate one night when she said she shouldn't because she was worried about her weight. He'd watched as she'd had her first real chocolate in almost a year. "You're not that way with me."

"I have a contract that states very plainly you *do* belong to me." He stared at her for a moment, and she had an unnerving thought that he could see right through her. "You're not afraid of what could happen to you after yesterday. You're afraid of what could happen between the two of us."

Well, he wasn't pussyfooting around the situation. "Like I said, it feels different than I thought it would. I feel more than I thought I would."

He moved in and she could suddenly feel his heat all over again. Not just his heat. Something really big and really hard was resting against her thigh. It was fairly close to where it should be. Could be. Might be soon.

"There's nothing wrong with that, Faith. Did you really want to sleep with a man you didn't know?"

That three weeks had been the difference. She supposed she'd expected they would get in touch but not a lot more. They would come together to play and have sex. It felt like more than sex. Being so close to Tennessee felt more intimate than actually having sex with Roger. "No. I thought I did. I thought it was kind of the right thing to do. Real relationships are hard for me. My career is kind of demanding."

His fingertips brushed over her collarbone. God, he was killing her. "Yes, it's demanding, but you know what I think?"

He leaned over and kissed the tip of her nose, a sweet gesture.

He was being so tender with her and she wanted to scream at him to jump on her and have his wicked way. Her body was getting primed. Her nipples were so hard. They might climb off her body and try to get between his ridiculously sexy lips. "I don't. I don't know anything right now."

Except the fact that she wanted him. It was probably a bad idea, but she wanted him.

"Then let me help you out, darlin'. You don't have to think for a while. Let's both stop thinking and follow our instincts for once." He moved in and his lips caressed hers.

Easy, thoughtful, at first he simply pressed his mouth to hers, letting them rub together as though taking stock of the feel of her. Ten didn't overwhelm her. He started slow. He let her sigh against him as he brushed his lips over hers and let her taste the mint on his mouth.

She gasped and pushed against him. "You already got up and brushed your teeth."

The most devilish look went over his face and he stopped playing. He rolled over and his body was on top of hers, his hips coaxing her legs to open wide. Before she really knew what he was doing, his cock was right on her core. "Yes, I did. I woke up and brushed my teeth and my poor sub slept the morning away. I came back out here and climbed into bed with you and waited for my moment. I'm going to eat you up, Faith."

His mouth covered hers and she couldn't fight him. It felt too good. His tongue surged and he seemed eager to devour her. His mouth slanted over hers again and again, his body heavy but in the best of ways. She loved his weight bearing her down into the mattress. There really wasn't enough space for the two of them, but they didn't need it. They simply nestled together until she wasn't sure how to untangle their limbs. His chest pressed down, warmth flaring through her as his tongue invaded.

He'd gotten up and prepared himself for her. Oh, he wasn't giving her the same courtesy, but he didn't seem to need it. He wasn't acting like a man who wasn't enjoying himself.

"Stop thinking, Faith," he growled against her lips. "You taste good. You're fucking perfect, and I dreamed about doing this all night. Best dreams I've had in forever. I'm not waiting for you to decide you're good enough for me. I'm telling you. You're perfect and I want to fuck you more than I want my next damn breath."

He took her mouth before she could respond and she kind of melted under him. There was nothing else to do. He'd taken control and she needed this.

He kissed her and his hands explored, running under her tank top and up to the under curve of her breast. His cock was right on top of her mound. Only her pajama bottoms, thin undies, and his boxers were between them. She could feel the hard line of his erection jutting between her thighs, dragging over her pussy in a blatant imitation of what he would do once he got inside her.

"Dreamed about this all damn night." He shifted off to the side and his hand suddenly cupped her, one thumb brushing over her nipple. "Hell, I've dreamed about this since we started talking, Faith, and I think you have, too. That's why you're acting so skittish this morning. You like me."

So arrogant and so damn right. She couldn't help but smile at him. "I do. I like you a lot, Tennessee."

He rolled her nipple between his thumb and forefinger. "Well, that's a good thing because I like you, too, Faith. See, we're already getting along fine. We're going to have fun these next few weeks and I'm going to take care of you."

His hand left her breast and he covered her mouth with his again. The man knew how to kiss. After his initial assault, he seemed content to slow down and take his time. He drugged her with lazy kisses, long and deep. His palm flattened over her belly, lingering possessively before his fingertips started to slip under the waistband of her pajamas. "I think these are going to have to go, darlin'. But first let me show you exactly how I intend to wake up every morning you let me sleep in your bed."

She gasped as his fingers unerringly found her clitoris. The sensation seemed to sizzle all along her body.

"Tell me how you like it, Faith. Long and slow and easy, or rough and hard. I can give you what you want." His words caressed her even as his hand was working to heat her up.

She shook her head. "I like it any way you want to give it to me. I'm not really picky, Ten. It's been a while since my last orgasm, so I'm not going to be choosy." She could barely breathe as he started rotating the pad of his thumb over and around her clit. "It's probably been a year since I felt this good."

The last real orgasm she could remember had been with Roger. The last time she'd felt a body pressed against hers and known she wasn't alone. She hadn't loved Roger, but at least he'd given her that comfort.

This was way past comfort. Actually, there wasn't a damn thing about this that felt comfortable. This was wanting. She needed more from him. She pressed her hips up and was immediately rewarded for her actions with a little slap to her pussy.

Yeah, that did something for her, too.

"No. We're going to start this out right, darlin'. Like I told you, plans have changed and I'm going to be more in charge than you imagined. Poor baby. She thought she was getting some pushover, sissy Dom who would let her take what she wanted."

"I knew your nickname was Master No. I really didn't think you were a pushover." She defended herself, but she could tell what he was doing. This was one more flirtation. Though she was pretty sure he wasn't what she'd bargained for. No, she'd thought she would find someone she could hold herself apart from, but it sure as hell wasn't a sexy as sin cowboy with a dirty mouth that threatened to melt her insides.

His hand slid back down. This time a single finger slid through her thoroughly juicy pussy. "I'll show you how little of a pushover I am tonight. We're going to Sanctum and I'm going to have fun showing off my pretty sub. You should behave today because there could be consequences this evening if you're not careful."

She was going to be at a club tonight with this man at her side. It made her want to glow. Clubs were one place where she could simply be. In a club, she didn't have to be a doctor, didn't have the responsibility of hundreds of lives. In a club, she wasn't Senator Hank McDonald's daughter. In a club, her background didn't matter. She got to be Faith, her own self.

Well, she also got to be Master T's sub, and that was another reason to glow.

His finger slid inside, his thumb finding her clit again. "Who gives you pleasure?"

"You do, Sir."

"Do you take it from me?"

She shook her head. "No. I'm sorry. I was eager. I'm usually better behaved than this, but now I think it was because I didn't want my last Dom the way I want you."

"Oh, I gotta say, I do love a manipulative brat. That kind of praise is going to get you what you want." His lips lowered again, moving against hers as his hand found a rhythm. "But don't try to take one from me again. I'm the Master here. I'm the man who takes care of you here."

He added a second finger, fucking her while his thumb pressed down. There was nothing to do but let him have his way. Yes, this was what she needed. He was right about that. All her inhibitions melted away. She didn't need them.

"Look at me. Don't close your eyes," he commanded.

She looked up into his serious blue eyes. He was so lovely, with his square jaw and blade of a nose. Her Master was the very definition of masculine beauty. "Yes, Sir."

His hands never stopped moving, and she was so close now as he watched her. "I want to see you come, darlin'. I want to watch you come for me and then it's going to be my time. Then you're going to roll a condom over my cock and I'm going to take you fast and hard. I won't be able to hold back, Faith. I want you, too. I want you more than I've ever wanted another sub."

His words warmed her, but she couldn't think about it for too long because her body was taut, right on the edge. She couldn't breathe as he sent her flying over it. Pleasure coursed through her, but when she opened her mouth to scream, he covered her. He kissed her, drinking down the sounds of her pleasure like a man dying of thirst.

So good. It felt so right to be here with him, and now she wished they weren't wearing so many clothes. She wanted to curl against him, skin to skin.

His hand eased out and he gave her one last kiss before bringing his fingers to his mouth and thrusting them in, tasting her with obvious pleasure. "Damn, girl. You make a man feel good responding to him like that."

She had to smile. "Yeah, I think that's a 'you' response."

It was only for him.

"We're going to keep it that way. After I have my time, I'm going to feed my pretty sub and then we're going to talk about moving to my place. But for now, how about we get out of all these clothes and get to know each other even better?" He was reaching for her tank top when there was a short knock and then the door opened.

"Hey, sleepy head, I brought you some coffee. Well, Theo's version of coffee. It tastes like shit to me. Oh, hey, Ten." Erin grinned. "I noticed you weren't on the couch. I thought you'd gone out."

Faith felt herself flush. She was likely a nice shade of red.

Ten just frowned at Erin. "No. I didn't leave. Now reach over there, pass me that box of condoms, and go away."

"Oh, that's probably not happening," Erin said with a rueful shake of her head. "Big brother's here. Apparently Tag knows who tried to kill Faith and he's all pissy about it."

"Yo, Ten," a masculine voice shouted. "Dude, I have my daughters here. Could we keep this family friendly? Get your ass out here. You're going to want this intel. And dear god, make sure you're dressed and calm and stuff. Sweet baby girls don't need to see that kind of thing, do they? No, they don't. Tell Uncle Ten to put away his junk. Yes."

"Oh my god. Fatherhood has turned him into a complete idiot." Ten groaned.

Erin tossed Faith a robe and put the coffee on the side table. "I tried to tell Tag you weren't here, but he bet Theo that you were likely in here, you know. Doing it. Though Tag doesn't say the words around the babies. He makes a deeply junior high gesture." She made a circle with the thumb and forefinger of one hand and inserted a finger into it.

Ten rolled out of bed. "He's an asshole." He put his head out the door. "You're an asshole. A cock blocking asshole, and this intel better be good."

"Dude, language around the girls. And it's fucking really good," Theo's brother replied.

"It can wait ten minutes while I take the world's fucking coldest shower. I hate him." The door to the bathroom slammed shut.

Erin sat down on the bed. "So you totally…"

"Nope. I mean I had a pleasant morning, but we didn't get as far as that." She sat up, now happy she hadn't gotten naked. She couldn't help but grin back at her totally juvenile friend. She knew she should be a bit more interested in whatever information Theo's brother had discovered, but she kind of wanted to leave that to Ten. It was more fun to talk to Erin about relationship stuff. Of course, she could only do it because she trusted Ten to take care of the security aspect of her life. Maybe she shouldn't, but her every instinct told her she could trust this man with her life. "But seriously, when you make that gesture and you're talking about Ten, you should use two fingers. Maybe three."

That skinny finger Erin was using didn't describe her Master in any way.

100

"I can hear you, Faith," Ten growled through the door.

Her poor Master. She dissolved into laughter with her friend.

* * * *

"God, you're a bastard, Tag." Ten strode into the kitchen ready to kill someone, but Tag had his bulletproof vest on, and by bulletproof vest Ten really meant there was a damn baby in his arms. Even he wasn't horrible enough to shoot through a tiny, wriggling baby.

Tag's face split in a shit-eating grin. "Hey, remember when you tried to cock block me in India? Payback's a bitch, brother."

He didn't like to admit it, but when Ian Taggart called him "brother" it made Ten want to kill him less. With Jamie gone, Tag was the closest thing he had. "Yeah, well, I remember you greeted me at the door with a revolver and threatened to shoot the next person who came between you and your wife."

"See, I taught you, but you didn't listen. You should have shot Erin on sight."

"Hey," Theo said with a frown as he entered with the second baby in his arms. Tag's actual brother shook his head Ten's way. "No shooting my girl. No matter how much she deserves it. This one's diaper is changed. Jeez, man, what are you feeding her? That was horrible."

Maybe he didn't want to be Tag's brother if it meant having to change diapers. "He should be paying you to do that, and you do understand that this is an op, right? We're alone. You don't have to keep your cover up. Erin took Faith out to pick up a few things she needed."

"Hey, this might be an op, but she is my girl. And this stinky thing is my niece. I have a blood obligation to ensure her backside is clean while her momma is at yoga class." Theo shifted the baby on his shoulder. The little girl seemed to settle in for a nice nap. "I personally think it's great that Charlotte is finding her Zen. She's going with Phoebe, Eve, and Avery."

"Serena and Grace claim they have a prior engagement. I happen to know they meet every Saturday morning for mimosas and beignets. It's their form of relaxation. I'm kind of with them on that one." Tag took a drag off his coffee. "And this isn't a cover for Theo. He's in love."

"Tell me you're not serious." The last thing Ten needed was his backup operatives having their own soap opera going on.

Tag laughed as he shifted the baby and dragged the rag on his shoulder off, wiping down her mouth. "This is my child. I mention the word love and she barfs."

Theo rolled his eyes while Tag cleaned up his unromantic child. "Erin and I are good. That's all anyone needs to know. Erin and I are going to be perfectly fine after the op is over. She even likes the house I bought for us."

"Yeah because you totally used this op to seduce her," Tag shot back. "You better keep her happy because I'm firing your ass if she sues us for sexual harassment."

"There's no harassment. There is some truly beautiful lovemaking though," Theo explained.

Tag's face screwed up in a truly disgusted expression. "Oh, god, Kala, I think you're going to have to clean Daddy up this time."

Ten was done with the drama. "Is anyone going to explain why the two of you thought it was important to screw up my morning? I would like to point out I'm the one who actually needs to fuck someone for his mission."

The minute the words were out of his mouth, he wanted to take them back. They felt wrong, which was precisely why he stood strong. It was the truth. No matter how good it had felt to sleep with her the night before, she was a mission. Faith McDonald was a means to an end and nothing more. He wouldn't let her be anything more. It didn't matter that she responded to him so beautifully or that he was crazy about how open she was.

It could all be a lie. It could all be a way to draw him in, and he would do well to remember that.

"Oh, I've found Erin is so much easier to be around when she's been sexually satisfied. Trust me, I'm doing us all a favor." Theo's face lit up with a supremely satisfied grin. "Mostly me though. That woman is hot as hell and she's all mine. She might not know it yet, but that honey is going to marry me."

Tag shook his head. "You'll have to forgive him. He's overly pleased with himself."

"Hey, she's happier now. She's less caustic. She smiles more," Theo said. "She simply needed to know she's lovable."

Ten groaned. "Are we on a secret Oprah episode?"

"Fine. Fine," Tag allowed. "I'll get to the good stuff. You, my friend, are dealing with the Ukrainian mob."

"That's the good stuff?" He and Tag had very different definitions of good. "Explain."

"We got a hit on your corpse. As we thought, he was already in the system." Tag slid a folder across the table to him. "He's an American with Ukranian ties. His parents emigrated when he was a kid. His father was a minor figure with the San Francisco based part of that Odessa mafia. You killed John Kozak. He's been nabbed for murder for hire. Yes, you got yourself an actual mob assassin. Fun way to start your day."

"Shit. What the hell do they want with Faith?" Even as he asked the question, his gut twisted.

"Should I enumerate all the ways she could be in bed with them?" Tag said with a hint of nauseating sympathy in his voice.

"Don't. We need to look at her financials. And I'd like to see her vaccination programs." It made him sick to his stomach, but he understood the con. Faith's sister's company would be convinced to donate vaccines and drugs to her clinic. The mob would be the ones running the transportation company that handled the shipment, and they would switch out the real drugs for placebos. They would take the real drugs and sell them on the black market for fun and profit that they might or might not share with a doctor who tipped them off on the shipment.

Could Faith be working a con? She wouldn't be the first doctor to do it. She certainly wouldn't be the first naïve idiot to think she could make something of herself in Africa only to be ground down and left barren.

It could have happened. She could have taken the bait when she needed money. Or she could have seen a good deal and taken it. She could be looking out for number one.

"You think Faith's working with them?" Theo patted the baby's back as he paced.

"No, I think she was working with them and now they've decided she's expendable. We need to figure out why." No matter

103

what she'd done, he needed to keep her alive until he'd gotten the dirt on her father. He had to figure out how she'd fucked over the Ukrainians and protect her until such time that he no longer needed her and then they could take her.

Or he could take her and punish her and bend her to his will and make damn sure she never did anything criminal again. He could keep her all for himself once he'd properly spanked the criminal out of her.

"That doesn't sound like Faith," Theo said, a frown on his face.

It struck him that Faith had liked Theo. Faith had asked about Case because she liked Theo so damn much. She'd obviously charmed him to the point that he couldn't see her as a criminal. "So she should have given you a pamphlet detailing her crimes? Is that what you expected? Did I train you at all?"

Theo's eyes narrowed. "Of course you did. You trained me to make judgment calls. To really look at people and figure out what they're capable of. She's not capable of this. She wasn't working with the mob. What would she do with them? You think she was selling drugs? Because I've watched that woman beg and plead for anything she can get for her patients."

Of course she did. She was likely Mother Theresa in public. She was likely very useful to her father as well. Being able to parade around his saintly doctor daughter would be good PR. "I want Hutch to pull absolutely everything he has on the relationship between Faith and her father."

"She's got a love-hate relationship with the man," Theo replied.

"I don't want to hear about your perceptions." It was obvious Theo had taken a big dose of Faith's Kool-Aid. Of course, Ten himself had woken up this morning basically vowing to protect her. "I want solid proof. I want their e-mails to one another. I want anything I can get my hands on. These people are smart. They won't show their colors in public."

"McDonald certainly won't," Tag agreed. "He's been a politician for almost forty years. He started in state politics when he was straight out of college."

Tag wasn't telling him anything he didn't already know. "McDonald's family is political royalty. His family has held a seat in congress or the senate for the last fifty years. There's talk about Hope eventually following in her father's footsteps. So this is a family who knows how to keep the skeletons hidden. We need to dig deeper. We need to figure out how Faith is involved in her father's schemes."

"Or we can accept that she's not." Theo laid the baby he was holding down in her carrier thingee. When he stood back up, his hands were on his hips, judgment plain on his face. "I think she's exactly what she looks like. She's been nothing but kind to everyone we've met up with and she's done wonders with Erin. I don't think Erin's ever had a female friend like Faith, so you need to understand that I'm going to look out for her. Erin cares about her, and that makes her my responsibility."

Tag looked down at the baby in his arms. "It's time to vomit again, Kala. Uncle Theo's going to break into song."

"She's not your responsibility. She's the target and now I'm worried that I have to work against my own team." He faced off with Theo, who he'd trained. Theo had been trained to see deeper, to view the world through the filter of the mission. It seemed to Ten like Theo had gotten too comfy with his target. "I know you've spent months with her. I know you care about her, but even if she's not involved with her father's business, you getting emotional about this is going to get Faith killed. I'm going to ask you some serious questions and I want you to answer me like the operative I know you can be."

Theo's jaw had tightened, his shoulders straightening as though he couldn't help himself. "Yes, sir."

"Can you give me one good reason for the Ukrainians to send an assassin after her?"

Theo's eyes closed briefly and they were colder when he opened them. "She's gotten involved in something that could compromise their operations."

"And what do the syndicate's operations consist of?"

"Obviously they're criminal enterprises, Ten. I know where you're leading. You want me to add one and one and come up with two. If she's involved with the mob, then she's involved with something criminal."

The boy could be led to the proper conclusions. "And if she's involved with criminal operations, it only makes sense she's also involved with her father. It would be awfully coincidental if her father kept her in the dark, but she still managed to find her way to his lifestyle. Can we connect the senator with the mob?"

Tag sighed and sat back, his big hand cradling the baby. She rested along her father's forearm, her head in that strong hand. Her eyes were closing because that baby wasn't worried about anything. She was completely certain that her father would take care of her.

Ten had read the reports about himself. He'd been a fussy baby, crying even when held, as though he'd never once trusted the person who held him. It had been a factor in moving him from home to home even as an infant. No one wanted a fussy baby.

Faith had curled in his arms, as though she totally trusted him. The night before she'd turned over in her sleep and draped her body over his like they'd been sleeping together for years. He'd been stiff at first and then he'd relaxed, enjoying the way she felt. Well, everything but his cock had relaxed. That looked like it would stay stiff all fucking day.

He'd just learned she was involved with the mob and he still wanted to be inside her.

"I've got Markovic on it. Apparently he's got some ties there," Tag explained. "He was calling some people this morning, and hopefully he can figure out why they put the kill order on her. I put a call in to my *Bratva* contact. He might have heard something. I'll ask him about Faith and the senator when he calls back."

Ten chuckled. He was fairly certain Big Tag had never expected that his wife would come with a full set of Russian mafia in-laws. "You're still in touch with Dusan?"

Dusan Denisovitch was Charlotte and Chelsea's cousin. He was also the head of the Denisovitch Syndicate, one of the most successful of the *Bratva* or the Brotherhood. Dusan had risen to the head when the former leader had been murdered. Ten was fairly certain he was currently in the same room as the man who had killed Dusan's father. He'd often wondered if Dusan thanked Tag for clearing the way.

"Yep. I can't get rid of anyone," Tag complained. "The good news is Dusan's actually fairly rational for a criminal. He'll call back when he's done doing whatever he does. I try not to ask. I'll have a report for you on Monday."

He would have to get through the weekend before he found out the truth. He looked over at Theo. Theo believed Faith, but Theo hadn't seen the things Ten had seen. Theo'd never nearly been gutted by a woman he'd recently finished fucking. Yeah, that had happened to Ten more than once. Theo thought Erin was a handful. He'd never had to go hand to hand with an MSS agent who tried to take off the cock she'd just sucked.

He couldn't believe in Faith. He had to keep himself apart. It was simply proving more difficult than it usually was. Usually it wasn't difficult at all. Damn but he wished he knew what it was about Faith that called to him. Her innocence? That could be false. She wasn't the most beautiful woman he'd ever slept with, but he couldn't think of a single one he preferred to her. Maybe Theo wasn't the only one who needed to remember what the hell he was doing here.

"Get me the info I need, Tag."

Tag's eyes met his. "I will. What are you going to do about the girl if she's dirty?"

"Whatever I have to." It was the only answer he was willing to give. He sighed. "I should get ready. She'll be back soon. I want to move her over to my place. I can keep better track of her there. Has she eaten yet?"

Theo shook his head. "I asked her to pick up some cereal while she was out."

Poor Erin. She wasn't getting a cook out of Theo. "Do you have eggs? I don't eat cereal."

Tag's eyes lit up. "Hey, I could eat."

Ten sighed and opened the fridge to see what he could do. Maybe cooking would take his mind off the fact that he might have to turn Faith over to the authorities.

Or depending on how bad the situation was, he might have to kill her himself.

CHAPTER SIX

"It has to move fast, Erin. I only have a few weeks off," Faith said as Erin turned toward the house she and Theo shared. It was in an older neighborhood with plenty of trees. Everything seemed green and pretty.

"I'm not being judgmental. God, don't think that for a second. I'm simply pointing out that you've only known Ten for a few weeks. I don't want you getting hurt."

"And I thank you for that, but I know the score." She actually didn't like to think about the fact that she would have to leave him in a few weeks. She'd never really thought about it with Roger. She'd enjoyed their time together, but she'd always been ready when it was time to go back to work. The thought of leaving Ten kind of made her heart clench.

It was because it was new and he was so gorgeous. He was different. Surely she wouldn't feel this way after a few weeks of spending tons of time together. After she'd actually slept with him, she would likely yawn and go back to her real life. Yeah. That was going to happen.

God, she was going to get her damn heart broken.

She put on a smile. "We're just having fun. We're not serious. Not everyone is as suited as you and Theo."

Erin's hands tightened on the wheel. "I'm thinking of breaking up with him."

Faith turned in her seat. "What? Why would you do that?"

"It won't work," Erin said, her voice small. "Isn't it better to rip the bandage off?"

She shook her head, her heart hurting for Erin. What was going on behind the scenes?

"No. Nope. As a doctor I can tell you plainly that it's a bad idea to rip the bandage off. It tends to do more damage. And what do you mean it won't work? You two are perfect for each other."

"I don't think I'm perfect for anyone," Erin muttered. "It's not him. He's a great guy. I'm not cut out for a long-term relationship."

Something else was working here. "How long have you two been together?"

She hesitated for a moment before answering. "A year now."

That was longer than most of Faith's relationships. "Have you ever had a relationship last this long?"

"No."

"Then you're nervous because everything's going well." Faith actually knew the feeling. She felt a bit of it this morning. Waking up with Ten had been a revelation. It should have been awkward and weird but it had felt...right. It felt like they'd been sleeping side by side for years. "You need to relax. He's madly in love with you."

"I don't know why."

"Then ask him." Communication was important. The lifestyle mentors she'd been around had preached it incessantly. How could a Dom know what worked if the sub never talked to him about it? Sure they were talking about scenes, but Faith had always known when she met the one, she would use that belief in her relationship. She would be open and honest about what she needed.

Was Ten "the one?" Was he the man she might give up her clinic for? She'd always thought she would work until she died, giving her service to the world around her. What if she could have more? What if she could have a family and a husband and love?

"You think I haven't done that?" Erin's question pulled her from those dangerous thoughts. "He gives me some bullshit about being strong and feeling like I complete him. I don't complete anyone, Faith. He doesn't...he doesn't even know everything. He's never met my dad or my brothers."

"Why haven't you introduced him? You're living with the man."
Was she going to introduce Ten to her family? Sure they would be on
the island, but there was a difference between "hey, this is my date"
and "hello, Dad, I'd like you to meet the man I might be falling for."

She sounded like such an idiot girl in her head.

"That so wasn't my idea," Erin replied. "And I don't think it's a
good idea for Theo to meet them. I don't have much contact with my
family anymore, but he's started asking about them. I don't want
those two worlds to collide."

Ah, so there was the issue. She knew there had to be one buried
deep. "You would rather break up with him than have him meet your
family."

"Yes," Erin answered in a flat tone.

"Tell him. He'll understand." She hesitated to bring anyone into
her weird family, too. It had been easy up to this point.

"No, he'll get nosy. Theo's sticky. He's everywhere. He won't
just have sex. He's gotta get all involved and stuff. I've gone along
with it, but I don't want to talk about this. I got over it a long time
ago. Theo's not going to let it sit so I should break it off now. Well,
soon. I don't know. I shouldn't be talking about it anyway." She
frowned. "I think someone's following us."

Faith turned in her seat, but all she saw was another car, driving
sedately down the street. At that moment, Faith's cell phone trilled.
Her sister. "Why do you think we're being followed?"

"Because that car turned when I did. It's a Benz. We don't have
those on this street. I think it's been following us since we left the
drugstore."

Faith slid her finger across the screen. Her stomach knotted. Was
she putting them in danger again? It was so easy to sit back and let
Ten handle all the nasty stuff, but she had to seriously consider that
she was endangering everyone she cared about. "Hey, Hope. I'm
going to have to call you back."

"Or you could stop the car and say hello. Hey, I think you're
speeding, sis. Are you sure you're okay?"

Faith turned in her seat. Sure enough, she could see her sister's
blonde hair through the windshield. She let out a long breath. At least
no one was trying to kill her at the moment. "We're being followed
by my sister. I think it's safe enough to go home." She put the phone

to her ear again. "Hope, why are you behind me?"

One hand came up and waved vigorously. "I have a seminar at Presbyterian on Monday and I thought I'd say hi."

"How did you know where I was?"

"Oh, I totally track your cell phone."

"You what?" She shouldn't be surprised, but there it was.

"Hey, I once lost you to a rebel army in Ghana. I track your damn cell phone. If I could put one of those pet scanner things under your skin, I would. So let's get to wherever you're staying so I can hug you."

She put her hand over the phone. "It's my sister. Is it all right for her to come in? If not, I can go with her."

Erin pulled into her driveway. "No, you can't. Unless your sister is a trained bodyguard, you won't be going anywhere alone with her, or have you forgotten?"

She had kind of forgotten. The morning had been more about kisses than someone shooting at her. She hadn't thought twice about leaving with Erin. Now she wondered. "Are you carrying a gun?"

Erin put the car in park. "Of course. I've got one on me and another in my bag. A knife, too. A girl's gotta accessorize. So you're sure that's your sister pulling up in front of my house?"

Hope was already out of the car. It was a Saturday but she was dressed to the nines in a sheath that showed off her slender body and what looked to be five-inch heels. Likely straight from a fashion label's trunk show. She was carrying her Chanel bag and smiling brightly. "My baby sister! I had to track you down, but I found you."

She couldn't help but smile back. When Faith started forward, Erin reached for her elbow.

"Not here. Let her come up. We've got cover up here but none in the yard."

Had Erin really been scoping every place they'd been this morning for assassins? Faith shivered at the thought but did as Erin asked. Her sister strode up the walk. "Hope, I'm surprised, but it's good to see you."

"Well, you weren't coming to me," her sister complained. "I had to come to you." She threw open her arms and enveloped Faith in a hug. "I'm so glad you're home and safe. Tell me you're never going back there."

Her sister smelled like money. It wasn't bad. She smelled really good, but it reminded Faith of everything she'd left behind. She loved her dad and her sister and she didn't doubt that they loved her, too. But they were all right with the world the way it was. They kind of approved since they were the ruling class. Faith couldn't live that way. Faith pulled back. "It's good to see you, too. But of course I'm going back. I'm here through my birthday. I'll be going home after that. Hope, please meet my friend, Erin Argent. Erin, this is my sister, Hope."

Erin nodded. "Nice to meet you."

Hope stared at her for a moment. "You were my sister's bodyguard?"

"She's still kind of my bodyguard." Faith didn't want to explain Tennessee, but she was probably going to have to.

Erin simply smiled. "I'm watching out for her while she's here. You know with your dad being who he is, I think it's important that Faith has someone looking out for her."

Hope reached out, putting her hand on Erin's shoulder. "You have no idea how long I've tried to explain this to her. Daddy's got some pull. It places her in a bad position. My god, the girl got kidnapped. You would think she knew this. It's so nice to meet a woman who gets it. So you're Erin? She talked about you in her e-mails."

"Really? God, I can't imagine what she said." Erin started moving toward the entry. "Why don't you come inside? Faith's staying with me until we head out to the islands."

Faith followed behind. "I invited Erin and her boyfriend to come with me."

She hoped Theo was still Erin's boyfriend by the time they got to the Caymans. They were too sweet together. Erin and Theo did a great job of hiding it, but they were the kind of D/s couple she would like to be part of. Theo was a loving top. Erin was a true partner to him. They cared for each other and gave the other what they needed. In and out of bed.

Could she find the same thing with Master T?

Hope smiled. "The more the merrier. As long as I get to spend some time in the sun with my little sis, I'm happy."

They both started to follow Erin inside.

A heavenly smell hit her nose. It smelled like she wouldn't have to eat that granola cereal she'd bought. Erin had gotten a box of something a five-year-old would eat for her and Theo. But whatever was cooking now truly smelled magically delicious.

"Hey, you're in time for breakfast." Ian Taggart was sitting in Erin's kitchen, a baby in his arms.

Her damn stupid heart nearly melted. There was something about a big strong man and a baby that got to her.

Of course, there was also something about a man who knew his way around a kitchen that did something to her girl parts, too. Ten was standing at the stove, flipping what looked like pancakes with an expert hand. Theo was pouring a cup of coffee.

It was a lovely domestic scene.

"But we bought cereal," Erin said.

"Which we no longer need," Faith added quickly. "It smells heavenly, Sir."

"Sir?" Hope stood beside her, her eyes wide. "Oh, Faith, tell me you're not. Oh. Hello."

Hope had gotten a good look at Theo, and for the first time in Faith's memory, her sister seemed to go completely blank. She would practically swear her sister was drooling.

Theo nodded her way, but held his hand out for Erin. "Hello. Baby, Ten decided he could do better than our sad cereal. He's making pancakes and bacon and eggs. I have to say I'm really surprised that he's got that skill set. So, why don't you introduce me to the new girl?"

Erin waved her way. "Apparently Faith's sister is a paranoid freak who keeps close tabs on her."

Faith felt all eyes on her. "This is my sister, Hope McDonald. I recently found out she tracks my cell phone. Hope, this is Erin's boyfriend, Theo, his brother, Ian, and my…friend, Ten."

Ten turned and held out a hand. "Timothy Graham, but my friends call me Ten. And I'm obviously more than her friend. For now, let's just say your sister and I are involved. It's nice to meet you. Would you like some breakfast?"

Hope took his hand and shook it. "It's nice to meet you, Mr. Graham. Do I call you that or is there some weird lifestyle thing I should call you? Sorry. My sister doesn't tell me much, but she called you sir so I figured it's one of those things."

Faith could feel herself turning beet red. "Sorry. She's very vanilla. I've tried to explain."

Ten shook his head. "It's not an issue. Hope, it's very nice to meet you."

"And you," Hope said, though she was still looking at Theo.

Erin seemed to notice. Her arm went around her man's broad shoulders. "Yes, welcome to our place. Any relative of Faith's is certainly welcome into our home."

Theo kissed his girl's cheek. "Damn straight, baby. Let's eat."

Ian slapped a hand on the table. "Now you're speaking my language, brother. Ten, I'm going to need a fat stack of those pancakes."

By the time an hour had passed, Faith had found herself completely surrounded by Theo's crazy family. The women had shown up about fifteen minutes in. Charlotte Taggart had led the way. The gorgeous redhead had strode in, complaining that someone better put a baby on her boobs because her milk was letting down and it had made yoga class very interesting. She'd pulled out a boob and started nursing her baby at the long dining room table. Phoebe Murdoch had simply grabbed a plate and a cup of coffee and texted her husband to join them.

It was a joyous chaos that somehow filled her soul. It reminded her of the way meals went in her clinic in Africa. They all gathered around and talked and ate and complained about the day. The only difference was these people knew each other. Intimately. Completely. They were a family. They didn't rotate out every six months.

Dinners at her father's house were quiet affairs. She could barely remember her mother. She'd been five when her mother had been murdered by a mugger. So when she was actually home and they sat down to eat, it was her father, her sister, and Faith talking quietly about how their day had gone.

There were no women breastfeeding. No men ribbing each other. No one marched in and started making out with his wife while he stole her bacon. Phoebe had vowed revenge for the loss of her precious protein.

She'd loved every moment of it. She'd especially loved it when Ten had sat down beside her, putting a plate in front of her before digging into his own. She'd waited for him. He'd tried to give her the first plate, but she'd stood by him, helping him. It was her place.

She really liked being Master T's sub. There was something soothing about it. He was a man who put others first. Someone needed to put him first. He needed to know he was important.

This was what had been truly missing from her other relationships. Master T needed her for something more than sex and submission. He needed someone who really cared about him.

"Those people are crazy." Hope stepped into her room and away from the chaos. "Everyone but the cute one."

Faith had to shake her head. Ever since the moment she'd introduced her sister to the gang in the kitchen, Hope hadn't been able to take her eyes off Theo. "I'm completely shocked. You totally have a thing for Theo. You know he's taken, right?"

"By that ridiculous tomboy? I have no idea what he sees in her." Hope shook her chicly cut hair.

"Well, they're happy together so you need to back off." She'd been shocked at how aggressive Hope had been. She'd sat by Theo, asking him about his former Navy SEAL days and practically preening like a schoolgirl with a crush. She hadn't actually eaten anything, simply drank three cups of plain black coffee, smiling whenever Theo would refill her mug.

"He's former Special Forces," Hope said with a sparkle in her eye.

"Yes, I know. I hired him." It was so odd to see her super-serious sister with a full-on crush.

"But you don't really know what it means." Hope's eyes narrowed as she seemed to be thinking something through. "I've been working a lot with soldiers lately."

"I thought you were working with orthopedics. Are you developing new prosthetics?" God, that would mean her sister was doing some good in the world. Her sister had been the single most gifted surgeon she'd ever seen. Top of her class at Johns Hopkins, she was board certified in two fields, but Faith didn't know of a surgery her sister couldn't master almost immediately. What did she do with her gift? Was she at a teaching hospital? Was she innovating? Nope. She'd left surgery behind. She worked on whatever paid the most money, and that tended to be things to aid in weight loss, lose wrinkles, or help the overstressed cope. Not that those were bad things, but the world needed better prosthetics, too.

"Something like that. It's pretty complex. Let's say I'm developing an overall program to aid soldiers in doing what they need to do. Someone like Theo is the perfect candidate. Healthy. Well adjusted. Strong family background with lots of support. He's exactly the kind of man we like to work with."

"Well, except he hasn't lost a limb, thank god." Theo seemed to have come out of his Navy days intact. Of course one never knew what was bubbling under the surface, but Theo seemed to have it all.

Hope shook her head as though clearing it and turned back to Faith. "Of course. And that really is a good thing. So who is this Ten person and what kind of name is that?"

Oddly, she didn't want to go into it with Hope. The story behind his name was so intimate, she didn't feel like sharing it with anyone. She had to wonder how many people knew Ten's real history. It was easier to brush it off. "It's a nickname. I don't think he likes Timothy too much. He's ex-military, too. You know they all call each other by their call signs and stuff."

"How well do you know this man?" Hope asked, her mouth curling down.

Ah, the judgment was back in full force. She might pay Theo to strip off his shirt to distract Hope long enough that she could get away. "I know a lot about him. I've spent the better part of a month getting to know him."

"I don't like it one bit. I want to put a PI on him. You can't take him out to Daddy's place without a full security check."

"I know that." She was supposed to submit the names of her traveling companions so her father could run them through various places and ensure himself that they weren't serial killers or even worse, Democrats. "I'll send him the names in a week or so. They've all agreed to jump through Dad's hoops. I told them it's worth it since Dad's bartenders don't go easy on the good stuff. So stop worrying. Besides, the club does its own background checks."

"Yeah, we'll have to agree to disagree on how much we should trust some kink club to protect you. I don't like that man."

"Ten? What don't you like about him?"

"He's cold. Far too cold for you."

"He's not cold at all. He's quite charming." It was why she couldn't understand how the other subs had taken to calling him Master No. He had a ready grin and a quick wit. He looked far more like a cowboy than the ex-soldier he was. Master T was surprisingly sweet. Even after that jerk had tried to kill her, he'd held her and allowed her to feel safe. There was nothing cold about him.

"Oh, he's charming, but it's all an act. That one's cold. He's got you fooled, sis. There's a snake under that sexy smile. I would love to look into his background. I bet he was more than a mere foot soldier. As a matter of fact, I would bet that one has some intelligence work in his background."

"Don't all Special Forces?"

She shook her head. "Not really. They're muscle. Intelligent, well-trained muscle, but they don't actively form missions. They carry them out. Your guy, he sent men in. He made rough calls."

"How would you know that?"

Hope shrugged. "I don't for sure, but I've been working on this project for five years now. I've gotten to know military men of all kinds, and he doesn't have the same demeanor. In fact, I wouldn't have said he was ex-military at all if you hadn't told me. There's something about the way a military man stands, holds themselves...I don't know. It's hard to explain. But your Ten doesn't have it and that makes me interested in him."

Hope's Smarty Pants was showing through. She'd done this all their lives. She always knew more than Faith. It was best to brush it all off. "Well, you'll get the chance to delve into his background soon enough. I think Dad's security team will have the reports in the next few weeks. He won't send the plane out until he's satisfied. Score one for controlling fathers."

"And that's a bad thing? You can't blame him after what happened to mom."

They sat for a moment, their shared loss between them. Faith's mother had been killed in a mugging. While their father had been on the road campaign stumping, Alice McDonald had chosen to stay behind with her sick daughter. The way she'd been told, Faith had taken a fever and her father had a very important speech to give the next day. He'd left Alice with the girls in a hotel in New York, not wanting to put Faith on a campaign bus. Alice had gone to get a prescription filled and was murdered by a man who took her purse and left her to die in an alley.

When she thought about it, it made sense her father was a bit overprotective. He'd lost his wife and then nearly lost her when she'd been taken in Ghana.

"My friends are all right. They'll pass any tests Dad puts them through."

Hope sighed. "Good. Now tell me how the vaccination program is going. I heard you had some trouble. I promised my company good press from this. What's happening?"

"Ebola was happening, sis. Sorry a little hemorrhagic fever outbreak messed with your PR plans." It actually felt better to get back to their semi-caustic relationship. Anything was better than the web of grief that came down on them when they talked about their mother.

"Well, you would think those poor people would appreciate our efforts."

"I'm sure they would if they felt like they could actually make it to the clinic." It had been the hardest thing to deal with all year. Even harder than dealing with the outbreak was knowing a whole group of children was being exposed to illnesses they didn't have to because their parents were terrified of coming to the clinic. She'd even tried to go door to door, but many wouldn't open their doors for fear of infection.

They'd lost five babies she knew of to preventable illnesses. And two of those babies had actually had vaccines, which made her worry.

"How much do you know about black market vaccines?" Faith wasn't sure she wanted to have this conversation with her sister, but she needed a few answers.

"I know it's a growth industry since big pharma stopped producing them. Especially flu vaccines. We're down to what? Two producers? Which is why you're lucky my company is one of them and you should give us good press. We went into the red to help you out last season. If you can't give marketing a boost by telling the world how kind we are, they might not send you another."

She nearly growled. "I'll do whatever you need me to, though this year's batch will likely go almost unused. Even the ones I did end up using were oddly ineffectual. I lost several kids and three elderly patients to influenza and they'd been vaccinated."

Hope shrugged. "You know it doesn't catch them all and the vaccine isn't one hundred percent."

"I had them typed after death. The vaccine covered the flu strain these patients died of. I know it's still not a hundred percent, but it shouldn't be this bad. I can see one or two patients, but I need to know what went wrong. I have my suspicions."

"Which are?"

She looked over to ensure no one was listening. She didn't want her time with her friends taken up with yet another case to investigate. If Erin heard word that Faith was anxious, she would go and talk to Theo, who would talk to Ten, and they would take over. They would take care of her, but she could handle this one all on her own. "I think the shipment was derailed at some point and I got fakes."

Hope went still. "You think someone stole our shipment and sold them on the black market in Africa?"

"I think someone stole them and sold them here in the States. There was a shortage last winter. They could make infinitely more money selling them here. I think they were likely switched before they ever made it out of Kronberg facilities."

"You think we have someone working on the inside?"

"Well, I think the criminals do."

Hope rolled her eyes. "Funny. I can't imagine it. We have about a million security protocols. And how are you going to prove it? You probably ran through that shipment in a month."

Hope never did listen carefully. She'd probably been thinking about getting into Theo's fatigues. "Hello, Ebola. People stayed away from the hospital. I have half the shipment left. I'm waiting on the test results. I sent a couple of vials to a testing facility I know. They're slow though. I should have an answer in a few days."

A look of pure disgust crossed Hope's face. "I can't believe they would do this. I swear to god I'm going to take someone's balls off over this."

"I'll hand you the scalpel." Because hey, she'd taken the

Hippocratic Oath, too, but Hope had never taken oaths very seriously. If Hope wanted to bust some balls, Faith would give her the big old thumbs-up.

"Are they shipping the results back to Africa? I want to know what you find out as soon as possible. If someone's fucking with vaccines, who knows what else they're capable of screwing with. We would have to check and recheck everything that has gone out in the last year." Hope had turned a nice shade of white. "God, our stock could plummet."

And people could die, but Faith knew where to focus. "Let's stay calm. We don't know anything yet and I doubt they're stealing drugs meant for the States. It's too easy to detect. It was really only the Ebola outbreak that made it possible to even check. I would have gone through those vaccines in no time at all if the clinic hadn't become ground zero. They would have been gone long before we started losing patients, and I wouldn't have been able to prove anything. I want to know what's in there. I don't think it's simply a placebo because a few people had some odd side effects."

"Like what?" Hope asked. "You have to tell me because we could be looking at lawsuits."

"From Liberia? I doubt it. But I will tell you because you need to know. I didn't put it together until later but a couple of my patients had memory issues."

"How could you tell if it was babies and the elderly? One has no memory and the other is kind of known for forgetting stuff."

Ah, but flu vaccines went to everyone. "I gave out those vaccines to almost two hundred people. Twenty-five of them showed back up complaining of weird memory loss. Like they were dreaming and couldn't tell what was dream or reality for a few days."

"Odd. Did anyone present with fever?"

Faith shook her head. "Not enough to be statistically important. These were healthy people with the same complaint. Some of them thought it was years later and they'd only slept for a night. But they insisted it had been longer."

"That doesn't make a lick of sense. They must have had some form of dementia. Were any of them Ebola patients?"

"Two ended up dying, but that was later. And the effect was temporary." She could still remember one man. His eyes had been haunted. He'd claimed to have lived years in a single night.

"Sounds like a psych problem to me. What about the other doc? Don't you have another one with you?"

"Yes," Faith replied. "Nate Harrison. He's a GP out of California. I've done a couple of tours with him. Nice guy. He gave out another two hundred vaccines, but he didn't have the same problems with his patients that I did."

"So are you still known as the pushover doc?"

It was something that other doctors had called her all through her residency. She'd been the doc to come to if you wanted someone to listen to your problems and give you attention. She wasn't going to apologize for giving a shit. "They weren't asking for attention. And not a one of them asked for meds. I don't think this is a psych issue and I'm going to get to the bottom of it."

Hope finally sat back, shaking her head. "Well, let me know what you find out. I need to let the PR people get ahead of this. Can you give me that much?"

Her sister had been good to her. Despite her desperate need to enrich her own bank account, Hope had tried to help out with Faith's clinic in the only real way she knew how. "Yes. I'll let you know what the lab says. I'll even keep my mouth quiet if it turns out I'm wrong and it's a placebo. But I'll expect at least twice as many doses next year and Kronberg has to find the criminals."

Hope sighed. "You drive a hard bargain, sister."

She so rarely did. She usually just busted her ass to try to make things work. "I do try."

A loud laugh came from the other room. Masculine. Sexy. It sounded a bit like Theo. She wondered how it would sound if Master T made it. He chuckled from time to time, but never let loose a full-throated laugh.

Hope looked toward the door, the sound catching her as well. "So you're bringing Theo with you when you come out to the islands for your birthday?"

"Yes, but I'm serious about you keeping your hands to yourself. Erin won't take it kindly if you're pawing her boyfriend."

Hope's eyes turned thoughtful. "I don't paw anyone. I'm quite polite. And if I decide I want that soldier, I'll take him."

"Really? You're not exactly the most charming woman in the

world. I've never seen you try to seduce anyone."

"Seduce?" Hope huffed. "That's a silly word. And I can be very persuasive when I want to be."

The door to her room opened and Ten was standing there. "Darlin', we've got someplace to be this evening and I need to prep for that. Theo's going to bring you along and we'll talk when you get there, all right?"

He needed to leave, but he wasn't going to take her away from her sister.

"Should I pack?"

His eyes heated. He hadn't liked being interrupted earlier. "Yes. You should pack. Take care. I want you safe and happy when I see you tonight."

When he would take her to Sanctum and no one and nothing would interrupt them.

There was one thing she needed to know. She stood up and walked to him. They hadn't had a chance to talk, but this wasn't a question she wanted to ask in the open. She walked straight into his arms, loving the way they went around her, the strength of the man holding her. She went on her toes and whispered in his ear. "Should I stay inside?"

His hands found her hair, masking his voice. "The attacker was a man known to have a beef with your father. He was a lone crazy, so I'm certain it won't happen again, but don't you leave here without Erin or Theo. I want you safe. Do you understand?"

He would blister her backside if she walked out of here alone. He wanted her to himself. The thought made her heart pound. It made her pussy soft and ready for him. He was willing to protect her, to take care of her. It did something for her.

She nodded and brushed her lips against his. "I promise, Master."

His lips quirked up. "And I promise you're going to have a good time tonight."

He kissed her again, winked, and then walked away. Faith couldn't help but watch that man's super-fine muscled ass. It really was a thing of beauty.

There was nothing cold about that man. Her sister was wrong. Ten Graham was exactly what he seemed to be—a lovely man with dominant, protective instincts.

And she was rapidly falling for him.

"So why don't you tell me more about Theo," her sister said, patting the seat beside her.

Faith groaned. "I'll tell you all about Erin, who's going to kick your ass if you keep flirting with her man."

At least she wasn't the only one losing her head over a boy.

CHAPTER SEVEN

"It looks good, doesn't it?" Theo asked as he joined Ten. There was a stupid happy-puppy grin on the younger man's face that told Ten he'd probably gotten lucky at some point this afternoon.

"It's certainly more high tech than it was before. Tag invested a lot of money in this place. Makes a man wonder where he got it." Ten looked out over the playroom floor. Tag really should thank him for the whole Ace incident. Ace had been a sleeper planted by a man working with the senator. He'd blown up Tag's first club and damn near killed a bunch of the team, but Ten had to admit the new Sanctum was a work of art.

And so was Faith McDonald. He'd caught a glimpse of her walking into the women's locker room with Erin at her side. Her dark hair had been in a ponytail, but he'd given her strict instructions that it was to be left down this evening.

Tonight she was utterly under his control. He made the decisions. He chose what they would do and how they would do it, and she would comply.

He had to admit it was enough to get his dick going.

"I don't know," Theo said, shaking his head. "Tag makes good money through the company. Big brother is wealthy, if you know what I mean."

Ten snorted. The kid was naïve. "I'll eat my leathers if this was financed through his profits from McKay-Taggart. I always thought he gave up Charlotte's money too easy. Bastard. I blame the Brits. They were eager to close the case and split that ten million. I bet Charlotte had double that put away."

"I don't think Ian would lie to you," Theo said solemnly.

Fuck yeah Ian would lie. He would lie to protect his wife and family. Those millions would give him a whole lot of security. If he really was honest with himself, he'd known it at the time. He'd signed that deal and wished Tag and Charlotte well.

Maybe he was the naïve idiot.

No matter what Tag had spent and how he'd gotten the money, Sanctum was impressive as hell. The building was three stories tall, with a bar lounge and locker rooms on the ground floor. Above was a dungeon built for play, and finally privacy rooms and aftercare centers.

He meant to have Faith in one of those privacy rooms by the time the night was through.

"What's the plan?" Theo asked. "Should Erin and I stay close?"

"I need you two to scene. Something hot. Faith likes to watch, from what I can tell. I'd like to spend some time alone with her."

"You won't hurt her, right?"

He sent Theo a look that had sent many junior operatives fleeing for their lives. "No. Obviously I'm not going to hurt the girl. I need her. I'm going to fuck her and make her mine. You knew this was going to happen."

"I guess I thought you would like her more than you do."

Like? It was a ridiculous word. He didn't "like" Faith. She was the target. He didn't like targets. Of course he didn't normally crave the target, either. "I'm going to make sure she survives this mission. That's all I can promise you."

He glanced at the clock above the bar. She wasn't scheduled to meet with him for another twenty minutes. Apparently it took subs longer to get ready than Doms. Probably all that pretty corset stuff had something to do with it. He'd rather have her naked.

It did give him time to clear up a few things. He spotted Damon Knight in the lounge. The big Brit was sitting with the Russian and another man. Kai Ferguson. Damn. Ten liked to avoid Kai. There was something about the man he found a bit unnerving. Like Kai could see right through him. Still. He had a mission and he needed information the Brit had.

"Is Case going to be here tonight?"

Theo shook his head. "He's tailing the sister. The last I talked to him, he was hanging out in the parking lot of an expensive steak house on Lemmon. He's getting shots of everyone Hope McDonald is meeting with and he'll try to identify them by morning. I think it's awfully interesting she happened to show up in Dallas."

Ten had spoken to Hope McDonald briefly. She'd made her disdain for him plain. She obviously wasn't a big fan of the lifestyle. "Have we confirmed the conference she's attending?"

"Yes, but she wasn't on the attendee list before yesterday morning. I think she came here to see Faith. The question is was she being an attentive big sister or is there something else going on."

Could she be working with Faith? She could be the inside man at the pharmaceutical company. "She seemed to like you. Maybe you should spend time with her."

Theo seemed to turn a little green, or perhaps it was the lighting from the human hamster wheel. Some sub was making that wheel turn and hard. It changed colors based on how fast it was spinning. "She gives me the creeps."

Ten had been forced to fuck worse. "Suck it up, buttercup. I wasn't telling you to screw her. Talk to her. Ask her about work. Get a feel for her."

"Fine, but I'm not sleeping with her. I'm not doing any of that. Ever. There's Damon. Let's see what he's got for us." Theo started toward the bar.

It must be so fucking easy to be young and so pure he couldn't ever imagine whoring himself out for information. Ten felt about three thousand years old as he watched Theo walk away. He felt a momentary wish that he could have been that naïve once. He'd always known his body was another tool to be used in service of his country.

He strode across the space between them, utterly ignoring everyone in his path. It was a trick he'd learned. He could hyper focus and allow everything else to fall to the side.

Except he was struggling to do it around Faith. She seemed to invade his thoughts, visions of her coming into his head at the oddest times. He'd been driving earlier, his brain working on the Ukrainian situation, when an image of her all soft and dewy from sleep had whispered across his brain, disrupting his thoughts.

He'd been useless from that point on. He'd had to go home and meditate before he could clear his brain of her.

Meditation was a useful tool and one not many people would associate with him. Franklin Grant had insisted he take transcendental meditation classes twice a week, and he'd kept up the practice.

At first Ten had believed the old man had done it to help him focus, to center a young man in need of discipline. Now he understood that Franklin Grant had given him that gift for one reason and one reason only—so he could take the pain that would later be handed to him. So he wouldn't break when other men would. So he would be the perfect operative. So he could die with the country's secrets intact.

Like his brother had.

He knew Phoebe was at complete peace with Franklin Grant, but Ten had issues with their adopted "father." At the end of the day, Franklin had always been Ten's handler, even when he'd been a shit-out-of-luck teenager on his way to self-destruction. Franklin had simply shown him a better way. Why destroy himself when he could destroy someone else?

He was nothing more than an animal who had been trained to protect. A guard dog for the country.

And then suddenly he could feel Faith, the way her hair tickled his chest and how warm she'd been in his arms.

He ruthlessly quashed the image. He had a damn job to do.

"Knight, have you learned anything at all?" He was well aware his tone wasn't the most pleasant.

An elegant brow arched over Knight's eye, and that was when Ten realized they weren't alone. A pretty woman with blonde curls sat at Knight's feet, her head on his lap as he petted her, his hands moving possessively over her.

Damn it. He'd been rude. If there was one thing these men didn't like it was a man being rude around their women.

Actually, he didn't much like the thought of anyone being rude around Faith.

"Please excuse me. Penelope, you look stunning tonight. How

are you this evening?" He managed to ask the question in his "charming" tone. That was how he thought of it. He'd been taught to shove his inner asshole deep and make himself pleasant to be around.

"Better," Knight allowed.

Penelope Knight grinned at him. "I'm lovely, Mr. Graham. And yourself?"

Penelope Knight was former MI6. She wouldn't drop his cover or misstep.

"I'm doing wonderfully and looking forward to the evening. May Theo and I join you? Faith isn't due for another couple of minutes and I thought I would get caught up on what everyone's gathered this afternoon." Polite. He could certainly play that way.

Knight gestured to the seat in front of him. Theo took the seat to the left and Ten joined him.

"I've been talking to Ferguson here about his impressions of Faith," Knight said. "He spent some time with her this afternoon."

Kai Ferguson had been with Ten's sub? Faith had spent time with the casual, charming younger man? Kai Ferguson didn't have a body covered in scars. He didn't have a load of undiagnosed mental issues. Hell, Kai helped people with their issues. He was a therapist dedicated to helping soldiers coming back from war.

There was no help for an operative because the war never ended for him. It kept rolling along.

Kai held a hand up. "I only talked to her, Ten."

"He came over and helped me install the fire pit in the backyard," Theo offered.

"And you didn't think to mention that to me?" Ten was well aware of the chill in his voice.

Kai took over, his eyes somberly watching Ten. "Tag thought as long as I was there it would be a good time to get a personal view of the woman. Eve's in the locker room doing the same thing, but two viewpoints are better than one, and it's helpful to get both a masculine and feminine viewpoint. Some people act differently around men versus women. I don't think Faith is one of those people. She's lovely, by the way, and she speaks highly of you. In my opinion, she believes she's falling in love with you."

"Good," he said, trying to cover up the fact that hearing those words gave him a sense of satisfaction they shouldn't. He should be pleased because a woman in love was so much easier to deal with. She would turn to her lover when the going got rough. Oh, he had no illusions she would choose him over her family, but he might get some play out of her emotional state.

Or he could soak it in and enjoy her for every second they had left. He could bask in her warmth and pretend it was all real since he wouldn't find anyone like her ever again. He could move her into his place and play house, pretending for the next few weeks that they were exactly what they appeared to be—a couple finding their way, learning each other because they were invested in their relationship.

He could let everyone else worry about recon and intel, and he could spend all his time sinking into her, bonding her to him.

A tempting thought, but he wasn't the kind of man who let his fellow operatives do all the work.

Don't trust anyone but your brother and your sister, Tennessee. Not even a partner. Definitely not a woman. It's fine to enjoy one, but that's not how your life is going to go. They'll always turn on you. It's the way of our world.

His adopted father had practically beaten those words into him. Not physically, but he'd said them enough that they should have been ingrained in Ten's brain. He was simply far stupider than Franklin Grant gave him credit for.

"Are you with us?" Ferguson asked, his eyes narrowing. "Do you need to talk about something?"

Where the hell was Tag when he needed him? A good punch in the face might force him to focus. This was all Faith's doing, but he would put it on a proper footing tonight. He would be the Master. "I'm fine. Markovic, did you learn anything?"

The big Russian looked perfectly comfortable in a set of leathers. There was a woman at his feet as well, a lovely brunette. She wore an emerald green corset and killer stilettos. He tried to remember her name. Desiree Brooks. It was a porn star name for an MI6 agent, but according to all the reports on her she was quite deadly. She looked happy to be hanging on to the Russian's leather-clad leg.

"Is there a reason MI6 is here?" Ten asked.

Theo looked down at the woman. "She's MI6?"

Markovic shook his head. "She is with us now."

"I decided it was time to leave the service," the woman replied in a quiet British accent. Not too upper-crust. There was a bit of the country in her. "I came over to bring the boss some information on a few ops we have running and Nick decided he needed a girl for the night. He's worried his beauty will drive all the women insane."

The Russian shrugged. "They have never seen such a man before. I cannot be loving them all, so it's better they think I am unavailable. As to your problems, I do not believe the assassin was working for the Odessa mafia."

"What do you mean?" He thought this had been established. He simply wanted to know why they were after Faith.

He'd been almost relieved. If Faith was dirty, he couldn't really hurt her. If Faith was a criminal, he wouldn't have her on his conscience for the rest of time.

"My contacts tell me Kozak has not been an active member for a long time. He's been in hiding and working independently."

"So he was affiliated with the Ukrainians but the mafia wasn't paying the bills?" Theo asked.

"That's what Taggart's contacts claim as well," Knight stated. "There's no order from any of the usual suspects. I can't find a syndicate that wants her dead. I'm looking into some of her contacts in Africa, but that's going to take a bit more time."

"Who would want her dead if she's not disrupting a criminal practice?" He said the question aloud, but it was more to himself. His mind was whirling, working through the problem. He needed to check into the land her clinic was built on. It was possible someone was trying to eliminate a problem and ease the way for their own profit. Money tended to be at the heart of most crime. Money or passion. "We looked into the ex-boyfriend. Are we sure he's the only one?"

"She was with him throughout the last part of her residency," Theo replied. "There were a few lovers while she was in med school according to Erin, but nothing serious. She got into the lifestyle during college and seems to use it almost as stress relief."

Theo wasn't telling him anything he didn't already know. "I'm more interested in her business. This smells like money to me. From what I can tell, Faith hasn't been very passionate about anything except her job."

Up to this point. She seemed fairly passionate about him. He couldn't forget the way she'd come to him the night before, offering affection and kindness.

Shit. He wanted to believe she was real.

"That doesn't mean someone wasn't passionate about her," Penny said.

Now that he could see. He could certainly understand someone getting obsessed with her beauty and grace. "Look into everyone in her background again. And I want a close eye kept on the sister. Do we have eyes on the senator?"

Knight nodded. "One of my men is working with Michael Malone. They're in DC at the moment, but that could change. The senator has a private jet. It can be difficult to follow him if he decides to leave spontaneously. So far all we've got on him is that he visits a woman in a DuPont Circle condo twice a month."

"So he's got a mistress."

Markovic shook his head. "How is this a scandal? Politicians in Russia have many mistresses. It is cold country. Many women are required to keep a man warm."

"Really?" Desiree said, an elegant eyebrow arching over her right eye.

Markovic put a hand on her head. "It is different here. This is warm country. Only one woman required."

So they obviously had something going on. Ten didn't understand it at all. Operatives didn't have relationships in his world. They were loyal to the mission, to the Agency. Not to each other.

He really wanted to get back to the world he understood. Things were clear at the Agency. Things made sense. He knew his purpose there.

"Besides, we can't really call her a mistress," Theo said. "The senator isn't married. She's more like a girlfriend. I don't think we can spin it to hurt him, but I've got Michael looking into her. So how do we handle Faith now that we know it's not the mob after her?"

He'd already dealt with that. "I told her it was safe. I want her to feel comfortable enough to go about her business the way she normally would. I want to see where she goes and what she does."

But that wasn't what he'd really done. He'd totally intended to do exactly what he'd said when he'd spoken to her earlier. He'd meant to let her off the leash and see where she led them, but the words that had come out of his mouth hadn't been the ones he'd meant to speak. He'd told her that despite the fact she was safe, she should stay with Erin and Theo until he could protect her himself. He hadn't corrected himself.

What the fuck was he thinking?

Theo frowned. "We don't know that she's safe. I don't like this plan, Ten."

Ten wasn't used to having his own team question his decision making. Despite the fact that he could easily put Theo's worries to rest, the idea of telling anyone how he'd screwed up rankled. "You don't have to like the plan. You merely have to follow it, soldier."

"I'm not a soldier anymore." Theo's eyes had narrowed. God, he looked like his brother, and Ten could remember that same stubborn tone of voice coming out of Tag's mouth. "You should know I'm going to watch out for her."

"And you should remember why we're here. Have you forgotten what her father did to Jesse Murdoch? To my own brother? What he'll continue to do to our servicemen if we don't stop him? You might not be a soldier anymore but does that mean you no longer give a shit?"

Theo sighed. "Of course not. I haven't forgotten anything, but I also don't think it's a good idea to leave her unprotected. We don't know that Kozak was the only one coming after her. He was likely hired, and that means whoever wants her dead can hire someone else."

At least he could think with something other than his apparently tender heart. "Which is why you shadow her if I can't. Actually, you and Erin should shadow both of us when we're together. You might be able to see things I can't. And that's all I'll say on the subject for now. Just get me the information I need, Even Littler Tag."

He used the nickname the rest of McKay-Taggart had started using to describe the youngest Taggart. It got the rest of the group laughing and let some of the tension out of the room. He didn't need the rest of the team thinking he and Theo couldn't get along.

Theo growled. "I hate that. How about Even Younger Tag? That's more fitting. And trust me, by tomorrow you'll have more data than you can handle."

Ten liked data. Data was actually one thing he could handle.

Then he saw something he was fairly certain he couldn't.

Faith stepped into the bar, her arm through Erin's as they talked together. Delicious. She looked utterly edible in a scarlet red corset and tiny thong. Fishnet thigh-highs covered her legs and led his eyes down to a truly spectacular pair of fuck-me shoes. Her hair was down, tumbling softly around her shoulders. She'd curled it, giving her glossy waves.

"Your girl is lovely," Knight said.

"Yes, she is," Theo replied as he stood up.

Ten frowned. For a second he'd thought Knight was talking about Faith. He kind of wanted to point out that Faith was the most stunning woman in the room and any man who couldn't see it was fucking blind.

But she was only the mission and his fellow operatives knew that so they reserved their brotherly praise for Theo, who looked like a goddamn groom waiting for his bride.

Theo put out a hand, gesturing Erin forward.

Erin looked like a completely different woman. With her fiery red hair up in a demure twist, she looked oddly ladylike in her sapphire blue corset and matching thong. Her long legs had been left bare and she wore nude five-inch heels that made them look like they went on forever.

Still, for all her height she only came to the top of Theo's shoulders. She stepped into his embrace like she belonged there, her whole body seeming to relax as he put his hands on her.

"You look absolutely gorgeous, love." Theo's fingertips found her chin, lifting her gaze to meet his. "I'm the luckiest man here, and one day you'll believe everything I tell you because I'll keep saying it."

Ten could almost swear he saw a fine sheen of tears in Erin's eyes as she nodded.

"Of course you will. You don't give up on anything do you, Theo Taggart?" Erin asked in a low voice.

"Not anything that counts," he agreed before brushing his lips over hers.

"I love watching them together," a soft voice whispered in his ear.

Faith. She was standing next to him and he'd been watching

133

Theo, trying to figure out what the hell was going through that boy's brain. Erin was trouble. Falling for anyone was trouble, but Erin Argent was more trouble than most.

So why did Theo grin like a loon when she walked into a room?

Why had Jamie done the same with Phoebe? Sometimes he wondered if Jamie and Phoebe would take it back had they known what would happen. Would Phoebe have spared herself the agony of loving James Grant if she'd known he would die?

Ten kind of thought he would. The ache still felt fresh sometimes, like Jamie had died yesterday and Ten was still searching for his brother's body. Like he'd just found it and realized how little the universe cared. Jamie had been tossed away like a piece of trash, like he hadn't mattered.

A hand found his, warmth drawing him back into the real world. When he looked down, Faith was staring solemnly up at him.

"Can I help you, Master?"

Just once he wanted to give in. It was only one night. "Kiss me, Faith."

She didn't hesitate. She went up on her toes and placed her lips on his, her hands cupping his face like he was something precious, and somehow it washed away the dirt from his mind. Somehow when she kissed him, he could forget about everything but her warmth, her sweetness.

Maybe a few days. It looked like she wasn't involved with the mob. It didn't mean she wasn't dirty, but it did mean the jury was out and he could fool himself.

Other voices cautioned him not to. His adopted father's voice blared out a warning. His own voice reminded him that the sweetest-looking woman could turn deadly.

And then there was Jamie's voice deep inside.

You go, Tennessee. You take her and don't fucking let her go. Take the chance.

God, he hadn't heard Jamie's voice in his head in years. All he would see when he closed his eyes was Jamie's dead body, left for the vultures. But in that moment, in the fraction of a minute when Faith pressed her lips against him, he could see his brother on Jamie's wedding day.

I'll do this for you one day. You just watch.

When she eased back down, he realized he wasn't ready. Not for that kiss to be over. He reached out and dragged her close, loving how small she was against him. She was a lovely handful, but small compared to him. She was someone he could protect, could hold close and be a barrier between her and the rest of the shitty world.

For a little while.

He devoured her, not playing around. He let his hands find her hair. For these few weeks she was his. His sub. His girl. His to play with and fuck and protect and pretend that he was normal for once.

Her mouth opened for his, allowing him in and welcoming him with the silky glide of her tongue. Heat suffused him and his hands were suddenly in motion. He couldn't stay still. He needed to touch her, to slide his palms over her curves and know that every inch of this woman belonged to him.

For now.

A masculine chuckle shattered his focus and brought him back to the real world. He broke off their kiss, but settled Faith securely in his arms before looking over at Knight.

"You know there are privacy rooms, chap." Knight's smirk told him a lot.

The men he worked with were going to give him hell about this one.

So let 'em. Let them joke, Tennessee. It's all in good fun. You know you would rib them about not being able to take their hands off the hottest, sweetest sub in the club. Jealous bastards.

He kind of liked hearing Jamie's voice again.

He settled down. There weren't many scenes up and running yet. It was the time of the night when they greeted each other and talked before hitting the dungeon floor. It was a time to anticipate the evening. He pulled Faith down onto his lap, settling his hand on her knee. She curled up against him as though she belonged there, as though this was just what they did.

"We'll get there eventually, Knight." He noticed Markovic had left quickly, taking the British beauty with him. They would disappear since he would go back to working on the island in a few days. Faith wouldn't remember ever seeing the Russian.

Her eyes had been on Ten the whole time.

A good girl should be rewarded. He let his hand travel up to her

Lexi Blake

thigh. He didn't have to be a gentleman here. Here she belonged to him.

"So tell me about business, Knight. How's it going?" Ten began asking innocuous questions, nothing that would give up their covers. Knight could talk about operating the London office and it wouldn't tip off Faith.

The truth was always the best cover.

Faith sighed and nuzzled his neck sweetly. His free hand moved on her hair.

The truth was he liked having her close. The truth was he could sink into this cover and maybe never want to come back out.

He would. He would get what he needed from her and come out on the other side, but for the first time he wondered if he could have it all. If Faith wasn't dirty, then perhaps proving her father was would rightfully devastate her. She would need someone then.

She would need her lover to comfort her.

Tennessee Smith suddenly knew one thing. He intended to be that man.

* * * *

Faith watched the scene in front of her with a smile on her face. And hard nipples. Really hard nipples. It was a hot scene they were watching. Yet there was a tenderness to it.

She and Master T had walked the dungeon floor. He'd taken her up to the second floor, showing her around and patiently answering her every question. She was fascinated with the size of the club and the level of attention to detail that had gone into designing it. There were playrooms of all kinds. She'd watched a medical scene where a doctor had taken his very naughty nurse to task. It was one of the things she'd loved about the lifestyle. She'd met the "nurse" earlier in the evening, and Eve McKay had seemed so staid and intellectual. Nice, of course, but it showed another side of the woman when she'd allowed herself to be spanked and brought to orgasm by her gorgeous hubby.

The lifestyle was where she'd first learned she didn't have to be just one person. She didn't have to always be the in control doctor. She could find the other sides of herself and indulge them.

Like Erin was right now.

Erin was wrapped in silk rope, the gorgeous pattern forming a dress around her body. She was kneeling, her breasts on display. Theo had taken his time as he bound her. His fingers had moved slowly, lovingly creating the tortoiseshell pattern that covered Erin's flesh. It had been easy to watch Erin slip into subspace as he worked the ropes over and over her. Her eyes had become soft, her muscles relaxing.

Once Theo was satisfied his submissive was properly bound and trussed, he'd begun his sweet torture. He'd taken a cube of ice and run it over the nape of her neck, causing her to shiver and writhe.

Sensation play. Faith loved it.

Master T shifted behind her, one arm around her waist as he leaned in, whispering in her ear. "I scheduled a room for us. I want to play with you."

She felt those words across her flesh as though he could impart warmth to her with only his voice. He'd scheduled a private room for them. That meant he had plans. Plans he hadn't discussed with her. Oh, he knew her hard and soft limits. He knew what she liked and didn't like. So it didn't bother her. She rather liked the idea that he'd spent time planning and plotting how they would play together. It was one of the things she loved about the D/s relationship she'd had before. She'd never felt used. Her Dom thought carefully about what would bring them both pleasure. Sex was careful, thoughtful, never taken for granted.

She was going to have sex with this amazing, gorgeous, wonderful man. It made her want to melt. Instead she nodded, letting him know she was ready whenever he was.

On the stage, Erin gasped as Theo attached a really nasty-looking clamp to her right nipple. The clamps were lovely, with pretty emeralds dangling from the end. Theo rolled the left nipple between his thumb and forefinger before slipping it on.

She would be so aware of her body. The ropes would hold her tight, clamps biting into her sensitive skin. For some people it would be torture. For people like her and Erin, it was the highest high. The endorphins would be flowing, mixing with crazy arousal and flooding her system.

Theo's hands went to the laces of his leathers. Nice. Oral scene.

That was sure to get her completely hot. Yes, she was crazy about Master T, but that didn't mean she was blind. Theo Taggart was a total hottie. She'd been looking forward to seeing him without his clothes on. She'd seen him without a shirt, and that was one phenomenal chest. From the racket Erin could make, Faith had a hunch her friend's Dom had a nice package and she was going to…

A hand came over her eyes and she was shocked to find herself manhandled away from the scene. She was trained well enough that she didn't call out. She knew exactly whose strong arms were around her and she had a sneaking suspicion why.

Was her Master the tiniest bit jealous? He'd told her to pack her bag. He'd been explicit in his instructions that she would be coming home with him, and earlier in the day he'd frowned Theo's way when he'd walked through the house wearing nothing but a towel.

When he settled her back down and took his hand off her eyes, he stared down at her.

"I didn't think. Did I frighten you?" He was so serious as he looked her over. They were far enough from the scene that they could speak, though in Sanctum one was never very far from something interesting.

"Frighten me?" She could hear the sounds in the background and knew Erin and Theo's scene had totally moved on to something interesting, but she knew better than to turn around and look back. She had to think of her Master's apparently tender feelings.

He liked her. He wanted her to like him. Only him. It was all right because she'd noticed he didn't ogle other women. Despite all the lovely female flesh on display, Master T seemed to have eyes only for her. He would tip his head and comment on a sub's loveliness, but there wasn't heat in his eyes. That was reserved for Faith. Master T knew how to make a sub feel secure. So why would he think he'd frightened her?

"I'm fine, Master. I'm not frightened."

He straightened up. "I didn't think about the fact that you've been kidnapped before. I covered your eyes. It could have brought back bad memories."

"Oh." No, she hadn't been thinking about that at all. It was nice to not think about it. The truth was once Theo and Erin had been brought on as her security, she'd been able to relax. She'd trusted them from the start. Every instinct she had said those were two people born to protect and defend those weaker than them. Master T was the same way. "No. I'm fine. No PTSD for this girl. And actually, they never blindfolded me. I think they wanted me to see all the horrible stuff." She shook her head as a couple of horrific images entered it. "Okay, maybe I spoke too soon on the PTSD."

He wrapped her up in his arms. "I'm sorry. I wanted to get you alone and my hand slipped."

She barely managed not to laugh. Doms had their egos, too. "It slipped? Over my eyes?"

"Yes." His sure voice practically begged her to argue with him.

Which she had no intention of doing. She was going to have a lovely evening with a man who couldn't stand the thought of her looking at another man's probably really large penis. She was totally going to look at Master T's penis. And do other stuff with it. "It's not a problem, Master. I'm perfectly fine and I'm ready for anything you would like to do."

His smile turned distinctly sensual. "Anything?"

"Anything."

A warm hand cupped her shoulder as he stared down at her. "And what if I told you I want to go sit in the bar with you at my feet."

He didn't want to... She nodded. "Of course."

He chuckled and lowered his head, kissing her swiftly. "Not on your life, darlin'. But that sad look in your eyes...well, you make a man feel ten feet tall." He got close, his mouth next to her ear so she felt the heat of his breath. "Do you have any idea what I'm going to do to you?"

Oh, she had ideas. "None, Master."

"I'm going to make you scream for me in the sweetest way possible. I'm going to tie you up and have my way with you. I'm going to lick and suck and touch every part of you until there isn't an inch that hasn't felt my skin or tongue or cock. By the time this night is over, you're going to know what it means to be my submissive. You're going to be mine body and soul."

Her ovaries practically vibrated. "Yes, Master."

"I like the way you say that. Yes, Master. Keep telling me yes. All night long." His face turned serious again. "I don't want to share you tonight. I know you have an exhibitionist streak, but this first time I want to be alone with you."

It was a little scary. She could see now that her exhibitionist streak served a purpose. It kept things oddly casual. What Master T was asking for was true intimacy. He wanted her all for himself. It meant something. It moved them beyond mere play and into something more.

Did she want that? Hell, yes. Her inner voice didn't even hesitate. She was crazy about this man and it was likely a really bad idea. It would be so much safer to back off, to find someone more like Roger. Someone she could hold herself away from.

She wasn't going to do that. She was going to do something truly stupid and jump into this big old scary pond with both feet. "I'm good with that, Master. I want you to myself, too. I see how the other subs look at you."

His hand caressed her cheek. "You are awfully good at making me feel like a man. I'll be right back. I want to make sure the room is ready. You stay here. And don't you dare look at Theo Taggart's dick. My hand slipped so you wouldn't see that."

She suddenly had zero interest in seeing Theo Taggart naked. "I will keep my eyes on you and you alone."

He touched his fingertip to her nose. "See that you do."

When he strode away, she watched that hot backside.

A giddy feeling took over. It was silly but she'd never felt this way about a man. Not even her silly, she-was-so-stupid-over-him high school boyfriend. Nope. Only Master T had ever brought out the giddy girl in her.

She wondered. They might not be together for long. It didn't sit well, but it might be true. They really only had the next few weeks, but he'd already given her so much.

What could she give him? Beyond her submission and her body, she wanted him to have something so much more. She cared about him. It might not be forever, but it was more than enough for her to dream about the rest of her life. She'd always known she would give her life in service. She'd wanted to be a doctor for as long as she could remember, and not the kind who made millions and drove fancy cars. She'd wanted to be the kind who saved the world—one patient at a time.

So she wanted to give this glorious man a gift. She simply needed to figure out what it would be.

Faith did exactly as she'd promised. She kept her eyes on her Master as he strode toward the desk that led to the upper levels. Everywhere one went in Sanctum there was security and customer service. Sometimes both. The man at the counter had a ready smile and a body that told her he could handle himself if things got rough. She doubted things often got rough at Sanctum. It was the single nicest club she'd ever been to.

It was the kind of club a girl could call home.

For the first time she wondered about working in Dallas. Not in a hospital. If she stayed here, she would open a clinic. She would serve those who couldn't afford health care. She would fight the good fight.

Her mother had taught her that. Faith barely remembered her. Her mother was a sweet face and a kind smile, but Faith remembered her words. Fight the good fight. She'd lived her life by those four words. To honor the woman who had given birth to her. But maybe she could fight that grand and glorious fight and still have a family, too.

He'd done this to her. God, she was a silly, stupid girl, but she was hoping Master T was "the one."

He spoke a few words to the man at the station and the host got on the phone.

"How are you enjoying Sanctum?"

She looked to her left and Theo's brother was standing there. Ian Taggart was a wretchedly large man. The Taggarts seemed to only come in extra-large sizes. Still, he'd been sarcastic and personable this afternoon, and it was hard to feel really intimidated by a man who was so madly in love with his wife and two babies. She'd watched him nuzzle his babies and blow raspberries on their baby bellies. She beamed up at him. He was a safe Dom to talk to. He would respect the limits. "It's like heaven, Sir."

Taggart smiled. "It is that. I built this place to be a safe haven. For me and my wife and my friends. How's my friend treating you?"

She didn't even try to hold back the glow she felt. "Master T is wonderful. He's been very good to me."

"I'm glad to hear it." His eyes were on the scene playing out to their left. They flared briefly, as though he was seeing something truly amazing, but she refused to look that way. Maybe Master T wouldn't see it, but she wasn't going to risk hurting him that way.

"Thank you so much for having me here. I know you don't take many applicants."

"Thank you for all your money. I hear you're only going to use a portion of your yearly fee."

That was something she was thinking about. "I don't know. I've been ruminating on how to deal with it. I think I'm going to let it ride for now. We've got a month or so before I need to decide. I like Master T. He's making me wonder if I shouldn't stay here in the States."

Taggart's blue eyes were suddenly on her. "Are you serious?"

He didn't believe her? "Yes. I really like him. I'm glad we had that three weeks to get to know each other. It's made the rest of our time together so much easier. You did a very good job pairing us. I think we're really compatible."

"Of course. We consider a lot of factors when we pair Doms and subs." His face split in a grin. "Actually we roll the dice and you two looked pretty hot together, so that seemed to be a good way to go."

He was an ass, but a likable one. "Good to know."

He was quiet for a moment, but it was an oddly companionable silence. Faith liked quiet. She could tell as much about a person from their silences as she could from their words. Ian Taggart was comfortable with himself, with his space. He owned the space around him, but not in a super-aggressive way. More like a benevolent king watching over his kingdom.

Up ahead, a woman approached Ten. She was dressed in what looked like a latex bodysuit.

"I thought you could be good for him," Taggart said finally.

She looked over to the big blond Dom. "Really? How could you know?"

"Theo. I asked his opinion. I trust my brother's instincts and I've read all the information on your background. In my business, you learn to size people up fairly quickly. I thought you could be very good for Master T. He's had it rough."

"I know. He had a hard start to life, but he seems fairly undamaged by it." Master T seemed willing to accept affection in a way some people wouldn't after being abandoned as a small child.

He was charming and open.

"He buries a lot, Faith. Don't think you see everything. There's a hell of a lot of pain bubbling under his surface. Just take care."

"Did he ever find her?" It was something she'd been wondering about.

"Who?"

"His mother." She glanced back and the woman was still talking to Master T, thrusting out her chest.

"No," Taggart said. "At least not that I know of. I don't think he ever looked. He slipped through the cracks of the system, but he was adopted as a teenager. He has a sister. You met her this morning."

And that adoption might have been what saved him. "Yes, Phoebe's lovely. I like her a lot."

"Has he mentioned his brother?"

She shook her head. "Brother? No. I didn't know he had one. I only knew about Phoebe."

"Ah, well, that would be one of those things bubbling under the surface. Forget I said anything. That's his story to tell. Just know that you're welcome here at Sanctum. Whatever happens between you and Master T, you're a member now. You have rights. Oh, and you should probably go deal with that."

Her jaw dropped. That woman was putting her hands on Master T. She was looking up at him and obviously pleading some kind of case because she was acting like a supplicant. Anger flared. God, she was jealous. She'd never been jealous before. Not like this, and she was stuck with the rules of the club. "I suppose I should let him handle it."

"Only if you want every woman here to think you're a door mat. Sorry, I mean that in the most politic way possible, but you should know the subs here at Sanctum aren't exactly big on letting other women paw their men."

That was good to know. The other clubs she'd been at had been a bit harder core, and the subs weren't permitted to solve things on their own. It was the one thing she'd disliked. Sanctum, it seemed, valued its submissive members and their rights. And it was her right to kick some ass.

"Doc, if you break her, are you going to fix her?" Taggart was grinning from ear to ear as though he was really enjoying himself.

Damn Hippocratic Oath. "Yes. But I won't use pain meds."

"You're going to fit in here, Doc."

She stalked toward her prey, aware that every eye was on her.

Master T took a step back from the girl in front of him. Even from where she stood, she could feel the arctic blast from his stare.

"I simply wanted to offer myself to you, Master," the woman said, her voice shaking prettily. She was a thin thing, her body graceful and lovely.

"If you touch me again, I'll see you thrown out of this club. Is that clear?"

The sub went to her knees. "Please don't, Master."

"Sir. He's Sir to you," Faith said.

Ten's head whirled around. It was obvious he hadn't seen her standing there. For a second, she wondered if she wasn't about to get into serious trouble. She would have allowed Roger to handle a clingy sub in a heartbeat, but she was rapidly realizing she hadn't been invested in Roger. Not at all. She'd started this whole relationship because it would be relaxing and an amusing way to spend a few months. There was nothing relaxing about the ache in her gut at the thought that Master T might tell her to go away, might punish her.

He held his hand out, gesturing her forward. "Faith, I was about to explain to Shawna that I am not available."

"But you trained me," Shawna said with a pout.

"No. I worked with you on a few occasions, as did several of the other Doms. Now I've explained that I won't play with you in the future. I have a submissive."

Shawna wasn't letting go. "I don't understand this place. You're the Dom. You can play with whoever you like. Tell your sub to accept it."

"My sub is very good with a scalpel, so I'll ignore your advice. Perhaps you should find another club. We don't play that way here. Our submissives are cherished. Even if Faith wanted to invite others to play with us, I would refuse because she's mine. And if she's mine, that means I'm hers, and I won't accept other hands on my body. So go."

The man with sandy blond hair named Kai strode up and put his hands on Shawna's shoulders. "Hey, why don't we go somewhere and talk for a bit? I've explained that I'll help you find a Dom, but you have to be patient. Why don't you go to the bar and I'll call your sister to come down."

Shawna stood, her eyes teary, but there was some anger in there, too. "Of course, Master Kai."

Master Kai winced as she strode away. "I'm sorry, Ten. She's a handful, but she's my assistant's sister. Kori is an important member of the club, so we allowed her sister in, though she's obviously got some issues. I hope she didn't ruin your evening."

Ten shook his head. "Not at all. We were about to go upstairs."

There was a tightening to Kai's face she didn't understand. It was only for a second and then his face was wiped clean and a blank, polite expression took root. "Enjoy yourselves."

She started to turn to watch him walk away, but Master T drew her attention back to him.

"You didn't stay where I left you," he said, his lips curling up.

"She was molesting you."

He stared down at her. "And you were going to ride in on your white horse and save me? I think I like that. But it also gives me a very thin excuse to punish you in a way I think is going to please us both, so thank you on both fronts, darlin'. I think we should play a game."

That got her heart rate up. "What kind of game?"

"The kind where I torture you and you scream for me. Come on. I want you to myself."

He held her hand as he led her to the elevator. Faith felt her heart beating hard in her chest and knew deep down that this night would change everything.

CHAPTER EIGHT

Faith felt the slightest bit vulnerable as she stepped into the privacy room. Like everything at Sanctum, it looked like it had been designed with care and thought. There was a large, four-poster bed and someone had prepped it. The comforter had been turned down and there were ropes already attached to the ones on the headboard. A crop lay on top of what looked like soft sheets.

She had to force herself to swallow. He was going to tie her up and use that crop on her body.

"What's your safe word, Faith? I have zero intentions of making you use it tonight, but I need to hear it. I need to know you'll use it if you feel frightened."

"My safe word is red, but I'm not frightened. Not really, but I will use it. I have before. I'm not one of those subs who thinks it's something to be ashamed of."

His face hardened. "When did you have to use it?"

"My old Dom spanked me a little too hard. When it got too rough, I safeworded and we talked. He apologized, though he didn't need to. Everything went the way it was supposed to. We found my limit and he respected it from there on."

"Did he bruise you? I don't mind some redness, but I prefer not to bruise my submissives. I want to know if you think I'm leaving marks."

"All right."

They stood there for a moment. This was the first time she'd been utterly alone with him. No one could interrupt and there was nothing to stop them from taking the next step. This was what she wanted, but now she hesitated. She'd spent three weeks getting to know him, another few days in his actual presence. What had begun as something casual felt more intimate.

"Don't be afraid of me." He crowded her, his hands finding her hair and tangling in it. He gently tugged on it, pulling her back so she had to look into his eyes. "I'll take care of you. As much as I can, I promise you that."

It sounded solemn, like he was making an oath to her, and she couldn't help but respond. He was giving her a safe place to play and explore and be the Faith she so rarely was.

It didn't mean she had to get her heart ripped out. No one could know what would happen in the future, but Faith knew the future didn't happen at all if she never took a leap.

"I'll take care of you, too. I want to spend this time with you. I want it more than you can know." She went on her toes and brushed her lips against his. He had a slight five-o'clock shadow, and she loved how the bristles felt against her skin.

"I want to show you something first. You should know what you're getting into. You didn't get a chance to really see them before. I want you to take a good look." He stepped back and pulled off his vest, turning so she could see his back.

She couldn't help her startled intake of breath. His back was a maze of scars, a collection of all the ways this man had been abused. Ian Taggart's words floated back through her head. There was a wealth of pain bubbling under Master T's calm surface.

He stood there, his back to her. His shoulders slumped slightly as though he'd felt the weight of that gasp, had expected it and was already accepting her choice.

Except she was fairly certain he didn't understand her choice at all. She moved to him and immediately placed her hands on his ruined back, her fingertips tracing the scars.

"You were burned."

"Yes," he replied, his voice gravelly.

He'd likely been young because the cigarette burns looked older

147

than the rest. It wasn't anything she hadn't seen before, but it always made her heart ache. It hurt more because she knew this man. "Foster care?"

"I had some good and some bad. That was a bad one, but if you look a couple of inches down, you'll see a scar I got when I was trying to get through a barbed wire fence. I got stuck and the man who found me was one of the finest men I ever met."

"He found you?"

"Like I said, I was stuck and I wasn't moving. Barbed wire hurts like hell. Papa Jack. He took in kids from time to time. His wife made the best pie in the world. He was a former Marine and I learned more about American history and how to serve my country from that man than I did from years in…the Army. I still miss that old man."

"What happened to him?"

"Cancer," Ten explained. "Child services wouldn't let him keep me when he got sick. I got sent to a group home after that. I just wanted you to know that it wasn't all bad. I had some good people in my life, too."

Those good people had obviously served to shape him into the man he'd become. She ran her fingers over some surgical scars. "Knife wound?"

He nodded slowly, but offered nothing else.

She moved down his torso, studying each scar, marveling at the strength of the man that could take such pain and still stand.

Master T's body was strong, but sometimes even the strongest bodies housed souls in need.

"I think you're beautiful." She leaned over and kissed his back, moving along his spine. She let her hands move, palms against his skin. She'd thought the wrong words. His flesh wasn't ruined, merely transformed by pain. There was still such beauty to it. She'd learn to find it everywhere. There was beauty in the worst scars, in places she'd never imagined beauty could take root.

"Thank you, Faith. I'm sure you've seen worse." He turned, obviously happy to have gotten through those moments.

"I have, but I think you're beautiful. Your body isn't something I can handle, Master. It's something I'm coming to crave. Please understand that. Your scars don't make you less beautiful. They make you more."

His jaw tightened and she could see he didn't believe her, but he also didn't argue. He took a long breath and then the charming smile was back on his face. "I want to see you. Let me get you out of that corset."

He turned her, brushing her hair off her shoulders. The intimacy that had frightened her before now cocooned them, and she shuddered when he kissed the back of her neck. "You're the beautiful one."

His hands began to move, working the laces of her corset with a slightly unpracticed hand. He hesitated as though trying to figure out which thread to pull, but slowly and surely the corset loosened.

She took a deep breath. This was what she loved about putting on her corset. She enjoyed the way it curved and made her look and feel so very feminine, but she always looked forward to this moment when she could breathe again, when she could relax and feel her body shift.

"Lift your arms, darlin'." When his voice got deep and that Southern accent took over, she couldn't help but sigh.

She complied and he lifted the corset over her torso, freeing her. She could feel her breasts move, nipples puckering, and then she was standing half naked in front of him. She remained still. Her back was to him, but he would tell her when he wanted her to turn. This was his time. He got to rule in the bedroom. He'd been courteous and kind, allowing her to take the lead in their conversations. It had been odd at first because her old Dom had dominated any talk with his own stories. He'd taken the whole Dom/sub thing seriously, which was why she'd never considered a full-time relationship, but Master T didn't seem to need it.

Which was likely why she was considering staying with him past their prescribed expiration date.

His hands came around from behind, cupping her breasts and making Faith sigh. Her skin felt electrified. Every molecule of her body seemed to come alive for him.

"Do you know how long I've been waiting for someone like you?" His breath was warm against her ear.

She leaned back into him. "At least as long as I waited for you."

He chuckled as his thumbs ran over her nipples, stiffening them further. "Not at all. You've had a Dom before. How long did you have a Dom?"

"A couple of years, but only for a few weeks at a time," she answered honestly. And then what he'd said really penetrated her brain. "How many subs have you taken?"

"Not a one. You're the first, sweetheart. You're absolutely the first woman I've desperately wanted to top." His tongue ran along the shell of her ear.

How was that possible? And yet it made a kind of sense. "I can't tell you how happy that makes me. Why did you get into the lifestyle?"

His hands moved down over her shoulders and to her waist before moving up her torso again. He didn't seem to be in a hurry, preferring to take it slow and easy. "I've been surrounded by it for a long time, but I kind of resisted it. What can I say? I'm stubborn."

She sighed back against him as his big palms cupped her breasts. His warmth surrounded her. "What made you change your mind?"

He breathed her in, his thumbs rasping over her already stiff nipples. "I think watching Tag get so invested in building this place made me think I should give it a try. It wasn't like I had tons of control in my relationships before. And none of them worked. I'm like every other man in the world. I'm looking for something that works. Now turn around and let me look at you."

His hands were gone, his warmth taken away as she heard him move behind her. When she turned, he was sitting in the lone chair in the room—a comfy-looking thing she could imagine straddling him on. He was truly delicious with his strong chest on display while leather pants and boots covered the rest of his body.

He was clothed and she wore nothing but her heels, fishnets, and a tiny thong she was sure she was about to lose. She wasn't sure why, didn't care to delve deep into her psyche, but this feeling of vulnerability did something for her. It only worked when she wasn't really vulnerable. She knew what it meant to have her life hanging in the balance, but this fantasy always got her blood pumping.

"Like I said before, you're a stunning woman, Faith. Give me the thong and lose the hose."

Yep. She'd called that one. She slowly rolled the hose off each leg, taking her time because he didn't seem to be in a hurry. He seemed determined to take his time, and she was more than all right with that.

"How long has it been?" Master T asked.

She folded the hose and thong and placed them on the corset, leaving her shoes there as well. If he wanted her to wear them, he would ask. Cool air caressed her skin. How long? How long had it been since she'd been comfortable being naked? A long while. She showered and redressed very quickly at the clinic because something was always going wrong. She slept in full pajamas there, too, because she couldn't be certain someone wouldn't need her in the night.

She couldn't be sure a small army wouldn't show up and drag her off into the jungle either. If that happened, she would rather be dressed.

How long had it been since her skin heated and she concentrated on her body as something more than a simple tool for her brain to use? Almost a year.

How long had it been since she'd felt this way about a man? Never. She wasn't sure why he called to her. Perhaps it was the mixture of Dominant male and lost little boy that tugged her his direction. Or some odd mix of hormones and pheromones in the exact chemical combination that seduced her. She didn't want to overthink why she wanted this man more than the others. She simply wanted him.

But she answered the question she was fairly sure he was asking. How long had it been since she'd been with a man? "Almost a year."

"So there's no one in Africa? Stop right there. Let me look at you."

She complied, remaining still and allowing his eyes to roam over her body. She felt nothing but acceptance coming from him, nothing but the sure heat of his gaze. "No one in Africa. I'm the only constant. I have other doctors and nurses rotate in, but they never stay for more than six months at a time."

"Turn around." When she did, he continued. "Six months is more than enough time to take a lover."

She had to chuckle at the thought. "Six months is a blur in Africa. I work twelve-hour shifts, sometimes sixteen depending on what's happening. When I'm not working, I sleep. I get to know the doctors' practices, how good they are in surgery, in the field. I rarely know much more than their specialty and why they came out to

Africa."

She always got the speech. Every newbie doctor made it at some point in time. The doctor would sigh and nod his or her head, and Faith would know what was coming. They came in order to give back to the world or because they'd always felt the calling.

And they left, ninety percent of them never to return.

The call didn't last very long in the face of the reality of Africa.

"Step forward." The deep command of his voice heated her flesh. She stepped forward and he sat up, studying her like she was a work of art.

One hand came out, tracing the curve of her hips down to her thigh. "So none of the other doctors ever tried to climb into your bed? I find that hard to believe. I would have been all over you, darlin'."

If he'd been the man McKay-Taggart had sent to be her bodyguard, she likely would have tossed aside all her very important rules about not getting involved with temporary people and fallen in bed with him. She was only now realizing that it had been easy before because she hadn't found a man who threatened to set her on fire with a single look from his bright blue eyes. She'd never really found a man she lusted after. Oh, she'd thought she had. She'd told herself how good sex had been with Roger and the boyfriends she had before him, but this was a different scale. This wasn't something a girl understood until she felt it.

She wanted to submit to this one man, to be his.

His hand cupped her breast and then she gasped at the pain that flared when he twisted her nipple. It quickly morphed into heat, flashing through her system.

"Faith, I want you here with me. I asked you a question. Don't try to deflect me. If I ask you a question it's because I want to know the answer."

He had asked her about other doctors. It was funny. She didn't like to talk about her job when she wasn't working. That was the point of these months. But he was interested and she wanted to give him anything he desired. Foolish girl, but there was the truth. "A few have come on to me. Only one ever got aggressive about it."

His eyes narrowed, but his hand softened, a sure sign she was pleasing him with her honesty. "Who?"

Shit. She didn't want to get into this. She wanted him to make love to her, but he was a freaking chatty Dom. "Does it matter?"

She hadn't really meant to sound so bratty. She'd meant it more like—hey, I don't want to concentrate on the bad stuff. Let's make good memories. It came out more like—God, you're boring me and I'm rolling my eyes like a sullen teenager. Mistake. Yep. That was a major mistake since his hand withdrew and his whole body hardened.

"Go to the bed, palms flat on the mattress."

"I'm sorry. I didn't mean it like that."

"But I did mean what I said. Go to the bed."

Shit. This was likely going to hurt. And feel good. God, she was a freak but she'd accepted this part of herself a long time ago. It was the hurt she'd seen in his eyes that made her hesitate. She wasn't going to hurt him more by disobeying when they were playing. She'd already figured out he could handle a great deal when they were in their everyday lives, but like all Doms, he needed some measure of control. He needed it here, and though her infraction had been minor, she intended to give it to him.

She was the impatient one, wanting to move more quickly than he was comfortable with. Damn it. Now he would likely slow down and all because she was trying to avoid intimacy again.

Palms flat on the bed. Spine straight. Calm. Collected. She waited for him this time. Breathe in and out. Accept what was coming because it led to something she loved. Pain could be transformed. It was another miracle of the human body. Endurance was rewarded with endorphins, with pleasure, with satisfaction and a release of tension.

Stress was the enemy. Acceptance her weapon of choice.

She relaxed as the first stroke of the crop hit her flesh.

It flamed along her skin and she tensed once more, every cell tightening before it came—acceptance. She breathed in and the flame turned to warmth.

"I asked you a question. Why wouldn't you answer?" The crop came down again, but she was ready for it this time. This time she opened herself to the pain, knowing where it led. The crop stung against her flesh, the leather slapping. She took in the sound, the pain, the scent of leather.

Honesty was easy when she was in this place. There wasn't a reason to hide here. Here she was naked and vulnerable, but it was all right to be both of those things. "I thought it would be different. I thought we would be play partners and not much more. Talking about my past makes me feel vulnerable."

Another slap, this one softer, as though even the crop was pleased with her answer. "You thought we would have sex and play and go our separate ways when the time came? I did, too. I don't know that still isn't what we'll do."

He found a rhythm, but after the first few, he seemed to lose interest in the punishment portion. The strokes of the crop seemed to be more about keeping her with him in the moment than truly teaching her a lesson. Master T, it seemed, didn't need to prove his point.

"We might," she agreed. The thought of never seeing him again hurt, but she couldn't be the girl who threw out her whole career for a guy she'd known for all of a month.

Even though she'd already started bargaining with herself, trying to find some way to keep him. God, her friends from med school would be beside themselves. The great and mighty Faith putting a man in front of her precious cause. Her sister would have a laugh.

And none of that mattered if she decided this was what she wanted. All that would matter was the two of them, and that was scary.

"I'd still like an answer to my question," he said as the crop hit the backs of her legs.

She had to think to remember exactly what he'd asked her. He'd asked if there had been anyone who got handsy with her. "One doctor. He was slightly older than me. He thought he knew a lot. One particularly long night he showed up on my doorstep. He said he wanted to talk to me about the new shipment of supplies. I let him in."

She felt his palm cup one of her cheeks. "Did he attack you?"

"He was aggressive. Said something about how much I could obviously use a good lay. Then I explained that he could use a good urologist and kicked his balls into his body cavity," she admitted. "The sad thing was we didn't have a urologist on staff. I had to fix the jerk. Sometimes it's hard to be a doctor."

He stopped and she was pleased with the deep chuckle that came from his chest. "Do you want more? I didn't give you a prescribed amount and I'm satisfied with your answers, but I can also smell your arousal. Do you want more?"

"God, yes."

"Then get on the bed and let me tie you down," he commanded in that dark chocolate voice of his. "I'll give you what you want as long as you play my games."

"Games?" She could play some games with the gorgeous Master T. Lots of games. Games that involved his mouth and hands and lovely parts of the man she hadn't explored at this point.

His hand caressed up and down the length of her spine, reminding her of what he'd done. Every inch of her skin felt sensitized to this man's touch. "Sure. Pleasure for information. I want to know more about you. I know you would rather we simply enjoyed each other's bodies, but I don't play that way. I want to know you. I want to know your history, how your mind works. So please me and I'll pleasure you."

That was a bargain she was perfectly willing to make.

* * * *

As Faith climbed onto the bed, Ten was well aware of what a bastard son of a bitch he was. Let's play a game? Pleasure for information? It wasn't a game for Faith, not really. She was trying to please him because he'd told her lie after lie.

Would she believe him for a second if he explained that giving him this information would help him protect her? Fuck no. She was a smart girl, his Faith.

Not his. Never his. The best he could hope to get out of this was to be the bastard who left her one morning because he'd gotten all the information he needed out of her. If he was lucky, she would think he was an asshole who used her for sex and then dumped her. If he screwed up, she would figure out how bent his soul was and she would hate him for the rest of her life.

God, he didn't want her to hate him.

"Like this?" Her voice was soft as she looked up at him.

She was his wet dream, lying on the bed like she'd been placed there with no thought beyond his pleasure. He could definitely see why this called to Tag. A smart woman, strong and secure in herself,

155

and she was submitting to him and only him. It made a man feel about ten feet tall.

And as small as a little piece of shit because he was going to damage that lovely security.

"Yes," he said, unable to take his eyes off her curves. Faith was built on generous lines. Her breasts were a sweet handful, her waist flaring into hips he could hold on to, and a truly spectacular ass. Round and juicy, those cheeks were meant to catch a man's eye. His eye. He kind of wanted everyone else to keep their damn eyes to themselves.

Would she understand if he stopped everything right this instant and explained what he was doing and why? Would she forgive him? Or would he be in need of a good urologist like that fucker who'd tried to hurt her?

She would choose her father. She would choose her family. She would choose anyone but him. If there was one thing he knew in the world, it was that truth.

The least he could do was give her pleasure, give her his true and honest praise. "You're beautiful, Faith. You might be the most beautiful thing I've ever seen."

Her lips curled up. "Thank you, Master. You make me feel that way."

She didn't argue with him. She took his words as the gift they were. It made him like her even more. He could look at her all day. He liked the low light of the room. It made everything seem slightly unreal, like if he could simply keep his eyes on her, he might be able to forget he was here to do anything but make love to her.

He grasped the rope and began working it around her wrists. It was better this way. She wouldn't be able to touch him. There would be distance between them. He could still give her everything she needed, but he wouldn't have her arms around him. He wouldn't wake up with her tangled around his body like a vine climbing up a tree.

He would be in control and that would remind him of what he needed to do.

"So you worked with this man for six months?" The idea of some doctor pawing her in the middle of the fucking jungle made him want to wrap his hands around the asshole's throat. "Where was your bodyguard?"

She wasn't giving him a name so he had to figure out a way to narrow the time frame down. If he asked again for a specific name, she might grow wary—might think he was going to do something he shouldn't. He was really trying to figure out who would potentially want to hurt her. If that near assassination had been about a pissed-off rejected suitor, he could at least handle the problem for her.

It was becoming harder and harder for him to buy that she was really dirty. He might be an idiot, but he had to admit to himself that she was potentially innocent in all of this.

She glanced up at him as he tied her left wrist to the bedpost. So trusting. There wasn't any fear in her body. She expected him to take care of her. "I didn't have a bodyguard then. That was only after what happened in Ghana. And no, Doctor Hines left as soon as the swelling in his testicles went down. I was on my own for a good three months."

Excellent. Now he had a name and she was looking luscious, a treat secured and laid out for him. His cock was already erect, but looking at her like this made him stiffen painfully. She wasn't staring at his scars with revulsion. She was looking at him like she could eat him up. It was time to make her feel good, too.

He took the crop in his hand. It was a flexible one, the leather at the tip soft. He brought it lightly down on her right nipple, the sound worse than he suspected the sensation was. Of course when he'd had a crop taken to him, it had come from that bastard Taggart, who'd had a field day holding Ten to the Sanctum rule that no Dom got to play with toys that hadn't been used on him.

There was a reason he didn't have an anal plug ready for her. There was only so much a man would do for a mission.

Besides, he was really only interested in her pretty pussy at this point. Pretty, likely tight as hell, definitely aroused. He could see the signs glistening in the low light.

"But now you have bodyguards," he continued. "You should have had them all along. That's a dangerous part of the world. I'm surprised your father didn't insist on it."

She winced as he tapped her left breast. "My dad and I had a falling out, and I kind of wasn't talking to him at that point in time."

Oh, that was interesting news. He dragged the crop tip down her body, brushing it over her pussy and enjoying the way her toes curled. He was going to taste her tonight. He was going to get inside of her in more ways than one. "I thought you were close to your father."

Her eyes were on the crop. He'd left it directly on her mound, covering it with the leather. "We've never been really close. He's always been closer to Hope. They think alike. My father was always working, always on the road. He didn't agree with my decision to open a clinic in Ghana. He would have preferred I went the same route as my sister."

Her sister, who was connected to a suspected Collective company. He gave her the lightest tap and loved how her whole body shivered. "He still paid your ransom. He must have been very angry when you went back. But you're still talking, obviously. You come home once a year and you told me you always see him. Aren't we supposed to go to his place in the Caymans?"

A harder tap this time and she was writhing. Faith was well disciplined though. Her voice was hoarse but she answered his questions. "Yes. My dad and I are all right. He's always making a deal, but he loves me. Oh, god. That feels so good." Another rougher slap. "He wasn't happy when I decided to go back, but he made amends. He threw a fundraiser when a fire destroyed my only operating facility. Fifty thousand dollars. It was a godsend."

He moved to her thighs, tapping them with force. The skin went a light pink. Fifty thousand was nothing to a man like Senator McDonald. He could probably shit out fifty K in his sleep and not notice. If he threw a fundraiser, fifty thousand would be a disappointment.

There was something to look into. He would look into the fundraiser and see if there was anything hinky about it. Finances were something solid he could deal with.

"It's good to have family to depend on. I'm glad you got close to your father again." A lie. He wished she was far away from the man, but then he wouldn't have an easy way in. He doubted Hope would be as pleasant to spend time with. Faith's sister had a chill to her he'd seen in some of the most ruthless people he'd ever met.

He smacked at her breasts again, twice to each in rapid succession. Her nipples were rigid as hell.

"It's been nice the last few years. After what happened in Ghana, we had a huge fight about opening the clinic in Liberia. I used the last of what my mother left me to do it. I couldn't have kept it open without his help, and now my sister's company is pledging vaccines and supplies. Please, please do that again."

He raised the crop again and brought it down a bit harder, watching the blood rush to her chest, giving her the sweetest rosy flush. So her sister and father had recently shown an interest in the clinic. That was intriguing. He would take a second look at the clinic's finances when it came to fundraising and the connection to Kronberg. The vaccines had come from there. Even though it seemed like there was no longer a connection between the clinic and the mob, he was still interested.

But he'd asked enough questions. He could likely keep this up for hours, but his cock was aching. Oh, he wasn't going to use it on her yet, but he was definitely moving this play session along.

Play. He would remember the word. They were playing. He was playacting. Yeah, he was getting really good at fooling himself when it came to her. He gripped her ankles and dragged them up. She was fit and flexible, her body moving easily into the position he wanted it, legs almost to her chest. He could see her pussy, glistening and wet. All for him, and he knew what she liked.

When he looked back at her, trying to find trepidation or fear in her eyes, he couldn't. There was only hot anticipation. Her hands curled around the ropes tethering her to the bed as though she was getting ready to hang on for a long ride.

"This isn't about punishment, Faith. I'm not really that Dom. I want to give you what you need and I think you need this." God knew he did. He brought the crop down on her round cheeks, the sound whipping through the air and then cracking. Her skin pinkened immediately. He brought it down again and again, finding a rhythm. She was completely vulnerable to him in this position. There was nothing she could do. She'd placed herself at his mercy, and the thought caused his dick to jump. So soft and sweet, and she had no idea how hungry the big bad wolf really was. He was going to eat her up. He would devour every last bite.

He brought the crop down again and again, sensitizing her skin. The moans and groans that came from her told him it was working.

She was breathing in pants, but she didn't fight him in any way. Faith wanted this. She needed this to feel whole and alive, and he felt more connected to her in that moment than he'd ever felt to another person. There was almost a flow of energy that began with each stroke, a wave he started and she gave back to him.

When her tears began to flow, he eased up and touched her heated flesh. "Is it enough?"

She sniffled and nodded. "I loved it, Master. I love that I'll feel it tomorrow, and all day long it will be like you're with me."

He let her legs drop, the words filling him with some unnamable, unwanted emotion. He didn't want to feel so soft around her, so fucking protective. He wasn't sure he could walk away from her, and that was a very bad thing.

He shoved it all out. One night. A week or two tops. He would convince her to go out to the islands early so they would avoid her father. He would get the information and then find a way to ease out of her life.

Or he would send her father to hell, get his position back at the Agency, and she would never know he was the one behind it all. He was good at covering his tracks and there would be no public trial for the senator. No jail time. The Agency would end him quietly, and Ten might even let someone else do it. Plausible deniability. He could tell Faith what he wanted about his job and see her when he could.

It might work.

He didn't care tonight. He wanted to get inside her.

"My time now, Faith. This is my time and you're going to obey me. Am I understood?" He was the one panting now because she was so ready for him. So fucking ready for him.

"Oh, yes, Master." She spread her legs, inviting him inside.

That was an invitation he didn't intend to refuse.

CHAPTER NINE

Her whole body felt like a live wire. When Master T had held her ankles and forced them up, leaving her backside available to the smack of his crop, she'd nearly cried out in pleasure then and there. It had been so long since she'd felt like this, felt herself sinking into subspace, giving up all the tension and stress and emotion of the last several months to the whack of a crop. Most people wouldn't understand and she'd stopped trying to explain it, but the pain freed her somehow. The pain allowed her to float for a while, unencumbered by what she'd seen and experienced before.

And the man brought her right back down to earth. She could admit that in the past she'd sometimes traded sex for dominance. It wasn't that the sex hadn't been decent. Her partners tended to be knowledgeable and experienced, but sometimes she would rather float than be in the moment with them. It was selfish, but then both partners had known the score.

She wanted to connect with Master T. She wanted this to be more than sex, more than a trade between them, so she forced herself to focus on him.

He'd given her so much, and she needed him to know that she was fully in the moment with him. When she spread her legs, making a place for him at the core of her body, she was satisfied with the way his eyes flared and how quickly his hands went to the laces of his leathers.

She watched him with greedy eyes as he kicked out of his boots and shoved the leathers off his lean hips. He was a beautifully made man. Even the scars did nothing but give him character. Without them, he would be too perfect, almost untouchable, as though he needed the imperfections to remind his lovers he required affection and a soft touch.

His cock sprang free and she realized that touch hadn't lied to her. Master T was a big guy on every level. His cock was long and thick, jutting up toward his navel. She wanted to touch him, to feel the silky skin covering that erection and taste the pearly pre-ejaculate that clung to the head. Her palms nearly itched with the need to touch him, but this was his time. She would give him what he needed even if it was a quick, hard fuck to satisfy the obvious ache in his dick. He'd been so patient with her. She could do the same for him.

He reached over and dragged open the nightstand drawer, pulling out a condom and tossing it on the bed.

He was going to take her. It would be rough and hard. Like the man himself, and she would simply ride that wave and give him everything she had.

He climbed on the bed, his muscles working like a predatory cat's. Lean, strong, graceful. There was a darkness about the man that she might never be able to penetrate, but it drew her to him like a moth to the flame.

His hands went to her thighs, pressing them open. When she thought he would reach for the condom, he dropped to his belly, his mouth above her pussy.

Her whole body tightened. God, he was going to kiss her. He was going to tongue her and taste her. This was what he considered "his time." She kind of thought she was going to seriously enjoy his time.

"You're so fucking gorgeous, Faith. Do you have any idea what it does for me that you spread yourself wide and don't fight me on what I want?"

If he wanted something that would hurt her, she would fight, but Master T had given her nothing but pleasure. She would give him a lot of leeway when it came to his own desires. And she wasn't a shrinking violet to protest that sex was dirty and they should turn the lights off. Sex was natural, and it felt even more so with this man. Sex was necessary and she took it seriously. She wasn't the most beautiful woman in the world, but every body was lovely in its own way. She truly believed that and she believed that thinking poorly of herself didn't help anyone. If a lover didn't like her body, he could find another woman.

She was rapidly wondering if it would have been the same with Master T. Would she have so easily sent him packing? Would she have felt some momentary regret that was quickly overcome with work? Or would she have mourned the loss of his potential?

The good news was he thought she was gorgeous and she felt that way. She felt like a pretty BDSM princess about to be taken by her Dom king. Ah, the fantasies she could play out with him.

A light happiness took over, mingling with the headiness of desire as she felt the heat of his breath.

"You look happy." He was staring at her.

"You make me happy. I'm happy to be here with you." She'd learned to acknowledge these moments. Moments she could hold in her heart when the times got bad again. They would go bad—everything did—but she would have a well of happiness to draw from.

"Then let me make you even happier." He dragged his tongue over her clit and she nearly came off the bed.

Heat sizzled through her veins and her head dropped back. She had to hold on to the ropes he'd tied so sweetly around her wrists. It was a good thing, too, since she would likely be clutching his hair if he hadn't. She would be shoving her pelvis up and trying to get him to lick and suck, and then she would get another spanking. So she was really glad for those ropes now. They enabled her to hold on and give him his way.

His big tongue ran over her pussy, dragging upward through her labia. He parted the petals and seemed intent on devouring her. So good. He felt so good. He sucked one side of her labia into his mouth with a juicy smack and then gave the other side the same treatment. All the while she could feel his fingers starting to breach her.

He teased his way inside as he sucked and licked the outside. She looked down and watched as his golden brown head worked over her. She couldn't help the gasp that came from her throat when he scraped his teeth over her clit. The sensation screamed along her spine, making her want to beg for more.

"Tell me you like this." It came out of his mouth as a command, a deep, husky order.

"I like this." It was an easy order to follow because she was already kind of addicted to Master T's brand of dominance. She usually had to give, to bend to the Dom, but Master T seemed to need exactly what she did. Dominance in the bedroom and a friendship outside of it. Maybe a real partnership. This was what she'd been looking for. She'd accepted less before, thought she had to compromise. This was perfection. "I love this. I can't get enough of this."

The smirk on his face did something to her heart. He was an arrogant man, but he needed her approval, her praise. As long as he kept it up, she would tell him how amazing he was on a regular basis. Hell, she would write him notes about how talented his tongue was.

His fingers foraged deep, curling inside her.

He found a rhythm that got her blood pumping hard. He found that perfect spot and she couldn't stay quiet. Thank god he hadn't given her any orders about silence because she screamed out as she came.

"That's what I like to hear, darlin'." He kissed her one last time and then got up to his knees.

Even in the haze of her orgasm, she had to stare at him. He was so gorgeous, with his cut body and handsome face. He reached for the condom, tearing it open and rolling it over his cock.

"Please, Master. Can you let me out of the bonds?" She wanted her arms around him, wanted to hold him.

He frowned as he stroked himself. "I like you like that. You look beautiful."

There was something about the way he said it that made her wonder if he was telling the truth, but then he was pushing his cock inside her and she couldn't think another second. He remained on his knees, his eyes on her as he tilted her hips up and started to force his way inside. "I like you this way, Faith. I like you vulnerable and needy. I want you to need my cock the way I need you. I've been needing you for weeks and weeks, and I don't want to hold back another second. After tonight, you're mine. For as long as this relationship lasts, you're my submissive. You're mine to take care of, to indulge, to fuck exactly the way I like it."

So full. He was pulling on her hips, impaling her with that big cock of his, and if she hadn't been so aroused, it might have been too much. As it was, it felt like perfection. She relaxed and let him take over. "Yes, Master."

"I won't hold back anymore, Faith. I'm serious. I'm going to be on top of you three times a day." His jaw was a hard line, arousal plain on his face. His hips flexed and she felt her body heat all over again.

How could he do that? How could he make her feel this way? "I won't complain. I'll take you as often as you want me."

"Famous last words." He leaned over, settling himself on top of her, his mouth hovering above hers. "Do you know how good you feel to me? If you don't believe a damn word I say, believe that I've never wanted a woman the way I want you."

He kissed her swiftly before shoving back up and taking her hips in his hands. He held her tight, his hips moving in a hard rhythm. He fucked in and out, his pelvis grinding against hers on the down stroke.

There was nothing she could do but take everything he had to give her. She would have sworn she couldn't come again. She'd never been one of those screaming multiple orgasm girls, but Master T was bringing it out of her.

He thrust in and his hips swiveled and she went over the edge again. She wanted to hold on to him, but all she could do was take what he gave. She shouted out his name as another wave hit her. This one was hard, rougher than the first. The pleasure crashed over her, leaving her breathless and exhausted, but she forced herself to stay with him. She wanted to watch him, wanted to see the moment she gave him the same pleasure he gave her.

His eyes closed, head dropping back as he held himself hard against her. His whole body tensed, but he didn't make a sound. He thrust in a few more times, obviously in the grips of his orgasm, but there was a distance that disappointed her.

When he pulled out, she wanted to reach out and touch him, but he was pretty good with the bondage thing.

"Give me a minute," he muttered and moved off the bed, disappearing into what she thought was likely the bathroom.

He'd left her. He'd fucked her like she was the last woman on earth and then he'd walked away.

Why would he do that? Faith felt the beginnings of tears and forced them down. She didn't know this was a rejection. People had odd reactions sometimes. She had to be patient and figure out what the problem was. Diagnose the issue.

Ten had been through a lot. His body attested to his rough life. Something could have triggered a bad reaction.

Or he could have not enjoyed the sex.

God, Faith, go to the worst-case scenario much? The man told you he wanted you more than he'd ever wanted a woman. Give him a minute to process.

Deep breath. It was going to be okay. They were learning each other's quirks, and she wasn't going to let her own insecurities derail what was turning out to be a really good relationship. If he felt the desperate need to run and hide in the bathroom moments after orgasm, then she would deal with it.

She wasn't going to immediately think that the world was over. Positive thinking. Negativity never got her anywhere. Nope. It was going to be all right.

What was she going to do if he dumped her after one night?

The door opened and he strode out, a smooth smile on his face. "Extra large, my ass. I'm going to have a serious talk with Tag about the condoms he uses. I damn near filled that one to overflowing." He started to work the ties off her wrists. "Or I was incredibly inspired. Sorry I left you in these. I didn't want to make a horrible mess."

She sighed as he got her free and drew her into his arms. He rolled over and cuddled her to his body.

"Can you forgive me?" He kissed her nose and smoothed back her hair.

She was warm again. She hugged him tight. This was what she'd missed during sex. She'd never really needed it before, but she craved this kind of intimacy with Ten. Warm and naked and safe. She rested her head against his shoulder. "Totally forgiven."

"Will you come back to my place?"

Would she spend every minute with him until they had to decide what to do? Until reality invaded? Hell, yes. "Absolutely. My bags are packed and waiting."

"Perfect," he murmured.

Faith breathed him in, loving the smell of his skin mixed with the musk of their lovemaking. She relaxed and realized she would do almost anything for this man.

It wasn't as scary a prospect as she thought it would be. She looked forward to the next few weeks and trusted that everything would work out the way it should.

* * * *

Ten stared at himself in the mirror and wondered what the fuck had happened in there. All around him the locker room was buzzing with sound and life, but he was focused on those last few moments with Faith, when he'd forgotten about anything but the silky feel of her skin, the hot clasp of her body. He'd closed his eyes because looking at her had been too intimate, too close. He'd never felt as close to a woman as he'd felt to Faith in those moments, and it had been far too much.

He'd been an ass. He'd practically jumped off the bed and run the fuck away. He'd stood in the bathroom, trying desperately to stop his fucking hands from shaking.

He'd covered it well. He'd forced himself to behave like an actual operative and not some lovesick idiot. He'd strode back out, made a joke about a condom, and pulled her into his arms. She'd settled in like she belonged there and all was right with the world.

Except he kind of hated himself.

"Just tell her."

He turned and noticed Liam O'Donnell had left the man cave section of the locker room for the quieter changing stations. Big Tag had kitted up the men's locker room with a widescreen LCD and a bunch of state-of-the-art lounge chairs. A good portion of the crew was currently sitting around the TV discussing the game that was on. The Rangers were up by two, but according to Tag it was all going to fall apart because the pitcher had a lazy arm or something and it was the top of the eighth.

He was never really one for sports.

"Tell who what?" He forced himself back into friendly mode, plastering that smile on his face that he thought let everyone know he simply enjoyed the world around him and wasn't he the nicest guy?

O'Donnell's eyes narrowed and Ten was fairly certain the Irishman wasn't buying his crap. "Tell Faith the truth. Decide right now if she's innocent or not and tell her what you're doing. It's the only way this turns out all right, or you should learn to get on your knees and beg."

The last thing he needed was O'Donnell's interference. "You're not assigned to this op, Li. I think I know what I'm doing."

O'Donnell chuckled and crossed over to the locker assigned to him. "Yeah, you got no idea, boyo. And you're not going to listen to a bloody word I say, are ya?"

Ten turned back to his locker, this time avoiding the mirror on the inner door. Why had Tag put those there? Were all his Doms prima donna divas who needed to check that their guyliner was on properly? He pulled out his shirt, shoving his arms in. "You don't know the op so I think I'll keep my own counsel."

"I might not know the op but I know what it feels like to hate meself for what I'm doing to a woman I care about."

"Faith is simply the target. Actually, she's not even the target. She's the means to get to the target."

"That's very Agency of you, Ten. Did they teach you that dialogue? Because it's all a piece of shit. You like the girl."

He wished O'Donnell would go away. "She's a likable woman. I'm still not sure she isn't involved in her father's business." Bullshit. That was complete and utter bullshit. This was a woman who had given medical aid to the asshole who had assaulted her. She'd tended to wounds she'd inflicted, but he really thought she was running around selling out soldiers?

He wanted to follow his instincts. Everything he knew told him Faith was innocent. The trouble was, his instincts had been wrong before. Very wrong.

"Does it matter if she is?" O'Donnell's voice had gone a bit softer and had an almost nauseating sympathy to it.

Why? Why is it nauseating for a friend to feel for you? Jamie's voice was back. He really hoped Ferguson never found out that Ten's dead brother from another mother talked to him.

Was O'Donnell his friend? "Of course it matters. If she's involved with her father's business, then she's responsible for my brother's death."

And that isn't a world you want to live in so it's not true.

So said the dead guy. Unfortunately, Ten knew it could be true. And yet he really didn't want to believe it. If it wasn't true, she could potentially be in danger. What would she do if she ever discovered her father's scheme?

What would he do?

"Well, then, I guess I was wrong. You seemed very cozy with her tonight. I thought there might be something there. Sorry. I'm a married man. I want everyone to be as utterly miserable as I am." It was said with the grin of a man who was far from miserable. Liam O'Donnell was a happy man with a baby boy and a wife he couldn't take his eyes off of. "I'll also be glad when this op is over and I get my partner back. Although I'm pretty sure Theo's turned her into a girl. Ruined a perfectly good drinking buddy. I swear that girl could cuss and drink with the best of them. Now she's probably going to want to talk about her nails or decorating or something. Still, she'll probably be more reliable than Boomer."

"Tag put you with Boomer?" Boomer was a first-rate sniper, but Ten hadn't hired him for his brains. He was loyal as the day was long, but he wasn't built for intelligence work.

"Been working a missing persons case. The boy was a fighter. I've been posing as Boomer's trainer to get close to the missing kid's friends. Turns out he wouldn't take a dive and the mob took exception." O'Donnell shook his head. "I hate it when I have to give bad news, but at least they have closure and the bad guys are currently being loved on by even badder guys in the state pen. Boomer was excellent at taking a punch, but I damn near lost him. Wandered away looking for a snack right before the bad shit went down. Came roaring back in with a hot dog in one hand. Let me tell you, don't come between that kid and his food. It's lucky those boys made it to prison after what Boomer did to them once they'd made him drop his lunch."

Ten couldn't help but smile. He missed his team, but it looked like they were fitting in at McKay-Taggart. Even the ones who hadn't left the Agency were talking about moving to the private side. "I'm going to have to get a whole new team when I get back. Start from scratch, I guess."

"You're going back?"

"Once I've proven the man who had me burned is a fraud and gotten rid of the Senator's inside man, yes, I'll go back." If he survived. It was all he knew. It was literally the only job he'd ever been trained for.

"You would go back to a place that didn't fight for you?"

"It's not like that. The Agency isn't good or bad. It simply is. And I always knew no one would fight for me. That's not how it works."

"You know, I bless the day I got burned. I wonder how my life would have gone if I hadn't left G2." O'Donnell had once been an operative with Irish intelligence. A joint mission with the CIA and MI6 went south and O'Donnell had been on the run for years before the situation had been fixed. On the run? Not so much. He'd found a home with McKay-Taggart.

"We're not all cut out to be in for the long term."

"Do you ever wonder if maybe this is a sign that you should get out?"

"And do what?" Ten asked.

"What the rest of us do. We work. We live. We have lives."

And barbecues and picnics, and they all held hands and ran through fields of daisies. Yeah. "That's not for me. I'm a lifer. I need a mission."

O'Donnell's eyes narrowed. "I've got a mission. Don't think for a second that I don't have a mission."

"I'm not talking about temporary assignments. I'm talking about something to focus my life on."

"So am I. Those temporary assignments, they aren't missions. They're work. Just work. My mission is something far greater, something I really would give me life for. My wife. My child and any more we're blessed with. My friends. Protecting them, being good for them, that's a mission worth taking."

It didn't compute. The words didn't really make sense to Ten. They sounded like a wave of domesticity. What O'Donnell was talking about wasn't a mission. It was retirement, and Ten couldn't do it. Still, when the Irishman closed up his locker, Ten felt the need to keep him talking.

"She wouldn't believe me."

O'Donnell shoved his keys in his pocket. "You don't know until you try."

"That's easy for you to say. If I fuck this up, everything falls apart. This isn't simply about revenge."

"I know that, Tennessee. I also understand that it was hard for you not to take care of the situation the way you wanted to. Did you think about it?"

"Did I think about murdering the man in his sleep?" A bitter laugh huffed from his throat. "I managed to get into his hotel room. I distracted his bodyguard with a hooker. Those are hard to come by in Saudi. McDonald was staying in a four-star hotel with some of the best security you'll find, but I got around all of it. I hid in a closet while he held a meeting with a Saudi company interested in buying roads in the US. They come in and turn public roads into tollways. Then the states can use the money for god knows what, the politicians get kickbacks, and taxpaying citizens pay four dollars to drive ten miles to work."

"Shit, brother. Why is he still breathing?"

"I stood over him after he went to sleep and I slit his throat in my head about fifty times before I walked away because if I don't find the name of the men he's working with, then none of it matters."

"And that's why she'll believe you." O'Donnell put a hand on his shoulder. "You're not a bad man, Tennessee. You have tunnel vision. I'm working on something in the senator's background. Something that might bring her to your side."

"What?" If he had something that could buy Faith's loyalty, he would take it.

"I'll send it to Erin when I'm done. It could be nothing, but I don't think so. Something isn't right with the investigation of his wife's death. I don't like it. I think she knew something and he killed her for it. Faith seems like the kind of woman who would want justice, too. She needs to hear this from you though. If she finds out from anyone else...well, I wish you luck."

"If I tell her too soon, she'll choose her father and I'll lose my chance. I have to convince her to go out to the islands a little early. I want to be out of there before he makes it to the party."

"Because he'll kill you on sight?"

"I doubt that. He won't want to dirty his hands, but he could cause me trouble with Faith." Faith had become the wild card. "I don't want her hurt."

O'Donnell shook his head. "There's no way she doesn't get hurt. That girl's in deep with you. It's going to hurt, but she'll forgive you more easily if you tell her yourself. Think about it. Don't walk away from her. She could be good for you, and that's about all a man can ask out of life."

"What if I'm not good for her?" He wasn't good for anyone.

"Then change. Be a man and be good for her. It's your choice. I know in the past you haven't had many of those, but this is very much something you decide. And I'm not stupid. You think your chances of actually getting your job back are next to none. You don't think you're going to survive this and you're all right with that. That's a choice, too, Ten, and you're making the wrong one. Night."

O'Donnell stepped out and brushed by Theo, who was walking in. They nodded at each other as they passed.

"Damn, he looked all kinds of serious," Theo remarked. "Of course you're probably going to look the same way when I tell you what I have to tell you."

His blood went slightly cold. "What do you have to tell me?"

Theo pointed. "Yep. I was right. All kinds of serious."

"I'm going to seriously set you on your ass if you don't start talking." Was it about Faith? Had they found something bad about Faith?

He didn't want to hear it.

"Someone broke into my place tonight."

He was oddly relieved. For a moment he'd had visions of Faith telling Erin she knew all about her dad's plans and hey, wouldn't she like to be a part of an evil army, too? Stupid, but he couldn't help it. "Did you catch them?"

"The security cameras did. Whoever it was they were good and very fast. They were in and out before the police or Hutch could get there. I didn't want to go screaming out in case you planned on keeping Faith out of the loop. Again."

The youngest Taggart was also the most judgmental. "You know why I told her it was over."

"Yes, so she'll act normally, and by normally you mean commit some kind of crime."

"Could you please tell me about the break-in?" The tiniest Tag's discipline had gone to shit since he'd started working for his brother.

"From what I can tell from the cameras, he knew what he was looking for. He entered through the backdoor—which will be getting a serious upgrade tomorrow—and went straight for the bedrooms. He glanced around the master and then headed for the one Faith had been using. When he realized she'd packed up, he left in a hurry, tried to cover his tracks. I doubt we'll find any evidence. He was wearing a ski mask and gloves. I'm thinking about getting a dog. A nice sweet puppy who'll tear off the balls of anyone who breaks into my house. Erin could have been there."

"And she would have taken the balls off the guy," Ten pointed out. "Shit. I have to go through Faith's things. She's got something someone wants. I'll need Erin to distract her."

"They're supposed to go to lunch in a few days with Phoebe. They're planning some kind of shopping trip."

Ten felt his brow rise. "With my sister?"

Theo grinned. "Yes, with your super-supportive sister. I think you'll find she's Team Faith all the way. Also, who's Dawn? Because she said after someone named Dawn, Faith was an angel sent from heaven."

He felt himself flush. "Dawn was a double agent who lived with me for a year and then sold me out to a terrorist cell who tortured and nearly killed me."

Theo gave him a thumbs-up. "You're totally doing better this time, boss. And it's cool. I'll come by at some point and you can distract Faith so I can go through her bags. Plausible deniability if we get caught."

And an excuse to beat the shit out of Theo. If Faith caught Theo going through her bag, Ten would be forced to kick his ass. It would be part of his cover. A really fun part of his cover.

Theo frowned. "I don't like the look on your face."

Which proved he wasn't a dumb shit. "Don't worry about it. I like this plan. You check her purse before they go and then we'll go through her bag and laptop while they're at lunch later in the week. I want to figure out what she has and why they want it. I want this over with before we head to the Caymans."

"Erin is going to start softening her up for leaving a little early," Theo said as he opened his locker.

"I know she doesn't like doing it, but it really is for Faith's protection." He suddenly felt the need to make Theo understand. It was unsettling, but he couldn't not follow it. "I'm going to take care of Faith. I'm going to try to take care of her even after the op is over."

Theo's eyes went wide. "Seriously?"

Ten nodded. "I said I would try. I didn't say she would let me. I'm going to have to play it very carefully. It's why it would be best if we could get in and then find a reason to get out before her father gets to the island. I might have a shot at protecting her from the fallout if I can ease her into the truth."

O'Donnell was wrong. If he told her now, he would lose her, but once she saw what her father was involved in, she wouldn't have a choice but to turn to him, and by the time she found out who he really was, she would be so tied to him there wouldn't be anywhere to go.

It might work. It would require a lot of deception, but it was all meant to protect her—from her father, from pain.

"I'll help you anyway I can," Theo promised.

Ten believed him. God, working at McKay-Taggart was making him soft, but he really did believe Theo.

He walked out of the locker room to find Faith laughing with Phoebe.

Soft. He was really going to have to deal with that.

CHAPTER TEN

"**I** like shoes," Erin argued over her enchiladas. There was a massive margarita in front of her.

"No." Phoebe shot back with a grin. "You like boots, and not the cute kind. You like combat boots. The salesperson at Nordstrom nearly cried when she saw what you're wearing."

Faith found herself smiling. She'd never been the girliest of girls, but she seemed to fit in with Erin and Phoebe. They weren't ones to spend all their time talking about Hollywood stars and their sex lives or makeup. Even this shoe conversation was more about teasing Erin than it was really discussing the latest Prada line.

It was good to fit into a group in the real world. Sometimes it felt like she'd been through too much, seen too much to ever really belong in nice places where bad things rarely happened to good people.

"I'm with Erin. I like my boots. I prefer sneakers, but I learned really fast not to wear them in the jungle. They're too easy for snakes to bite through." Faith felt herself flush. This was why she didn't fit into polite feminine circles.

"Yeah, those suckers have some serious fangs, but I'm still thinking the hooded vipers we had all over the bases in Iraq win the nasty reptile war. I've never seen so many Special Forces dudes cry like girls," Erin said, sitting back.

"I think you two are wimps. I've worked intelligence my whole life. Did they give me body armor? No. They gave me a Victoria's Secret pushup bra. Try stopping a bullet with that. No boots for Phoebe. No. Learn how to run for your life down the streets of Beijing with four operatives shooting at you while you're wearing five-inch Chanel heels. Seriously though, if you have to choose, those Chanels were really comfy. And you haven't lived until you've seen some of the bugs in Southeast Asia. Ewww."

There was a reason she fit with these women. They'd asked about her work and hadn't flinched when she talked about blood and gore. It was kind of their world, too, though they seemed to have come out on the other side of the truly dangerous stuff. Faith caught sight of Phoebe's husband sitting at the bar, slowly nursing a single beer while he watched the baseball game on the TV. He'd been the perfect chauffeur, polite, respectful, quiet, but it was easy to see the way his eyes would shift to his wife and slowly heat. Jesse Murdoch looked like a happy man. But apparently he was the type of man who believed women who intended to drink multiple margaritas and shop needed a driver.

She rather thought Ten, Theo, and Jesse had drawn straws over who got the duty. These were "protect the women" kind of men. Living with Ten had proven that to her. She'd never had a boyfriend who was as thoughtful and protective as Tennessee Graham. He was working from home while she was here, but he took time to spend with her. He cooked breakfast every morning and dinner in the evenings. He tended to take her out for lunch or she would make sandwiches and they would sit at the bistro table on the balcony of his small, neatly kept condo.

Her days were spent relaxing, catching up on movies and TV shows she enjoyed and reading books. So many books.

The nights were all about him. There was one moment every day when Ten Graham turned into Master T. He would walk into the living room and the look in his eyes would let her know it was time. She would sink to her knees in front of him and oh, how they would play.

He would tie her up and spank her until she was hot and ready and then he would tease and taunt her in the most delicious ways before making good on the promises of his crop and cane and fingers and mouth.

Still, she felt an odd distance from him. She couldn't complain. He was the most extraordinary lover she'd ever had, but there was a distance she couldn't quite overcome no matter how many times he made her scream.

Not since that first morning when she'd woken up and he was wrapped around her had she felt so close to him in bed. It gave her a restless feeling, but she might have to admit that despite having the time of her life with him, he wasn't the magical one. She would miss him, but she knew what she needed and that was a real connection to a man, a feeling that she was needed for more than sex and submission.

She had to deal with the fact that she'd gotten exactly what she'd wanted. She'd gotten an amazing Dom to spend a few weeks with and some of the most relaxing days she'd ever had. She would remember the vacation forever.

Why did she want more?

"So are y'all really going to the Caymans?" Phoebe asked. "My brother is not exactly the islands type."

There it was—an insatiable curiosity about the man. He didn't talk a whole lot about himself, and Erin seemed to know him more as a coworker than a friend. This was why she was restless. She knew she wanted more than Ten seemed willing to give her. She prided herself on being a smart girl, but she was in a load of gorgeous-man quicksand, and it muddled her brain. Every time she tried to distance, he would walk in the room and she would reach out again. She'd thought about leaving early and without him, but she knew she wouldn't. She would take every single second she had with him. "Why? Ten seems like a man who likes to relax. There's nothing as relaxing as lying on the beach."

"Unless someone's mortaring the beach, and then it kind of sucks. You know, sand is hard to run in," Erin explained with a perfectly straight face.

She was going to be fun on the island.

Phoebe ignored the war talk. "Ten likes to relax, though he doesn't do it much. I'm talking about the fact that my brother doesn't really like to take his shirt off much."

"Why?" The question came out as a disbelieving huff. "If I had a body like that I would never wear a shirt."

"He's pretty hot," Erin admitted. "Not as hot as Theo. I get paid to say that."

Sure she did. "I'm just saying having seen the man fully naked, he should have zero insecurities."

Phoebe shuddered. "Okay, wow, I guess I didn't think through this particular part of the bonding experience. Despite the whole no blood between us thing, he's really my brother. And I was talking about the scars. When he was a preening teenager, he used to go shirtless whenever he could. I swear every appropriate female in the area got a glimpse of Ten's physique. A whole lot of inappropriate ones, too. I'm not even going to tell you what I caught him doing with my Mandarin tutor. I was too young to see that."

Faith could see him being a horny teenaged boy. "The scars aren't that bad. He doesn't talk about them though. I got him to tell me one story, but he shut down about the rest of them."

Phoebe nodded after taking a drink of the frosty margarita in front of her. "There's a reason for that. I think in your world it's called trauma. We call it an occupational hazard. He got caught by the bad guys once and most of the scars are from that experience."

"He was tortured?" She'd suspected it, but couldn't stand the thought of that man being vulnerable and hurt. He was so big and strong, and the idea of someone taking it from him…well, she knew what it meant to feel helpless.

"I heard it was bad," Erin said quietly. "He's a strong guy, but I think it's the strong ones who take it the worst. I always knew I could be hurt, you know. It wouldn't be a shock to my system."

Phoebe's eyes hooded. "Ten knew he could be hurt. I don't know the whole of it, but his childhood pretty much sucked ass."

"Which is why he got strong," Erin replied, her eyes grim. "He got stronger than everyone around him, and more powerful, and it still didn't work. I was never stronger. No matter how much I worked out or how good I got at my job. Welcome to being female in the military."

Something about the cocky grin on Erin's face made Faith wonder if she was really talking about the military—or her family. She'd caught some behaviors that made her wonder about Erin's home life as a child.

Phoebe shook her head as though shaking off bad thoughts. "Anyway, Ten doesn't like to show off the scars."

"I've seen them. They don't make him any less beautiful," Faith said quietly.

"Which is precisely why I like you," Phoebe replied. "You make him relax in a way I haven't seen in forever. I know he can be difficult."

"He's not. He's damn near perfect. He's treated me like a princess." She wasn't going to have Ten's sister think he wasn't a great guy.

"All right. I'll put it a different way," Phoebe began. "He can be an emotionally closed off bastard when he wants to be."

Shit. Were they going to have this talk? Was she even ready to have this talk? "We're just getting to know each other. He doesn't have to open up about everything. He says all the right things actually. I'm enjoying my time with him."

"But?" Phoebe was like a dog with a bone.

"But nothing. It's going well."

"It's probably really hard for Ten to be open to anyone." Erin sat back, a blank look on her face that didn't fool Faith for a moment. "Sometimes what it takes is a whole lot of patience to get through to a guy like Ten. Not that I would want to. I'm really better at punching things than being patient."

Phoebe's lips curled up slightly. "Lucky for you Theo's patient."

"He is not. He's a manipulative bastard who uses every given opportunity to force me closer to him even when I don't want to be." She sipped on her margarita before begrudgingly continuing. "Didn't want to be. Guys are bad news. You think you can have a little taste and it'll be okay. You'll be able to walk away all whole and shit. A Venus flytrap. That's what Theo is. I'm this fly and I'm flying and happy to be single and then he baited his trap with a pretty smile and really nice abs, and now I'm stuck and he's closing his man jaws on me and I can't get out because it's nice in there, you know."

Phoebe was staring Erin's way, her jaw slightly open. "That is the most words I've ever heard you say."

Erin's eyes rolled. "It's not my fault I'm not good at this shit. I never planned to be part of some icky couple thing. He bought us matching coffee mugs. They say Theo and Erin on them. I'm not kidding. I kind of want to break them, but then he would get the feels and…I don't get guys."

"You've never been in love before." Poor Erin. She was so confused and scared and Theo wasn't about to let her get away.

"I never wanted to be."

"But then you kind of miss the point of life, don't you?" Faith asked. How did she make her friend understand? "One day when I was working in Ghana, this man was walking up the road. It was obvious he was from one of the outlying villages. He was dressed in traditional wear and he was carrying something. I rushed out to help him and I found out he was carrying his wife. He'd carried her over thirty miles wearing no shoes. I have no idea how he was walking. His feet were so torn up and infected. She had a terrible case of pneumonia." She could still remember the elderly woman and the way she'd clutched her husband's hand even as she'd died. "I couldn't save her. But he wasn't mad. He cried and held her and he told me he had to try because she was precious. He stayed with us while his feet healed. I put him on suicide watch but he laughed at me. He told me why would he die when he could still walk where they walked. He told me he had so many good memories and he could live on those."

"That sounds awful," Erin said with a frown. "That's a really good reason to not do the marriage thing."

She didn't understand. "No. That wasn't what I thought. I thought he was so lucky. He was feeling that pain because he'd loved someone with his whole heart. The rest of his life he would know that he'd done what he was supposed to do. He'd loved. He'd been loved. Wouldn't it be empty if we didn't feel the loss? It would mean we'd never felt the love."

Phoebe reached for her hand and there were tears in her eyes. "At some point my brother is going to fuck up and I'm going to beg and plead with you in advance to give him a chance that you don't think he deserves. He's had it so rough, but he smiles around you in a way I haven't seen in years."

She'd stepped into it, but the look on Phoebe's face nearly caused her to cry, too. "I don't think it's quite as serious as you think it is. I think he's having fun."

"He's not," Phoebe insisted. "He's in deep with you but he

doesn't know how to express that. He's utterly lost. No one taught him how to love. No one really taught him what it means to be loved. He can't trust it and I'm worried if you walk away from him, he might never find someone like you again."

Erin stood abruptly. "I'm going to hit the head. I'll be back."

Faith got the feeling she'd said something wrong to Erin. And to Phoebe. "I don't think he feels that way about me. He wants me. He likes me. I don't think he's in love with me. We haven't known each other long enough."

"Sometimes it doesn't take long when the right person comes around. Sometimes it's fate," Phoebe said. "I was married to Ten's brother, Jamie. Ten calls me his sister, but I was really his sister-in-law. Jamie died on assignment in the Middle East. Jamie was the only person in the world who really got Ten."

"And he died." This was the brother Taggart had talked about. Ten hadn't said a thing about him.

Phoebe nodded. "Ten doesn't trust any of this. You think he's merely having fun, but Ten doesn't have fun. Even when you go back to your clinic, maybe you could still talk to him. He might tell you it isn't necessary, but he'll miss you. He'll never say it, but you'll be one more person he lost. Think about it."

Faith's cell trilled as Jesse Murdoch came over to talk to his wife. Faith looked down. It was her dad. Because she needed that right now.

"I've got to take this, but I will think about what you said." She stood and started for the front of the restaurant. The conversation with Erin and Phoebe had made her restless.

She wanted him. More than she would like to admit. Thinking about the old man in Ghana made her long for something she wasn't sure she would get, and it was obvious she'd upset Erin. She was tempted to tell Erin to pull up her big girl panties and deal with the fact that an amazing man was in love with her, but no one ever really knew what was going on under another person's surface. She had no real idea of what pain was bubbling up in Erin.

Damn, she shouldn't have had two margaritas.

"Hello," she said after dragging her finger across the screen. Now she had to deal with her dad and she was already emotional.

"Hey there, baby girl. How are you doing?" Her father's voice boomed over the cell.

Sometimes it wasn't easy having a larger than life father. "I'm good, Dad. How's DC?"

"I'm in London for a conference this week. Paris the week after that for some meetings, and then I'm coming to see my girls."

She had to smile. Her father had always had a busy schedule. The truth was after her mother had been killed, she'd been raised by nannies and her older sister. Her father felt like a kindly distant relative most of the time. "I'm looking forward to seeing you."

"Good. Because you can tell me who the hell this man is you're bringing with you. Where did you meet him? Because it damn sure wasn't in Africa. He's been in the States for years. According to the report I got on him he hasn't been outside the country since he left the service. And he's not a doctor. He doesn't even have a damn degree, Faith."

Snobs. She sighed. "I met him through mutual friends, Dad. He's a good guy. I thought you would be thrilled I was dating someone who served in the military. A good Southern boy."

"I don't like his background," her father said, stubbornness clear in his voice. "He's looking for money like all the rest. What happened with that nice Roger fella?"

"He dumped me for a more convenient woman." She walked out of the lobby, in front of the restaurant. This wasn't a conversation she wanted to entertain everyone with. The air was hot, the sun right overhead. Definitely shouldn't have had those margaritas. She was ready for a nap. A nice nap cuddled up against her guy. "He's a good guy. I like him. If you don't approve, I can stay here in Dallas."

"Now don't get all bent out of shape. You know no man's good enough for my baby girl."

"I'm sure you put him through a variety of intrusive background checks. Is there anything you want to tell me?" She'd expected this call, though later in the process.

"He was arrested for drunk and disorderly in New Orleans."

Sanctum had sent her its own report on Master T back before she'd accepted him. "Yes and he was twenty-two at the time and on leave. Drunk and disorderly is practically a souvenir from New Orleans."

Her father's voice went low, his sympathetic "man of the

people" voice. "He was raised in foster care, honey. Men like that have serious psychological issues."

This was her father's world. Everything was stated in absolutes. In her father's world, every person raised in foster care was obviously damaged—until he needed them to not be in order to move his current campaign forward. She had news for her dad. Everyone was damaged in one way or another. "I like him a lot. You're not going to convince me to dump him. If you don't want him around you, I understand."

Her father sighed. "I suppose he actually looks good on paper. Former decorated soldier. Raised himself up by his bootstraps. I could probably work with that. I need you to keep a lid on the weird lifestyle stuff, though. I suspect he's one of your...I can't remember what you call them."

"Doms, Dad. Yes, he's a Dom."

"See, in my days a Dom was an amusing fat guy who backed up Burt Reynolds in movies. Now, your sister tells me you had some trouble with Kronberg's vaccines. I'm meeting with some executives in a few days. Do I need to talk to them?"

She should have known her sister would go straight to their dad. Typical. "I haven't gotten the reports back. I sent a sample to the lab. I'm expecting the results in the next few days. It's probably nothing and I'm not planning on holding a press conference and denouncing anyone."

"Good because Hope is working on a very important project, and I would hate to have her funding cut because her sister sent the company stock into free fall. I can count on you. Right, honey? You'll let us handle it in-house if something's wrong?"

"In-house" meant sweeping everything under the rug. It made her suspicious. "Dad, is there something going on here?"

A pause came over the line, and she could practically see the expression that would be on her father's face. He would be trying to deal with her, trying to figure out the best way out of the situation he found himself in.

"I'm simply trying to watch out for both of you. What do you suspect is wrong with the vaccines, Faith?"

"I have no idea. It could be any number of things. I could have gotten a bad batch. The batch could have been switched out for a placebo." The mob was known to do it. They typically took the original batch at a transportation site and switched it for something else. God only knew what she'd been putting in her patients. She was starting a new protocol. No one got a vaccine until she'd tested part of the batch. Every damn dose was precious, and now she would have to use a few to make sure she wasn't giving her patients a shot of saline. Or worse.

They'd been confused, their memories odd and sense of time off. Saline wouldn't do that to a person.

"But Kronberg was trying to do a good thing," her father insisted.

And Kronberg obviously had a decent lobby. "Of course, Dad. I'm not accusing anyone. I just want to know what happened. I'm not calling a press conference and throwing my sister under the bus. You know I keep a low profile."

"I do. And you know I'd love to have you at my side when I announce I'm running for president. Have you thought about the ramifications for you and your work?"

Only a bajillion times. "Oh, yeah. It's going to make my life hell. If you win, I get Secret Service guys, don't I?"

"Pessimist. I was talking about more pleasant aspects, Faith. How do the words surgeon general sound to you?"

Like hell. The surgeon general was a figurehead. "How does the word nepotism sound to the press?"

"That's the beauty of the presidency," her father insisted. "Nowhere to go from there. I can do what I like, help who I like, and it doesn't matter. Now, you think on that for a while and I'll see you in a few weeks. I've told my assistants to clear my schedule. No working while I'm with my baby girls. Though you should expect I'll want to get to know this Ted Graham person."

She didn't correct him. Ten didn't go by his real name anyway. She hadn't heard a single person call him Tim. If she told her father he preferred Ten, she would likely get an earful about how the name Tennessee would alienate voters not from the south. She would let her dad call him whatever he liked. "I'm sure you will. Love you, Dad."

She hung up with the strange certainty that Ten could handle her dad. He might not like her father, but he would be able to deal with him. Of course, Roger had dealt with her father by being a preening sycophant anytime he walked in, but Ten wouldn't do that. No way. Ten wouldn't care what her father could do for him. It was nice. All her life she'd had to worry about people getting close to her so they could be near her father and his influence. She didn't have to worry about that with Ten and Theo and Erin.

Erin wouldn't go anywhere near politicians to save her life.

She felt something bump her hard. She whirled around, barely managing to stay on her feet. A figure in a black hood jogged away, and that was when she realized she'd dropped her phone.

"Jerk." She sighed. Manners were lost on people these days. She glanced around, searching for her phone. Nothing. There was nothing on the concrete except a few cigarette butts, a gum wrapper, and someone's receipt for lunch.

Damn it. He'd stolen her phone. She needed her phone. She started to take off after him.

"Hey! What are you doing out here?" Erin strode out with a frown on her face.

"That guy stole my phone. I'm going after him."

Erin got a hand on her elbow. "No, you're not." She looked back in the restaurant. "I'm going to kill Murdoch. He was supposed to be watching you."

"Why? I thought he was here to make sure we could have a few cocktails with lunch."

"Go and find them," Erin ordered. "I'll see if I can nab the guy who took your phone. What did he look like?"

"He was wearing a black hoodie. About five foot nine, big build. I didn't see his skin tone. I should come with you."

"No. Stay here. Ten's orders are for me to keep you safe. Do it."

"I already called security." Jesse Murdoch had a nice pink flush to his face. "Sorry, Erin. I thought she was walking into the lobby and then I got a call from Tag. I took eyes off her a minute and then it was too late."

Erin sent him a look that could have frozen fire and took off toward the parking lot in the general direction the thief had run.

It looked like her life wasn't so far from the one with her father as she would like. She stared at Murdoch for a moment. "Are you supposed to be watching me?"

Ten had told her the whole thing was over. The guy who had tried to hurt her had been a lone crazy person.

Then why would he send one of his friends to watch her?

Murdoch shook his head. "It's not like that. I was watching all three of you. I took responsibility for all three of you when I agreed to be the driver. Phoebe's my wife, but you and Erin belong to my friends. I know you don't understand the military, but Ten and Theo are my brothers. I watch out for their women. The only reason I'm letting Erin go off after the guy is she's trained, and she would probably put me on my ass if I tried to stop her."

It was perfectly reasonable. So why was she suspicious?

And why was that phone call from her father still nagging at her?

A uniformed security officer rolled up in a golf cart. "You Murdoch?"

Jesse nodded and started to take care of the official details.

Phoebe stood beside her. "I'm sorry if I made you uncomfortable. I meant to make this day a bonding experience. I'm just worried about my brother."

Some of the words Phoebe had said previously were penetrating her brain. It had been an awkward talk, but she understood Ten better now. After everything he'd been through, he might require more patience than other men, more time.

Or he might be a lost cause. God, she hated those since she never seemed to be able to let go of them.

She sighed and put an arm around Ten's sister. "I'm never uncomfortable."

It was a lie, but only a tiny one, and most of the time it was true. Seeing the things she'd seen it was hard to get truly uncomfortable in a situation where no one was trying to kill her.

"I like your brother," she assured Phoebe.

Phoebe leaned in, obviously happy with the affection and willing to give it back. "I'm glad because he likes you, too. I like you, Faith. I think you could do a world of good for him."

Despite the clusterfuck of the last twenty minutes, the world seemed a bit brighter. Doing good was kind of her stock-in-trade.

She let Jesse handle the details and wondered how Ten would take the news.

CHAPTER ELEVEN

"**A**re you still mad?"

Ten turned and saw Faith in the doorway to the bedroom. She was wearing one of his shirts and looking so fuckable he could hardly breathe. "I was never mad at you."

He might crush his brother-in-law's balls however. Apparently everyone had gotten upset over some conversation the girls had been having and Jesse had allowed Faith to walk out of the damn restaurant.

"It's all right. Now I have a new phone and that guy Hutch said he would make it so no one could use the old one. He's a weird guy. I offered to pay him but he wanted Red Vines from the corner store. That was all."

"He's never gotten over his smoking habit. He simply traded cigarettes for candy." One habit for another. No one ever really got over their addictions. "And I'm glad you like the new phone."

She thought it had been a crime of opportunity. He wasn't so sure about that. Erin had missed catching the guy in his car, but managed to get a plate. Naturally it showed up as stolen.

"I got it just in time, too." She walked in, a brush in hand, running it through her silky strands. "That was the lab. Apparently my flu vaccine was actually flu vaccine."

He stopped. This was the first he'd heard about a lab. "What do you mean? Why would it be something else? You sent your vaccines to a lab?"

She sat down on the bed. It was a massive king-sized thing Phoebe had ordered for him when he realized he would be staying in Dallas for several months. He never stayed in one place for too long. At first the condo had been stifling, a symbol of all the freedom he'd lost when McDonald had him burned. Now, it felt cozy. Nice. Now Faith had places she liked to sit and her side of the bed. Now when he looked around, he saw her.

"I got somewhat suspicious," she explained. "Paranoid, as it turns out. Several of the patients I vaccinated in the last year came in complaining about odd side effects. Memory issues."

"They lost time?" There were certainly drugs that could do that.

"No. It was weirder than loss. It was like time had slowed down for them. They thought more time had passed than actually had. The effect went away after a few days."

"Some form of group dementia?"

Faith shook her head in the negative. "No. They were lucid. And these weren't the types of people to take drugs. I have to wonder if something didn't get into the water. If I have the time, I'll do a study of it when I get back because it obviously wasn't the vaccine."

Everything seemed to revolve around that damn flu vaccine. He'd dismissed it when he found out the Ukrainian was no longer working for the syndicate, but now it seemed to be back in play. Or he was grasping at straws. "The vaccine was from Kronberg? Where your sister works?"

"Yes. My father will be thrilled to know there wasn't anything wrong with it. Kronberg is a big supporter, naturally."

Kronberg was also very likely a company involved in The Collective. His mind whirled, putting pieces together. "Do you trust this lab?"

"Sure. It's a highly respected lab."

"Darlin', was the name of the lab in your phone?"

Her eyes widened. "Yes. Why would you ask that?" The brush fell out of her hand. "She would tell me. That's what you think, right? My sister showed up unannounced. She asked me a bunch of questions about the vaccine. Then someone steals my phone. Those things aren't necessarily connected. We have this saying we learn in med school, Ten. When you hear hoofbeats, think horses, not zebras.

188

Well, unless you're in Africa. Then I can think zebras. The point is, the simplest solution is almost always right."

"Theo's house was broken into the first night we went to Sanctum, and the only thing the robber was interested in was the guest room." He saw the opportunity. It was right there and he wasn't even considering letting it get past him.

Her eyes widened. "You didn't tell me."

"I didn't want to scare you."

"So that's why Jesse was really with us today. You don't think this is over at all. How about yesterday when I went to the store?"

"I was behind you the whole time. I shadowed you. Faith, I'm sorry and I was probably wrong, but I didn't want you to be afraid. I wouldn't have allowed anything bad to happen to you, but I also didn't want to ruin our time together with fear. I couldn't be sure the two events were actually connected, but three times really is the charm." He didn't believe in coincidence. He believed in conspiracies because he'd seen them time and time and time again. If Faith's sister was involved, then Kronberg was involved, and that meant he had a clear connection between The Collective and Hank McDonald.

"The lab says the vaccine is fine," Faith insisted. "They sent me a chemical breakdown of all components. I checked it. Everything looks perfect."

She was missing a few key facts. "Yes, they sent that a few hours after your phone and all the data on it was stolen. Did you tell your sister the name of the lab while she was here?"

Her mouth closed, lips turning stubborn.

"Faith?"

"No. All right. No and I didn't tell her because I didn't trust her not to bribe the lab if the results made her company look bad. My sister is all about the bottom line. If she thought her precious research was in jeopardy, she would do almost anything."

"Even have you killed?"

The room went dangerously quiet for a moment. Faith took a deep breath before she continued. "Don't be ridiculous. I thought you said the guy who attacked me at Neiman's was someone who hated my father."

He had to step delicately here. "He was, but it would only have taken a nudge to set him off, and no one knew where you were. How did the nutjob know where you were?"

"I don't know."

"What exactly did he say when he was trying to take you?"

She rubbed her forehead as though the entire conversation was giving her a headache. "He said he wanted information and he had something I needed to understand. He said when he was satisfied, he would let me go."

Actually, now it was all coming into focus. What if it wasn't the mob that was concerned about the vaccines? What if it was Kronberg? Had that first hit man been sent to kill Faith? Or get information about the lab so they could manipulate the results? What if this latest incident was simply a subtler play at getting what Hope had wanted all along? "How did your sister know where to find you?"

Her face had gone a bit ashen. "She had a tracer app on my phone. Ten, she wouldn't. She couldn't. I'm going to call her."

He moved to stop her from going for her phone. "Do you honestly think she's going to tell you everything?"

Faith glared up at him. "I think she's my sister and she better tell me what the hell is going on."

"She's also a politician's daughter and she can talk her way out of anything. She's likely very good at not incriminating herself. Faith, if you want to find out what happened to your patients, you have to let me investigate. If you let Hope have even an inkling that you think something's up, she'll bury all the evidence and you won't ever know."

She stood there, staring up at him, and he wondered if he hadn't made a huge mistake. He put his hands on her shoulders, willing her to listen to him. Maybe if she listened about her sister, she could believe him when he told her about her father.

After a moment, she stepped back, her eyes sliding away from his. "You're insane and I don't want to talk about this anymore."

She walked into the bathroom they'd shared and shut the door. He heard the audible click of the lock.

It was laid out, a clear line from incident to incident. Faith was a logical woman with a brilliant mind. But she was like the rest. She chose family.

His mind immediately slid away from the ramifications of her choice. It didn't matter. If she wouldn't get him on the island, then he would find a way. There was always another way. He had assets already on the island. Markovic and Des were there. He wouldn't be able to get onto the grounds himself likely, not by any legal means, but there was always a way. During Faith's birthday bash, they would have to hire outside caterers and waitstaff. That might be his way in.

He needed to know the security around the building.

He would try harder.

Ten walked out of the bedroom, leaving it to her. It was late and she wouldn't be able to leave until the morning. He strode down the hall to the second bedroom. Phoebe had set it up as an office for him. There was a secure computer and all of his intelligence. He wouldn't get any sleep tonight so he could use the time to start digging deeper into Kronberg. They were the key.

He sat down behind the desk and stared at the screen, his hands not moving.

Faith was going to leave him. She would walk away and never think twice about it because he hadn't really meant anything to her. He'd been a convenient lay and good with a crop. She liked the crop.

The door to the office came open and she was standing there, still dressed in nothing but his oversized shirt. It hung down to her knees. He'd seen her naked and in next to nothing. The girl had some seriously sexy lingerie. So why did the sight of her in his shirt do something funny to his insides?

"Ten, we should talk," she said in a quiet voice.

There really wasn't any reason to piss her off more than he already had. It was over. He'd fucked up. He'd pushed too hard when he knew he'd needed a delicate hand. Now wasn't the time to argue or make a fuss.

"I'll sleep on the couch tonight unless you would rather go back to Theo and Erin's. I can drive you."

Her face fell. "You want me to leave?"

He looked back down at his computer screen. "You certainly don't have to. Like I said, take the bed. I've got a ton of work I need to get through."

Faith sighed and walked into the room, standing in front of the desk. "Ten, I'm sorry. I was harsh. I know my sister can be a lot to take. She's not the easiest person to get along with. She was probably rude to you."

He composed himself. It looked like she wasn't ready to get rid of him. There were a couple of weeks left on their contract, and it would likely be difficult to find another Dom. He might still pull this back. "Not at all. I don't have feelings about your sister one way or another. I was simply putting things together in my head. You're the expert here. If you say it isn't possible, then I'll drop it."

"She wouldn't hurt me," Faith explained. "It was all coincidence. Besides, it all turns out to be for nothing because the vaccine was exactly what it was supposed to be."

Unless her sister had gotten the name of the lab and bribed or coerced them to change the results. He kept that bit of logic to himself. She wouldn't want to hear it. She'd made up her mind. He had to be satisfied with the fact that it didn't seem she was going to turn out her temporary Dom.

Cold. He felt freaking cold.

Why had he pushed?

"You're right." It was time to smooth everything over and get her back into bed. Once he was inside her, giving her as much pleasure as she could take, she would let the last few minutes go and they would be right back where they needed to be. He would convince her to go to the islands in a few days instead of weeks and they could get this whole thing over with. He would investigate the sister, of course. He was right about her. And he'd been right about Faith. She chose her family and would do it again. "I've been working this job for far too long. I won't mention it again."

Her teeth worried her bottom lip. "You don't understand my family."

"No, I don't." He should move close to her, overwhelm her. So why did he find himself stuck in his chair? "I'm going to clean up some paperwork. You should rest. If you're still interested, we've been invited to a private session at Sanctum on Monday. Think about it."

"Please don't push me away."

He stopped. "I'm not pushing you away. I'm going to get some work done. Go to sleep. We can talk more in the morning."

He felt her hand on his back and heard her sigh. "You are pushing me away, Ten. I know you were only looking out for me. I came off as harsh, but I wasn't judging you. Can I think about what you've said? Do I always have to agree with you?"

He didn't like anything about this conversation. He'd rather be anywhere but here with this nasty, restless feeling roiling in his gut. Why wouldn't she leave well enough alone? "Feel free to think about what I said, but also know that I won't mention it again." He forced a smile on his face. "Hey, we're just having a good time. I apologize for making you uncomfortable."

Her hands were fists at her sides. "God, you're making me crazy is what you're doing. Stop. Stop with the whole thing. Do you think I don't know what you're doing? You're placating me. I don't want that."

"I've apologized," he said, his voice going cold. "What more do you want from me? Perhaps you should think about it and write out a list so you don't forget."

"Well, at least that's honest," she shot back. "You're mad. You're pissed off that I put myself in danger again and now I won't listen to you."

"Don't forget the fact that you questioned my intelligence." Really more like his sanity, but hey, he wasn't being picky.

She nodded. "I did. I did all those things and if you had tried to tell me how to treat a patient, I would have told you to go to hell. I tried to tell you how to do your job."

He attempted to relax. He didn't want to escalate past where they were. He was angry about a lot of things she couldn't really control. "You're not my client. How about we agree to leave business out of things. I'll back off."

"You won't. You'll be more careful next time though." She eased her way around the desk. "If you really think I'm in danger, you'll do whatever it takes to protect me."

He moved back, sliding the chair away from the desk so he could face her. "Maybe you don't know me as well as you think you do."

She took advantage, easing down into his lap. His cock responded immediately, lengthening, hardening, preparing for her. She looked up at him, those innocent eyes kicking him in the gut. "I think I know you pretty well. You're one of the good guys."

She was either incredibly naïve or she knew exactly what to say. No. She was naïve. He was going to stop fooling himself. She wasn't involved. She wasn't some agent who would stab him on the way out the door. She wasn't Dawn. She was Faith, and despite the fact that she would pick her family over him, he didn't want to see her hurt.

"The fact that you can say that proves you don't know me at all, darlin'. I'm not a good man, but I'm your man for as long as you want me."

Her hands found his face and she seemed to be looking for something there. "Do you mean that?"

Every word. He simply happened to know that she wouldn't want him for very long. "I do. I have zero interest in the relationship ending. I would like more time with you. Maybe even more time away from work. Why don't we go somewhere? We can invite Erin and Theo and go relax somewhere. No work. No problems. Just you and me and some friends."

As he said the words, he realized he really meant them. In that moment, if she'd said she wanted to go to the ass end of Thailand, he would have gotten on a plane with her.

"We could go out to the island," she offered. "If we wait, it's going to be crowded with family and my dad's friends. If we leave in a couple of days, we'll have the place all to ourselves for a week or so."

He let his hand slide along her thigh, his mind already fuzzy from lust. "I'll pack tomorrow. I want to be with you, Faith. And no, you don't have to agree with me. I'm sorry for how I reacted."

"Me, too, Master."

He felt the shift in her. Her eyes softened, her body curling into his. She wanted to play, needed to play.

Fuck it all, so did he. He needed this. It started as a cover and he'd gone through the motions with the submissives he'd trained on, but it had rapidly become something he craved when it came to Faith.

He let his hands curl in her hair, loving the soft feel of her tresses against his palm. So soft. And he was hard. In every way possible. He tightened his fist, watching her eyes. He saw the moment her scalp started to burn. That much and no more. He only wanted to give her the pain that was required to jump-start her pleasure. She liked having her hair pulled. He would tug on it and those eyes would soften, her pupils dilating in a way that let him know she was responding.

"You want to play with me?"

She nodded. "God, yes, Master. I always want to play with you."

"And if I'm feeling rough tonight?"

"I think I can handle it. I'm sure I can. I think it would be a good way for both of us to relieve some tension. I could help you with your stress, Tennessee."

Oh, she certainly could. He tugged at her hair, eliciting a sweet moan from the back of her throat. "You'll do as I tell you to, Faith. Who's the Master here?"

"You are."

He let go of her hair. "Take off the shirt."

She obediently tugged it over her head and sat naked in his arms. She was so fucking beautiful, and every inch of her was his—for now. He shoved that thought out of his head. It didn't matter. Time was meaningless. He was going to live in the now, and the now included playing with his hot sex toy.

"Sit on the desk." He reached over, shutting the laptop and moving it to the side. He kept a neat desk with nothing on top but his computer, a lamp, some pens, and a pad of paper. They were easily shifted to make a place for his toy.

Faith moved to the desk and sat down, never questioning him, never showing any sign that she was uncomfortable in her skin. To the contrary, she always seemed to calm when he got her clothes off. He'd taken to ordering her to be naked during the day. When no one was around, she would relax and read without the encumbrance of unneeded clothing. He would work and catch glimpses of her, heart-stopping sightings of her breasts or that pretty pussy. He made sure there was a robe or a pair of her yoga pants and a T-shirt always around in case someone knocked on the door.

It was a nice way to live.

"Lean back and spread those legs."

She did as he asked, her knees moving apart with grace and offering up the petals of her sex for his perusal. Already they were soft and puffy with arousal. He could slide inside her body and ease his own need.

But that wouldn't be much fun. Damn. Tag had ruined him for vanilla sex.

"You know there was a time when penetration was really all I needed," he grumbled. "Now I need something more. I need you to moan for me." He reached out and gripped a nipple hard, twisting it until he got what he wanted. A low moan came from her and the nipple was a lovely shade of pink. "Spread your legs wider, Faith. All the way."

She moved her knees farther apart, as far as they would go. Her body was open to him, begging him to play with her. He sat back. There was no rush. There had always been a bit of a rush before. Sex had been something to get to, to drive toward. Now he finally realized sex was something to indulge in, to sink into and occupy for long stretches of time.

Faith didn't speak, merely allowed him to stare at the beauty of her body. She was a work of art with her lovely breasts, pink-tipped nipples, soft skin. He took in the way her shoulders rounded, hair brushing her collarbone. He even liked her belly button and her knees. Parts of the body he never thought of as erotic were spectacular because they belonged to Faith.

"Tilt your pelvis up."

Her hips moved, shifting so her pussy was slightly elevated. Full pink and coral colored petals were revealed. Glossy with her own arousal.

"You're wet and ready to fuck, aren't you, Faith?" He asked the question in an academic fashion. He knew the answer but he really did like to hear her say the words.

"Yes, Master."

"I'm not ready." A lie. He could fuck her hard, but he was in a mood. "My toy bag is back in the bedroom."

"Should I go get it for you? I could do that."

She would. She would happily run off and come back with all her favorite things. He wanted to get a little more creative. "I think I can find some things in here. This is a fully stocked office, you know."

She ran her tongue over her lips. "I'm sure you have many interesting things, Master. But I could have the toy bag in here very quickly and you'll probably need some condoms."

"Oh, is my submissive trying to tell me something? What are you trying to tell me? That I don't know what I'm doing? That I'm not prepared to take care of you anywhere we happen to be?"

Her skin flushed a pretty pink. "No, Master. Not at all."

"I think you were. I think you don't believe I can handle you without a set of perfect toys. I think I should teach you the error of your ways." He reached over and opened the drawer, pulling out a foil-wrapped condom. "They're all over the place. I made sure of it when I realized your enormous need to be fucked."

Her lips curled up in the most delicious grin. "Such a kind and thoughtful Master."

"I'm going to be a creative Master." He pulled out a couple of binder clips and started to work with them. They were super tight. He had to loosen them up to do what he wanted with them. Faith enjoyed a bite of pain, not being wholly consumed by it.

"What are you doing, Ten?" Her eyes had widened. Yes, that got his dick jumping.

He smirked her way. "Making some pretty jewelry for you, darlin'."

"Oh, god." Her pupils were so large he couldn't tell where her irises began.

He worked the metal until he was certain he wouldn't hurt her. Not too much. They would bite and pinch but not do any damage. "Stay still. I don't want you to move. If you do, I'll have to punish you and start all over again. Do you understand?"

She bit that bottom lip again. So fucking sexy. "Yes, Master. I'll stay still."

He stood, the binder clips in his hands. Something had settled deep inside him and now he could focus on her. It was a good feeling to narrow his focus to her and only her. The world was a fucking gorgeous place because it only included Faith. Her body, her pretty face, her sweet soul—they filled his world in those moments when he allowed himself to sink into topspace. He only topped her. He would only ever top her.

He would probably see her face right before he died. Even as an old man, he would see her like this.

He shoved aside the maudlin thoughts. Live in the now. She'd given him reason for that earlier. He snapped the clip her way, enjoying the way her nipples seemed to peak in anticipation. He gripped her right nipple between his thumb and forefinger, rolling it. When he was satisfied with how round and hard it was, he slipped the clamp on.

She hissed and it was obvious she was stopping herself from cursing. A good thing since it would have given him the perfect excuse to punish her.

He gripped her other nipple. This wasn't punishment. This was play. Hell, none of it was really punishment. He clamped her other nipple and then grabbed two more clips, these the larger of the two sizes found in his desk. He sat back down and began to work them, loosening them up.

"Master?" Her voice was a breathy huff.

He didn't look up. He had work to do. "Yes, darlin'?"

"What are those for?"

He chuckled. "I think you know."

"Master, I think we should talk about this."

He glanced up, his eyes narrowing. "Where are we, Faith?"

"We're green. Still green. Oh, are you really going to clamp my clit?"

"Nope. Not at all. So you can relax." He was a bastard and he knew it. He was also ready. He dropped to his knees in front of her. The desk put her pussy right at the perfect level. "I'm not going to be so mean to your clit. I'm going to clamp your labia."

He parted her pussy, sectioning it off. Too wet. She was so wet. Something had to be done about that. He leaned over and dragged his tongue over her. So sweet. He loved the way she tasted. He could fucking eat her pussy for hours and never get his fill. She mewled and whimpered above him, but it was all sweet background noise. He slid the first clamp on and went to work on the other side, cleaning her with his tongue before easing the clip on.

Perfect. She was held wide for him. This way he could see the pinks and corals of her flesh, appreciate how her clit strained from its hood. It was a perfectly creamy pearl, begging for his attention.

"How do you feel, Faith?"

"Open. Vulnerable. So hot I can hardly stand it."

"But you will stand it, won't you? You'll take it for me."

"Yes, Master. I'll take it for you. The clamps make me ache, Master."

Likely in more ways than one. She was so beautiful like this, straining to maintain her composure, on the cusp of sexual pleasure.

Her pussy continued to be coated with the sweet honey of her arousal. He eased a finger inside her. He knew damn well it wasn't enough. It was a tease.

"Can you tell me what you want, Faith?"

"You. I want you."

"Oh, I want you, too, darlin', but I need specifics. This position, these toys, what do they make you want?" He'd selected them for a purpose, but he needed to know if they'd done their job properly.

Her voice was shaky, proving how on the edge she was. "I want your tongue. Please, please put your tongue on me. Suck on my clit. Please, Master."

"Since you asked so nicely." He added a second finger, curling up inside her. He knew exactly where to touch her to get her moaning. His fingers slid easily in and out. So wet. No other woman had ever responded to him so readily, so generously.

He'd clamped her so he could easily get to her clit. He wanted her aware of her body, wanted her to feel him as though he was touching her everywhere the clamps bit into her flesh. As though it was his fingers or teeth making her nipples and labia throb.

He finger fucked her, the muscles of her pussy tightening around him. She was close, but he wasn't done with her.

"Faith?"

She groaned as though she knew what he was going to say. "Please."

"You aren't allowed to come."

"Oh, god, Tennessee. I'm so close."

"Then you should work very hard to back off from the edge or it's going to be an awfully long night for you." It was so fun to torture her like this. It was a game. He knew what real torture was and this was a game between lovers, something to bond them.

He sucked her clit into his mouth and decided to be a bastard. He stroked her sweet spot with unerring accuracy and gave her a hard suck. Still, she was valiant, whimpering above him.

More. She needed more.

He gave her one more finger. She was tight around him. Slow and steady won this race.

"I can't, Master."

Of course she couldn't. He'd set her up to lose this round, but it was a game where no one really lost.

He flattened his tongue, licking up her cream, and a soft gasp let him know he'd done what he needed to.

Faith screamed out his name as she came around his fingers, her tangy taste exploding on his tongue.

Satisfaction rode him as he brought her down gently. He knew the punishment he wanted from his pretty bondage princess and it would be a while before she came again. So he let her enjoy, licking and sucking until he'd had his fill.

He backed off and Faith was flushed to a sweet pink, her whole body affected by the sex.

"Do you have any idea what I'm going to do to you?"

She shook her head.

"Good. You know I like to surprise you." His dick tightened and he got ready to play.

* * * *

Faith could still feel the blood pounding through her body. It had been a wildfire in her system. The clamps bounced as Ten stood up, his hands on her knees. He looked like a decadent god standing over her. A sex god. Nothing had ever felt quite as good and right as submitting to Tennessee Graham.

Though it was rough on her pink parts.

"Before we get to your punishment, I'm going to take these off because despite what numerous people might say about me, I'm not a sadist. Take a deep breath." He released the first clamp on her labia, leaning over to immediately suck the flesh tenderly into his mouth.

There wasn't a ton of pain. Ten had worked the large clamps so they were really only there to draw the flesh back and reveal her clit. She sighed as he moved to the other side, giving her the same sweet treatment there. His tongue felt so good. Even after the orgasm he'd given her, she could feel her body begin to heat all over again. She had a never-ending capacity to take pleasure from this man.

Of course, she was going to have to work for it this time, but then he'd known damn well what he was doing to her, known that she couldn't possibly hold out against such an overpowering assault to her senses.

"These are going to be a bit worse," he murmured as he looked down on her breasts. He was standing between her legs.

At least she'd followed orders that much. She'd held her body in the position he'd asked. He reached down and flicked her left nipple, making her hiss as sheer fire seemed to scorch her.

He sat down in his chair. "Come here and straddle me."

She did what he asked without thinking. She wanted so badly to be close to him. She straddled him, easing down onto his lap. His cock was practically crawling out of his pants. Her Master was hungry, but it was obvious he wasn't going to satisfy himself until he'd played for a while.

Should she listen to him about Hope?

She shoved the nasty suspicion aside. This wasn't the place for it.

"You can scream if you need to." A wicked smile crossed his gorgeous lips as he unclamped her right nipple.

She didn't scream, but she did feel a tear slip from her eyes. The pain flared through her system as blood spiked back into the flesh. Her body warmed once more and Ten eased the eager bud with his lips and tongue. He was gentle with the nipple he'd tortured, his hands drawing her close before he did the same with the left.

He brushed his hands up her back to the nape of her neck and she could feel his power. Callused and rough, Ten's hands were working hands, his body a marvel of masculine strength. He could crush her, could control her, but all he did was gently tug her down for a long, slow kiss.

Ten's kind of dominance was the ultimate for her.

"You were a bad girl, Faith. You came when your Master told you not to."

"My Master is very good with his tongue. It's impossible not to come when my Master put his hands and tongue on me."

"Not going to save you, darlin', but I appreciate the try." He drew her down again, kissing her long and slow.

Their tongues played and she couldn't help but sigh against him. He enveloped her in these moments. She ceased to be Faith and became something else, someone who fit like a puzzle piece with him.

"I'm going to slap your ass silly, Faith." He whispered the words like a promise against her lips. "I'm going to teach you not to disobey me." He kissed her again, this time an affectionate peck. "Or maybe I'm going to teach you that it pays to disobey me. I'm not sure which."

She'd been with Doms who couldn't laugh, who preached the lifestyle like it was a religion. Again, in Ten she'd found her perfect fit. "Very likely, Master. Somehow your punishments always bring me pleasure."

"Stand up. Hands behind your back. I'm going to make you uncomfortable before I bring you more pleasure. This is for me. I like to tie you up. I like the way you look when you're bound and stretched for my pleasure."

And she liked the way it felt. Her nipples still ached from the rough use, but she enjoyed the feeling. She liked the sensation and hoped it would last for a while, reminding her of how Ten had played with her. It was his form of worship. He worshipped her body with his mouth and hands and cock, with his dominance.

She stood and placed her hands behind her back. Was he going to get his bag now? He kept the rope in the leather kit he took with him to Sanctum. He used it around the condo, too. Her Master's endless bag of wonders. He didn't move to leave the room this time. Instead, he pulled the power charger out of the side of his laptop and then tugged the other side from the wall.

He'd told her he didn't need fancy toys to discipline her. He'd definitely proved that with this session. She felt him begin to bind her hands behind her back. The cord was smooth, a little cool. Ten tied her tight, but not to the point of real discomfort.

That was coming next, she was sure.

"Bend over," he ordered. "Lay your torso on the desk. I'm going to spank you until I'm satisfied, Faith. You have a safe word. Use it if you need to."

He pressed on her back, his palm covering the skin between her shoulder blades. He moved her until she was flat against the desk, one cheek turned to the side. She could feel a bit of the moisture she'd left when he'd tongued her to completion. It was warm against her belly. And she was making more even as he moved around to the side of the desk. She glanced up and there was something in his hand.

A ruler. He was really playing up the office theme today. It was a slappy yardstick he must have had behind the desk.

She gave him a nice whimper because that really was going to burn.

The first whack nearly made her cry out. She took the pain, letting it morph into heat. Her Master meant business though. She'd barely had time to process when he struck again. Over and over she felt the slap of the ruler against her backside. He peppered her with smacks, lighting her skin on fire. She could feel the heat. She lost track of how many times he struck. He would stop every now and again, lightly rubbing a hand over her flesh, inspecting her before getting back to business.

Tears dripped from her eyes, cleansing and freeing. She relaxed, letting the ache take her where she couldn't go alone.

The ache seemed to fade to a slow pulse. Her focus shifted, the world turning nice and fuzzy. This was a special place. She'd been here before, but it wasn't the same as it was with him. Him. Her Master. Her Tennessee.

She was becoming addicted to him. Dangerously so, but she couldn't seem to do anything about it. She wanted him too badly. She'd nearly panicked when she'd realized how poorly she'd handled things earlier. He'd retreated back behind that placid stare of his and she'd known if she let it go on, she would lose him—at least the part of him she was getting to know. The man didn't let many people under his armor. She understood that, but she meant to be one of the few.

"Have I lost you?" His hand trailed up her back.

She sighed. "Happy place."

"Ah, your backside is a lovely shade of hot pink, but my sweet sub is in her happy place. Have I mentioned how much your freak flag turns me on? I'm going to help you get on your knees." He lifted her up, turning her in an easy show of strength.

Her whole body felt languid as she drifted to the floor, her knees hitting the soft carpet. He stood over her, his hands finding her hair and tugging lightly, gaining her attention.

"You're not done yet, Faith. Not even close. Pay attention." He worked the fly of his jeans, shoving them off his hips and freeing his cock.

That gorgeous monster sprang out, bobbing in front of her face.

She licked her lips at the thought of torturing her Master for a bit. She leaned forward. Without the use of her hands, she had to concentrate on staying upright and getting her very important work done. That cock needed some affection.

She licked at the head, satisfied when she heard a long groan from her Dom.

"That's what I've needed all damn day." His hands found her hair again, this time sinking in with a gentle bite.

If she was happily in subspace, it looked like her Master was deep into topspace. She licked the round head of his cock as he planted his feet and settled in. His fingers ran over her scalp before tugging again.

"Lick me. Run that hot tongue all over me, Faith."

She did as he asked, licking him from base to tip before lightly sucking the head. She tasted the salty goodness of the pre-ejaculate already seeping from the tip. Spanking her had gotten her Master as hot as it had her.

He took it for a few moments. He allowed her to explore, running her tongue over the silky skin covering his dick. She let her tongue find the smooth surfaces, the ridges and hollows, learning his cock and the way he tasted. She licked him over and around until she made her way down to his balls. They were already tight against him, preparing to give up their juice.

"Fuck," he muttered when she began to lick the heavy sacs. "You're the sadist, darlin'."

She didn't bother to mention what that made him. It made him perfect for her.

He tugged on her hair, pulling her up. "Suck me, Faith. If you don't, I'll find something worse than the ruler. Trust me, I can find something nasty to slap your ass with if I don't get what I want."

He was staring down at her, heat in his eyes.

"What do you want, Master? I want to make sure I give you exactly what you need." He always made her ask for what she wanted because he loved to hear her talk dirty. She kind of craved it from him, too. She loved the way his Southern accent made everything sound so polite, even the nastiest of demands.

"I want to fuck your mouth, darlin'. You relax and let your Master have your mouth. You want to do that for me, don't you?"

Hell, yes. She simply gave him a sweet smile. "I want to please my Master in any way he would like."

His hands tightened in her hair, right to the point of discomfort. A sweet burn along her skin that brought her back to him. "I'm going to hold you to that. Until we get on a plane for that island, I'm going to keep you naked and ready to take my cock."

He didn't wait for her to reply. He lined up his cock and began to press inside. He fed her his cock, pushing past her lips.

So full. He was a big man and she had to open wide. She let him move her, guiding her up and down on his dick. She whirled her tongue over and around, fighting the tight fit. She relaxed and opened her jaw wider, taking him deeper.

She could barely breathe, but that was all a part of this particular game. How much Tennessee could she handle? She intended to handle all of him. Every last gorgeous inch.

Faith worked with him, letting him fuck her mouth. He found a hard, relentless rhythm. She hummed around his flesh, adding another layer to the sensation he would feel.

It seemed to break something in Ten. He growled and his hips moved faster, pushing her harder. He thrust in until his cock found the back of her throat, and he held her there as he began to come.

She swallowed around him, taking in everything he had to give her. He filled her mouth, nearly drowning her in his essence. She drank him down, licking and sucking even as he softened.

"Do you know how you make me feel?" His voice was a low growl, his hands softening in her hair.

She kissed his cock again. "I hope I make you feel as beautiful as I do when you're around."

He stepped away and pulled up his jeans. "You make me feel like a king. When I fuck you, I'm the king. I'm powerful and wanted. That's how you make me feel. You remember that. Always. No one ever made me feel the way you do."

She stayed where he'd left her, her body flush with pleasure. This was what she could give to him. This and one other present. She'd called Ian Taggart earlier. Theo's brother had been happy to take her credit card information and her request.

She would let this man know how wanted he was if it was the last thing she did. Whether or not they were together three months from now, she wanted him to know how special he was.

"I'm going to treat you like a king when we get to the island, Master." She was going to take the next few weeks and figure out if they could make this work. Figure out if he was the one worth coming back home for. She loved her work, but she wanted to love someone else more.

He moved out of her line of view and she felt him at her back. With a few quick moves, her hands were free and he was hauling her up and into his arms. She loved the way he picked her up with no effort at all. She let her head fall against his shoulder as he strode out of the office.

"And I'll make you feel like my sub," he vowed as he carried her into the bedroom they'd shared for a week. "I'll make you feel sheltered and protected and worshipped."

She already felt that way. And it was making her reconsider everything she'd said to him earlier about her sister. Maybe she should have him look into it. It didn't mean she was disloyal. It meant she was careful.

But first she was going to spend the night in her Master's arms. Nothing was more important than that.

CHAPTER TWELVE

Two days later, Faith stared down at the text she'd received. The private plane had touched down not two minutes before and when she'd brought her phone back online, the message had been sitting there.

Problems at the clinic. Small fire. Lost the entire shipment of influenza vaccine along with a few boxes of supplies. Sorry I hadn't told you. Didn't want to interrupt your vacation with bad news.

She'd woken up the morning after her fight with Ten and decided to do some more digging. On her own, for the time being. Her first stop had been to leave a message for the doctor running the clinic in her absence. She needed another few samples of the vaccine if she was going to run another test. She'd requested that he send three samples to three different labs this time. She was going to do this right and put her mind at ease.

Her mind wasn't easy at all now.

"I like rich people flying." Erin announced.

Theo shook his head her way. "Don't get used to it, baby. Remember who your man is, but I promise the next time we have to fly without Faith's private airline, I will treat you to one of those sweet, sweet premium coach seats."

Erin's nose wrinkled up. "I think I'm ruined now. I need a rich dude."

Theo had her out of her seat and in his lap in a heartbeat. "Not on your life, baby. You're stuck with me."

Erin looked uncomfortable for a moment, but then seemed to give in. She cuddled up on Theo's lap as they taxied toward the private hangar. "I don't like rich dudes anyway. And I always said you were sticky."

Ten's hand slid along hers, finally meeting to tangle their fingers together. "You all right?"

This was supposed to be their quiet time. Just her and Ten and Theo and Erin. They were going to spend the time until her dad and the rest of the family and friends got here for her party in a state of hazy bliss. They were going to drink and play and sit on the beach.

Her problems could wait. She would have to admit there actually seemed to be a problem at some point, and her backside would probably ache a few short minutes later, but she wanted her Master in play mode, not work mode. It wasn't anything that couldn't wait.

"No. It's some stuff with the clinic. Nothing important."

He leaned over and kissed her forehead. "Good. I'm ready to relax for a while. Didn't you say there was a resort close to the house?"

She glanced out the window. From the airstrip she could see the green of the jungle all around them, but she knew the ocean was never far away. "Yes, but honestly we never need to leave the house. We have everything right here including a private beach and there's surf and scuba gear and the boat. I say boat, but it's really more of a yacht. It's even got a two-person submersible to explore the reefs in. My father likes his toys."

"I'd still like to see the resort. I read something about it having the best seafood in the Caribbean. Also, they have the golf course," Ten pointed out. "I didn't lug those clubs here for nothing."

She was going to lose him to golf. He and Theo had dragged their golf clubs along with their kits. Golf and kink. At least she liked one of his hobbies.

"I already called and you both have full use of the country club. Erin and I will be in the spa." Unless… "Erin, you don't golf, do you?"

Erin grinned at her from her Master's lap. "I could kick both their asses. I have a seven handicap. My father forced the sport down my throat. I hate it. I'll totally do the girly-girl spa thing. I'm looking forward to lying on the beach and not doing a damn thing except drinking margaritas and reading a book."

"Oh, you'll be doing some other things while we're here." Theo ran a hand up her thigh. "I can promise you that."

Tennessee leaned over. "So will you. I bet the one thing this place doesn't have is a dungeon, but don't you forget that I don't need fancy toys to play with you."

His words heated her skin. He'd kept her naked for a full day after the night they'd fought. She'd packed for the trip without a stitch on and when Theo and Big Tag had come by, he'd denied her a robe. Both men were used to the lifestyle and hadn't blinked an eye when Ten had talked business with a naked woman on his lap.

She hoped the staff was used to nudity since Ten seemed to think she would spend a lot of time naked here, too.

It would be nice to play Adam and Eve. There were several bungalows and buildings on the property. Maybe they could set up a temporary dungeon and get some playtime in before the horde descended.

The brilliant sunshine was muted as the plane entered the hangar. From here it was a long walk up to the main house, but her father's well-trained staff would handle all the luggage and she could start to show off the grounds to her friends.

She shoved aside her worries. There wasn't a place for them here.

"Is that who I think it is?" Erin moved off Theo's lap and stared out the tiny window. "I thought you said we would be alone."

Ten's eyes narrowed as he looked past Faith. "That's an unexpected surprise."

Maybe she wouldn't be able to set aside those worries so easily. The plane came to a stop and her sister was standing in the middle of the hangar, smiling and waving. Her sister, who was supposed to be in Houston finishing up work before vacation. Her sister, who Faith hadn't mentioned a word to about this trip.

So many coincidences.

The door was opened and the stairs leading down to the ground released with a hydraulic hiss as the pilot nodded their way and wished them well.

God, she hoped her father wasn't here, too. She grabbed her

purse and started out.

Hope was dressed as casually as she ever did, wearing a neat pair of khakis and a prim white shirt. Stylish sandals covered her feet. She hurried forward to give Faith a long hug. "Hello! I was so excited when they told me the plane was coming in today."

She hugged her sister back. "I thought you were working in Houston."

Hope pulled away slightly, looking Faith over. "We ran into a snag, but I'm getting it worked out. Administrative stuff. I hate it. I thought I could use some downtime so I came out here a few days ago. And then I got bored, so I'm thrilled you're here. I even put together a lunch for us, though I thought it would be you and me and your…guy." She stepped back as Theo came down the stairs. "Hello, Mr. Taggart."

Theo grinned. "It's Theo, Hope. Unless you want me to call you Miss McDonald."

Hope shook her head. "Not at all. Casual is better among friends."

"Mr. Taggart is fine with me," Erin muttered.

Ten's arm slid around Faith's shoulders. "Don't worry about it, Hope. I have a solution. Theo and I will head to the country club after we get settled in and you can have a nice lunch with your sister and Erin. Theo and I have been dying to hit the links, if you know what I mean."

Erin turned a dull red, but Faith was happy she managed to not let loose the multitude of curses she was sure her friend had flying through her head at that moment. Ten had actually solved a ton of problems, including keeping her sister from fawning all over Theo. It would also give Faith time to figure out exactly what her sister was doing here and what had happened with Kronberg.

And what was going on with her vaccines.

"That sounds wonderful," Faith said. "Let's show them around and then eat. I'm starving."

An hour later, she sat down at the table by the pool. The sun was shining down as Hope nodded for the server to open the champagne.

"Where's your friend? What was her name again? Erica?"

Faith rolled her eyes. "You know her name. And she'll be here in a few minutes. She was seeing her boyfriend off. I bet you remember his name."

"I make it a point of remembering beautiful specimens," her sister said with a shrug. "Theodore Taggart. Did you know he wasn't aware of his older brother until a short while ago? He thought his twin was his only sibling."

"Have you been checking into him?"

"I did a little digging. Well, I read Dad's security reports. Theo and his brother flew through BUD/S training and then up and quit the Navy after less than a year in the SEALs."

"He decided to work for his brother."

"And that's where he met the girl. Apparently they've been together for a year or so. It's a little icky."

"Be nice." The last thing she needed was for her sister to start a fight.

"I'm not nice," Hope pointed out. "I'm practical, and that woman doesn't fit with him. He's smart and polite. He could go places. She's going to drag him down."

"He's in love with her."

"I don't know about that. Sometimes relationships are all about comfort and stability. People fear the unknown. He hasn't asked her to marry him. You would think they would know if they're compatible after a year. I think he's in a rut. Sometimes it takes a jolt to the system to get out of a rut. I'm going to feel him out about a job at Kronberg."

"He's not in the medical field." The idea of Theo in some stuffy lab was ludicrous. "I think he's happy working with his brother and he's very settled in Dallas. He bought a house not more than a month ago."

"He can buy another one in Houston. I need someone of his experience to work with the veterans in my study. I talked to him for a while at his house when I was in Dallas. He has valuable insight."

Maybe she didn't understand her sister's research. "You said it yourself. He wasn't in the military for very long. I know he saw some combat, but he doesn't have any major injuries. I don't see how he could help with prosthetics."

Hope frowned and her fingers drummed along the table as though she was trying to decide something. "It's more than prosthetics. Look, I can't really go into it without you signing numerous nondisclosure agreements, but I'm working on something some of Dad's friends started. It's a whole-body type of treatment for soldiers. There's more going on than simply an injured limb. What I'm working on can treat the mind and the body. It can create better soldiers."

Something about the way her sister was talking gave her the creeps. "Okay, now you sound all Frankensteiny. Create soldiers?"

"You are so sarcastic. I swear you lose manners every month you spend out in that jungle. I was simply talking about helping soldiers be the best they can be. At home. In the battlefield, for those who choose not to leave the service. I want the mind and body to work together, and I think Theo's the kind of guy who could help me."

"And you say you don't have a crush on him."

Hope was quiet for a moment. "Like you never took one look at a man and wanted him, knew he could be perfect for you. Tell me you don't feel this way about that Graham guy. I see the way you look at him. You never looked at Roger like that."

"It's different. I spent weeks getting to know Ten before I even met him in person. Yes, I saw his picture and thought he was attractive, but it's deeper than that. We fit together somehow. Also, he doesn't have a girlfriend." Who would be out here any minute, although she'd made it plain she meant to have revenge on the men. Erin hadn't been happy being left behind. She could imagine the words she and Theo had when the door to their room had closed. Ten had merely dropped off his bags, kissed her senseless, and told her he would be back soon.

She guessed he wasn't terribly worried about Hope anymore. Or maybe he was giving her what she'd asked for. He'd backed off and hadn't mentioned his suspicions again.

"Girlfriend. Not wife." Hope sat back, crossing her legs and looking every inch the lady of the manor.

"You know I don't think you'll be able to break those two up. For all the time they've been together they act more like a new couple than anything else. They're very loving with each other. They don't seem to like to be apart often."

"Doesn't she seem a little old for him?"

"She's the same age as you."

Hope fiddled with her glass. "Not that it matters. We'll have to agree to disagree on the matter. Would it help if I promise you my true motivations are all professional when it comes to Mr. Taggart? If during the course of our working together something happens to come about organically, I wouldn't refuse it. But I'm concerned with what he can do for my project. It doesn't matter that he deserves someone better than his current companion."

Naturally Erin chose that moment to step out. Hope was facing away from her.

"He needs someone educated. Someone who can really elevate him," Hope continued.

Faith saw the moment it hit Erin what they were talking about, but Erin seemed to shake it off.

"Everything smells delicious," Erin said, sitting down beside them. "I'm sure the boys are going to enjoy themselves, but this view is spectacular. Thanks so much for having me."

"I'm thrilled to get to show it to you," Faith assured her.

Erin accepted the champagne the server gave her. "So, Hope, the last time we met you were talking about some kind of project you were working on. Something about soldiers?"

"It's one of those boring things laymen rarely understand." She nodded to the servant, who began to serve the salad course. "I'm sure what my sister does is so much more exciting. Besides, I'm taking a short break."

"It sounded important. I hope nothing's wrong," Erin said politely.

Hope sat back. "Sometimes family affairs get entangled, if you know what I mean. This issue of Faith's has everyone worried at Kronberg. I was supposed to push forward into the next phase of trials, but now they're rethinking the project."

Were they? "The vaccine came through the lab work fine. It's real flu vaccine, according to the lab."

There was something about the way her sister hesitated before turning her way. Something odd. It reminded her of how Hope used to act when she wanted to throw their nannies off the scent of something she'd done wrong. Likely no one else would have noticed.

Her jaw dropped and her eyes widened perfectly, but for a second there had been an upward tug to her lips. A fraction of satisfaction in her sister's face. "You didn't tell me. When did you get the news? Damn it, Faith. How could you not mention this to me?"

"I got the call a couple of days ago. I told you I wasn't going to do anything drastic."

Hope stood up, her hand already on her cell. "I know what you said, but if it got out that our charity work was being undermined or that we'd made some kind of terrible mistake and poisoned people in Africa, it could send the stock plummeting and the board would blame me. Maybe I can get a meeting next week. You two enjoy. I've got to make a few calls."

She walked off, chattering into her phone about getting the vice president in charge of research on the line.

Faith looked down at her chilled shrimp salad but her appetite was gone.

When she looked up, Erin was staring at the door Hope had walked into, a speculative look on her face.

"Do you think she was lying to me?" Faith asked quietly.

Erin turned. "Why would your sister lie? I'm sure she was surprised, that's all. I'm sorry. Ten asked me to stay away from this subject with you. Apparently you're not in synch when it comes to your sister."

"Why would Ten talk to you about...did he leave you here to protect me?"

Erin's lips curved up slightly. "Well, he didn't leave you here alone, did he? Ratfink bastard. I'm sorry. I don't like your sister very much. And yes, she was lying to you. I would bet anything she knew about the lab reports, which makes me wonder why she's here. Can you redo the tests? On another sample?"

"Nope. Oddly enough, there was a fire at the clinic. All the samples are gone."

"That's convenient for her."

"Yes, isn't it?" She wouldn't be able to wait. It was time to tell her boyfriend she'd been wrong about her sister.

* * * *

Ten teed up on the second hole, the world green and perfect all around him. It was a veritable Eden. And like Eden, it was occupied by a snake. "Tell me what you've learned about Hope McDonald."

Nikolai Markovic stood to one side, dressed in the pleated shorts and golf shirt of the country club's well-trained caddies. "I can tell you for certain that she hasn't been here for days. She got in early this morning. After you filed the flight plan. It would have been easy enough to get the information. She's actually her father's secondary contact on all business practices. She likely received notification that the jet was being used. She then came in on a Kronberg private jet."

"Which means McDonald knows, too," Theo said with a frown. "Do we have eyes on him?"

"My intelligence puts him in Paris." The second of their caddies was even bigger than Markovic, and he didn't have the Russian's talent with accents. Brody Carter was at least six foot seven, with a wingspan bigger than a flipping condor. And he was as Aussie as they came. Theo's set of clubs looked like a play set in his hands. "Walt's been monitoring him from London. I've got a report on everyone he's met while he's been in Europe. The ones on and off the books. He's a bloody bastard, that one is. I can't prove it because the hotel he's meeting at doesn't have a video feed for us to hack into, but at least three men with suspected terrorist ties have been in that hotel with him."

McDonald was a slippery sucker. He knew how to hide his tracks. There was a reason he'd gotten away with this shit for decades. "No photos of them together. No audio recording? We still haven't gotten to anyone on his team?"

Brody shook his head. "They're all seemingly clean. He keeps a tight rein on his men, and I suspect only the two closest aides have any idea what he does at these meetings."

"How about a woman? He keeps a mistress. Let's shove someone in his bed." It was the way they did it in the good old CIA.

"Already talked about that. No one wants to send our female operatives into that kind of a mess. Try talking Taggart into doing it. I'm betting Theo there won't let his girl go any more than Nick is going to let Des," Brody shot back.

"I left Russia because of games like this. No female I know is going to be treated like a piece of meat. Not while I'm walking. This is not the way we do things here. You should get back to the Agency where morals have no meaning." There was a chill coming off the Russian that was colder than a fucking Siberian winter.

If Faith was an operative, would he ship her in to coldly gather information, using her body as a tool? Hell, no. "I'm sorry. I didn't mean to offend. It was the way we did things at the Agency. I suppose you think what I've done with Faith is wrong, too. It makes me wonder why you're still here backing me up and if I need to find someone who gives a shit about my back."

Theo sighed. "Dude, unwad your manties for a second. Nick's a good guy."

"Who thinks I'm a bad guy." It wasn't far from true.

Nick held up a hand. "It's different thing. McDonald is dangerous. He would kill any woman. We have proof of this now. You're protecting Faith. Am I wrong? Are you going to kill her on your way out?"

He felt himself flush. "Of course not. I'm not going to allow anyone to hurt her."

The Russian's shoulder shrugged negligently. "See. It's different. If one of our female operatives felt she needed to protect an innocent by being in his bed, this I would support. Not Des though. She has to settle for being in a not so innocent man's bed. And what are manties? Sometimes you Americans are as hard to understand as the Aussie."

"I'm bloody simple, you rat-arsed bastard," Brody shot back.

Theo ignored the two as they started to bicker. "Chill, Ten. No one thinks you're the bad guy here. You're going to take care of Faith."

"As much as she'll let me." He had to get them back on track. "I need to know if there's any movement from McDonald. Try to get someone in that hotel. Bribe an employee. I don't care. I want it done."

"Right. Will do, boss. For now, though, it seems like he's going to hang around in France until the party," Brody explained.

"Let me know if that changes." He lined up the shot, planting his feet and preparing for his swing. Another thing Franklin Grant had taught him. He'd been taught to play golf and tennis, to properly ride a horse, precise and proper etiquette. Everything he needed to fit into polite society. He'd also been taught how to fit into criminal society. Why did they feel like one and the same?

Lately, the only time he felt real at all was when he was making love to Faith.

He swung back and connected, sending the ball down the fairway. If anyone was watching, all they would see was two buddies and their caddies. The golf course was actually perfect for this meeting. There was a line of sight in every direction, and it would be difficult to hear without being in close.

He stepped back and allowed Theo to move in. "I would prefer actual eyes on the man. I need to be off this island before he gets here. I can pass a computer check and I've done a lot to conceal my identity, but if he sees me up close, the likelihood that he'll recognize me goes up. No doubt about that. Pictures are different than the real thing."

"We'll have you out of here before the bastard comes to town. Walt's been keeping an eye on who's gone through your cover. He thinks it's going to hold," Brody assured.

Hutch thought so, too. No one had gone past the initial reports. They weren't trying to scratch past the surface on any of the operatives. It was a good thing, but he had more to worry about than McDonald figuring out he was coming.

He had to figure out what to do with Faith. It had been simple at one point. Get the information he needed. Get away and then use it on the fucker. Get his job back or die trying.

Dying suddenly didn't seem like an option, and neither did a clean getaway.

He wanted Faith in his life, in his bed.

The Russian took over. "Des and I have done reconnaissance on the buildings in the compound. I've sent it all to you. I managed to get my hands on the schematics. There are a couple of buildings on the property that look to be interesting, but I think you're right. I think the main workshop is where he keeps his office. No one goes in there. It's locked with some fairly substantial technology."

Theo took his shot and Brody took the club, placing it back in the bag.

"Hutch got in about twenty minutes ago, and from his text it sounds like he's settling into our island house," Brody explained.

"Nick and I sleep here at the resort, but Big Tag found us a place on the south side of the island. It's off the grid with the exception of an Internet connection that Hutch says uses a sat line he's bringing himself. He's staying out there."

At least they had a decent base of operations. "Do I have a way out?"

Nick nodded. "Yes. We've got both a boat and a small plane out at the house. According to island records, it's a beach house owned by a wealthy British family. It actually is, but the family happens to be connected to MI6, and they're allowing us to use their setup, so it should be safe."

"And we've got new identification for you. Passports. Driver's licenses. They won't be able to track you as you leave the island. You'll be able to get back to the States and handle the information as you see fit," Brody explained.

It was all lined up. All his ducks neat in a row, and he was worried that none of it mattered if he didn't come out of this with Faith at his side.

And where did that leave Jamie? A stinking corpse with no vengeance.

I'm a stinking corpse anyway, dumbass. Do you honestly think I want vengeance more than I want you to be happy? Do you even remember me, brother?

He strode down the fairway toward where his ball sat. He could clear the hole in two. It was an easy par three, but he'd powered through to where he only needed a putt to sink the ball.

He and Jamie had enjoyed playing. If Jamie were here, he would have joked about everything. The game, their jobs, their girls.

"I think I should go to the safe house right away." Theo stepped up beside him. "Erin was pissed that we left her behind with that crazy bitch. I'm actually scared about what she's planning. She mentioned hanging me by my balls."

Maybe he still had a brother. A few of them. If he let them in. "I'll talk to her. It was my call. I need someone watching out for Faith. I'm almost certain her sister was behind the attempt on her life. I want a sample of that vaccine Kronberg shipped to her. Something's not right."

"Good luck with that," Nick said. "There was a fire at the clinic a few days ago. Damon has been keeping an eye on it. He thinks it was arson. You should be getting his report sometime today. I would bet anything that vaccine is gone, and the next time Kronberg sends them a shipment, it will be exactly what they say it is."

Shit. He was dealing with two fronts here. He strode to where the little white ball sat. If only the world were as simple as golf. He saw the target, lined it up, and sank his putt. In the real world, a lion popped out from behind a bush, ate his ball, and then turned on him. "She can't be left alone with Hope."

He sunk the ball. One under par.

Theo stood fifteen feet behind him. The boy needed to work on his game. "We'll make sure she's fine. We'll take some up-close shots of the building tonight and get them to Hutch. At least he can tell us exactly what we're dealing with. Damn it."

His shot went wide. He strode over, trying again.

Brody came to stand beside Ten. "There's something else. Liam O'Donnell sent me some reports and asked me to get them to you. He didn't want them on your phone or laptop in case Faith saw them without you preparing her."

His gut took a nosedive. O'Donnell had told him he was working on something. "What?"

"He thinks he can prove that the senator was involved in not one but two crimes involving his own family members as the victims." Brody stared out over the green, a grave look in his eyes. "If he's right, you can bring the senator down without getting into that building."

"His wife's death?" He'd wondered about that. It seemed so coincidental that his wife had been murdered.

Brody nodded. "Apparently Liam has discovered a witness who claims her husband was hired to kill McDonald's wife. Naturally the husband is dead. Shanked in prison sixteen years ago. Before her death, Alice McDonald visited a divorce lawyer. She'd also hired a PI who disappeared under mysterious circumstances a week after Alice's murder."

"That's all conjecture. It makes a great story, but it won't put McDonald away. I need proof." Could he be satisfied if he put MacDonald in prison for the rest of his life? "What's the other crime he's looking at?"

Brody hesitated. "McDonald was behind Faith's kidnapping."

Ten felt his jaw drop and an unholy rage threatened to take over. The man wouldn't make it to prison. He would strangle the senator. He would wrap his hands around the fucker's throat and squeeze and squeeze until he turned blue and then purple, and then Ten would squeeze some more. Would that be too humane? Maybe gutting the man would be more satisfying. Playing in his entrails. Or feeding him to some mangy mutt. Yeah, that would be better.

"Are you breathing, mate?"

"What did you say to him?" Theo seemed to have gotten the ball in the hole and was now studying Ten with a look of horrified wonder on his face. "Dude, you are really red."

"Ah, you told him about senator's part in Faith's kidnapping." The Russian nodded approvingly. "See, this is why I'm not worried. He is in love with her. No man turns so red unless he's in love. Well, or he drinks too much vodka and someone insults his mother. My mother was good woman."

"Shit." Theo handed Nick his putter. "Why would he do that?"

Ten tried to force himself to calm down. He couldn't murder the man here. He needed time and space to think about how to properly punish the senator. "Politics or money. It's all the senator cares about."

"He likes to combine the two, and Li thinks that's what her kidnapping was about," Brody explained. "A manufacturing company had plans to open a factory in Ghana. They would have competed with a rival company for workers and incentives."

"A Collective company." Ten wasn't asking a question. It was a statement. The senator was a puppet for The Collective.

"Yes." Brody hefted the heavy bag with no problem. "The kidnapping scared off the rival and left The Collective firm with a clear field in the country. Li found a wire transfer to the general who took Faith."

"That only proves he paid the ransom."

Brody shook his head. "The transfer was three days before her kidnapping."

Shit. It would kill Faith. She loved her father. He knew he had to bring the man down. It was imperative.

"Li thinks we should lay all this out to Faith," Brody continued.

"Show her and bring her over to our side."

And break her heart. It would be broken when she learned what her father had done, but not this way. This way would mangle and scar her heart forever. At least his way, she still believed the man loved her. A monster, yes, but she could still look back on her childhood and know she'd had a parent who cared. Ten took all of that from her if he used this intelligence.

He could bring her to his side. He could chain her there, but he ran the risk of changing her, of hurting her so deeply he might not recognize the Faith she'd been before.

"No. Bury it. Faith doesn't ever need to know about this."

"Shit, you really are in love with her," Theo said, his eyes wide.

He wasn't sure he'd go that far. He wanted her. He wanted to protect her. "I promised she wouldn't get hurt by this. I can't protect her by walking away. The senator has hurt too many people, and he'll go on doing it if we don't bring him down. If we can prove he was behind selling out troop movements, he'll go to jail for the rest of his life. I have to be satisfied with that."

"I'll sit on it, then. Don't worry about it getting to her. The only other people who have the report are at McKay-Taggart. This is your call. And the third hole is a walk. We should get going or those tourists behind us will catch up." Brody started up a hill.

"It doesn't have to be me." He said the words almost as though he was tasting them on his tongue. "I don't have to be the one who brings him down. All that matters is he goes to jail."

Nick had walked behind Brody, leaving him and Theo alone for a moment. Theo put a hand on his shoulder. "No. It doesn't have to be you. Someone else can do all of this, brother. Someone else can break in and get those files and you can walk away with the girl."

Could he? Did he even deserve the girl? "We have to do the recon. No one else will get this close without tipping off the senator. If I leave this to someone else, they'll get one shot at it."

"And they'll do the job." Theo breathed in the air, obviously enjoying the island. "When everything goes down, you'll be there to take care of Faith. She never has to know we were a part of any of this. She'll lose one family. A shitty one, if I do say so. And she'll gain another. We'll close ranks around her and take care of her and she never knows. She never has to feel that pain."

Was that fair? What really was the truth? It was all subjective. He cared about her. Did it matter that they started out in a way she didn't completely understand? He cared about her now. He chose her.

God, he chose her. He loved Jamie. Jamie had been his brother, but he was going to choose Faith.

As it should be, my brother.

Something settled in Tennessee Smith and in that moment, he let his brother finally rest. Justice. Not revenge. He would go after justice.

And Faith. He would get his small part of the job done and then he would take Faith home. He would leave all this shit behind and start over. He would be the man she needed him to be.

For the first time in his life, he understood what it truly meant to belong.

CHAPTER THIRTEEN

Ten watched as Faith stepped onto the balcony. The light from the massive moon made her skin glow. It was late, but he didn't want to sleep. There was a restless feeling in the pit of his stomach.

"Hey, I woke up and you weren't in bed," she said.

No, he'd slipped out shortly after she'd fallen asleep and he'd been standing here, trying to ensure the evening's operation went as planned. Theo had kept Hope up, playing chess over a couple of fingers of Scotch while Erin had claimed she was tired and gone to bed. He and Faith had done the same. Once Faith was asleep, he'd texted Erin with the go-ahead and then watched from the balcony as she made her way out of the house. She'd been nothing more than a shadowy figure, staying close to the buildings and hugging the dark spaces. If he hadn't known what to look for he never would have seen her.

Not ten minutes before he'd seen her make her way back to the main house.

Safe and sound. She'd texted him good night—code that told him the operation had been successful. She had the data Hutch would need to crack the security system.

Once Hutch was satisfied he could get someone in, Ten could walk away. He trusted Big Tag. Ian would get the job done, and all Ten would need to do was take care of Faith. He could take her someplace private and they would ride out the scandal that would engulf her father.

She didn't have to know how close he'd come to destroying them all.

"I couldn't sleep." He opened his arms and she walked right into them, nestling against his chest. Yes, that was what he needed. That felt right. He kissed the top of her head. "I stared at you for a while, but then I decided that was probably creepy, so I came out here for some air."

"I think I've gotten too used to sleeping next to a furnace," she mumbled. "I woke up because I was cold. It never gets cold here."

She'd put on a robe, but he could get her out of it soon enough. He let his hands cup her shoulders, running down her arms and up her back. He didn't fight the urge to touch her anymore. She was his and she was going to remain his.

He felt his cell vibrate. Likely Theo giving him hell for leaving him to watch Hope. Her creepy fascination with the youngest Taggart meant Erin pretty much had the run of the place. The staff was minimal and most went home at night. Hutch had already hacked into the security feed, so Hope had been their biggest issue.

He ignored the text. The ringer was off. He didn't want anything to interrupt his time with Faith.

He kissed her, letting his mouth play against hers. He could take his time, make it last. They had nowhere to go tomorrow. They would play on the beach and have some fun. He would keep them here and then Big Tag would call with an excuse to get them back to the States before the senator was due.

He simply had to make sure that when he needed to go home due to an emergency, she packed up and went with him.

When he let her up for air, she looked up at him, concern in her eyes. "I actually can't sleep for a couple of reasons."

Did she know about the fire? He'd noticed she'd been distracted earlier in the evening. At dinner, she'd been fairly quiet, only commenting when he prompted her. When he'd taken her to bed, she'd gone willingly into his arms, but she hadn't slipped into subspace the way she normally did. Something was going on in her head, and he'd let it play out. He hadn't mentioned it because he was supposed to be backing off. Unfortunately, he couldn't. Not when she was potentially in danger. It looked like Hope was getting everything she wanted, but Ten couldn't take the chance that she was lying in wait. He smoothed back Faith's hair. She was the loveliest thing he'd ever seen and he had to wonder why he'd fought her. If he'd been born a different man, he would have dropped to his knees the minute he met her, but he was stupid and took his time. He'd still come to the same conclusion.

She was the one for him. She was his prize at the end of this hellish nightmare.

"What's wrong, darlin'?"

"I know I said some things to you that night when we fought over my sister."

So she did know. He wondered how she was going to play this. It didn't matter. He would take care of her any way she went, but he wanted so badly for her to ask him. He wanted for her to need him. "It doesn't matter. We worked that out."

"It kind of does now."

"What do you need from me, Faith? All you have to do is ask."

She looked up at him, seeming to search his face. "Really? You're not going to make me grovel because you were right and I was wrong?"

He leaned over and kissed her again. "No. I'm going to help you because that's who I want to be for you. I want to be the man you come to. No questions. No groveling." He grinned. "Though I do like you on your knees."

She hugged him again. "I was worried. I thought you might make me work for it."

"You're precious to me, Faith. I won't ever make you feel less than precious to me. I promise. I'll look into the situation with your sister in the morning. I want you to be careful around her. I know you love her, but keep your eyes open. I think she might be involved with some very ruthless people."

"Maybe that's it. Maybe she's involved in something she can't control."

"If that's the truth, then I'll help her get out of it." It wasn't, but he also wasn't lying. If it had been true, he would move heaven and earth to keep a smile on Faith's face. Unfortunately, The Collective wasn't the same as a "bad crowd" a teenager could fall in with. They were the baddest of the bad, and if Hope belonged, then she'd done unimaginable things in the pursuit of money and power.

Faith's hands found his, tangling together in a sweet way. "I can count on you. Did you know that's really the first time I've been able to say that to a man?"

He needed to make her understand how serious he was. "You come first, Faith. I know we haven't been together for a long time, but I'm willing to put you first in my life. In everything."

She would never know what he'd sacrificed for her. It was funny that he'd found a peace with it. Once he'd realized how important she was, it was easy to put her first. It was the way of the world. Phoebe had come first for Jamie. This wasn't a betrayal of Jamie's memory. It was an actual true remembrance of the brother who had cared for him.

She was quiet for a moment, the sound of the ocean the only noise between them, but he felt oddly calm. Since he'd made the decision to choose Faith, he'd found an inner peace he'd never had before. This was what Liam had talked about. He didn't need a mission. He had her. Or rather, taking care of her was his true mission.

"I think I would like to have more time with you." Her voice was quiet, almost halting, as though she couldn't quite believe what she was saying.

He wasn't sure what she was saying, but his heart jumped a little. "I want that, too. I was thinking that maybe I should go to Liberia with you. I've heard you're out a bodyguard."

Her eyes flared. "Are you serious? You have a job, Ten."

"I would have a job with you," he reasoned. A job that paid next to nothing and had none of the power he was used to, but that was all right. He'd made his decision. There was a saying he remembered from the religion classes the Agency had him take as a young recruit. He couldn't remember the exact wording from the Talmud, but it was something about when you saved one soul, you saved an entire world.

Faith saved lives. She saved worlds. More than he'd ever managed to do at the Agency. He'd kept the balance there, but she was actively trying to do good.

She deserved someone dedicated to her comfort, her protection, her good.

He was her knight in really tarnished armor.

She went up on her toes. "I would love for you to go with me, Tennessee. I need to figure out a few things, but we can take our time and make some decisions together."

They could decide their future together.

His cell vibrated again, but he ignored it. Theo was likely fucking with him, and he had better things to do. Faith would want to know why Theo was texting him after midnight. He was only keeping his cover. He kissed her long and slow.

Soon he wouldn't need a cover with her. He would tell her anything she needed to know. He would remake his life for her. He drew her in, his mind planning a long and slow seduction.

Their tongues mated, rubbing against each other, playing. His hands roamed down her back right to that glorious ass of hers. He rubbed his cock on her. It was all right. He didn't have to be polite. She was his. He could throw aside all that polite shit and be Tennessee Smith. She belonged to him and he was hers.

Fuck. He was hers and that was such a goddamn good thing to be.

He started to maneuver her back toward the bedroom. He would get her on the bed and torture her for a good long while. He would make her scream before he gave in. He would tease her.

He gripped her ass cheeks in both hands and easily lifted her to his chest. He loved her weight in his hands, loved how she gave over and let him handle her. He made his way to the bed, his mouth still on hers. He fell with her on the bed, giving her his weight.

She giggled, the sound making his soul light. "I think I might love you, Tennessee Graham."

Oh, that was what he wanted to hear. "I want nothing more in my life than for you to love me, Faith McDonald." He stared down at the honest beauty of her face. "I'll follow you. Where you go, I go."

For the rest of his life.

He'd been an idiot. How could he have wasted weeks on suspicion? He should have been loving her without reservation all this time.

He spread her legs, making a place for himself. His place. His freaking home.

His cock was rock hard and he stroked himself against her pelvis. He would get in there soon and he would show her his affection.

"I'm fucking crazy about you, Faith." He crushed his chest to her breasts. "You're all I think about now."

Her arms wound around his neck and she rubbed her nose against his in a sweet gesture of affection. "I'm crazy about you, too. Tell me something, Ten. When you're my bodyguard, are you going to protect me from all invaders, foreign and domestic?"

He felt his lips curl up in a genuine smile. She made him so freaking happy. "All invaders. Every single fucking one. This belongs to me." He stroked against her and then felt his face soften. "I'll protect you with everything I have, Faith. Everything I am. I will rule you in the bedroom, but you should also know that I am your slave."

He started to pull off the robe she was wearing. It was her only clothing because she rarely wore any around him. Her body belonged to him and he didn't want it covered. He wanted to be surrounded by her beauty, her feminine loveliness. He began to reveal her soft skin when he heard the door slam open.

He sprang up to his feet, his hand going for a gun that wasn't there.

The men walking into the room didn't have the same problem. They were well armed.

Faith gasped and he moved quickly to get her behind him. Damn it. His SIG was in the nightstand. He hadn't wanted to scare her by leaving it out in the open, and he had no place to put the damn thing in his pajama bottoms.

Adrenaline flooded his system. "Faith, you stay behind me. Is that understood? When you get the chance, you run and go find Theo."

"I'm afraid the younger Taggart has already fled the building, Mr. Smith," a deep voice said.

Ten felt his whole body tense as Senator Hank McDonald strode in. He was wearing a business suit, but there were boots on his feet. He was backed up by two more guards carrying serious hardware.

Someone in the London office was going to get his ass kicked.

"Dad?" Faith tried to move from behind him.

Her father's face softened marginally. "Hey, sweetheart. I need

228

to talk to you and I would rather do it without the interference of a rogue former CIA operative with a grudge against me."

Shit. Shit. And more shit. "Faith, I need you to listen to me."

There were suddenly four guns pointed straight at his head.

"Dad, what the hell is going on?" Faith asked. "And who is Mr. Smith? This is my boyfriend. You got his files. His last name is Graham. Timothy Graham, though his friends all call him Ten. Could we please stop with the extreme fear tactics? I know you like to say you're a protective father, but this is a bit much."

She still didn't understand. And he wasn't sure there was anything he could say at this point. He'd waited too long.

Her father shook his head. He was a barrel-chested man in decent shape, but then he didn't have to spend much time in the gym since he seemed to have a small army around him. "This man's name is Tennessee Smith. He was a CIA operative until he sold out his country. I was the one who brought him down. Now he's using you to get to me."

"That is the single most ridiculous thing I've ever heard," Faith said. "Have the goon squad put the guns away and let me get dressed. I know you don't appreciate my lifestyle, but I'll be damned if you treat a man I care about like this."

He could practically feel the rage vibrating off her. Would she turn that rage against him when she discovered he'd lied? Was there any way to get the hell out of here? He could make it to the balcony, but he didn't trust her father not to hurt her in the crossfire.

"Faith, darlin', I need you to know a few things." Ten hated that he couldn't look at her, but he had to keep his eyes on the snakes that surrounded them. They could bite at any moment.

Faith's hands were on his shoulders. "Ten, we can pack and be out of here in no time. Since my father's hospitality is lacking, we'll go to the resort for the night and then head home in the morning."

"You won't go after you see the evidence, baby girl." Her father shook his head in seeming sympathy. "I'm so sorry he brought you into this. If I'd known, I swear, I would have had this bastard assassinated. How dare you bring my daughter into this, you traitor."

"He's not a traitor. He was in the military." She kept trying to move, to get around him.

His gut took a dive. The next few minutes were going to be the hardest of his life. He did the unthinkable. He turned his back on the guys with the guns, leaving himself utterly vulnerable, but he had only seconds to make her understand.

He cupped her cheeks. "Faith, I love you. I've never loved anyone before. I've never said those words to another woman in my life, but I love you. Please believe me."

Her body went still. "Ten, what's going on?"

If he brought her into this, her father could kill them both. If she believed Ten, her father would have no choice, and he'd already proven he didn't mind killing the ones he loved. He'd murdered her mother because she'd been planning to divorce him. What would he do to a daughter who could threaten his career?

Sometimes choosing her meant walking away. Meant sacrificing himself.

"I love you, Faith. It might have started out as a job, but I love you." He stared at her, praying he could memorize every inch of her face. So much time he'd wasted. He wished he'd met her years before, but he wouldn't have trusted this feeling then either. Sometimes he wished the cold had taken him when he was a baby. Now he was glad it hadn't because this love for her was so fucking warm. He was warm for once in his life. "I hope you can forgive me."

He had to walk out of here. They would almost surely kill him as soon as they were out of range. He might have a shot at getting away because they wouldn't want Faith to see his murder. He would walk out and the senator would show her his trumped up evidence and Faith McDonald would hate him.

But she would be alive. She would be in the world even if he wasn't.

He turned back to the senator. "Do you have a car ready for me or am I walking to the airport?"

The senator met his eyes and for a brief moment there was a silent understanding between them. The senator nodded. "I've got a plane ready for you. You can leave tonight."

He would be in a shallow grave before dawn.

"He's not going anywhere. Not until I understand what the hell is going on." There was a fine sheen of tears in Faith's eyes as she put her hands on his arms, keeping him close. "Ten, what is happening? What do you mean by job?"

He had to sell this because if she believed for a moment that her lover was in the right, she would back him. She would go up against her father and she would pay the price. "Your father had me burned. I was a career CIA agent and he cost me everything. I intended to give him payback. I know he'll have plenty of evidence against me and he'll be more than happy to show you, but I need you to hold on to one thing. I love you."

Maybe he should have pretended to not care, but loving Faith might be the one good thing he'd done in his miserable life. He couldn't. He couldn't die lying to her, couldn't leave her thinking she hadn't touched his soul.

"You were the best thing that ever happened to me, Faith McDonald, and I would give a whole lot to go back and be a better man for you."

"I don't understand any of this."

He leaned over and kissed her forehead, likely the last sweet moment of his life. He prayed Theo would watch out for her. Erin liked Faith. Theo would do anything for Erin. Theo would make sure she didn't get hurt. "You will and I hope you can forgive me. Have a good life, Faith." He turned back to her father, his enemy. This was the man who had killed Jamie and as he stood there in front of the bastard, all he could feel was a sense of panic that he might hurt Faith. "I'll leave quietly, McDonald."

"If you do, then we won't have a problem." McDonald nodded to one of his goons, who moved behind Ten. "You'll understand if I have one of my men escort you."

Because he wasn't leaving this island alive. It was him or Faith. There was no choice. "Of course. Luckily I hadn't unpacked."

He grabbed his bag. He wouldn't need it, but he had to make it look good.

"Ten, tell me what's happening. Please tell me this isn't true." Faith was clutching her robe around her body. This was the bad kind of vulnerable, and he was so sorry he'd made her feel it.

"This started out as a job, Faith. I intended to use you to take your father down. I sent Theo and Erin to soften you up. They herded you to me. There were no other Doms who would have been options at Sanctum. Only me because it was all a setup to get close to you."

Tears rolled down her cheeks, causing his heart to crack. Fuck, he hadn't realized it could do that. He started to reach for her.

She stepped back. "You didn't want me."

"I wanted you the moment I saw you." He wasn't going to lie to her about that. Never. "I fell in love with you, but I have to leave."

She nodded. "Yeah, you have to leave. Do you honestly think I'll believe a word you say? How could you? How could you use me like that?"

"It's my job," he said. He had a shitty job.

"Go. I can't…I can't look at you." Her jaw firmed and it was obvious she was trying to hold it together.

But he could look at her. So pretty. Someday a man who was worthy would come along and take care of her. She glowed when she was well taken care of. He could see her on her knees, submitting with that sweet passion of hers, giving him everything she had.

He would hold on to that.

He felt a hand on his arm and then the hard shove of metal to his spine.

McDonald stopped him before he made it out the door with his "escort."

"This is far from over, Smith," the senator said under his breath.

A thrill went through his system. He nodded, saying nothing, and then he was in the hallway. Far from over? Did the senator have plans? Some torture, perhaps? He could handle it. Time was what he needed. The longer he had before they put a bullet in his brain, the more time his team had to find him. Theo would call in Ian and Ian would take over. Eventually, if he stayed alive, Big Tag would ride in and save the day.

If Ian found him, he could find her. He could explain. He could protect her.

God, all he fucking cared about was Faith.

They pushed him along and Ten got ready for the fight of his life.

* * * *

Faith stared at the door where Tennessee had been. One moment she'd been safe and happy and in his arms, and the next there had been guns and accusations, and how the hell had he lied to her?

Hollow. She felt hollow.

"Baby girl, I need to talk to you." Her father was the last one left in the room. His guards were gone, likely shoving her lover on a plane that would take him back to Dallas.

She wouldn't see him again. Wouldn't hold him. Wouldn't touch him.

He'd made promises. He'd lied.

"I want to go to bed." She didn't want to listen to her dad. She didn't want to hear how she'd fucked up and brought more trouble into his life.

How was he gone?

An urge to go after him overtook her. She needed to get dressed and go find his ass and have it out. That hadn't been a good-bye. That had been an excuse, a fucking apology. She didn't want an apology. She wanted his balls. She could keep them in a jar of formaldehyde and always know she'd had her revenge on him because the very thought of that man moving on and finding some sweet sub to fuck made her completely crazy. When she was done with him, he wouldn't be able to fuck anyone. Ever. Again.

She could do it. She could take his balls.

God, she wanted to see him. There was more to this. There had to be.

He couldn't walk away.

She started toward the door. She didn't need to get dressed. He liked her naked. At least his dick did. He couldn't lie about that. Sure, maybe he got hard any time a woman walked into the room, but she could use that.

"Faith, you can't go after him." Her father stood in the way. It was easy to see he'd prepared for this meeting. It was after two o'clock in the morning, but her dad was pressed and shiny in his two thousand dollar suit that could feed all the families who visited the clinic for a year.

"I need to talk to him."

Her dad didn't move. "I can't allow that to happen, Faith. He hates me. I know what he said to you and I know it sounded very believable, but that man will do anything to bring me down. I found out he was working with the enemy last year. My aides gathered information and when I presented it to the CIA, they immediately disavowed the man."

"They disavowed him?" She knew her father. She knew his tells. There was something he wasn't saying. "One would think if he was the traitor you say he is, they would arrest him."

Her father stood over her, looming in a way that made her feel about five years old and in need of protection. "I've got a file on him. I'll let you read it. Faith, I know you won't believe me, but I didn't know until earlier today. He showed up on the security feeds and I might have missed it, but he turned just the right way, so I recognized him. He hates me. He admitted it himself. You were a job to him. I'm so sorry you got dragged into this."

He'd also told her he loved her. Why would he do that? Maybe she could understand it if he'd stood his ground and asked her to choose, but it seemed cruel to tell her he loved her when all he was planning on doing was walking away.

He didn't seem like a cruel man. Oh, she could believe he would hurt someone if he thought they deserved it.

Could he hurt her if he was out for revenge? Was telling her he loved her his final act of vengeance?

"I need to talk to him. If only to plant my foot in his balls." She was going to have this out. He didn't get to walk away scot-free.

Her dad blocked her once again. "No, Faith. He's dangerous. This is a man who sold his own brother out for cash."

Phoebe's husband? Phoebe's words flitted through her brain.

At some point my brother is going to fuck up and I'm going to beg and plead with you in advance to give him a chance that you don't think he deserves.

Had Phoebe been trying to tell her something?

"I still want to talk to him."

"Do you know some of the things he's done? I wouldn't let my dog be alone with that man, much less my daughter. Do you remember Dale Albertson?"

She nodded. He'd been her father's aide for a couple of years. She remembered him as a lanky man. He hadn't made much of an impression. He was only interested in politics. The few times she'd met him, he'd wandered off the minute she started talking about her job. Still, she remembered her father had told her he was trustworthy and useful. That was practically a declaration of love from her dad.

"Yes."

"Tennessee Smith tortured him. He brutally beat him for information about me. Dale killed himself because he couldn't get over what Ten Smith had done to him. I wanted to take the bastard to court, but the CIA covered it up. It would have been embarrassing for the Agency. So in my mind, he's gotten away with murder."

"I don't believe it." Not her Ten.

Her father reached into his pocket and pulled out a thumb drive. "Then believe this. This is a file on Tennessee Smith and everything he did to hurt me and mine. It includes irrefutable proof that he was with Dale shortly before he was abducted in Dubai. Since then he's been after every single member of this family. I suspect he's the one behind the trouble with your vaccines."

"That's ludicrous. How would he even do that?" She couldn't even fathom a world where he did that to her.

"He's a resourceful man and he's determined to bring down my entire family, including my girls. He's found it hard to get to me so he switched to targeting you and Hope."

"But the vaccine was clean."

Her father was quiet for a moment. "No. It wasn't. Baby girl, Hope called me in a panic. I bribed the lab to say it was clean because I didn't understand what was going on. The vaccine was a trial drug. I don't even know how the bastard got it, but he did. It's a memory drug your sister's been working on. Smith intended for you to find it and go to the press. He was going to claim that your sister and Kronberg were testing their drugs in a manner the FDA would utterly disapprove of. That would have decimated your sister's career and taken down your clinic and all your good works. He knew how to really get to me. Through you and your sister."

She wanted to believe him. God, he was her father, but she'd never felt for anyone the way she did Tennessee Graham. Smith. He'd lied about his name. How much more would he lie about?

Her father put a hand on her shoulder. "Will you read the file? Can you give me a chance? If you run off after him now, he'll use his charm on you. He'll pull you back in. I can't stand the thought of losing you."

She glanced toward the balcony. She'd found him out there not ten minutes before. She'd woken up and missed him. Would she wake up tomorrow and every day after missing him? He'd lied to her. They'd all lied to her. Theo and Erin. Ten. All the people at Sanctum. One big lie. She'd thought she'd found a home and all she'd found was betrayal.

"I'll read it." Maybe it was better this way. If she confronted Tennessee right then, she wasn't sure if she would really cut his balls off or cry in his arms and beg him to take her with him. She might melt at his feet and take him any way she could.

She was pathetic and she wanted to believe what he'd said. She wanted to believe that he'd loved her.

She should try to be rational. Logical.

Her father handed her a thumb drive. "Everything you need to know is on here, sweetheart. Read it and we'll talk about it all in the morning. I can't tell you how sorry I am that you got dragged into this. I love you. I know we've had our problems, but I would do anything to protect you, Faith. When your mother died, I vowed to her that I would protect you. I vowed it on her grave and I failed today. I let that man hurt you."

Hurt. It was a silly word for what she felt. Hollow. Scraped raw. Her very bones seemed to ache with the loss.

Her father sighed heavily and stepped back toward the door. "I'm going to give you some time. Don't be surprised if you see more security around the island for a few days. I'm worried about you and Hope. I can't trust that man not to try to hurt you in a physical way."

Had he already? Had he been the one to send the man who tried to kill her? Her mind whirled with conspiracy theories. Ten could have hired the assassin and then taken him out himself in an effort to send her right into his arms. He had the backing of one of the world's elite security companies. McKay-Taggart could have sent agents to set her clinic on fire.

"He tried to burn down my clinic."

"Bastard. I knew he was going to try something like that. He's had men working in your clinic for months. I'm sure one of them set the place on fire to hurt you. Don't you worry. We'll rebuild what he destroyed." Her father's eyes widened. "I should have killed him."

"Maybe you should have." She turned away. Now she really wanted to be alone. She would read everything her father had on Ten Smith.

The question was what could she believe when her father had just lied to her?

She'd said he'd tried to burn down the clinic. She'd wanted to see what her father knew and he'd stepped right into it. She hadn't told him she'd lost a building and yet he knew. Beyond that, Tennessee had zero reason to burn down the clinic. He would have wanted it whole if what her father said was true. He would have wanted those vaccines so she could test them again and begin his nefarious campaign against them all.

But her father hadn't batted an eyelash as he'd let the man take credit for the crime he'd very likely committed himself. If her father had lied about that, what else was he lying about? She wasn't an idiot. She knew her father was capable of doing nasty things to keep his position.

"I love you, baby." The door closed quietly as he left.

And she was left with a million questions and a very broken heart.

CHAPTER FOURTEEN

Well, he'd made it inside the building. It wasn't exactly the way he'd thought it would be. Far from it. He'd envisioned a covert operation. Sneak in. Sneak out. Not that he would be hanging from a hook, battered and beaten once again.

"Would you like to tell us where your friends are. Smith?" The head of the torture squad was far more slender and refined looking than any man wielding a cattle prod should be.

"I would love to tell you." He was still feeling a bit feisty. He needed this session to last for a good long while. He thought about how long it would take for Big Tag to get from Dallas to the islands. He might need a week. Could he make this last a week?

Where was Faith? Did she hate him now? The first woman—the only woman he'd ever loved and she would likely go to her grave hating him.

"We're waiting. Mr. Smith." The prod in his hand crackled with energy.

Yes, they were all waiting. This was a waiting game now. "I would love to tell you, but I don't know. They're probably halfway to Dallas by now."

"They aren't. We're monitoring all aviation on and off the island. They're still here and your life is going to be so much easier if you simply tell us where they are."

"I've always preferred complicated. So much more interesting."

"Tell me something. Do you find this interesting?" The asshole touched the cattle prod to his side.

His whole body clenched, muscles firing off in seemingly impossible patterns, bones threatening to break. At least that's what it felt like. Sucked to be a cow.

The prod was removed, but his body continued to shake. He hated this. Hated the loss of control. Loathed the vulnerability.

He wanted Faith. He wanted to be in bed with Faith, to roll over and find himself in her arms. Safe and warm and wanted.

"Interesting enough for you, Mr. Smith?"

His teeth were chattering too much to reply.

The door opened and through the haze of his pain, he watched as Senator Hank McDonald walked down the stairs and into his torture chamber followed by Faith's evil sister. Too bad she wasn't a stepsister to complete the fairy tale imagery.

"You told me I could have Theo," she complained as her heels clacked against the concrete floor.

"You should have gotten him before he slipped away," McDonald shot back. "I told you to secure those two before I got to the house."

"Somehow they knew you were coming. I got to their room with four guards, but they were already gone."

Smart Theo.

The cattle prod-loving guard traded his favorite torture for Ten's cell phone. It had been in his pocket. Useless. He'd been too interested in Faith to answer what was likely a heads-up from Theo. He wasn't sure it would have changed the outcome. Would he have left her there with no explanation? Would he have tried to take her with him? He wouldn't ever know.

"Apparently Romeo here was too busy to read his texts. Some super spy," the guard said with a snort.

"That's his phone?" Hope stepped forward. She was still far overdressed for so casual a place, but then so was her father. Evil, it appeared, had a dress code. No casual Fridays for The Collective. "I could call Theo and get him to exchange himself for Smith."

"No." He wasn't about to change places with Theo. He'd done this before. He'd been in this position and he knew what it could do to a man. He'd sent men in before, back when he'd run a team. There had been times when he'd known the likelihood of a positive outcome was grim. Sometimes it was necessary, but he'd be damned if Theo took his place. Theo was still all shiny and shit. There was nothing like days of pain and mindfucks to take the shine off a soul.

"I'm going to have to agree with our friend," McDonald said. He took off his suit coat and neatly hung it over a chair. "Smith is the prize here. There are actually several foreign governments who would like to have a word with him."

He had to laugh. It bubbled up out of nowhere. Some things were so dark, so black, they required laughter. "Please send me to Tahiti. I really pissed off those fuckers."

He'd never actually been, but he could see himself there with Faith in her bathing suit, running out into the ocean and scampering like kids who had nothing to worry about.

"I was thinking more along the lines of China." The senator obviously didn't appreciate his black humor. "MSS would love to get hold of you. There are also a few Middle Eastern groups who would like some face time with you." He turned back to his crew. "After we're done, I'll sell him on the open market. You won't believe what he'll go for, so I want him to feel the pain, but don't damage him too much. I need him healthy for his eventual death."

Hope pouted like a toddler denied a toy. "I wasn't going to actually trade him. I was going to set a trap and then we'll have both. Do you really think I'm an idiot?"

"No. You've already done enough. How could you let your sister find out about the vaccines? I told you to use another clinic for your trials."

Hope's face turned a bright red. "I couldn't find another clinic. And she never would have known if it hadn't been for the Ebola outbreak. She would have run through the shots and my man on the ground would have taken care of the patients who came in complaining. She might have heard a few, but things got crazy during the outbreak. I couldn't control the study."

Ten stared at Hope. "You're testing your drugs on Faith's

patients. Nice."

Hope shrugged. "I'm doing something the FDA might not approve of. And it's just people in Africa. No one gives a shit about them. My preliminary trials have proven very promising."

"Poor Mr. Smith," McDonald said with nauseating sympathy. Though to be fair, pretty much everything was nauseating after the cattle prod. "You know you almost had me. I believed the Timothy Graham persona. Working at McKay-Taggart got my back up a bit, but it's a large enough company. Do you want to know where you screwed up?"

In oh so many places. His arms ached. He would have more nerve damage to deal with. "Sure. Let's have a debrief. I seem to have plenty of time."

"You have no idea how true that is," the senator replied enigmatically. He undid the buttons at his wrists and began to roll up his sleeves. "I use facial recognition software, too, Smith. You did a good job of avoiding my cameras. Well, the ones you found. There's a stuffed bear in Faith's bedroom."

Taken down by a fucking nanny cam. Wouldn't Tag have a laugh at that. "You spy on your daughter?"

"Of course." He pointed to Hope. "This one in particular requires watching. She's what psychologists call amoral. Hope is a bit of a sociopath. I find it useful at times, but often she finds it difficult to curb her hungers. I got her the job at Kronberg after I found her testing her drugs and surgical techniques on homeless people. Kronberg has done an exceptional job in focusing her skills."

"It's good to know you have a Dexter protocol."

"I care about my daughters. I give a damn about their careers, their ambitions. And I take care. When I realized you were using my daughter, I traded places with one of my security guards. It's amazing what makeup and knowing where the cameras are can do for a fellow. I think your brethren still believe I'm in Paris, and I have alibis coming out of my ass. The CEOs of four different companies will all be willing to testify that I was with them in Paris today."

"I'm sure you do." It didn't surprise him that the senator had his ducks in a row. "I'm sure you've done everything you can to cover up your crimes."

"I like to think I'm prepared." He circled around Ten's body.

Ten tensed again. The senator had a lean and hungry look. The whole day was starting to feel like a Shakespearian tragedy. "Preparation won't save you from what you've done. People will figure it out. You can destroy the evidence, but it's still alive in the victim's bodies and it will be for a while. So it doesn't matter. You'll get caught eventually."

"We're taking care of that," Hope explained. "I put a plant in Faith's clinic a long time ago. I clean up after myself. That particular experiment has already been terminated."

Ten rarely found himself shocked by the evil people could do, but Faith had made him soft. Kids. Hope was terminating children's lives to hide her experimentations. Faith would be devastated.

"I'm going to kill you." He would get out of this clusterfuck and he would reap a righteous vengeance on these people. He would go biblical on their asses. Rage filled him, drowning out the pain. His sight went a misty red.

"Pass me that." The senator's eyes hardened as he took the cattle prod. "I think our guest is getting feisty. Don't underestimate him. He's deadly."

"I'm damn straight going to be deadly to you," Ten spat.

The senator shoved the cattle prod in his side and pain exploded through him. His body convulsed, shaking so badly he couldn't see straight. His vision faded and a blessed blackness threatened to overtake him. He wanted to go there. He could be with Faith there.

"Don't let him pass out," a nagging voice said. Hope slapped him back to awareness. "I want to see how he handles this."

There was a stinging sensation in his leg and that crazy bitch pressed down on the hypodermic needle.

His vision went hazy as they hit him with the cattle prod again.

And time seemed endless.

* * * *

Faith could feel the sunshine on her face, but it didn't move her. The sound of the ocean was never far on the island, and here in the tourist district, it was practically the soundtrack to life. It was a peaceful day with happy tourists walking around, enjoying the shops and restaurants before heading back to the resorts or the cruise ships that had brought them here.

She walked through the small market, out of the house and alone for the first time since Ten had left. She'd slipped past her father's guards, and she knew she wouldn't have very long. She needed to be alone, needed to process what Ten had done to her, what her father had done.

Maybe it was time to think about going back to Africa. She could sink into her work and one day she wouldn't think about Tennessee Smith every second of her waking hours. She was fairly certain she would dream about him for the rest of her life.

She could hire someone who could help her find out what had happened at her clinic. She didn't buy a word her father or sister had said. A day and a half. She'd spent most of that time in her room, but they'd nagged until she'd agreed to eat with them. She'd sat there and talked and they'd both been lying to her. They knew something, but if she called them on it, they would do whatever they needed to do to cover it all up.

That's what Ten had said. He'd advised her to be quiet until she had proof.

Good advice or had he simply been covering his butt, too?

She caught a glimpse of herself in the mirror. There was a haunted look to her eyes, and she would swear she looked older.

She missed him. It had been not more than thirty-six hours since she'd read that file her father had left for her.

She'd learned a lot about Tennessee Smith. She'd learned he was a career CIA operative who had moved up the ranks quickly because he was both ruthless and deadly. He'd been responsible for some of the deadliest missions in the history of the Agency. He had a genius-level IQ, and according to the psychologist's report, he was a potential serial killer. The report talked about his childhood issues and inability to bond. According to the report, he'd even been the one to kill the only woman he'd ever been serious about. He'd killed her when he thought she'd turned on him.

That's what the report said.

She didn't know what to believe.

"Excuse me, miss?" A deep voice brought her out of her misery.

She looked up and there was the most massive man she'd ever seen standing in the aisle. He was a gorgeous hunk of man, towering over her. He had to be over six and a half feet, and there wasn't an ounce of fat on him. He was dressed in a pair of board shorts and a white T-shirt that clung to his every muscle.

He wasn't Tennessee Smith though.

"Yes?" The word felt dull coming out of her mouth. It was like the last few weeks had been filled with color and now she had to go back to black and white.

"Can you tell me where the coffee shop is?" He had a thick Australian accent. He brushed a hand through his super-short hair and looked around as though completely lost. "I can't find a thing in here."

She looked around. There was a coffee shop close by. It sold gelato, too. She realized she'd managed to walk to the edge of the market. "Well, you're going to have to walk back to the east. You're on the edge of a residential district and that's probably not the safest place to be. I should go back, too. I'll help you find it."

At least she could get one good deed in. The man was intimidating, but some of the residential sections of the island were known to be violent. Even at his size, he could be mugged or worse. The police were too busy protecting the tourists to pay much attention to some sections.

"Or you could come with me quietly, Faith."

She turned back, her skin going cold at the sound of her name. She hadn't told him her name. She started to walk away, but a woman blocked her path. She was dressed in a filmy white skirt that covered the bottom half of her slinky bathing suit. A big hat covered her flowing dark hair and she carried a big beach tote bag. She looked every inch the wealthy tourist out for a jaunt, with the single exception of the gun she held on Faith.

"Sorry, love," the woman with the English accent said. "I'm afraid you're going to have to come with us."

"You weren't supposed to scare her," the Aussie shot back.

The Brit shrugged. "Ten isn't around to give us orders. I'm following my instincts. My instincts tell me this one is going to require a bit of persuasion to come with us. Besides, we need to move. Her father's goons are looking for her. We've got maybe two minutes until they're here." The woman's stunning green eyes narrowed. "Tell me. Did they kill Tennessee Smith? Did you watch them?"

"Hey, Erin said she wouldn't do that," the man argued.

They knew Ten? And Erin? She looked around, but she'd managed to get off the beaten path. The nearest people were far away. She wasn't sure they would even hear her if she screamed. She wasn't sure she wanted to scream.

She wanted answers. "Is Erin still on the island?"

It was stupid. She didn't even know Erin. Not really. Erin was apparently a big part of the conspiracy against her father, but she wanted to look at the woman and tell her how she felt. She hadn't been able to do that with Ten.

"She is. None of us leaves without Ten. Or his body," the Aussie said with grim determination.

That was a bit dramatic. "Put down the gun. I'll go with you. I want to talk to my…friend. It's good to clear the air sometimes. Are we walking or do you have a car somewhere? We really should go. My father's men will look for me and they might not be so polite when they find the two of you here."

The British woman nodded to an alley. "My partner is waiting."

She placed the gun in her tote bag, likely thinking Faith wasn't much of a threat. Which was correct. She had a tiny bit of self-defense training. The likelihood that she could stand up to these two was miniscule. The Aussie alone could kill her with one hand.

Which was why this was a horrible idea, and yet she followed the woman in white down the alley that could potentially be the site of her ignominious death. Or another kidnapping meant to force her father to do whatever these people wanted.

Would Tennessee Smith be at the end of this road? Would he be the one holding a gun and sending her into a cell until her father coughed up the money or information he required?

She had to know. In that moment, it didn't matter that she could die. She had to know if Ten Smith would be the one who killed her. She had to look at her friends and tell them what they'd done to her, how deep their cuts had been.

When a big man with inky black hair opened the door to a van that really should have had *property of a serial killer* painted all over it, she got in.

Because nothing seemed to matter anymore.

Twenty minutes later, she knew all three of their names, but not where they were. The Aussie, Brody, had blindfolded her lest she be able to direct her father and his nefarious men back to their Bat Cave.

Des was the woman, and Des had gotten a stern lecture from the Russian god, Nikolai. Apparently no one wanted a gun pointed Faith's way at this point. It was obvious they were going to play good cops and bad cops with her. She wondered which one Erin would be.

"We're here," Brody said. The big man had sat in the back with her after he'd made sure she didn't have a cell phone on her. She'd left it behind and considered seriously destroying the thing since her sister had probably put a tracker on this one, too.

Brody had been strangely gentle with her, making sure she was buckled in and that she didn't get jostled too much after they'd turned off the road and onto what felt like a dirt path. He'd asked if she was comfortable and told her that they would feed her or get her something to drink once they'd made it to the meet point.

He was a polite kidnapper.

"Don't get scared," Brody said. "I'm going to take the blindfold off now. We're here. No one's going to hurt you."

"Sure. That's what all you guys say." She blinked as the sunlight hit her eyes. The Russian was standing in front of the door, his hand out to help her down. Behind him, she saw a canopy of green and a gorgeous house in the background.

It could only be one of a few of the private homes on this part of the island. On this very exclusive piece of beachfront, there were twenty or so homes kept by wealthy investors or intensely rich people. They stayed away from the resorts, preferring parts of the island where no one would bother them.

Ten had money behind him if he could afford to use a place like this as his base of operations. Money and power.

"Is he in there?" Faith's heart was actually racing at the thought of seeing him, of getting a chance to tell that motherfucker what she really thought.

Of seeing him one last time.

"Who? Theo?"

"No, Ten."

Brody frowned. "He's not in there. Why do you think we brought you here? We're trying to find him."

"I thought that was all a load of bullshit meant to soften me up." She hadn't bought the whole "did you watch Ten die" crap. It looked like Ten had betrayed more than her. "He left the island on a private plane a day and a half ago. Call him in Dallas."

The door to the big house opened and Erin stood there. "No private plane has taken off from your father's airstrip for days. According to his tracking device, he's still at your father's compound."

"Tracking device?"

Erin nodded, her eyes weary. It looked like the redhead had gotten very little sleep. There were dark circles under her eyes. "Yes. He had it implanted before this mission. I think he felt naked without his. Big Tag doesn't require it, but he agreed to monitor one for Ten. It's subcutaneous. I doubt your father will have found it. The trouble is it hasn't moved since about an hour after he was taken."

"You're lying." It was too much to take in. All the spy shit didn't make sense to her. Why would someone need a freaking locator device implanted inside his body? Only a paranoid freak would do that. Or a man who'd been taken before. A man who desperately wanted someone to give a crap about where he was in the world.

"Why would I lie?" Erin asked, her voice heavy. "Look, I know you hate me right now and you have every reason to, but I need to find my boss. Whatever we did to you, we did it for the right reasons, and I can prove it. Hate me later. Help me now."

"Why would I believe a word you say? You've lied to me all along. You've used me to get to my father. And so did Ten. God, Erin, you set me up. You're the one who put the idea in my head. Did you like playing the pimp?" She wouldn't have gotten into bed with Ten without Erin's prompting. She would be lonely, but she wouldn't ache the way she did. She would have gone back to Houston and picked out a Dom and spent a few weeks playing. The man wouldn't have touched her soul, but he also wouldn't have ripped it out of her body and spit on it.

Had Ten really done that? It depended. It depended on why he'd told her he loved her.

"I liked the fact that both of my friends were smiling," Erin allowed. "I liked the fact that they obviously cared about each other."

Faith moved up the steps leading to the house. To her right she could see the path leading to the boathouse and the ocean. It shouldn't be a surprise that they were prepared. Hell, they'd been preparing for this for a while it looked like. Anger flared through her as Theo stepped out, leaning against the doorway. He was watching, allowing Erin to handle this, but Faith had no doubt he wouldn't let Faith get too close to his precious girl.

"Cared? In my world people who care about each other don't use each other. They don't lie to get their way. They don't set up their friends."

Erin's eyes went cold. "I don't think you know your world as well as you think you do."

She should have known this would happen. "I suppose you have a file on me."

"Not you," Erin replied. "I mean, there is one on you and all it told me was you're innocent."

"Innocent of what?"

Theo stepped onto the porch. "He gave you specific orders, Erin. You were not to give her those reports."

Erin flushed, but her jaw went stubborn. "I'm not going to. Brody is. Brody is willing to disobey orders and you know damn well what Big Tag would do in this situation. Call him. Let him make the decision. With Ten out of the game, we should call home and request new orders. We should have done it the minute he was taken."

Theo's jawline hardened. It was obvious they'd gone over this before. "I am in charge and I don't need my brother to save me. Ian made me second in command because he trusts my judgment. I think my brother would honor what Ten wanted. Faith is Ten's. He makes the decisions regarding her."

Erin's eyes narrowed. "He can't make a decision if he's a fucking corpse, Theo. We're running out of time. He could already be dead."

"He's not dead," Faith insisted. He couldn't be. Even as angry as she was, she couldn't think about a world that didn't include his lazy, sexy smile, his strong arms. "My dad got him off the island. He wanted all of you gone."

"Is that why he tried to kill us?" Theo regarded her seriously.

"Maybe Erin's right. Ten's going to kick my ass, but Erin's not going to leave this island until you're safe. I know you're pissed, but the minute Ten fell for you, you became one of us, and we don't leave a man behind."

"He wouldn't have really hurt you." Not her father. How far would he go for revenge? Not nearly as far as he would go for money. There was never enough for her father.

Erin pulled up the hem of her shirt. There was a bandage wrapped around her midsection, blood staining through. "I wasn't fast enough."

"Shit. You need to be in a hospital." This she could handle. Finally something she could handle.

Erin let the hem drop. "Not until we find Ten. And Theo patched me up all right."

"Not if it's bleeding through. Go inside." She looked to the helpful Aussie. "I need hot water, any kind of first aid kit you can find."

"Needle and thread," Theo said grimly. "She promised she would let you stitch her up. She wouldn't let me."

"Like you can sew," Erin complained under her breath.

"You're going to find out what I can do when you're well enough, my love," Theo promised. "You disobeyed direct orders in the field and you've been the worst patient in the history of time. Let's hope Faith knows how to cool a backside after it's been spanked about three hundred times. You move. You do what she tells you to, Erin. I'm done with this shit. You let Faith take care of you or I'll ship you back to my brother so fast it will make your head spin. You won't go in the field for years."

Erin stopped in front of him, her eyes flaring, and then she shut down. She walked into his arms. "All right, Theo. I'll do what she says." She kissed him before stepping back. "And I was right to do what I did. I gave you time to get that text off to Ten. For all the good it did us."

She'd felt his cell phone vibrating. She'd thought it was nothing more than an e-mail or some stupid social media thing. Hers did the same thing all the time. He'd ignored it because he'd been kissing her. She'd told him she thought she might love him. She'd watched his eyes flare with victory and he'd ignored Theo telling him to run.

He hadn't run. He hadn't fought. He hadn't shoved her away and tried to save himself.

He'd told her he loved her and not to ever forget that.

She followed Erin into the house, her brain a wrecked mess. What the hell was she supposed to believe? She washed her hands and then took a good look at Erin's wound.

Someone had shot her. That didn't make any sense. She would have heard someone shooting.

Her stomach tightened and she thought about that night. Her father's men. She closed her eyes briefly, remembering what she'd seen. There had been four of them and they'd all had guns. Guns with long barrels. No. Not barrels.

Silencers. Her father's men had been carrying guns with silencers. There was no reason to do that unless they'd intended to shoot and make sure no one heard.

What the hell was going on?

Erin's wound was a through and through. It was on the side of her torso, right above her hip. An inch to the right and she would have needed serious surgery to repair her large intestine. As it was, she needed about three stitches to truly close the wound. Theo had done his best with butterfly closures, but she still bled when she moved.

"You were lucky." Faith looked through the kit Brody had brought her. They were prepared. The supplies included a suture kit. "This is going to hurt without a local."

Erin shook her head. "Local hurts, too. I can handle it."

"God, you're stubborn, girl." Theo sat on the bed beside where Erin lay. "Hold on to me."

Luckily, she was damn good with sutures in the field. She worked quickly and before Erin could really break Theo's hand, Faith was bandaging the wound.

"She'll heal." Now that the job was done, she felt more centered, calmer, and more ready to deal with the situation she found herself in. "Is this tracer device the only reason you think my father has Ten?"

"Lie down, Erin." Theo barked the order as his sub attempted to sit up.

"Erin, you need to rest. You'll pull those sutures if you're not careful." Faith didn't want to put her through that again. "Rest for the day. You'll be up and fighting again tomorrow."

"But," Erin began.

Theo was having none of it. "You promised me. You promised to do what the doctor said. I want to find Ten, too, but understand that you are now and always will be my priority in life. Think about that. I'll scrub the entire mission to see you safe."

"Which is precisely why we shouldn't be partners," Erin shot back.

"You can get back to Li when this is over, though you should know I intend to have a conversation with him about taking care of you in the field. So lie back down or get to the plane and I'll take you home."

Erin turned a bright red, but she laid back. "You're a bastard, Theo. You're as bad as the rest of them."

Theo sighed. "Yeah, I know, baby. Come with me, Faith, and I'll lay out what we've learned about your father's organization. Ten will kick my ass, but if we're going to get him back, I think Erin is right. You have to know."

"Can you give us a minute?" Erin asked.

Theo stared at her for a moment as though not completely sure of what he should do. He finally stepped toward the door. "Brody will be waiting in the hall to lead you to the office."

When they were alone, she looked at her former friend. "What do you want, Erin?"

Erin huffed and sat up with a muffled groan. So stubborn. "I want to be the woman I was before I had to go to Africa. I want to not give a shit about you or Theo Taggart or anyone else. It was easier. I didn't have to compromise. I hate this compromise shit."

"Well, guess what, sister. You don't have to care about me at all." With the exception of Tennessee, Erin was the one she was most angry with. She'd been comfortable with Erin. It was a precious thing. Friends were a little like lovers. She was picky about them. She could spend time with people and enjoy it, but she didn't connect with many people the way she had with Erin.

Now she had neither friend nor lover. She was afraid she didn't have any family either.

Why, oh why, would those guards have silencers on their weapons? And why would her father and sister lie about the vaccines? Had she been a naïve idiot all these years?

Erin made her way to the window. She stared out at the lush green of the garden. "I don't make friends easily. I know. It's a huge surprise. I'm so sweet and open that everyone should love me." She snorted, an inelegant sound. "I'm crass and closed off and I can be a little mean at times. I get it. I was raised in a family where if I wasn't tough, I got walked on. Hard. None of that matters. I hate this. I hate being vulnerable."

"Well, I hate being lied to." She forced herself to say the words because she was already softening. Her impulse was to sit Erin down and talk to her. The redhead looked so lost, so out of her element.

Faith reminded herself that she was the victim here.

"Yeah, I know. Theo thinks we're going to explain our mission and you'll understand and forgive us all. He's naïve. I know what's going to happen. We'll lay out the mission, you'll realize the truth, and you'll help us."

"You really think so?" She wasn't so sure.

"I know you, Doc. You won't be able to turn away, but you won't be able to forgive us either. Especially me and Ten. You'll look at Theo and the rest of them and be able to say they were doing their jobs. Not me and Ten though. Because you loved us. It's a stupid word, you know. People say they love you, but what does it mean? It's overused and overvalued and god, it goes away so easily. There should be some constancy to that stupid word."

"Love can be killed like everything else." She wasn't going to give in to the tears that were forming behind her eyes. She wasn't going to let Erin get under her skin again. And that went double for Ten Smith.

Please let him be alive.

"Yeah, I guess if anybody can kill it, I can. Ten never wanted you to know what Theo's going to tell you. He forbade us. He could have used the information you're about to receive to bring you to his side, but he chose not to. Do you understand what it takes for a man like Tennessee Smith to bury information that would help him achieve his goal?"

"I don't know Tennessee Smith at all. I knew a man named Ten Graham, but he wasn't real."

"I think he was more real with you than he's ever been with

anyone else. I understand Ten. God, I understand Ten better than I do anyone else on this crew. He has no idea who the fuck he is. He's been undercover for so much of his life, he's got no idea who the real Ten is. I think he liked who he was with you. It's the only reason he wouldn't use that information. The Ten I know is ruthless. He's hard as a rock, but he got soft for you. I hope he's still alive."

"My father wouldn't kill him." She couldn't believe it. It couldn't be true.

A vision of those thugs her father employed using their guns with silencers crossed her brain.

"Your father has killed. He's killed many times and he'll continue to do so. He killed Ten's brother, Jamie. Not directly, but he sold the troop information to the man who did. He was also indirectly responsible for the physical and mental torture of Phoebe's husband, Jesse. Your father killed or damaged the two men she loved most in the world. The truth is you lost your only family a very long time ago, and to the same man Ten lost his to. His mission should be yours, but he was willing to shoulder the burden alone because he loves you."

"What do you mean by…" Erin's words sunk in. Faith shook her head. "No. No. He loved my mother. He couldn't have. He would never."

"He lied to you. You weren't sick that day. Your mother didn't call the pediatrician to make an appointment. She had an appointment with a divorce attorney. She also had spoken to a lawyer at the Justice Department. They had opened a file on your father. After your mother was murdered, they closed it. Theo can show you everything. He'll also explain why your father was the man behind your kidnapping in Ghana."

Faith had to take a step back. She felt like someone had kicked her in the stomach. All the air seemed to rush out of the room and for a moment, her peripheral vision began to fade.

Erin was suddenly at her side, offering her support even though she still had to be in pain from the sutures.

Faith forced herself to stand. She couldn't count on Erin. She couldn't count on anyone.

"I want to see what you have." She walked out to the hall where Brody waited to show her where to go, wondering if she would have anyone she could believe in after the next few minutes.

And she wondered if any of it mattered because she already knew she would do whatever it took to get Tennessee Smith back. She would let him go, but she had to make sure he was alive.

CHAPTER FIFTEEN

"**I** should go with them." Faith stared at the monitor.

"Nope. You should stay right here with me." Hutch sat back and yawned a little as though a nighttime raid of a dangerous man's fortified home was really no big deal. The man who couldn't be older than his mid-twenties was the only one left in the van with her. He'd brought along his computer and some very high-tech equipment she didn't understand. Apparently he was some sort of hacking genius and had already broken into the security feed around the mansion. "They have to get in and out. You'll hold them back. There's a storm coming."

After the singularly named Hutch had gone over the multitudinous ways her father had betrayed both her and his country, he'd explained that they were on a timeline. A tropical storm was coming in a few hours and they had a very small window to get Ten and get the hell off the island. Even as it was a few would remain behind since the plane was small and could only hold four passengers and the pilot.

Apparently the Russian was also a pilot. So Theo had decreed it would be Nick piloting Tennessee, Faith, Erin, and Des off the island and back to the relative safety of the mainland.

She didn't like to think about the fact that Theo had talked about bringing back Tennessee's body if they had to.

He was alive. He had to be alive.

"You're a go on the south side, boss." Hutch had on a set of headphones and spoke into the microphone attached. He turned the screen of the computer so she could see four shadowy figures making their way along the south wall of the compound.

All four figures were dressed in black in deference to the darkness around them. The night before the moon had been spectacularly full, but this was a new moon night and in the absence of city lights, everything was dark around them.

There was a brief knock and the door opened. Erin climbed inside. "What's going on?"

Hutch shrugged. "Nothing yet. Shouldn't you have the Jeep all fired up and ready to roll?"

"Can't roll anywhere without my crew. When they start hauling ass back here, I'll fire up the Jeep. What's security look like?" Erin grimaced as she took the bench on the other side of Hutch.

They hadn't spoken more than a few words since Faith had gotten the four-hour report on the lie her life had been. Whoever Liam O'Donnell was, the man was thorough. She now believed that her father had her kidnapped to pave the way for an American corporation to keep its interests in Ghana lucrative. She'd seen the money trail. It was a money trail that led to her. Shortly thereafter, her father had used a portion of the same money to help fund her new clinic. She remembered that check like it was yesterday.

Her father's actions had led to Ten's brother's death. Tennessee Smith had been trying to right a wrong. He'd been trying to find justice for his brother.

She wished he'd told her that in the beginning rather than allowing her to fall in love with a man who didn't exist.

Her heart was heavy in her chest. Since learning the truth about her father, she'd been a walking bag of bones. Every movement was forced because all she really wanted to do was lie down somewhere and sleep. Maybe never wake up.

Her father had put out a hit on her mother. She'd been trying to expose him.

It was up to Faith now. Once she was sure Ten was all right, she was going to the press. If her father wanted to kill her, let him try his hardest. She intended to prove more difficult to kill than her mother.

If her sister got in her way, Faith would have to take her down, too. She would deal with Hope at some point if only to find out what she knew about the experiments at the clinic.

Of all the things she'd been told, the secrets revealed, the idea that Hope would experiment on non-consenting patients was the easiest to believe. Hope had always been about her research. Science required breaking a few eggs, her sister had told her. And in Hope's mind, some eggs were more important than others. Faith had been comforted by the fact that FDA regulations and little things like laws would keep her sister in line.

Hope had found a way around them.

"Security is only a tad different than what Faith said it would be." Hutch's voice brought Faith back to the moment. "The only difference is several more guards on the front entrance. See?"

Hutch clicked a button and the screen became four blocks of security feed. The entrances to the main house and several of the outlying buildings showed up on screen. Hutch pointed to the right uppermost block. There were five armed security guards.

"They're waiting on something. I don't like it. Call Theo back." Erin's mouth formed a flat line as she stared at the screen.

Hutch touched another button. "Boss, your girl here thinks this is some kind of a setup and wants your ass back here. There are three extra guards on the front gate. Apparently that means something to Erin."

Erin grabbed the extra headset with a growl. "Theo, they're looking for someone. Something's going down." There was a pause before Erin shot back. "Instinct, little boy. I've done this more than you. Yes, you're my superior on this mission, but I've logged more time in the field than you and Case combined. Something's wrong. Turn around now."

Hutch winced in a way that let Faith know Theo hadn't agreed with Erin.

"You're going to get everyone killed." Erin took off the headset and looked to Hutch. "I'm calling Tag. Get me a line out."

Hutch put up his hands. "Erin, I know you have many ways to disembowel a man, but in this one case, I'm more afraid of Theo than I am of you. This was Ten's operation and Theo's my teammate. He's in charge so I'm not going to pull that line for you. Relax.

They're professionals."

Erin sat back, her eyes staring straight ahead at the screen as Theo and the group made their way toward the outermost building.

"That building is supposed to be for the gardening equipment and all the stuff the maintenance team uses," Faith said, her voice dull.

"It's got some serious security measures on it for a storage shed. Someone really doesn't want the riding mowers stolen." Hutch reached for a bag of chocolate covered peanuts. "Want some? They're protein."

"No, thanks." She'd forced down a protein bar for dinner. It had been a little surprising that it hadn't come back up. She'd spent hours pouring over the evidence against her father. Much more time than she'd spent on Ten's records. If the McKay-Taggart team was lying, they were far more comprehensive than her father. She'd spent another hour comparing the evidence.

They could both be right. She believed some of the things about Tennessee Smith. The ruthlessness was true. No doubt about that. She could believe that he'd sent men out into dangerous situations, even out to die. But why would Jesse Murdoch vouch for the man? According to her father's report, Ten had sold Murdoch out along with James Grant. Yet Murdoch and his wife—who had also been James's wife—stood beside Ten.

The money trail told the tale in the end. Who had profited? Her father. Her sister.

When she looked deep into her soul and asked herself if she believed her father was capable of murder, she had to answer yes.

So she was here, ready to betray her family completely, and then she would be alone.

"How are they going to get into the building?" She hadn't sat in on the mission briefing. She'd been putting together a field kit and preparing, though they'd told her they planned to get in and out as quietly as possible.

If they couldn't get to Ten easily, they were supposed to regroup and wait for a better time.

That's what Theo had said. She wasn't sure she believed him. Theo seemed determined to prove himself in the field. If they were still friends, she'd talk to Erin about it. She'd sit beside her and lend

Erin her strength.

Not that she had any.

"Theo's got a program on his tablet I set up to run through a list of possible combinations. He's going to hook it up, give it two cycles, and then we'll call it. I'll have more data even if it doesn't work. It might take two or three tries, but we'll get in there."

"He's got C-4," Erin said flatly.

Hutch's eyes widened and he was playing with his headset again. "Boss, you're coming up on the building. You've got one guard to your right. I've been watching him, and if you give him two minutes, he takes a smoke break. I've watched him for a couple of nights. Once he steps out, you'll have about five minutes when that door is unguarded. I'll handle the cameras."

Faith watched as Theo moved in behind the guard and silently took him out.

"Shit," Hutch swore. "Don't do this, Taggart. Follow the plan."

"This is his plan," Erin said with a shake of her head. "It was always his plan. He was never going to leave Ten inside that building. Living or dead, he won't leave Ten behind."

Faith's heart sped up. "Are you sure Ten is even in there?"

Hutch's hands were fists. "His tracking device leads us there, but it hasn't moved since the night he was taken. He could be a corpse or they could have found the device and cut it out of him. There's zero guarantee Theo's going to find Ten. There's a one hundred percent shot that he's going to tip off your father and his guards that we're here if he blows the damn door."

"He doesn't care. He thinks he's smarter and faster than everyone, and I pray to god he's right," Erin said. "Because those guards at the gate are waiting for something and it's not a pizza delivery."

Faith watched the screen. The small group moved in now that the guard had been taken care of.

"Naturally I get a call I can't refuse now," Hutch said under his breath. "It's coming in off the sat line so it's going to come over the speakers." He went silent as he fiddled with the computer.

"Is he really going to blow the door?" Faith asked Erin as Hutch tried to answer the call.

Erin sat forward, the screen casting ghostly shadows over her face. "He's going to do anything he can to get Ten out of there. He can't leave his boss. He knows what's happening in there. Theo won't leave Ten to be tortured and killed if he thinks for a second that he can get him out, but he's not being careful."

Torture. She didn't want to think about it. It seemed like forever since Ten had walked out of her room and into her father's care. What had happened to him in that time?

"Chelsea? Are you there?" Hutch hit a couple of keys. "Damn storm is moving faster than we thought it would."

Faith had seen men who had been tortured. She'd treated the wounds to their bodies, but the ones to the soul never went away. "Theo cares about Tennessee."

"Theo wants to be the hero. He wants to be his big brother, but what he doesn't understand is that his brother wouldn't be this reckless. Not with a team on the line. He's trying to be Big Tag, but Ian has so much more experience than he does." Erin stopped and brushed her hand across her face. "He's going to get someone killed. And even if he doesn't, Ten is likely going to murder him for pulling this shit."

"He's saving Ten." Faith couldn't see how that would be a bad thing.

"Ten would never do this at the expense of his team," Erin explained. "Ten is a big boy. He knows the rules of the game. He knew going into this mission that he might not come out of it."

Her skin chilled. "Ten didn't fight my father when he came for him. He didn't fight or try to run away."

Erin turned serious eyes Faith's way. "He knew you could get hurt. He weighed the likelihood of getting away versus you being harmed and chose the path he was okay with. Theo's being too optimistic."

On the screen she saw Theo at the door to the building. He had something in his hands and he was placing it on the door.

"You there, Hutch?" A feminine voice came over the line. This wasn't the private line. This call came straight out of the computer's speakers. "Stop it, baby. You can't eat that. What's up with putting everything in your mouth?"

"What?" Hutch asked. It seemed he'd finally found a good line.

"Sorry, it's Satan's night out and Si and I got left with the demonlings. Did you know they don't sleep? I thought babies slept a lot. Also, they really like to hit keys on the computer. No, Kala. Auntie Chelsea needs that computer."

"Chelsea, this is really not a good time," Hutch said.

"No," Chelsea replied. "It is not. I wouldn't call this a good time at all. This one is a total poop machine, but apparently Si wants a couple of tiny humans, so I'm supposed to keep the demonlings alive and happy. Luckily they are really cute. Don't. Why do you want to eat that pen? Go back to eating your own foot."

Erin leaned in. "Chelsea, we're in the middle of an op. Could you can the baby talk?"

A long sigh came over the line. "Fine. Everyone's cranky. All right. I'll get to the good stuff. So I was showing Kala here around the Dark Web because what else am I going to do with a baby this late at night. That's when I found the auction. The closed auction. When were you guys going to mention that someone nabbed Ten? Because the Chinese paid thirty million for him, and according to the chatter baby girl and I found, the pickup is tonight."

The upper right-hand box caught Faith's eye. There was a light streaming up from the road, a car approaching the front gate.

"Shit and shit and fucking shit." Hutch closed his eyes and got back on his headset. "Theo, I need you to get back to the vehicles right fucking now. MSS is on the way and they will not be alone."

It was a little like watching a horror film. It was right there on the screen and there was nothing she could do about it. She could shout at the screen, but it wouldn't fix the problem.

A large SUV was waved through the gates followed by a second SUV.

"I'm not kidding, Theo. There are potentially ten to fifteen MSS agents on their way to you and they will be backed up by McDonald's guards. Get your ass out of there now."

Erin shook her head. "He'll just move faster. He won't stop." She opened the door to the van and hopped out. "I'm going to back them up."

Faith watched as her father stepped out to greet the newcomers. He had a phalanx of heavily armed guards and her sister at his side. The guards had traded their elegant handguns for assault rifles.

Something serious was going down.

Her father had sold a CIA operative to the Chinese?

Tennessee Smith was alive, but her father wasn't planning on that lasting forever. He was going to sell Ten into torture and death at the hands of his enemies, and Faith couldn't allow that to happen. She followed Erin out of the van.

A loud blast shook the air around them.

"Damn it," Erin cursed. "Stubborn man."

She took off running and Faith followed, praying they would get there in time.

* * * *

The sound of the world exploding barely brought Ten out of his stupor.

How long had it been? Days? It felt like days. A lot of days. Maybe even weeks. He'd been tied up in this position for what felt like forever. No food. No water. At some point they'd cut the clothes off him so they could torture every inch of his body.

He was nothing more than an animal now, and not one looking to survive. He had one mission. Keep his mouth shut. Don't give away secrets. The Agency might have given up on him, but that didn't mean he could betray his country, his friends.

So long. Did his friends even remember him now?

"What the hell?"

He heard the guard. There were two of them. It seemed like more, but now that he forced his eyes to open, he could plainly see only two men were in the room.

And he wasn't naked anymore. He was dressed in some sort of scrubs. When had that happened?

"Shit. Is he coming out of it? Doc said the drugs wouldn't wear off until the Chinese had him."

The words started to penetrate. Also, gunfire. Yeah, that was in play, too. There was the rapid blast of a gun firing through the building.

Drugs. He'd been given drugs. Something psychotropic.

His hands were bound in front of him, locked in a set of cuffs. He wasn't where he thought he was. In the building, yes. He recognized the walls around him, but he wasn't hanging off that hook.

How much time had passed? His senses deceived him. It had been the drugs.

"Come on, asshole. You've got a plane to catch. Bill, let's take him out the back. I don't know what's going on, but I don't like it. I'm not going out into the courtyard as long as there's gunfire going on." The second guard hauled Ten up.

He swayed on his feet. Someone had blown the main door. There was only one party who would blow that door.

Focus. Use the tools he had. That was what he had to do. He would concentrate on the pain later, but for now he pushed it aside. There was no ache in his shoulders, no burning along every inch of his skin. There was no weakness in his muscles from what felt like days of electrical torture.

Now there was only adrenaline coursing through his system, and he meant to ride that wave.

Hands. They were in front of him. Idiots.

"Let's go," the guard said as that gunfire got closer.

Ten brought his hands up, catching the fucker in the chin and sending him back on his ass. Ten propelled up from where he sat and found the world spinning. It made him nauseous, but he forced himself to move. He needed to find the keys, needed to get out and figure out where his team was, and he suddenly found himself in the middle of a war zone.

His vision was out of whack. He got clear sight of concrete and industrial walls before it went fuzzy again.

"Hey," a deep voice growled and there was a volley of cursing. "I'm going to need backup here. All hell's broken loose and our prize isn't as sleepy as promised. Get the doc down here now."

The doc. Not his sweet doc. Not Faith. The other one. The evil one. He hated that woman. She was the one with the drugs. The pain he could handle. That feeling of endlessness was another thing altogether.

He had to make his legs work. The muscle in his right thigh seized and he hit the concrete with a thud.

A hand found the back of his neck and started hauling him up. There was nothing he could do. His leg was twitching uncontrollably. His spine started to bow.

A loud crack sounded through the room and he fell back to the floor.

"I got you," a familiar voice said. "Can you stand?"

For a second he thought Big Tag was here. Saving him again. It took a moment to realize the man hauling his ass up this time wasn't quite as big as Ian, though he was proving just as stubborn.

"Theo, what are you doing here?"

"Saving you, boss. Des, clear a path for me. Tell Nick and Brody we're going to have to carry Ten out of here. I don't think his legs are working right now. Also, tell them we have incoming. We should expect to have to fight our way out."

Ten caught sight of the lovely Brit. She was wearing all black and looking perfectly competent as she raised her SIG Sauer and started moving back through the complex toward the stairs and the door that would lead them outside.

"Let's go. We've got a small army of MSS agents on the way in. Apparently they love you in Beijing." Theo wrapped Ten's arm around his broad shoulders. "Can you manage this?"

He could shuffle along now that the spasm had subsided. It would be back. "Leave me. Get the fuck out of here, Taggart. We don't have enough men and not a single one of you is wearing body armor."

They hadn't brought any along. It was supposed to be a quick get in, get out operation.

Theo gave him a reckless smile. "Body armor's for wimps. I've got two cars waiting. We'll make it."

God, he wished his head would stop spinning. He needed to think. He needed to know the odds. MSS was here to pick him up. They wouldn't have sent a single man or even two or three. They would send a contingent, and they wouldn't want to let him go without a fight. McDonald had a small army of guards here himself.

If they could have done it quietly, it could have been done. If they had more men, it could have been done.

"Theo, get your people out of here this instant." The words felt dumb on his tongue. He was sending away his only way out, but he couldn't live with the consequences. He wasn't about to trade his life for any of theirs. "That's an order."

Theo moved forward, dragging him along. "I can't obey that

order, sir. You're incapacitated and incapable of making proper decisions. You can fire me later, but I'm saving you tonight."

A little flare of panic seemed to wake his system up. His legs started moving, stumbling along at a brisker pace. "No. This is going to go south and it's going to go quickly. Dump me. Let MSS take me. Big Tag can find me later. Get our people off this island. Goddamn it, Theo, get Faith out of here."

Where was she? Was she inside the big house? Did she have any idea what was going on? He had to pray that McDonald cared enough about his daughter to keep her out of whatever the hell he was doing. Making deals with China's spy organization could be a double-edged sword. Unfortunately, Ten was fairly certain he would be gutted with that sword one way or another. He had to make sure no one else got hurt.

He tried to stop Theo's progress as they headed for the door, but he was weak again, his muscles drained. Useless. He was fucking useless.

"Stop this right now, Taggart," he said, using his best boss voice. "I order you to stand down and retreat."

"I am retreating." Theo kept right on moving into the hallway and began hauling him up the stairs.

"You coming?" A voice with a thick Australian accent called down. Brody was here. He would get to die with the rest of them.

Or maybe he was better trained than Theo. Perhaps Damon had done a better job with his men. "Brody, you're now second in command. Get your men out of here. Leave right this fucking second or I will make sure you never work another day in your life again. Am I understood?"

"Can't hear much. I think that C-4 blast might have done something to my ears, boss," the Aussie cracked. "We should move. I can see headlights coming. Maybe a minute and a half out. Des and Nick are in a holding pattern. They'll make sure the exit is clear."

Everyone was getting fired.

"You don't have any time," a soft voice said.

Theo turned, raising his weapon.

Fuck, his vision was finally clearing and he got to look at Hope McDonald standing at the bottom of the stairs in her crisp white coat. She apparently observed protocol even out here in the jungle. "Kill her."

Theo had his weapon pointed at her head. "She doesn't have a gun."

"That bitch doesn't need one." Faith would be safer with her sister dead.

Hope's hands came up. "Theo won't kill me. He's a gentleman. You should move. Father's men will attack from behind and the Chinese will come up the road."

"Why would you tell us anything?" Theo asked.

"Because it won't change the outcome. I really would like for us to work together, Theodore. I find you fascinating. Even more now that I've read your records. Mr. Smith was a good subject, but you will be a masterpiece. You should hurry. They're almost here."

"Kill her." Ten couldn't remember everything that had been done to him, but it had started with her. His true agony had begun with that needle she'd wielded. She wouldn't stop. She would keep her research going and others would hurt, too.

Theo started to drag him out into the night, leaving Hope at the bottom of the stairwell. "I can't shoot an unarmed woman, Ten. You can fire me later, but I can't."

Ten could kill her. He could do it easily, but right now he couldn't even grip a damn weapon.

Retribution was going to have to wait because none of his men had the sense to listen to him.

"Faith. Tell me Faith left the island."

Brody stepped up, peeling away from the shadows. For a massive man, he blended well with the night around him. He was dressed all in black. "I'll take him. And Faith is safe and sound back at the vehicles with Hutch and Erin."

He found his whole world upending as the big Aussie tossed him over his shoulder. God, he was going to be sick.

"Why is Faith with Erin?" Erin would watch out for her. Erin wouldn't let anything happen to Faith. "The last I heard she never wanted to talk to any of us again."

"I needed her intel," Theo said. He touched his earpiece. "We're on the move."

Brody took a couple of steps forward before stopping again. Ten couldn't see anything but the big guy's backside. "What's wrong?"

"Are you kidding me?" Theo asked. "Fuck. Erin and Faith are on their way in. Hutch is firing up the van and coming after them. It looks like we're going to have to squeeze into one vehicle. I'm going to have her ass."

There was the sound of gunfire and a curse.

"I'm going to need you to stand for a minute, Ten. Or at least sit. Keep your head down. Des, Nick, what's going on?" Brody no longer kept things quiet. It didn't matter. Hell was raining down around them.

Ten was surprised to find himself fairly steady as Brody set him down. He flattened his back against the side of the building, his palms against the material. Steady. He was going to get out of here and then he would recover and kick everyone's ass.

He would do it after they got home because this operation was over. He would find another way to take down McDonald.

"We've got incoming," Nick shouted back.

"We'll let them come in and sneak out when they raid the building. They can't see us here," Theo explained. "And Hutch just cut the power. We've got the cover of night on our side."

"Here, mate." Brody pressed a gun in his hand. "Try to hold on to it."

He had to admit, he felt better with a gun in his hand. He thought seriously about going back in and killing Hope.

Up ahead, he heard the sound of tires pounding over pavement. Unfortunately, Hutch couldn't cut the lights on the vehicles.

"Get back," Theo ordered.

"I can cause some chaos," he heard Des say. "Get ready to run toward the back. We can go up the trail to where we left the cars."

She swung out and two shots pierced the night before the vehicle entering the compound lost control and flipped, rolling into another one of the outer buildings.

Des turned and even in the low light, he could see the look of triumph on her face. "Let's get out of here."

Another shot rang out and she fell forward.

Ten watched in horror as they lost one of their own.

CHAPTER SIXTEEN

"Take the wheel," Erin said as they approached the compound. "I've got to take care of those assholes coming up on his flank or Theo's going to get caught in the middle. I'm going to kill him. I swear."

Faith's heart pounded in her chest. As far as she could tell, Erin was going to kill her and soon. She'd nearly taken off as Faith had jumped into the Jeep and she hadn't slowed down. Lucky for her, Faith knew the roads or they would have been overtaken by those black SUVs. For all Erin was angry with Theo, it was easy to see she was running on pure panic.

Though she seemed calm and professional now, as though having someone to target gave her strength.

Faith moved into the seat as Erin popped up and started firing at the group of five men who were bearing down on the building everyone was certain Ten was being held in. These men moved in from the west, obviously trying to sneak up on the team pinned down at the storage building.

Torture chamber, according to Theo. That building her father claimed was simply there to store the gardening tools actually housed a place for him to torture his enemies. According to the plans Theo had provided there was an entire bunker under what looked like an ordinary storage building. It was a lot bigger than it seemed.

Had her whole childhood been a lie?

Erin fired, never losing control. Faith's stomach turned as one by one those men went down. Erin wasn't wounding them or trying to take them temporarily out of the fight. She was taking kill shots with the cool of a professional. Which she was. It was a good thing as Faith nearly lost control of the Jeep as they came out of the jungle. The horrible sound of metal screeching filled the air and then the ground shook as one of the black SUVs rolled and then exploded.

"Shit!" Erin dropped back into the cab, hanging on as Faith regained control of the vehicle.

Faith forced herself not to panic. Ten was somewhere in that mess of smoke and fire and men with guns. She couldn't think about the killing part now. She wasn't naïve. She knew it was necessary at times, but it went against her nature. So she focused on what she could. Find Ten. Get everyone out as quickly as possible.

"Stop the Jeep," Erin ordered. "Hutch is on his way. You stay here."

She leapt out of the Jeep before Faith could stop it.

Faith's hands shook as she put on the brakes. The night was dark, but now it was illuminated by the fiery wreck that had been one third of the bad guys. That had to be a good thing.

Unfortunately, it looked like the other two thirds were taking exception to losing their men as the sound of gunfire split the air again.

She'd come around the back and had to reorient herself. The main storage building was to her left, the dirt roads through the jungle behind her. Up ahead was the road that connected the storage units to the main house. To her right were two secondary units, small in comparison to the one she was parked next to.

She nearly jumped out of her seat when she heard a car slam on its brakes behind her.

Hutch was out of the van in an instant. The happy-go-lucky hacker looked very comfortable with a couple of guns in his hands. He was firing before he got more than a few feet from her.

That was when she saw it. A figure stood out from the side of the building. She was illuminated by the light of the fire burning from the SUV. Faith was sure from the slightness of her frame that it was a she.

A big man started to reach out, to pull her back to the shadows. Her body stiffened, head snapping forward, and then she slipped to the dirt.

Faith blinked. She hadn't seen that. She hadn't seen a woman shot and falling to the ground. Her father didn't hire female guards. If a woman had been hit it had to be Erin or the British agent she'd met.

A masculine shout was heard and she saw a big figure move toward the body before another one hauled him back.

Faith hopped out and started running. She was the only person who could do what needed to be done. Gunfire erupted around her, but it wasn't her first time in a warzone. If she could do her job, maybe some of this would make sense.

Erin and Hutch were laying down fire as she made it to them.

The Aussie was holding the Russian. "Not losing you, too, Nick. Get it together, mate."

"We have to get to her." Theo sounded unsure all of the sudden, as though he knew what he needed to do, but couldn't stand to say it.

"She's gone," Erin argued. "That was a headshot. We get the fuck out of here before we lose someone else. Nick, I need you to remember your goddamn training."

"Faith?"

She stopped in her tracks. Tennessee Smith was leaning against the wall. They had so little cover, but Ten reached out and dragged her in, shoving her to the wall and covering her with his body.

"We have to get you back to the car," he said, his voice low. "I understand there are two. You're going to drive as fast and as far away from here as possible. We'll take the other one. Is that understood?"

Well, he was right back in Dom mode. She couldn't take that from him. Not now. "I have a patient."

"No. You don't. She's dead." Ten's voice had gone cold. "Erin's right. That was a headshot. The Chinese don't miss. We have to leave now."

Theo moved back, his eyes never leaving the targets. "I can't leave her body. We don't leave men behind."

"Cut the naïve bullshit, Taggart," Ten said. "If you take a step out from behind that wall, we're all dead. Des proved that. This is a clusterfuck situation and I assure you that we leave men behind when they're corpses and getting them back would produce more corpses. You've been in charge up until now. I'm back and we fucking retreat. Do you understand me?"

Theo's face was ghostly in the moonlight, lines forming that hadn't been there only moments before. He aged right in front of her. "Yes, sir. This is my fault, sir."

"There's time for recriminations later. Let's get our people to safety now." Ten sounded so much more solid. His hand found hers, fingers curling around tightly as though he was scared to let her go. "Markovic, we're leaving."

The Russian stood, his face turning smooth and bland. "Yes, sir."

What was it going to take for the man to leave his teammate behind? Worse. She was fairly certain the two were lovers.

Ten moved out. "Stay behind me."

"Can you walk?" Theo asked, moving to the front. "Brody, take our six."

"I'll make it and if I don't, you better leave me the fuck behind and get Faith the hell out of here. We're going to have a long talk about bringing her on this clusterfuck of an operation," Ten shot back.

"Why wouldn't you be able to walk?" Faith followed behind, shuffling to match their cautious movements. He looked grim and he wasn't wearing shoes. She wasn't sure why he was in scrubs, but she couldn't see any wounds on his body.

"Later, Doc. Move now or your father's men are going to cut us all down. They won't be able to tell who you are. They'll put a bullet in you with the rest of us. And watch your back. Your sister is still in that building." He glanced to the storage building, his eyes on the door as they passed it. The lock looked like it had been blown and there wasn't a handle anymore, but the big door had swung shut.

She clung to his hand. "I can handle it."

"Keep your head down," Ten commanded. "I think we got most of them, but I promise reinforcements are on the way. We need to move and quickly. You're lucky you came up the back or they would have torn you apart."

"They've got a sniper somewhere," Brody shouted out. "That shot at Des didn't come from the ground."

"He's likely on the roof of the main house. It's well within range and if I had planned a meeting with MSS, I damn well would have had cover. It would have been easy to switch positions and start picking us off," Ten explained. "Where are the vehicles?"

"Erin had me park on the side of the building," Faith explained.

"Good girl. More cover." Ten hunched over, obviously trying to make his tall body into a smaller target.

"Tennessee, I'm so sorry. I didn't know about the handoff. I didn't think about snipers or any of this," Theo said.

Ten was obviously not in the mood for apologies. "No. You were thinking about being the hero in front of your girl and showing big brother that you can handle yourself. Expect to be scrubbing the floors at McKay-Taggart with your fucking tongue after this."

"Ten, he was trying to save you." They had all been trying to save him.

Theo shook his head. "Don't. He's right. I fucked up and now Des is dead."

"Suck it up, buttercup," Ten shot back. "You can deal with the ramifications of your decision making when we're all off this fucking island. The op is over. We get the hell out. I'm not losing anyone else. Am I understood?"

He tugged Faith along. He wasn't moving with his normal grace. Something was wrong. He seemed to force his limbs to go where he wanted them to go. Then she felt his arm spasm, his fingers tightening on hers and jerking. He immediately let go and cursed under his breath.

"I'm going to need someone else to take the front. I can't move fast enough," Ten admitted.

"What's wrong?" Faith watched as a muscle in his face jumped.

"Later, Doc." He nodded to Theo, who moved ahead of him. Ten put a hand on the younger man's arm. "If I fall, you leave me. That's an order. You get her out of here. You get them all out of here. I am not worth this. Do you understand me?"

Theo nodded and then moved ahead. Gunfire splattered around them and the lights came back on suddenly.

"Shit," Ten said as he hit the ground. "Down." He turned back to her. "The shooters are behind the front wall, but they'll figure out that we're retreating so they will come over that wall and enter the compound. I want you to stay low and close to me."

She nodded.

"I got her back," Erin said from behind Faith. "When we get out in the open, head for the van. It's got the most cover. I'll drive since I know the road. Hutch can follow in the Jeep and Brody can keep everyone off our ass from the back."

"I will join him." The Russian's voice was bitterly cold, his eyes narrowing as he seemed to understand everyone was looking at him. "I will do my job."

Ten nodded, accepting the plan. "Brody, pop up and give us some cover. We go on three."

Her heart was racing, adrenaline pouring through her.

She glanced back, but she couldn't see Des anymore. Her body was lying somewhere about a hundred feet to her right, but just outside cover, just where they couldn't get to her. Had there been anything she could have done?

These people had lied to her, but it seemed like that was something everyone did. She didn't want them to die. No one had lied to her more than Tennessee Smith, but she wasn't sure what she would do if he'd been the one lying out there in the dirt.

Tears blurred her eyes. She had to stop that shit. She couldn't bring them down anymore than she already was. She had to do exactly what Ten had said so they could move. Then she would have a part to play.

"Go," Ten said.

Theo stepped out and there was the sound of a gun popping off. Theo raised his weapon and returned fire. "We're clear. Go."

But she watched as Theo looked down at his chest. He put a hand over his heart and when he pulled it away, it was covered in bright red blood.

"No!" Erin screamed the word and she was running toward Theo.

"Motherfuck." Ten stepped out, giving her cover.

The world seemed to slow. She could hear them yelling, heard the gunfire cracking through the air around her. The door behind her came open and then slammed shut again. They'd said her sister was still in the building.

Her sister was a brilliant surgeon. Better than Faith. Faith was more of a GP. Hope had done things in the operating room that could be called miracles. It had been a shame that she'd gone into research, but that was where the money was. Hope in a battlefield theater could have saved god only knew how many lives.

Now Faith only wanted to save one. Just one.

Faith turned and pounded her fist on the door. "Hope! Get out here. He's been shot."

She tried to pull at the door, but the way it had exploded had left nothing but a jagged mess where the handle had been. She needed someone to push it open from the inside. She tried to look through the hole that had been left, but the lights were off inside. She couldn't see anyone.

She hit the door again, so hard her fist ached. "Hope, please. Please. You know you can save him. Open this fucking door."

She needed someplace clean. Someplace to lay him out. Blood. She might need blood. God, where was she going to get blood?

Calm. Faith took a deep breath. Her sister wasn't coming out. She was alone and they were under fire and Theo had been shot. He didn't need her panic. He didn't need her insecurities. He needed the doctor, not the woman.

Erin dragged him back, Ten giving her cover fire.

Faith was on him, sure that the others would protect her. There was no question of protecting herself. She had a job to do and those fucking bullets flying her way meant nothing.

"It's bad, Doc." Theo looked up at her.

Assess. It was the first thing she needed to do. Evaluate the injury. She tried to view him as a patient and not her friend. Not half of Erin's heart.

"What can I do?" Erin asked.

"Hold his hand." Theo needed support. Erin tended to shut down when things got emotional.

Erin's eyes went wide, but she reached for his hand.

Blood. It was everywhere. The dark shirt he was wearing masked it, but the minute she touched him, her hand came back covered in blood. He had a massive chest wound.

"We need to move," Brody said. "They're coming over the wall."

"I can't move him." If she did, he was dead. She was surprised moving him back to cover hadn't killed him.

His breath rattled in his chest and Faith felt her stomach drop. It was a wheezing sound, like air escaping from a balloon. She pulled the shirt up and was glad the lights were on. She could see the bullet wound, estimate how close to the heart it had struck. Close. Way too close, but she had to worry about his lung first. If she was right, he had an open pneumothorax. Sucking chest wound. To top it off, he was bleeding profusely. She would bet his chest cavity was filling with a massive hemothorax.

"I need something to seal his lung," Faith said calmly, her hopes beginning to diminish. This was the kind of wound that was iffy in the best of conditions. "And then I need to get him to an OR. I need a chest tube to get this blood out. I can't see anything for all the blood."

"Get Erin out of here, Ten." Theo coughed and blood trickled from his mouth.

Erin leaned over. "Don't. Don't you dare do this, Theo. You promised me."

He reached up and brushed his fingers over Erin's face. "I did. Promised I'd love you until I died. Kept it, baby. Kept it."

Faith put her hand over the wound. "I need something plastic."

She could stabilize him. If she got something thin and plastic she might be able to stabilize the lung so he could breathe. Then she would work on the blood loss. Yes. She could do this. Her hands were coated in blood, but he was strong. She could do this. She had to stop being cynical.

"They're coming," Nick said, his voice calm.

"I'll get the van started." Hutch moved behind her.

She tried to focus on her patient.

Theo only had eyes for Erin. He ran his fingers over her face as though memorizing her. "Let Case take care of you. He won't...he won't know what to do. Took care of me so long, he doesn't know what to do with himself. Now go, baby. I'm done."

Tears dripped from Erin's eyes. "No. You promised."

What could she use? Maybe he was strong enough to make it to the van. She might have to risk it.

"Such a pretty girl." Theo's lips curled up, the blood on his face marring his perfection. He frowned suddenly. "Don't cry. You never cry."

"Don't do this to me." Erin leaned over. "You don't get to do this, Taggart."

"Erin, ask Tag…" He coughed again, blood bubbling up from his throat. "Fuck, ask Tag to forgive me."

"No." Erin's head shook. "No. You tell him yourself."

"Love you, baby. Forever."

Faith felt the moment he died. His chest rattled and then stilled, sinking in. Motion stopped and his face went slack. Something left Theo Taggart in that second. Something that animated him, made him human. It fled and she was left with nothing more than a body.

"Theo? Theo?" Erin shook him.

The blood flow had slowed. She hadn't noticed. His heart had stopped. It was no longer pumping, no longer moving.

She had to start CPR. Somewhere in the back of her mind, she knew he was gone. If he'd been close to an ER, maybe they would have a chance. If they had blood and all the technological wonders of a modern OR, she might have been able to save him, but she couldn't not try.

"Theo? Stop it. Fucking stop playing around." Erin shook him, trying to get some sort of response out of the man she loved. "Please. Please."

"Erin, move back. I need to start CPR," she said, shocked at how calm her voice was.

"Yeah," Erin agreed, her eyes glassy. "CPR. That's good. He needs it."

"Get the women. They won't come on their own. We have to move and now." She heard Ten speaking, but the words didn't penetrate. She could hear the gunfire getting closer. So much gunfire.

She got to her knees. Five compressions. She had to restart his heart. Nothing else mattered.

"No. No! Please don't. Don't make me leave him." Erin was yelling, but Faith had to focus on Theo. Every second that passed made it harder to bring him back.

There was movement behind her. Brody was gone. She pressed down. *One, Two, Three…*

Ten hauled her up and into his arms. His gun clattered to the ground. His body shook, but he held her tight.

"No. I have to give him CPR." She struggled in his arms.

He groaned and she felt him spasm, but he wouldn't let her go.

"He's gone, Faith. He's gone. Nick?"

Nick began to reach down for Theo's body. His shoulder flew forward and she saw what she hadn't before. There was a line of men coming up behind them. Nick groaned, but managed to fire behind him with the arm that hadn't taken a bullet.

"Move. We have to leave him," Ten ordered. "Move!" He glanced down at Theo. "Good-bye, brother."

He took off, almost stumbling, but he managed to keep his feet under them.

As he rounded the corner, she saw the door opening. There was a crack of light now and she saw a hint of her sister's blonde hair.

Too late. Far too late.

CHAPTER SEVENTEEN

Ten led her into the bathroom. Faith was like a doll he had to pose. If he let her, she would drift, her eyes becoming hazy as she almost surely found herself back in that horrible place where they'd been. Hours later, she was still in shock.

The only time she'd been in the moment was when she cut the bullet from Nick's shoulder. Even then, she'd been like an automaton, not even arguing with the Russian when he'd refused pain medication. Ten had been ready to hold the big guy down. He and Brody had been on standby, but Nick never moved. Never flinched or cried out. Even when Faith widened the wound so she could get to the bullet, even as she'd doused him with rubbing alcohol to clean the wound, he'd merely stared straight ahead. At the end, he'd said something in Russian about his gratitude and gone to his room, closing the door.

Erin was under watch. She might not realize it, but Hutch had orders not to let her out of his sight. It was easy because she wouldn't go back into the room she'd shared with Theo. She was on the couch, curled up with her gun, her eyes wide open though she'd told everyone she was going to sleep.

Brody was watching Nick. And Ten was going to take care of Faith, if his damn muscles would stop twitching.

He'd only been gone for two days. It had felt like weeks. How was it possible?

"Lift your arms," he commanded quietly once they'd made it to the bathroom. Outside he could hear the wind whipping around. The storm was about to blow in or he would have had them all on a plane or a boat off the island.

Her eyes came up. Normally they were so vibrant, but now they seemed dull. "I already washed off the blood."

He hated to point this out to her, wished he could simply put her to bed. Sleep would put a few hours between them and the horror of this evening. "Sweetheart, you washed off Theo's blood. Now you've got Nick's on you and we need to wash your hair."

There were matted places in her hair. She couldn't wake up like this in the morning. She needed to wake up clean, with at least her body back to normal. Nothing else would be, but he could give her this.

She caught sight of herself in the mirror and shuddered. "All right. I'll do it."

Good. At least he wouldn't have to fight her on that point.

She stared at him. "Why are you still here? Shouldn't you go back to your room?"

Ah, they had found something to fight about. "Not while we're on this island. I'm staying with you. I won't touch you if you don't want me to, but I'm not leaving you alone. You make bad decisions."

Her eyes narrowed and for the first time in hours, he felt like she was looking at him. Naturally, she looked irritated. "Like the decision to come rescue you?"

It was good that she understood. He didn't want to argue, but he couldn't move on this point. "Yes. Like that one. You never should have been anywhere near that operation."

His right leg seized and he damn near went to his knees. For hours he'd managed to ignore the weakness in his body, but the adrenaline was finally wearing off. He caught himself before he hit the floor, his arm on the sink. With shaking muscles, he got down to his knees. Faith knelt down and put her hands on his thigh, rubbing with a light touch.

"Does it hurt?"

He shook his head. "No. I know what real pain is. This is a weakness. My muscles keep firing off."

279

"Did they use electricity on you?"

He didn't want to get into this with her. No matter what, McDonald was still her father. It was bad enough that Ten was going to kill the man. "Take your shower, darlin'. We can talk more in the morning."

"I need to know what happened so I can treat you."

"I'm feeling great." He was feeling like shit, but he wasn't putting her through anything else tonight.

"None of us is great, Ten. Tell me what happened. Or maybe I could tell you. From the electrical burn on your arm, I would say they used something like a cattle prod. I suppose they could have gotten a violet wand and upped the amperage, but my father isn't known for his creativity. He likely would have used a cattle prod. Depending on how bad the torture was you're looking at anything from mild autonomic dysfunction to keraunoparalysis. I need to check the veins in your legs for vascular spasms."

She really liked to throw the big words around. None of it meant anything. His path was laid out and it didn't include a bunch of medical care. "I'm all right, Doc. They got me good, but I'm functioning for now. Take your shower so we can get some sleep. As soon as this storm blows over, we're getting you out of here. I need to get Erin and Nick back to the States before they do something stupid like go after your father for revenge."

A brow arched over her forehead. He liked to think of it as her judgmental brow. It was the left. Her right brow was far less holier than thou. "That's stupid? Isn't that exactly why you're here? Didn't you come after my father because of the role he played in your brother's death? Wasn't the whole point of romancing me so you could do the same thing Erin and Nick will want to do?"

He was so weary. There wasn't a lot of fight left in him and he wasn't going to waste it on fighting with the woman he loved. She might never forgive him, but he wasn't going to hurt her ever again. He leaned over and kissed her forehead. God, being close to her made him feel better. "Yes, that's what I'm talking about. That stupidity is what I'm trying to avoid for them."

"He killed your brother."

So Theo had shown her the file. He managed to straighten up and ran a hand through his hair. What a fucking mess. "I never meant for you to see that file."

"But you had it made."

"Before I knew you. Before I loved you."

She was on her feet again, getting into his space. "Don't use that word with me, Ten. You don't get to use that word with me."

He nodded. "All right. But don't think for a second it's not inside me. Just because I don't say it, doesn't mean it's not real."

She turned away from him and seemed to come to some decision. She reached down and pulled her shirt over her head. "It's not like you haven't seen it all anyway." She tossed aside her bra. "Why? Why was it stupid for us to try to save you? Do you know how horrible it was for Theo to hear that? You were awful to him."

"I was his superior officer and I was trying to teach him. I didn't know he would die on us, though I believe that was my point." The loss of Theo was an actual ache in his body. "He should never have attempted to rescue me. He went in blind."

"We thought we knew what we were doing. And we weren't blind. I know the area and Hutch did all the stuff on his computer. You know you were planning on getting into that building yourself. I don't see how what Theo planned was different. You intended to use the same people to get into the building. The only difference was we were getting you back instead of some data."

"I was going to get into a building that was guarded mostly by technological means," he explained. "The minute your father showed up, we were outgunned and Theo should have called his brother and handed over the operation to him. Theo has never been in charge in the field. The only reason he was my second was this was never supposed to end in combat."

"He couldn't leave you."

"He should have. He should have gone back to the States and let his brother deal with the problem."

Faith stood there, shaking her head as though she couldn't understand what he was saying. "I can't believe you're being so cold about this."

"Cold? You think I'm being cold? Baby, you don't want to know how I really feel about what happened out there. You don't want to hear me scream. Do you think for a second I don't want to use this storm as cover? I've already planned it out in my head. I can see the op. They'll have to leave the guards on the inside because of the weather and that will make them soft. I'll watch and the minute I can, I'll slip inside and take out whoever's in my way. No guns. They're too loud. I personally prefer a knife. More personal. If you're going to gut a man, you should have to look him in the eyes, you know. I'll sneak up the back stairs. Your father's room is at the back of the house. He'll have a few guards on him, but no one will be expecting anything tonight. They think we'll lick our wounds. So they won't expect me to slit their throats. And then, oh then, I can spend some time with your father. He owes me a debt. I could collect it tonight."

He'd played the scenario out in his head over and over. As he'd watched Faith pulling out a bullet from Nick, he'd thought about how he could mount her father's head on a wall somewhere, an eternal sign that he'd taken down the real predator.

In the end, he'd decided nothing mattered. Revenge wouldn't bring Jamie back. It wouldn't raise Des and Theo from the ground. It would simply get the rest of them killed.

When she was safe, when Faith was in the care of people he trusted, then he could go back, then he could do what he needed to do.

The only person he would risk from here on out was himself. There would be no happy McKay-Taggart job waiting for him. Not after he'd gotten a Taggart killed. There would be no little family for him or invites to dinners. He was done. He would walk away at the end of this because no matter how much he loved her, he wasn't good for anyone. He was the reason she was in the position she was in. He was going to cost her everything. Her family. Her memories. They would always be tainted now.

He'd cost her and had nothing to give in return. No family. No future. Just death and retribution.

"You sound very ruthless right now, Ten." She'd taken a step back.

"I am. Don't underestimate me, Faith. Did your father give you a file on me?"

She nodded. "I'm sure it was lies."

"And that proves how naïve you are. Don't you know the best cover is always the truth? Did he tell you I was a killer? Because I am. Did he tell you I've sent men like Theo Taggart out to die more times than I can count? Because I have. Did he tell you I'm not a man who stays? Because I won't."

"Why? You said you loved me."

"My love doesn't mean very much," he replied with all the honesty he had. "Take your shower. I'll be on the couch. We move out the minute this storm blows over."

He turned and strode into the bedroom. He could hear Faith turning on the shower.

Every muscle in his body ached. He ached.

Fuck. Why had Theo done it? Why the fuck hadn't he called his brother? Why the fuck hadn't Theo let the goddamn Chinese take him? It wasn't a fair exchange.

It was one more punishment. He got to live knowing he was alive because some shiny happy kid who could have had a future was dead. He was a piece of shit and he was walking around while Theo was lying in the rain.

He hadn't even gotten Theo's body. He'd had to tell Ian Taggart his brother had been left behind. He'd had Hutch open a line and despite the fact that it had been a rough connection, Ian had been able to hear. The op had gone to hell and Ten had lost two of Big Tag's operatives. God, he'd cost Theo his life.

"Understood." It was all Ian had said before the line had gone out. One word, but there had been an arctic chill to it.

Ian had been his only friend for so long. Ten hadn't been a particularly good friend. He didn't really understand how to be. Spending all these months at McKay-Taggart had changed him. They didn't run like the Agency. They might work in the shadows from time to time, but they didn't live in them. He finally understood why Taggart had walked away from his job.

He'd wanted a life. He'd wanted a place where he didn't treat men and women like chess pieces, deciding who to keep and lose based on how the game was going.

It was all Ten knew. It was the only place he fit.

The shower turned off. She'd moved quickly. He tried not to imagine her naked. The funny thing was he wasn't thinking about sex. His dick wasn't engaged at all. It might never work again after what they did to him. He was thinking about the feel of her skin against his, the warmth he would feel when she wrapped herself around him. He hadn't realized how cold he'd been until he met her.

He would take her to Dallas and then walk away. It was the best he could do for her. Despite the fact that he'd gotten Big Tag's brother killed, Ian would look out for Faith. He would watch over Phoebe. He would take care of the women Ten loved. They would be safe.

When the time came, Big Tag would bury him because that was the kind of man he was.

Ten wished he could be that man. He wished he could take back the last few hours. If he could go back to that one moment in time, he would have taken the lead and stepped out into the road. He would happily take the bullet that destroyed Theo.

If he had, would Faith have looked at him one last time? Would she have held his hand and cried? Would he have gone out feeling something more than bitterness and regret? Yes, that would have been a better outcome.

The door opened and she walked in wearing the T-shirt he'd left for her. It hung down to her knees. He hated the fact that she was wearing Nick's shirt. Something primal inside him wanted her wearing his, but he didn't even have that to give her. He was going to have to wear the scrubs or borrow something from Theo.

Fuck.

"You shouldn't sleep on that thing. It's too small for you." She had a towel wrapped around her head, showing off the graceful line of her neck. She looked so small in Nick's shirt. Small and fragile.

It didn't take very much imagination to replace the image of Theo with hers. Faith, silent and dead, all her goodness nothing but garbage in his wake.

"I'll survive." He wouldn't sleep anyway.

"All right." She turned to go back into the bathroom but before she made it to the door she whirled around, a stubborn look on her face. "No. No, it's not all right. Take off your shirt, Tennessee. Don't even try to argue with me. I'm the top in this particular situation and I won't let you order me around."

"This situation?"

"Yes, the situation where I'm the doctor and you're the patient," she explained. "You've just spent days being tortured. I'm going to take a look at you whether you like it or not."

Somehow the thought of her putting impersonal hands on him seemed cruel. "I'm fine. I don't need attention, Faith. I want you to save your energy for someone who needs it."

"Needs it? Or deserves it? I'm starting to figure out a few things about you. This whole tough guy thing isn't about you looking macho."

He felt his eyes widen in surprise. "I don't know what movie you're watching, darlin', but I got my ass handed to me. No. I am not trying to look macho or preserve my masculine mystique so you won't think less of me. I'm not going to give you a rundown of all the ways your father cut me down to size. You've been through enough."

She got down on her knees in front of him. "And so have you. I wasn't accusing you of being arrogant. The opposite. You won't accept care from me because you don't think you deserve it. Guess what? That means nothing to me. I'm the doctor and everyone gets my care. I swore an oath a long time ago and I take it seriously. So take off your shirt and pants. I want to see everything."

"Faith," he began.

She frowned at him. "I won't touch you if you don't want me to. Well, I mean not in a sexual way."

"What does that mean?"

"It means I don't know how I feel. It means everything is twisted up and the world kind of sucks and I know our time is almost up. It means let me take care of you. Not because you think you deserve it but because I need to do something. Please."

How was he supposed to argue with that? With aching arms, he pulled the shirt over his head and let her see the damage.

* * * *

Faith had to take a deep breath. Ten's body had been covered in scars before, but he had some new ones. Little circles of burned flesh surrounded by raised welts. He had to be in pain, but she was starting to think Ten was the masochist in their relationship.

She forced that thought aside. They didn't have a relationship. At least not one that would ever last. She couldn't be that girl, couldn't be the sad pathetic thing who ran into the arms of the man who had lied to her, used her.

It was easier to focus on the burns. "Someone cleaned these."

He nodded. "Your sister. She's quite the doc herself. I didn't understand why at the time. I kind of thought they were going to kill me so cleaning me up and making sure the wounds didn't get infected seemed counterproductive. Now I know they were saving me for MSS."

Despite her sister's efforts, all the physical activity of the evening had caused a few of the welts to open. She reached into the small first aid kit they'd brought along and took out the antiseptic. It would hurt, but any man who'd taken this and not gone insane could take the sting she was about to give him. Besides, if she was right, Tennessee likely welcomed the pain.

He didn't think he was worth saving, and now he was in a deep dive over Theo's death. She'd felt it herself, but it wasn't until she'd really listened to the man that she realized Ten's grief was actually guilt.

He hadn't expected them to come for him. He'd expected to die.

Despite all the pain he'd caused her, she had to acknowledge that he'd given her joy, too. Nothing had felt as real as making love with this man.

Why hadn't he fought the night her father had taken him? There had been a balcony to his left. It was entirely possible he could have made it. He was smart and strong. He was quick and beyond capable. This was a man who had been in tight spots before and fought his way out.

Yet when her father had come for him, he hadn't fought at all. In fact, he'd been polite to the man who had killed his brother.

Somehow, it didn't jibe with the reports she'd read on him.

He winced a little, but otherwise made no sound as she cleaned his wounds. Like Nick, who had been far too traumatized by seeing his lover killed to care about his pain.

How much trauma could a soul take before it shut down? Before it gave over and began to think the trauma was normal? The body often adapted in a search for survival. The soul did the same. Ten had come to accept pain was a way of life and that he deserved it.

The day had been so long. She wasn't certain of anything except that she couldn't let him sleep on this tiny couch. And she couldn't sleep without knowing why he hadn't fought.

"Your sister gave me some kind of drug," he said quietly. "You talked about your patients at the clinic. You know, the ones who received the vaccine. They had memory issues, right?"

She studied the veins of his legs. In extreme cases, electrical torture could cause vascular spasms and disrupt blood flow, but it looked like her father had been leaving that for the Chinese. "Yes. They thought more time had passed than actually had. After the episode, their perceptions of time went back to normal. Did she tell you what she was giving you?"

He shook his head. "No, but I know I got more than one dose, and apparently at some point I blacked out completely because I don't remember putting on these clothes. I vaguely remember being someplace white. There was a bright light and she was standing over me with a clipboard. She was talking about how well my system handled the drug."

Bitch. She had a clinic down there for her experiments, but she hadn't helped Theo and Des. She hated her sister in that moment, but she needed to know more. "How long do you think you were there?"

"I know it wasn't more than a two full days, but Faith, I swear it was forever. I've been in this position before. I was trained to be able to take this kind of torture, but when I was on that drug, I had no control and it dragged on and on. I couldn't meditate, couldn't force my mind to go anywhere else."

She sat back, her stomach clenching. "She couldn't. It's not real."

"What's not real?"

"What you're talking about." What had her sister done? "It's called time dilation. It's a future tech thing, a theory. They talk about it in science fiction. I know I've heard some people are making strides in memory manipulation, but we're supposed to be years away from something like this."

"Wait. I've heard of it. The Agency sent out some information on potentially dangerous technology being developed. One was a time dilation drug." He shook his head with a rueful grimace. "It's supposed to trick the brain into thinking more time has passed than actually has. I can now say that it's a very effective torture technique. Quite frankly, I'm surprised I'm not more seriously injured."

"You wouldn't have to be physically. Your brain gave you the pain. I can't believe she's doing this. She tested her drug on my patients."

"It doesn't shock me at all. I suspect your sister is doing what her company wants her to do. Kronberg is suspected of being in a group called The Collective. It's a loose association of some of the world's richest men. Think of it as a cartel, but they're aiding each other in business interests. They're a 'by any means necessary' kind of group."

"The Collective? I've heard that word before."

Ten sat forward. "Your father has mentioned The Collective? To you?"

She searched her memory. That word had caught. It was something she'd heard her father say a few times before. He wasn't as careful as he thought he was or he'd trusted that she would never understand what he meant.

"He kept a log. He called it his collection. Maybe it isn't the same thing. He would joke that he had a collection. It was names in a notebook. I was a kid. He didn't care that I was in the room. Hope and I would play in his office all the time when we were out of school, and I remember him telling me it was important to keep lists." She couldn't get the idea out of her head. Her father always had backups. He always had a way out.

She needed to find that way out and block it.

Otherwise, Tennessee Smith would have one more thing to hate himself over. He would kill her father and it would hurt him, like another wound on his soul.

She might not be able to be with him, but she could give him respite this once.

"Don't worry about it anymore." Ten brushed back her hair.

"Why did you come here?"

"Like I said, don't worry about it." He sat back.

"I want to know what you were really looking for." After everything she'd been through tonight, she felt like she deserved a debrief.

"I think your father's documentation is on a computer in the compound I was held in. I think I'll find all the evidence I need to take both your father and a good portion of The Collective down."

He was wrong. "He wouldn't put it on a computer. Never. Don't get me wrong. There might be something there, but it's going to be in code and he won't keep that on a computer. He would use offshore accounts and write them down. In longhand."

Ten's eyes closed briefly. "It no longer matters. I don't want you to worry about it. It's something I'll take care of."

She was sure he would. He would do whatever was necessary. She finished cleaning the last blister and sat back. "I'm so sorry about Theo. I know you cared about him."

Erin would be devastated. For all her words about breaking up with him, Faith knew Erin loved the man. They'd been happy together and now Erin was alone.

She knew the feeling. It was how she'd felt after she'd learned Ten had lied to her, except there was no recourse. Theo was gone. Erin couldn't yell at him. She couldn't scream and vow revenge for her broken heart. All Erin had now was sorrow.

There was no comfort for her friend. Erin hadn't even looked at her earlier. She'd stared through Faith like she was seeing something else.

Suddenly the lies didn't seem so big anymore. The betrayal a bit more insignificant. It wouldn't work in the long run, but for now they both needed comfort. The storm was raging outside. There was nothing more to do for tonight.

"You won't be comfortable on the couch. Please sleep on the bed."

His lips turned down. "I'll be all right."

"I won't. Look, Ten. Once we get back to reality, I know we're going to go our separate ways, but I do understand what you were trying to do. I wish you hadn't taken it to a physical level."

"I needed to be able to protect you."

She didn't buy that line for a minute. "Don't bullshit me."

"Fine, I thought getting into bed with you was the fastest way to get on this island."

Honesty hurt, but she'd asked for it. "If you had sat me down and laid out the evidence the way Hutch did, I would have helped you."

"Would you?" His eyes narrowed as he eased back into his shirt. "Let's say I show up one day out of the blue and lay out evidence against your father and sister. You're telling me you would have chosen to help me without ever talking to them? That's what I needed. I needed to blindside your dad. He couldn't see me coming, though of course he did in the end. You wouldn't have given them a call to ask 'hey Pops, you been selling troop information for cash? You working with corporations to protect their interests at the cost of indigenous people?' You take one look at that evidence and sell them both out without a single qualm?"

What would she have done if he'd walked in cold and laid out a case against her family? He wouldn't have had the information about the vaccines. She hadn't even known about those at the time. She wouldn't have watched her father cart her lover off to torture him. All of those things had led her to believe the evidence. If he'd walked in off the streets, she very likely would have told him to blow it out his ass. "All right. I would have called them. But you didn't need to sleep with me. You could have sent Erin in. She could have come down to Houston with me and I would have invited her and Theo down here. I would have believed her in the end."

"I doubt that, Doc." He sounded so tired. His head fell back as though he couldn't stand to hold it up a second longer. "And Erin couldn't be with you to protect you, though that wasn't my primary mission in the beginning. You take a lover once a year. From what I can tell, you don't have a truly emotional relationship with the man. Was I supposed to bring another civilian into this situation? It's a good plan, by the way. Taking the lover. The way you work, you don't have time for commitments. I get that. We're more alike than you think."

She liked sex. She wasn't going to apologize for it. Ten was right. It was easier to find a Dom to spend time with than it was to become attached when she knew she was going back out in the field. Some people in society might call her names for it, but they could bite her ass for all she cared. She'd learned a long time ago that what society thought didn't mean shit.

So why was she worried about what people would think of her? It had gone through her head that she couldn't be with this man again because everyone would think she was pathetic.

Who cared what everyone thought? Since when did outside voices get to dictate her life?

"I got emotional with you," she admitted.

His eyes opened, the hard line of his jaw softening. "Like I said, we're very alike, Faith. When I started this mission, I only cared about one thing. I wanted revenge. I intended to sleep with you as a way to get to your father. In the beginning, I didn't care what happened to you. You were a means to an end and getting into your bed was the quickest and easiest way to get what I wanted. If I could have gotten access to your father's compound some other way, I would have. Right up until those three weeks."

"When I was in Germany?"

He nodded slowly, as though the motion was difficult for him. "Maybe everything would have been different if we'd met and fallen into bed together. Maybe if that had happened I would have kept it purely physical, but I had to talk to you for three weeks without touching you. For the first time in my life, I had to…be intimate with a woman. Not in bed, but in other ways."

She could imagine a man as lovely as Ten could pretty much sleep with anyone he wanted to. He wouldn't have to charm women. They would fall into his arms, but she would bet they wouldn't touch him emotionally. With her other lovers, she generally chose them because they had a lot in common. They were almost always in the medical profession and when they weren't playing, they were talking business.

She'd been forced to talk to Ten about other things, to push past her own surface and reach deeper, give him more, find the things they had in common. "Those three weeks meant a lot to me, too. How many lies did you tell? We talked about the things we like. Did you make that up, too?"

She wanted to know the real man. She needed to know what had been false. It was a burning need.

"No. I really do love to read mysteries and I have a weird affection for movies with dinosaurs in them. I like to cook. It calms me. I like you. That's pretty much a list of all the things I like in this world. Like I said, if I'd had an easier path, I would have taken it right up to those three weeks, and then it didn't matter anymore."

"What do you mean?"

His gaze caught hers. "I was going to have you, Faith. I'd never wanted a woman the way I wanted you."

When he looked at her like that, she couldn't think straight. "I don't know that I believe you."

"Why would I lie to you now? I promised never to lie to you again and I won't. It's why I told you, well, that stuff I told you when your father came for me. I don't want to lie again. I want you out of this mess. When you're safe, I'll be able to breathe again."

That stuff he'd told her had been him saying I love you. She wanted to believe him so badly. Even when her heart had been battered, she'd wanted something between them. "Why didn't you fight when my father came for you?"

Ten sighed and sat up. "Because he killed your mother and if he had to, I think he would kill you. He'll do what it takes to protect his secrets, and you need to remember that. Until he's dead or behind bars, he's dangerous to you."

"You could have tried to get away."

He brought his hand up to brush against her cheek. "He's a smart man, darlin'. He would have known how to bring me back. All he would have to do is threaten you and I would have been back, so I was just being lazy in the end. I cut out all that useless running since I couldn't leave you like that."

Tears threatened because his words were so sweet. "I don't understand, Ten."

"I know," he replied, a sadness inflecting his tone. "Which is why I want you out. I want you to go back to Dallas and let McKay-Taggart protect you until this business is done. Then you get your life back. You can go back to your clinic."

She could. It was what she needed to do. Once all of this was over, that clinic would be all she had. When she thought about it, it was really all she'd ever had.

What did he have? What would Ten go back to after everything was done?

Something banged against the side of the house, making Faith nearly jump out of her skin.

Ten reached for her hand. "Hey, it's all right. It's only the storm. Hutch has the whole place wired with video. Even if the power goes out, the security system and those monitors are on a generator. We're safe here."

Only because her father had no idea where they were. "Once the storm blows over, he'll come looking."

"It won't only be him. Those Chinese agents won't let me go

easily. I'm not the only one who wants a little revenge. But we're safe for tonight. According to the reports, the storm should blow over by tomorrow afternoon. You'll take off tomorrow evening."

"I will?" She'd thought *they* were leaving, but then that had been Theo's plan and he wasn't here anymore. Ten was back in charge and it looked like the plans had changed.

"Yes. You and Erin and the rest of the team are heading back to Dallas. I have some things I need to clean up here."

There was distance in his voice that made her question if tomorrow would be the last time she would see him. "You're not coming back, are you?"

"No. I won't go back to Dallas again. I broke those ties by getting Theo killed. I'm not going to be a reminder to everyone of what they lost."

"Theo made the choice to go after you. You didn't get him killed. You didn't fire the bullet and you didn't order him to go to that compound." As far as she could tell, all Ten had done during his rescue was yell that he shouldn't have been rescued at all.

"But it was my op. It doesn't matter. He died on my watch and that's all that counts. Ian will watch over you until the objective is achieved, and then you can go wherever you want. I'm going to make it safe for you."

But he wouldn't be with her.

The lights flickered and then died. His hand gripped hers. "It's all right. It's actually better for us to go dark. Just in case."

Just in case her father's men had braved the storm to look for them. Just in case the Chinese agents were out there right now. She'd been informed that this was the safest location they could find and all the locals believed it was empty this time of year. They only had to survive a few hours and then she wouldn't see him again.

"Come to bed with me."

A low chuckle accompanied his movement. In the shadows, she watched him struggle to his feet. "You've never been safer from a man's advances than tonight, darlin'. I'm a little worried your father gave me an electrical vasectomy. Can they do that?"

She gasped. She'd told him to take off his pants, but he'd seemed fine. "I need to look at you."

He huffed a little as he maneuvered them to the bed. "No, you do not. I'm hoping it was like the rest of what he did. Better than it seemed. It was the drugs that made the pain worse. I want to sleep, Faith. I want to hold you. Can you let me do that?"

She shouldn't. He was going to leave her and no amount of anger would mask the heartache she would feel the last time she looked at him. Still, she needed his comfort, needed to give him some as well.

She curled against his body, looking for a spot that wouldn't hurt, but he merely dragged her close. He wrapped her arm around his torso.

"I want to feel you, Faith. I don't care about the pain. I want to know you're here with me."

She put her head on his chest and listened to the sound of his heart. Strong. Steady. Alive. No matter what her father had put him through, he was still with her.

It was enough for now.

CHAPTER EIGHTEEN

Faith stepped out into the hallway, her eyes adjusting to the dark. It was long past time for dawn, but there was only a dim light illuminating the walkway. She couldn't sleep. She'd left Tennessee, pulling away with reluctance, but she was so thirsty. There had been no little cups in the bathroom, but she'd seen bottles of water in the fridge earlier. She would slip away and grab one before Ten knew she was gone. He needed his rest after what he'd been through. He had more scars now, his body proving to be a map of the man.

She'd lain in his arms for hours, comforted by his nearness.

What was she thinking? He'd lied to her, used her, and she couldn't work up the will to hate him. Not after tonight. Not after everything they'd been through.

She knew how precious life was, held it in her hands time and time again, but it was different when it was someone she cared about. Theo had been her friend. She couldn't think of him as anything less. The way they met no longer mattered. Theo was gone and she would miss him.

When Ten was gone, she would mourn him. Likely she would mourn him to her dying day.

How long would it be before she tried again? She walked toward the kitchen, the problem on her mind. Would she try to find another lover while she knew Ten was still in the world? It was only a matter of time before some job he took put him in a dangerous position. She couldn't imagine that Ten would live to see old age. He was careful, but he placed himself in mortal danger again and again. At some point he would lose.

She wouldn't even know he was gone. Likely no one would tell her. She would simply spend the rest of her life wondering where he was and if anyone was taking care of him. She would continue with her work, the years going by in a blur of service.

Did she want to live her life that way? When she really thought about it, was honest with herself, she'd gotten into this type of medicine because she knew she could never compete with Hope's brilliance. Her sister was a master surgeon and when she'd decided to put her mind to research, there apparently wasn't anything she couldn't tackle. Oh, she was evil as fuck, but so smart Faith had always been in her shadow. Her father had been a larger than life figure, one of those people who moved the world strictly on his say so.

Faith had wanted something of her own and she'd found it in the far reaches of the world. She'd told herself it was enough, but there was a restlessness that had begun the minute she'd laid eyes on Ten Smith.

Was she going to let him go? It was really up to her. Yes, he was the Dom, but this went past play and into real life. This was their relationship, and he had no idea how to have one. She was the mentor in this case and she was allowing emotion and pain to inform her decisions.

She'd been angry, and anger was really good at clouding judgment.

She'd made the one mistake she'd promised she wouldn't. She'd reacted instead of acting. She'd allowed the actions of someone else to change who she was—who she wanted to be.

Tennessee didn't understand what it meant to have a relationship because he'd never had one. Life trained a person and Ten's training had taught him that he was expendable, that unless he was bringing something important to the table, he had no place there.

There was a crack of lightning and a ghostly figure was illuminated. Faith gasped and took a step back before she realized who it was.

Erin. She was standing in front of the big bay windows in the den. They were supposed to be shuttered, but one had come open and Erin was looking out over the ocean, the sky cracking around it.

"She blew out the candles," a low voice said.

Faith turned to her right and saw Hutch sitting at a table, his laptop off for once. He was sitting there in the dark keeping watch. "She hasn't slept?"

It had been almost ten hours since they'd lost Theo. The storm was calming, though there was still plenty of thunder and lighting. They wouldn't leave for Dallas until they had the cover of night. They should all be resting and trying to recuperate.

He shook his head. "No. Not for a second and I don't trust her not to try something stupid. So I haven't slept either."

Perhaps it was time to start acting like the person she wanted to be. After everything that had happened, no one would blame her for turning cynical. She could turn her back on the world and everyone who heard her story would understand. In some ways, it would be easier. Scar tissue could make a body tough. It didn't feel pain the way healthy tissue did. She could let her wounds scar over and not feel again.

Or she could be something more.

"I can't sleep either. I'll stay up with her."

Hutch shook his head. "Sorry, Doc. I put my money on her in a fight. Hell, she could probably take me, but at least I'm trained."

"I'm not going anywhere, Hutch." Erin didn't move from her spot.

"Which is exactly what you would say if you were going somewhere," he replied with a sigh.

"Please. Let me talk to her alone." Faith found one of the candles Erin had apparently snuffed out and relit it with the box of matches on Hutch's desk. The room was filled with soft light as she lit a few more.

"All right but if she leaves this house, Ten's going to…" Hutch stopped as though realizing what he was about to say. Too soon. It was far too soon to joke about killing anyone. "Please don't leave, Erin."

"I'm not going anywhere. I don't know if you've noticed but there's a storm outside. We can't get back to Dallas until it breaks."

Erin's words came out in a monotone.

"I'm going to put on a pot of coffee and pray there's a Diet Coke somewhere in this place." Hutch nodded. "Call out if you need anything."

He moved toward the doors that led to the kitchen, and she was alone with Erin.

"You got something you want to say, Doc?"

There was the tough girl. Faith was fairly certain the tough girl wasn't an act. There was a hard core to the woman that formed her personality. More scars. She wasn't sure where they'd come from in Erin's case, but now she could see them.

Scars could be removed. Oh, they'd try to come back and some people formed them more easily than others, but they could be cleaned away for new tissue to grow in the hopes that the patient would regain sensation, feeling.

"I'm not leaving." Erin finally turned around, her arms crossed over her chest. More protection. More defense. "Everyone thinks I'm going to do something stupid, but I won't. We've had enough stupidity today."

"I'm so sorry about Theo."

Erin shrugged. "Yeah, well, he was stupid. I believe I told him what would happen. No one ever fucking listens to me."

Her voice was flat, as though she was talking about Theo losing at some board game instead of his life. This was how Erin would deal with Theo's death. She would shut down, close it off, try to make herself believe it didn't matter because he'd been the only person in the world she could be vulnerable with. With Theo gone, Erin would lose her connection to the world because she didn't make friends easily.

Like Ten. Like Faith herself.

She couldn't leave Erin alone. She couldn't.

She moved closer. She had to be careful because Erin wasn't going to like this. "I forgive you."

A single brow arched as Erin stared at her. "For what? For lying to you? That's cool, Doc, but you should really be more pissed about that. Hey, I guess if Theo dropping means I get a free pass I should go with it, but you really don't have to. I'd do it again. I'll do whatever the mission takes, and if that means serving your pretty ass up to my boss, I'll do it. That's who I am."

Poor Erin. Most people would see a cold, hard woman standing in front of them, but Faith saw someone who hurt so much she couldn't acknowledge the pain. It was the most dangerous of all wounds. The one that didn't register. The patient would look down, see the gaping hole in their body, but the brain wasn't capable of handling that kind of pain. It would misfire, attempt to spare the body in its last moments. Pain unfortunately had its place. Pain could cleanse. If a body could still feel pain, it was capable of healing as well.

"I'm sorry about Theo." Tears had formed. God, it felt good. Faith had been numb. She'd been stuck in that moment and it hadn't been real. None of it had been real, but it happened. He'd died. Ten had been tortured. Her father was a monster. It was real and she had to face it.

For the first time, Erin's face changed from the bland, blank expression to something like trepidation. "Good for you, Doc. Why don't you go cry somewhere else? I want to be alone."

Erin would be alone for the rest of her life if someone didn't break through to her. Faith wasn't sure it was her place, but she seemed to be Erin's only real friend beyond Theo. Erin laughed and joked with others, but she'd been real with Faith. It hadn't all been a lie and Faith wouldn't throw it away because it hadn't come in the perfect form.

"I'm so sorry about Theo." She could barely see Erin as she walked toward her.

Erin backed away. "Don't you do this to me."

"You can't cry so I'll do it for you. Because we're friends. You were right. I was mad at you and Ten because I loved you." She stopped in front of Erin, searching her friend's face. "I do love you and I'm so sorry about Theo."

Erin flushed, turning pink and then red, her eyes brimming. She bit her words out, anger palpable. "Don't you do this to me."

Faith put her arms around Erin and let go. She cried. She cried for Erin and for Theo and everyone who loved him. She cried for Tennessee, who would never forgive himself. She cried for herself, for the family she'd lost.

Erin stood there for a long moment and then pushed her away.

A scream shook the walls, louder than the storm outside. Erin screamed, the sound coming from her soul.

Faith stood back and watched as Erin lost it. She picked up a lamp and tossed it across the room, brought her fists down on the table, breaking it. She pounded against the wall, her skin becoming bloody.

And finally, she dropped to her knees, tears replacing the anger. "He fucking promised me."

This time when Faith dropped down to join her, Erin reached out, grasping her like a lifeline. Erin squeezed her tight.

"He promised me."

Theo had promised her forever. Faith had heard him when they thought she wasn't around. Theo would pull Erin in and kiss her senseless and then he would tell her he would love her forever.

"I know." Faith held on to her, let her friend nearly crack her bones as she wept. "I know, sweetie."

There was nothing to say, no words that would truly comfort Erin. The only thing Faith could offer was her warmth, her love.

"I loved him. I loved him so much. I didn't want to love him," Erin said, her voice hoarse. "I didn't want to love him. Do you think he knows? God, Faith. I didn't tell him. He told me he loved me every day and I didn't tell him because I was too afraid."

"He knew." Faith smoothed Erin's hair back. Her mother had done this when she was a child and Faith had cried. She would smooth her hair back and rock gently. Faith started to move, as though her muscles remembered the rhythm of comfort. "He knew you loved him. He was so proud you loved him."

"I don't know why. I don't understand anything." She settled her head against Faith's shoulder and a long shudder went through Erin's body. "I already miss him. I can't stand it. I can't."

Faith let Erin cry, the moment lengthening, softening. The hardness she'd felt in Erin was gone and there was nothing but grief left.

Grief was good. Grief was true.

Faith looked up and every man in the house was staring at them. Brody and Nick had come out of their room. Hutch stood in the kitchen entryway. And Ten was staring at her, his eyes as soft as she'd ever seen them.

The knock on the door forced them all to turn and suddenly every man in the room had a gun out.

Erin stood, shoving Faith behind her and trying to wipe her eyes with one hand.

Brody went to the door, his back ramrod straight.

Hutch was back at his laptop. "Open it. It's fine. If those three are here to kill us, I'll lay down my arms and let them."

Brody opened the door and three large figures were standing there. They each wore raincoats and had backpacks with them. It took her a minute, but she finally recognized Ian Taggart.

She glanced over and saw Ten's shoulders slump.

It looked like his time as head of this operation was over.

* * * *

Ten set down his gun. He'd picked it up from the nightstand when he'd heard that horrible screaming. He'd known someone was in terrible pain and he'd sprinted in to try to save whoever it was, but nothing could spare Erin her pain.

He'd expected Erin's grief to go deep. He'd never thought he'd see her cry, but Faith had somehow managed it. Faith had gotten the soldier to let herself be human for once, to hold on to someone because the pain of losing the man she'd loved was too much.

He wasn't going to survive losing Faith. Walking away from her was going to be the hardest thing he'd ever done.

Then don't, asshole. Stop the martyr shit and be a real live boy for once.

Now that his brother was back in his head, it seemed he wouldn't go away. But the reasons he should leave her were many and varied, and one of them was now standing in the hallway.

Three of them really. Ian hadn't come alone. Sean and Case were with him. The Taggart brothers had come for one of their own.

Case pulled off the rain jacket he was wearing. It dropped to the ground and he walked up to Erin, standing right in front of her. "I've never seen you cry." His voice was utterly hollow and then his head dropped. "It's real. Oh, god. It's real."

He was shaking as Erin put her arms around him. Theo's twin. The two people in the world who had loved him most tried to comfort each other. Faith had made that happen. Without Faith, Erin likely would be cold and shut down and Case would have followed suit, the two separate and alone in their grief.

Big Tag looked grim as he stepped up. "Could I talk to you alone? Sean, can you make us all some coffee? I think we're going to need it."

Ten nodded. "There's an office back here we can talk in."

"Good. Hutch, call my wife and let her know we got in all right so she doesn't have to search the Atlantic for my body so she could pull my balls off and make rattles for the girls. Charlie wasn't happy about me coming here. She shows her worry through violence." He stepped away and held a hand out to the Russian. "Nikolai, please accept my profound condolences. I know she was more than a member of your team. Damon is already getting everything settled. Her family will be informed and her cover kept intact. I'm so sorry."

Nick nodded, his face blank. "I thank you. She was good woman. And your brother will be missed."

A muscle in Tag's cheek jumped, the only sign that he was emotional. "Thank you. Ten, let's talk."

Ten looked back at Faith, who had stepped away, giving Erin a moment with Case. She looked so vulnerable standing there. "Are you going to be okay?"

Faith nodded. "I'll help out in the kitchen. Maybe I can convince everyone to eat a little something. Are we still leaving when the storm blows over?"

"Yes." Ten and Tag replied at the same time.

Tag was about to have his ass and Ten would give it to him. If Tag wanted to beat the shit out of him and leave his body here for MSS, Ten would go along with that plan.

He led Tag back to the office and lit a few candles. Even though there was some light coming in now, it was still dark enough to need them.

"I should have known a little thing like a hurricane wouldn't stop Ian Taggart."

Ian sighed. "I have a friend at NOAA. He owed me and when he found out why we needed to get here, he offered us a ride in the big bird."

The National Oceanic and Atmospheric Administration tracked

hurricanes and tropical storms. They often flew straight into the storms, taking readings and measurements. "You must have gotten to Miami quickly. And how did you land? God, tell me you didn't parachute in through a tropical storm."

He wouldn't put it past Tag. He was larger than life and could move mountains when he wanted to.

Tag sat down in one of the big chairs, but he looked anything but comfortable. "The storm took a turn to the west. The east side of the island got a little rain but none of the really damaging winds. We were able to land on a private airstrip. There was a Humvee waiting for us. I still have contacts in the Agency. There are people there who are worried about you."

"Yeah, I bet they are." He bet they would love to know where he was. Maybe MSS wouldn't get a shot. Maybe Big Tag would turn him over to the Agency and he could get tortured by someone who spoke his language. That was a plus.

"Tell me what happened," Ian ordered. "I've already read Hutch's report, but I want to know what happened to my brother. I need to hear it from you."

Ten leaned against the desk. Despite the sleep he'd gotten, he was infinitely weary as he recounted what happened. He told Tag everything because the man deserved to know exactly how badly Ten had fucked up. He included the idiocy of not answering his damn phone because he was far too busy trying to get Faith in bed.

Though he wasn't sure if it would have changed anything. Even if he'd gotten the text, he likely wouldn't have left Faith there without knowing she would be safe.

Big Tag looked up, his eyes grim. "Theo was already in the compound when Chelsea called. According to Hutch, he was given the intelligence that MSS was on their way."

"He thought he could save me." Theo had been naïve.

"He should have left you. He should have let them take you." Big Tag was anything but.

"Damn straight."

Tag's eyes narrowed on Ten. "You know why I say that, right?"

"Yeah." Ten would have done the same thing. Hell, Ten wasn't even really part of the team.

Tag shook his head. "I've kept in touch with my Chinese

contacts. I called in several favors after Chelsea told me what was going on. I knew the time and date of your expected arrival in Beijing thirty minutes after Chelsea found out about the auction. I would have had a team in place and ready to take you back, but my brother didn't call in. He disobeyed direct orders. Tennessee, we've had our differences but I made my way down here as fast as I could because I had to settle my brothers' minds."

He understood that. "Case. You had to give Case some closure."

Tag nodded. "Yes. Case and Sean and I need to find Theo's body. We can't leave him or Des here. I came here because I thought I would find Erin in a catatonic state where no one could touch her."

"Faith got to her. Even after everything we've done to Faith, she still reached out when Erin needed her."

"Which is precisely why you should do the smart thing and never let that woman go again." Tag stood up and put a hand on Ten's shoulder. "And I came here for you, brother. I came here to tell you that this was not your fault. If there's one thing I know it's that you'll martyr yourself in a heartbeat if I let you. You would never have been okay with a rescue mission. I'm not stupid. Theo planned this on his own. He made a conscious decision to not call in and get orders."

The thought of Tag blaming his brother made him sick to his stomach. "He thought he was helping me."

"He was being reckless, and I knew he had that streak in him but I put him in the field as a second. You fought me. You wanted Erin, but I overrode you." Tag massaged between his eyes. "I wanted to push Theo. Case is solid. He's an obvious leader, but Theo takes too many chances. God. He took too many chances. I can't believe I'm referring to my brother in the past tense." He took a steadying breath before he continued. "Erin would have taken control and called in. None of this happens if you had your choice of a second in command."

"Please don't blame him. He was a kid trying to do what he thought was right."

"I know. I wasn't blaming him. I blame me. This is on me, Ten. I need you to understand that I don't blame you. I know what you've been thinking. I knew it from the moment you called and told me the news, and I knew I had to get down here before anyone did something stupid. Including you, Ten."

He couldn't quite be offended by the remark. After all, Tag wasn't punching him in the face and he still had a few of those left. "I'm shipping everyone out tomorrow. I'll handle things from here. I'll help you get our people back and then you're out of this. I'll come at the problem from a different angle. I need to figure out where the money is and how he's scrubbing it."

Tag chuckled. "You think you're in charge?"

"I think this was my mission and I'm taking it back." He wasn't going to risk anyone else.

"No."

Ten frowned. "What's that supposed to mean?"

"It's generally accepted as a way to communicate negativity. Your torture seems to have rattled your thinking process, though it was always a little off, brother. No means fuck no, you're not in charge."

So arrogant. "I get that you want revenge."

"I don't want revenge. I want justice. And that's where we differ. That's why I'm staying in charge and your ass is going to be on a plane back to the States in a few hours, so start packing."

"You can't dismiss me, Tag. You're not my boss."

"No. I'm your family and that means making decisions for you when you're incapacitated. You recently came out of thirty-six hours' worth of torture. You watched two team members die. You're not capable of thinking straight. That's the very definition of incapacitated, and if you don't agree with me, I'll take it a step further. I'll hold you down, dose you up—yes, I brought sedatives—and you'll still be on that plane. Charlie's waiting for you. She's got the guest room all set up."

Ten felt his jaw drop. "Are you trying to tell me you would hold me hostage?"

"I prefer to think of it as giving you time to come to the proper conclusions about the rest of your life. Don't discount the guest room. It's got a really nice bed and I've been told the restraints don't even chafe." Tag turned to him. "Or you could do the right thing and take door number two."

Ten knew he should be pissed. Tag was taking control where he shouldn't.

Or should he? If Tag actually cared about him, maybe this was his place. Ten wasn't stupid. He knew what door number two was.

"I don't have anything to offer her."

Tag's lips quirked up in a sad smile. "That's the funny thing about women. The good ones don't require anything."

This was the part Ten didn't understand. "I don't get it. I don't get the exchange. I know I can make her orgasm. She can pay for that. I don't trust the rest of it."

"Ask her. Ask her what she wants from you. Tell her what you need from her. I think you're going to find you have what she wants."

He didn't see how. "I don't even have a job."

"The good news is she does," Tag replied. "She's way smarter than you."

"That she is. She deserves better."

Tag's face twisted in a grimace. "Don't tell her that. Women don't like that shit. Let me give you some advice. 'Yes, baby.' That's all you need to say when you're not on a dungeon floor. Now when you're playing, feel free to get as nasty and caveman-like as possible, but in the real world, our two words for survival are 'yes' and 'baby.' Tell her yes, Ten. Walk away from this. I need one fucking good thing to come out of this. Look, if you don't love her…"

"I love her." He wasn't going to hide the fact. "I didn't know what it meant until I met her."

Tag sighed, a weary sound. "Then that's my one good thing. Because you know this is really all about me."

It was never about him. It might seem like it, but almost everything the man did was about helping someone else. "I don't understand you."

Tag stood up and put a hand on his shoulder. "You don't have to. All you have to do is follow my advice. Take your woman. You think you need revenge, but justice is so much more important. A really smart woman taught me that. Go home with Faith and we'll handle McDonald together. We won't let him get away with it, but we need to do this in a way that won't get us killed and bring more grief to the people we love. I've got Li on the money trail. We put together a solid case including the corporations funding him, bring in the press, and take them all down. Once McDonald is in prison, well, karma tends to take over there."

Karma being Big Tag. "I thought this wasn't about vengeance."

"Justice first, and then a little revenge is good for the soul," Tag said. "But nothing is more important than her. It can't be if you're going to be her husband."

Faith's husband. The idea that he'd once thought of proposing to Dawn turned his stomach. It was nearly sacrilegious to think of another woman. Faith was the one. It was stupid, and before he'd met her he hadn't believed in "the one." Probably no man did until he found her.

"I don't deserve her."

"I don't deserve Charlie and yet I have her and I'm grateful for her. So be grateful your lady has no taste and marry her before she changes her mind. Marry her and know that no matter what happens, you both have a home in Dallas." Tag was quiet for a moment. His voice was hoarse with emotion when he spoke again. "I can't lose another brother, Ten."

And that was reason enough. He owed Ian Taggart the world. He owed Faith his devotion. "I'll come home then and I'll bring Faith with me. Tag...I would do anything for you."

Ian gave him a manly hug. "Stand by me while I bury Theo. It's going to be a rough couple of months. I have to watch after Erin and Case."

"I'll be there." He realized something. He wasn't the only one. "We'll be there."

He would win Faith over. He would keep her. One good thing. It was all a man needed. One good thing could make the rest of life seem not so bad.

He stepped back, giving Ian his space. "I'll stay as long as you need me to, but eventually Faith's going to want to go back to Africa."

Ian nodded. "McKay-Taggart Africa. I like it."

"Hey, Knight got to put his name on it. McKay-Taggart Smith and you've got a deal."

Tag nodded. "I like to keep it in the family. Now go and get your girl. She's probably making Sean crazy by now. I want you two out of here by tonight. Sean and I are going to do some recon to find out what they did with our people."

With their bodies. "Ian, if I can help..."

"You're twelve kinds of fucked up. Go home and rest and heal.

307

Phoebe's all freaked out. She'll be over here if you don't get home soon. I'm sending you out with Faith, and the rest of us will be back as soon as we can. I'm letting Nick and Erin stay if they want. They deserve to help get their people back. I need Brody with us. You're injured and Faith's a civilian, so you two get to go home. Check in on my girls while I'm gone."

His girls. Ian's wife and daughters were the most precious things in his world. The fact that he was trusting Ten with them said something. "I will."

Ten moved to the door with newfound purpose. He had a job to do. He had people to protect. Suddenly, all that revenge didn't seem so necessary.

All his brother had ever wanted was for him to be happy. Jamie wouldn't have wanted vengeance. It was past time to honor his brothers. All of them.

"And Ten?"

He turned at the door. "Yes?"

"I'll take that two grand in cash."

For the first time since that awful moment in Faith's bedroom, Ten smiled. Tag had bet him two grand that he would end up married and damned if he wasn't. "She still has to say yes."

"Somehow, I think you'll work that out."

Ten walked out into the hallway. It would be best two grand he'd ever spent.

CHAPTER NINETEEN

Faith looked outside. The storm was abating, the winds dying down. Soon it would be time to leave. She wouldn't come back to this island again. She would be held at some sort of safe house until McKay-Taggart dealt with her father, and then she would be alone. She likely wouldn't see Ten again. Even if she did, he would hold her apart. He would treat her like a client because he didn't think he was good for her.

"Hey, I can't get anyone interested in food. Do you want some eggs? I think I saw some sausage in there. I can whip up a frittata or some kind of casserole for later, but I could get you something quick now." Sean Taggart wasn't as big as his older brother, but he had what she liked to call the Taggart presence. Even in his obvious grief, he was solid.

She shook her head. "No, I'm fine. I guess I'm with the rest of them. It's not a long flight back to the States. I'll get something once we're there. Besides, I have no idea how good a pilot Nick is. I don't know how well I do in small planes."

They would be using a four seater to get to Miami. From there they would catch a commercial flight to Dallas. According to Sean, everything was set up and she had false identification and tickets on a night flight. Once she got to Dallas, she would be staying with Jesse and Phoebe Murdoch.

Surely Ten would come and see his sister after he was done with his mission. She might get to see him one last time.

"It's about two hours to Miami. You'll be there in no time," Sean assured her. "And I think Nick's staying here. Some of our plans have changed, but you would have to ask Ten about those. He wants to make the decisions when it comes to you."

"Shouldn't I get a say in that?"

Sean's hands came up. "Hey, you always have a say, but I think you should work that out with him. He's your Master after all."

He gave that up when he decided to leave her. And the world was far more complex than some contract she signed long before she knew what was going on—and under false pretenses. Tennessee Smith thought he could have his cake and then not have to eat it, too?

The shock of the events of the previous day was starting to wear off and Faith thought it was pretty good timing. If she waited much longer to confront Ten, he wouldn't be around to argue with. He would shove her on some plane and tell her it was all for her good and then traipse across the planet on his revenge mission that wouldn't bring back anyone.

"I think I will," she vowed and turned to leave the kitchen.

She walked quietly through the living room, not wanting to disturb Erin, who finally looked like she'd passed out on the sofa. Case sat with Hutch at the table, looking over some kind of records.

That was when the door opened to the office and Ten came striding out. Despite everything he'd been through, he looked so gorgeous to her. With his tan skin and golden brown hair, he was the all-American hot guy. All that beauty masked his darkness, his need to stay in the shadows. His eyes caught hers and he stopped, his mouth turning down.

He wasn't happy to see her? Well, she could make that frown meaningful because he wasn't getting off so easily. She wasn't about to be shipped out without having her say. And maybe she wouldn't allow herself to be shipped off at all.

"Hey, I was coming to find you." His face softened. "Is everything all right? You look upset. Did Sean say something?"

"Sean said a lot of things that we need to clear up."

"Okay," he allowed. "We probably should. Faith, I do have some things to say to you, and you might have a hard time hearing them at first."

So he was planning on spending their last hours together telling her all the reasons why he was leaving her. "Can your speech, Ten. I think it's time you listened to me for once."

His eyes narrowed. "Do you forget who's the top, Faith?"

"Oh, the first thing we're going to talk about is our contract. Null and void. You voided that contract the minute you started lying to me, so don't pull the Master crap. Besides, this goes far beyond our D/s play."

He loomed over her. "Yes, this about the fact that we're still in a dangerous situation and whether or not you like it, I'm still the top here. You can throw that contract in my face all you like once we get back to the States, but you will not disobey me here. You will get on that plane when I tell you to and there will be no arguments and no negotiations when it comes to your safety."

She brushed past him because she wasn't having this conversation where everyone could hear her.

Ian Taggart was lounging in the doorway. "You should give him hell. He deserves it."

"What the fuck?" Ten cursed behind her as she moved along. "What happened to all that brotherly love shit?"

"I'm ridiculously mean," Tag allowed. "Ask anyone."

She wasn't getting involved in their male bonding. She strode into the room they'd shared the night before. She'd curled up beside him and accepted that he would be gone. She'd accepted it the same way she'd accepted things all her life. She was done with that.

No one ever fought for Tennessee Smith. Well, he was about to find out that she would, but she didn't fight fair.

She was about to find out if he'd been honest with her. If she had any real power in the relationship.

"Faith, what the hell is this about?" Ten closed the door and then crossed his arms over his chest. His shoulders broadened and for the first time since they'd rescued him, he looked every inch the Dom. "You should know that if you give me trouble about getting on that plane, I'll put you over my knee and no one here will stop me. You're getting on that plane one way or another."

She wasn't afraid of him. Not physically. He could play that card with her all day and she wouldn't back down. Now emotionally,

emotionally he could savage her. It was all he'd known as a child, and she had to show him another way.

Which unfortunately included getting yelled at by his sub because that was sometimes what people in love did. "You're an idiot."

Way to go, Faith. Way to build up his esteem.

One side of his mouth tugged up. "I've been told so, yes. You want to enlighten me as to how I'm an idiot this morning? I'm going to warn you. I'm feeling much better. I'm still sore, but it looks like my dick is up and running."

She looked down at his crotch. Sure enough, no amount of torture could keep that monster cock down for long. "I should look at it."

His head shook. "Not until I'm ready to use it on you. And it's fine. No scarring. Like I said, those drugs heightened everything and made it seem worse than it actually was, so I'll be able to fuck you hard after I've spanked your ass silly for this stunt."

"Stunt? You think this is some kind of stunt?"

"I think you're willing to do anything so I won't put you on that plane. It won't work."

Tears threatened. "Because you're a moron."

"You are digging yourself a deep hole."

He was so calm. It was infuriating. "You don't have any right to spank me. I will get on that plane and I will go back to Dallas. I'm not stupid. I know what can happen, but do you? Do you even care?"

"About what happens to me? I often have not," he replied calmly.

"Because you don't think you're worth anything."

His face was blank for a moment. "When you start life in a trashcan, it makes you question your worth. I will admit that. I went through so many homes, I couldn't help but think I was disposable."

"You're not. You have so much to give."

"What do I have to give, Faith?"

This was it. She would either convince him or lose him, and she suddenly knew she wouldn't survive losing him. No matter what had happened, she loved this man. He might have been a shit to her in the beginning, but he'd protected her at the cost of his mission. She had to make him see that it could work. "You're so smart, Ten. You're

312

smart and funny, and I like who I am around you."

His face softened. "I like who I am around you, too. I'm a better man around you."

That was good. "I don't think you should keep pursuing my father. Not like this. I think you could take him down through research. I'll help you. I'll give you everything I know because I want to stop him, too. But it's too dangerous to do it this way."

"You think we can take him down using good investigative work?"

She nodded eagerly. "Yes. I think if McKay-Taggart wants to find information, they'll find it. It simply takes patience. I know you want to take him out because of what he did to your brother, but could you be happy with sending him to prison?"

"Yes, Faith." His voice was sure. "I could be happy with that. But that doesn't change the fact that you're going to be on that plane this afternoon. You will go back to Dallas and you will lay low until I figure this out and I can be sure you're safe. I'm going to use the time to keep you naked as much as possible."

"Somehow I think your sister won't like that much."

"My sister can get used to it. As often as I've caught sight of her and Jesse doing it at Sanctum, she can get used to my wife being naked. And she knocks. We'll keep the door locked."

She stopped. "You said I was still getting on the plane."

"Yes. I did and you are. I will be your pilot for today, ma'am. You should know that I only accept tips from beautiful doctors."

Now the tears were flowing in earnest. "You called me your wife."

"I was hoping we could negotiate that contract, darlin'. I'm not getting any younger. I love you, Faith. Is there any way you can love me? Even a little. I know I don't have a lot to offer, but I'll give you everything I have. I'll be the man you deserve, and that starts with getting on that plane with you. It starts with choosing you. I choose you, Faith." He stepped forward and his hands cupped her face, staring down at her. "I pray that you'll choose me, too. Forgive me. I was an idiot."

He was coming with her? He was leaving the island with her. He was choosing her. It was enough. "I love you, Tennessee. I'll always choose you, too."

She went on her toes and brushed her mouth against his, her whole body coming alive again. It had only been a few days, but it felt like forever since she'd kissed him. His hands moved, tangling in her hair as he took control of the kiss.

His tongue licked at her lips and she let him in. Faith molded her body to his, feeling every lean muscle. She let her hands slip down, easing over his shirt. She wanted to feel his skin, his warmth. She could never get enough of him. His tongue rubbed against hers as his hands explored. They seemed to want the same things, she and her man. Flesh to flesh. She tugged on the bottom of his shirt.

And then remembered what he'd been through.

"I'm sorry. Did I hurt you?"

His eyes had darkened with desire. "Don't even try that shit with me right now. I want you. I might be the tiniest bit uncomfortable, but that is nothing compared to what you're going to be if you treat me like an invalid. I want to do something with you. Something I haven't done in a long time. I don't want any walls between us."

She shook her head. She didn't want anything between them either.

He backed up and pulled his shirt over his head. His chest looked so much better this morning. He would have new scars, but nothing could make Ten Smith anything less than gorgeous. She reached out and gently brushed her fingertips down his chest to the waistband of his sweatpants. They were slightly too large, having come from one of the other guys, so they rode low on his hips. His cock proved he was telling the truth. The man was feeling better, and she wanted to make sure he felt amazing.

"What do you want from me?"

He eased the shirt off her and her nipples immediately responded to the heat of his gaze. They pebbled for him, desperate for his touch. Her whole body was warming, softening and getting ready for him.

"Everything, darlin'. I want everything you've got. But first you're going to have to get me ready to fuck you."

Yes, he seemed to be having so much trouble in that area. She didn't complain though. She'd apparently had terrible timing. If she'd been the slightest bit more patient, she wouldn't have called her future husband a moron. Oh, he was at times, but it was kinder to let him think she didn't know. She dropped to her knees and slowly dragged the sweatpants over his muscled hips. He wasn't wearing any underwear, so his cock sprang free. Long and thick, he was right. It appeared they'd left this part of him alone. She sighed and studied him as she stroked his erection. There were a few places on his lower abdomen with healing spots from the day before. She leaned over and brushed them softly with her lips.

Her father had done this to him and he still wanted her.

She looked up at him. "Did you think I was involved in my father's business?"

For a spy, he could blanch quite quickly. She rather thought that was only for her. In the field, Tennessee Smith would have the world's best poker face, but here he was just a man who didn't want his future wife to know he'd doubted her. "I might have had some thoughts on the subject, but that was all before I met you and realized you were far too sweet to ever be involved in anything like that. Then all I wanted to do was protect you."

Yeah, she bet he did. She leaned forward and kissed his cock, warm brushes of her mouth over his flesh. "I wouldn't blame you, Ten."

His hand tangled in her hair. "Erin knew. She told me from the beginning I was a paranoid freak and you were innocent. I…I haven't had the greatest luck with women. Suck the head."

His hands twisted, right to the point where her scalp lit up and she felt the tug in her nipples. The man had learned her sweet spots.

"I can't imagine you haven't had hundreds of lovers. You should know I'm the last in that line, babe. I've got it on good authority that the women of Sanctum don't share." She gave the head of his cock a good long lick. It was perfectly plum shaped and a lovely shade of purply red. A drop of pre-come pulsed out, and she lapped it up before closing her mouth over his cock.

Ten shuddered. "Not hundreds and I wouldn't call them lovers. They were a way out of myself, an escape. A couple of them were near-death experiences."

"What?" Faith tried to talk more, but Ten guided her back to his cock.

"It's kind of in the job description, darlin'. If you're fucking for information you sometimes get burned. Or almost emasculated. Or sold to a terrorist group because the operative you're living with is a double agent. It's all an accepted part of spy life. Don't stop, baby. That feels so good."

"You're not going back to that job," she tried to say, but her mouth was kind of completely full of cock.

He chuckled and thrust in a little further before proving he could understand her. "I'm never going back to that job. I've got a new mission and that's taking care of you. You should know though that Ian wants me to run a small office in whatever craptastic country you're working in."

He was coming with her. She hummed her assent to that plan as she worked her mouth over and over his cock. McKay-Taggart obviously wasn't the CIA, and thank god for that. He could use that brilliant mind of his and still stay relatively safe and close to her.

But there was one issue they had to settle.

She came up for air, her hand going down to cup his heavy balls. "I need to stay in Dallas for a while. I need McKay-Taggart to figure out who on my staff was working with my sister. She couldn't have managed this without someone on the inside. She needed data from the patients she was experimenting on. My doctors rotate in and out, so it has to be one of my full-time nurses."

It hurt her heart to think that one of her nurses would do that to patients for money, but she had to be realistic.

"Stand up," he commanded. It looked like he'd only wanted a taste. She stood and his hands found her undies, and suddenly he was the one on his knees. "I'll talk to Ian when he gets back to Dallas. We'll work something out, but if you want to go yourself, I'll be beside you."

She shuddered as he pushed her back and onto the bed, her legs splaying. He gripped her thighs, pressing them open so her pussy was right where he wanted it. "I need to stay in Dallas for a while."

He put his nose right in her labia, breathing her in like she was the sweetest flower he'd ever encountered. "You will. You're going to be under guard until we deal with your father, but I'm hoping that won't take too long."

"I have to stay and help Erin through this." She wasn't sure why, but she and Erin had clicked. They'd become the type of friends that rarely came along, and she wasn't losing that. Love came in some strange forms, but it was too precious to toss out because it wasn't perfect. Ten wasn't perfect. He'd hurt her and likely would again because he was human. She would do the same, but if they made that vow to hold on despite whatever happened, they could have a life together.

Holding on. She'd let go of so many things in her life. She'd drifted, but he could keep her steady if she let him. He needed to be needed, craved it. He needed to understand that she wasn't going anywhere. She was the permanent part of his life.

And she was going to give her friend some stability, too.

Ten rested his cheek against her, sighing as though he'd found his place. "I love you, Faith. I'll go wherever you need to go. And I thank you for taking care of Erin. She's going to need it. She's welcome to stay with us. We'll make sure she gets through this."

He turned his head slightly and then his tongue rode over her delicate flesh.

She clutched the bedspread, trying not to scream out. Normally she wouldn't care, but given the things that had happened, she wanted to respect her friends.

"That's right. Keep quiet, but don't think for a second this is disrespectful. I love you. If it had been me, I would want my friends to find something good. Theo was a good man. He wouldn't deny us this."

She nodded. He wouldn't. Theo had been in love. If it had been Ten who had died, any of them really, Theo would have clung to Erin. They needed a reminder that there was still something good, that they were alive.

She relaxed back and let Tennessee take over. His tongue worked, caressing every inch of her pussy. He spread her wide and fucked deep inside, his mouth enveloping her. This was what she needed, what she would need for the rest of her life. This was what she'd been missing. All the times she'd surrendered before, all the play at submission had been nothing but a rehearsal for this man— her true match, her real Master, her partner and her husband.

"Let's make this fun. We've got hours before we have to go." He climbed on the bed with her, lying back. "Get up here and straddle me. I haven't had my fill yet. Have I told you how good you taste? How perfect you are for me?"

She started to move, to obey him, but he hadn't said how she should straddle him. She turned and before he could protest, she was on top of him, her tongue lapping at his cock again, but this time her pussy was right in line with his very talented mouth. Who didn't love a good old-fashioned 69?

"Fuck, I like how you think, Doc." A big hand slapped her ass. "You take me. You take every inch of me while I take what's mine."

He fucked her in earnest, his tongue going deep. It was hard to concentrate when her whole body felt like a live wire, but she had a job to do, too. She sucked his cock in long passes, loving how it seemed to pulse under her tongue. Salty pre-come leaked from his head and she sucked that down, too. Every now and then his big hand would come down, slapping at the flesh of her backside and sending ripples of sensation up her spine. Pain and pleasure. They combined and formed something new and sensational in her brain and body. She wasn't sure why she needed both. Long ago she'd given up trying to be "normal." This would be normal for them, the push and play of D/s in the bedroom. She would take this time she had with him while they were in hiding and use it to teach her man that he could count on her, that she would stay.

He was necessary to her, as necessary as her next breath.

"Stop." He slapped her ass again. "I don't want to come yet. Sit on my face, darling. Ride my tongue and after you come, I want you to ride my cock. I used to fucking love this. I'm taking it back. I'm taking it back with you."

She moved, getting into the position he wanted. He was making himself vulnerable to her. How many times had this man had some "lover" try to hurt him over government secrets? How many times had he offered up his body for something other than pleasure? "You are never going back to that job."

He'd done enough for his country. Tennessee Smith's shop was closed for business.

"I always listen to good advice, ma'am." He pulled on her hips, getting her into position.

Then she couldn't think anymore. When he speared his tongue deep inside, there was no more worry or pain. There was no loss to be felt, only the pure pleasure of joining with this man. She gave over to the incredible sensation of being Ten's lover, Master T's sub, Mr. Smith's wife.

Faith McDonald. She could be all those things for him and still be herself because loving him made her more than she'd been before. She'd been alone, her soul missing an inherent piece, and now she was complete. Even when he was away from her, she would keep a piece of him inside.

Even when they were truly parted, as all lovers were in the end, she wouldn't be alone because she'd loved him.

The pleasure burst across her and she bit her lip to stop from crying out his name.

He kept up the torturing, forcing her to come again under the sweet lash of his tongue, the sucking of his mouth on her.

Finally he let go, and she had to force herself to remain upright. After all, it was time to give her man the ride of his life.

* * * *

His cock was dying, but the rest of Ten Smith was perfectly satisfied. She'd come all over his tongue three times before he'd let her up. Her little pussy had ground down against him, demanding her pleasure, and he'd given it to her. Later, he would tie her up and make her come at least ten times before relenting and giving her his cock, but today he was too eager.

In the past that eagerness would have been the very pressure he needed to hold back, but he didn't need to hold back with Faith.

"Tell me again. Tell me you love me."

She moved down his body, bringing their faces in line. She touched their noses together in a tender show of affection. "I love you. I love you more than you can know."

It was all that mattered. The moment mattered. Nothing else. "Tell me you'll stay with me."

Maybe that mattered, too. It made him seem like a weak, pathetic child, but he needed the words.

"I'll stay with you for as long as we have," she promised, her mouth coming down on his. "And when our time is over, I'll find you. I don't know where we'll go, but I'll find you again."

She was crying, her tears falling to his cheeks as though he'd shed them himself. He'd given up crying long before, but Faith took up his slack. She could cry for him, be strong for him. And he would love her.

Loving Faith made it possible to love other people. It had happened with Ian earlier. For the first time, he'd opened and let the possibility in that he could be part of this weird and wonderful family. He'd claimed to love Phoebe, but he'd chosen revenge over being her brother.

He'd chosen revenge over truly honoring Jamie.

"I want to marry you and have kids with you. I don't know if I'll be a good father, but I want to try, Faith. I know what I want to name our first kid. Girl or boy."

She closed her eyes briefly and when she opened them, they were practically glowing. "James. Jamie. Yes, I think that would be perfect."

New life would honor the brother he'd lost. Not taking more. He finally got that. He finally understood that in order to really love someone, he had to make himself vulnerable.

He could be vulnerable to Faith because she was his home, his heart, all the good things he could do in life.

"Take me for once. I want to watch you take me." He eased her down, his eyes taking in every inch of her body and the way she moved. She was a sensuous thing, comfortable in her own skin in a way he would never be. Another thing to love about her.

It had been forever since he'd given a woman the power position. Years had gone by and he'd never allowed a woman to be above him, to have a chance to hurt him again.

He'd prepped himself to get through it, but now that she was smiling down at him, there was no trepidation. There wasn't an ounce of fear. This was Faith and she would never harm him, even when he deserved it. She came to him with open arms.

He would protect this woman to his dying day.

She took his cock in hand and everything fell away. There were parts of his body that ached, but he welcomed the pain because it meant he was alive.

"Do you want a condom? We don't need it. I take a shot and I'm going to be perfectly faithful to you," she offered.

He smiled. Nothing between them. One day when they were ready, there wouldn't even be that chemical barrier between them. He reached up and touched her face, brushing back her silky hair. "I'm clean and I'm never touching another woman for as long as I live. You're my end game, Faith."

He'd thought it would be something else. An early grave. She was a surprise, a gift he'd been given. He would take her. He might not deserve her, but he would become the kind of man she needed. He would be the brother his sister needed, the brother his friends wanted. Even if that meant taking a punch in the face from Tag.

Faith began to lower herself onto his cock. Pure heat raked over his body. This was what he'd needed since the day he'd met her. This was beyond sex. He hadn't realized it, but he'd been searching for it all of his life. Communion. Intimacy. Love.

So tight. She was tight and perfect and she knew how to draw the damn moment out. His girl took him in little passes, gaining ground and then retreating, tempting and teasing him. He watched, not giving in to the urge to take over. This was Faith's show. They had a lifetime to play, but this was a sacred act for him. Giving himself to her. Trusting her.

She sighed as she finally settled on his cock, every inch of his dick buried deep in her body. She clenched around him, making him bite back a moan.

"Are you all right?" Faith looked down at him.

She was a fucking goddess with her hair spilling over her shoulders and brushing her collarbones. Her hair pointed the way to her breasts. He couldn't help himself. He reached out for them. Round and perfectly sized for his hands, he was drawn to them. When he got her home and kept her naked, those breasts would always be ready for his mouth.

"I told you what would happen if you treated me like an invalid. Lean forward."

She bit her bottom lip but did as he asked, and he finally got that sweet treat in his mouth. He licked one nipple, aware always of the connection of their bodies. His cock was pulsing, begging to be set free, but he wanted the moment to last. He sucked her nipple into his mouth, loving the way she tightened around him. A little nipple torture was definitely on the agenda for his hot doc. While he sucked one nipple deep into his mouth, he pinched down hard on the other one. Sure enough, her pussy clenched around his cock. She needed this play and he needed to give her everything.

With gentle care he bit down on the nipple in his mouth while thrusting his hips up. Faith gasped and started to move against him. "Yes. That feels so good, Master. Give me more."

He would give her everything. He switched nipples, moving to soothe the pinched one with his tongue while he squeezed the other tight.

Her body practically vibrated over his. She whimpered and squirmed, every movement delighting his cock. She'd already come for him, but he could feel her body getting ready to go off again. This time, he meant to be with her.

He let go of her nipple and eased her back up. Those sweet pebbles were now red as raspberries, and her skin was perfectly flush with arousal again. She wasn't doing her duty now. She wasn't pleasing him because he'd pleasured her. She wanted an orgasm and she would fight for it. That was what he wanted.

He smacked her juicy ass, the sound further enflaming his senses. "Ride me. Take me hard."

Her head fell back as she began to move. He couldn't take his eyes off her. He watched as she started to bounce up and down on his cock. So much heat. So much fucking friction. She moved gracefully, her pussy sucking at him, drawing him back in again and again. He watched as her tits bounced, the sight causing him to reach for them again. He cupped her breasts as she worked over him. So gorgeous.

He let his hands skim her body down from her breasts to the curves of her hips. He wasn't going to last much longer. She was too hot, too perfect, and he could feel every inch of her pussy milking his cock. He slammed up into her, his hands pulling down as he ground up. He let his right hand find the spot where they were joined. The pad of his thumb rubbed over her clit as he started to fuck her with a furious intensity.

Her eyes widened and just when he thought she would shout out, he pulled her down and kissed her, drinking down the sweet sounds she made.

There was a tingle at the base of his spine and he let himself go. Pure pleasure raced along his skin as his balls drew up and he came inside her.

She fell on top of him and he bit back a groan. Real torture made a man a little sore, but he wouldn't change anything. He wrapped his arms around her. She was here with him. That was worth all the torture in the world.

He shifted, moving her to his side. "Sleep for a while, darlin'. We're leaving in a few hours."

Her eyes were already drifting closed.

He sighed and let sleep take him as well.

CHAPTER TWENTY

Time didn't stop. It kept going. When would they let him die? When would the darkness come? He liked the darkness, but whenever it would threaten to take him, someone would throw water on him or slap him awake or god, give him more drugs so he couldn't sleep.

The lights. He hated the lights.

The subject takes the drug quite well. Heart rate and blood pressure are all perfectly normal. Well, normal for a man who's in an enormous amount of pain. I need more time with him.

You don't have it. The Chinese are almost here. Get him dressed and ready for transport. I have to call Victoria and make sure she's ready for a package. If you damage the goods, I'll kill you myself.

When she looked down at him, the lights behind her made her look like she had a halo. An angel of death.

She looked him over with a shake of her head. Her eyes reminded him so much of Faith's in their color, but there the similarities ended because this bitch had some crazy eyes on her.

What I wouldn't do to open you up and see what makes you tick, Mr. Smith. Unfortunately, my father won't let me play. Not that you're the one I really want to play with. Let's get you another dose and you'll forget this ever happened. I'll replace the memory with some…hmmm, let's see how much your dick can take. My sister seems to love it so much.

She started at him with the needle again and he screamed.

"Ten? Tennessee?"

He opened his eyes and Faith was staring down at him. She'd gotten dressed. She was wearing a T-shirt that was the tiniest bit too small for her and a pair of jeans that hugged her curves. Ten forced himself to take a deep breath. "I was dreaming."

She sat down on the bed beside him, her hand easing into his. "More like a nightmare, baby. Are you all right?"

"He's got the damn PTSD. All my men have it," a sarcastic voice to his right said. He looked over and there was Tag, leaning against the doorway.

He sent Tag his middle finger. "You would have PTSD too if someone took a cattle prod to your dick."

Tag's eyes widened. "Holy shit, Ten. I take back everything I've ever said about you. You're a motherfucking hero. You were able to perform after that? Yeah, she tried to be quiet, but that bed squeaks. Seriously, every man alive should salute you. Can I see it?"

"No, you can't see it," Faith shot back. "What is wrong with you?"

His girl had his back. Or his dick, as it was. He sat up. Faith was looking at Tag like he was some kind of monster. He had to explain. Tag was just a dude. "It's no big deal. The only time men will look at another man's junk willingly is when it's been horrifically mangled."

"Gay dudes will totally look at another dude's junk. It's normal for them. They'll also look at a mangled one, since they're dudes, too," Tag explained.

"Why are we looking at junk? Has Ten finally come out of the closet?" Sean joined his brother.

Tag shook his head. "Nah. Part of his torture was a cattle prod to the cock."

"Whoa," Sean said. "Can I look?"

"Told you." The dream was starting to dissipate. And he was starting to wonder how much of it really was a dream.

He squeezed Faith's hand and sat up, looking at Tag. "The good news is the torture to my penis was virtual. She used some kind of drug to fuck with my memory. I think I even recall her telling me she was going to do it."

"It's not all virtual torture. You're covered in electrical burns," Faith pointed out and gave Tag a saucy stare. "And he really did perform admirably."

A ghost of a smile crossed Tag's lips. Despite his sarcasm, it was easy to see the man was still hurting. There were lines on Tag's face he hadn't noticed before.

"I am happy to hear Ten's still a functional male and that the two of you worked things out. Faith, I'm glad you'll be sticking around. It'll be good to have a doc on call," Tag explained. "My men do stupid shit. I swear if Boomer walks into that glass wall one more time, I'm having him put down. Where did you find him?"

"Where I find everyone. US military." Boomer wasn't the sharpest tool in the shed, but he had his talents. So did Ten, and one of them was putting things together. "I need to see the file on McDonald's mistress. What do we know about her?"

"She works in banking. She's some kind of VP at one of the international banks," Tag replied, getting serious.

"He's sending her some kind of package. We might want to intercept that." Now that the fog was clearing, he was more certain that it hadn't been a dream but a memory. McDonald had been concerned about Victoria receiving some kind of package. Maybe it was flowers, but Ten doubted it.

"I'll have someone watch her apartment," Tag promised. "Now, we're going to head out. Hutch claims this is the best time to do recon on the compound. We're going to go in quietly and get out the same way. It's strictly intelligence gathering."

What Tag wasn't saying is the intelligence they wanted was the location of Des's and Theo's bodies. They would keep to the shadows unless they had an absolute free ride to pick them up.

Tag would get the job done. He would bring his brother back and they would all go home to try to find a way through the grief.

Ten looked at the clock and stood up, stretching his body. "We'll be gone before you get back. I'll have a detailed report on the entire operation on your desk tomorrow afternoon, and I'll be ready to do anything you need me to do. Faith and I are going to stay in Dallas for the next few months."

Tag held a hand out. "We'll be more than happy to have you around. Be safe."

Ten shook his hand. "You too, brother."

As they walked away, Faith crossed her arms over her chest. "What were you talking about? My father doesn't have a mistress."

He hated being the bad guy with her. It was odd because he'd spent years being the bad guy with absolutely everyone in his life. "Sweetheart, your father sees a woman in DC on a regular basis. Her name is Victoria Chandler."

She shook her head. "He might see someone, but she's not his mistress. My father's been impotent for fifteen years. We've tried everything. Every new drug that comes out, he'd give it a shot. I did his checkup six months ago. Trust me, if he's got a mistress, he's not sleeping with her."

That made no logical sense. "He visits this woman on a regular basis, Faith. If he's not having sex with her, what would he be doing?"

"I would say maybe they're friends, but my father doesn't have friends. He has business contacts. He places zero value on friendship. If he was trying to keep up the appearance of being functional, why would he keep a mistress secret? My dad is the type who would pay a woman to date him and be done with it."

"He's run on family values platforms," Ten mused. "He talks about your mother in his speeches to this day."

"Yes," she said, her every word flavored with bitterness, "Dad is good at playing the grieving widower."

If the relationship wasn't about sex...

"She's in banking. That's how he's moving the money. We've been looking in the wrong place. We've been trying to tie him to the cash, but he's smarter than that. He's used this woman to launder his funds for years." Ten picked Faith up, enveloping her in a hug. "We're going to get him and we're going to take down everyone who helped him."

She hugged him tightly. "And my sister? Tell me you'll get her, too. She's dangerous, Ten."

He tempered his exuberance. Justice for Jamie meant Faith

having to see her father and sister in jail. No matter how much they deserved it, it was going to hurt her. He kissed her forehead. "Yes, I'll get her, too. I'll try to keep it as quiet as possible. I don't want to hurt your clinic, but we need to take down the executives at Kronberg who allowed this experimentation to go on."

She put her head on his shoulder, not letting go. "Yes. They have to be stopped."

They stood there for the longest time, gaining comfort and strength for the long journey home.

Twenty minutes later, Ten looked over the plane. It was a small plane, what he would call a puddle jumper. The couple who owned the place used it to get from Miami to here on a regular basis. He would use it to take Faith home. He settled the little luggage they had in storage. When they got to Miami, he would take Faith shopping so they didn't stand out from the crowd at Miami-Dade airport. She needed a purse. It was the little details that could trip a person up. A woman without a handbag would stand out. They needed luggage, at the very least carry-ons. TSA tended to question travelers who didn't fit the norms.

He turned, looking back at the house. Faith walked up the pathway. She'd placed a baseball cap on her head and held another one for him. Caps hid hair color. If they kept their faces down around security cameras, it was likely no one would be able to remember much about them.

He had to get her to Dallas. Once they were in Dallas, he could breathe again.

"I left a note for Erin. I told her I think she should stay with us when she gets back home. Being in that house without Theo is going to be so rough." She gave him a sad smile. "So I might need to not be naked for a while."

He pulled her close. Whatever she needed. "Just know that at some point, those clothes are gone. We're going to have a fully naked honeymoon."

"That should be fun." She looked up at him. "So you know how to fly this thing. The airstrip looks small."

"Hey, it's not made out of dirt, so I'm calling that a win. I've flown small planes many times before. It's all part of the super-spy school I went to. I got an A in 'using small planes to flee your enemies' class."

"I'm glad to hear that. Oh, god." She pulled away, her eyes widening.

Ten immediately went for the SIG in his holster, but as he turned, he saw what Faith had seen, what he'd missed before. Hutch had missed it, too, likely because of the storm and the brilliant way the small team had camouflaged themselves. They were dressed in dark green and eased out of the jungle with the long practice of predators.

"Mr. Smith, if you will come with us, we won't harm the girl," an accented voice explained.

There were six of them. No wonder they'd waited. He would bet they'd waited all night in the middle of a tropical storm. They'd likely followed the trail back and then MSS had proven themselves to be deeply patient bastards.

"Let the girl go free and I'll come with you." He couldn't take out six armed operatives. Not in a gunfight. Not out in the open. They had no cover and even if the plane had been up and running, MSS would simply shoot it out of the sky.

Faith wrapped her arms around his waist, staying behind him. "No. I'm not leaving you."

Shit. They would kill her. "You will if I tell you to. You'll go to our friends. You'll be safe with them."

It was as close as he would get to begging her to go and get Ian.

"You're talking about Mr. Taggart?" the leader said with a shit-eating grin on his face. "I believe we have a surprise for him as well."

There was a loud boom and Ten felt the ground shake.

"That would be your friends meeting a grisly death from our trap. You're alone, Mr. Smith, and you have nothing to bargain with. Come with us or we'll kill the girl."

He heard the sound of crunching gravel. He didn't want to turn his head. Never take your eyes off the snake that's about to bite you. Another thing Franklin Grant had taught him.

"Faith, please tell me that's our people coming up the drive."

"It's my father." Faith's voice shook. "And he's not alone. We're surrounded."

"Cowards waited until they could separate us from the rest of the team," Ten said, his heart racing. He was cool under pressure, but now he realized he'd been that way because he'd had nothing to lose. The idea of losing Faith made him sick to his stomach.

But he was going to. He knew the odds, could see the various scenarios play out in his head. He could take a few out, but without cover, he had no way to protect her.

No way except to pray her father wouldn't kill her.

"Mr. Smith, I'll take my daughter back now." McDonald's voice boomed across the yard.

Ten turned. It didn't matter. There was no option, no way to fight that wouldn't lead to the loss of her life. He saw McDonald and four of his thugs bearing down on them.

"She had nothing to do with this," Ten said. He had to try. "She didn't know a damn thing until you told her and then my people kidnapped her."

McDonald frowned. "Yes, of course they did. Faith has always been a bit rebellious, shall we say. If you're worried I'm going to murder my daughter, think again, Mr. Smith. I love both of my children. I'm going to make certain that Faith sees how much you've twisted the situation to your own liking."

Faith started to talk, but Ten quickly put a hand over her mouth and leaned in. He had seconds before the MSS operatives tore them apart. "Keep your mouth shut. Agree with whatever he says. I don't believe for a second Tag is gone, and he will come for you. You be alive when he gets there. I love you, Faith."

"Drop the gun now," a hard voice said. He was surrounded by six MSS agents. He let the gun fall to the ground. There would be more waiting back at their plane. He would have to look for some way, any way to get out.

McDonald got a hand on his daughter's arm and yanked her to him.

Ten found himself with a gun shoved at the base of his spine. Faith looked so scared, but she kept her head held high as she was walked back to her father's SUV.

I love you, she mouthed before she disappeared inside the vehicle.

"Torture the hell out of that motherfucker," McDonald said, spitting his way. "I swear, I should have killed him myself."

"We'll take care of things from here on out." The MSS operative pulled back the hood of his jacket and shook his head as McDonald's SUV took off. "Tennessee Smith. Alone at last. Do you know how long I've waited for this day?"

Shit. Naturally it was a fucking reunion. "Lei Gan. I can tell you exactly how long you've waited for this day. It's been since I gave you that scar. It's looking good, by the way. And you really didn't need your peripheral vision."

Lei Gan was an operative he'd come up against once. Exactly once, but the man hadn't forgotten the encounter. Then again it was probably difficult to forget the man who'd nearly gutted him and taken an eye. Lei Gan was the operative who'd spent time with Phoebe Grant when her cover had been blown. Ten and Jamie had taken care of him.

Lei leaned in, letting Ten get a good look at the eye patch he now wore. "When I get through with you, you're going to wish you'd killed me that day. And I've already sent a lovely note to your sister. I've promised to send you back to her. In small pieces, of course."

Nice.

He bit back a groan as one of the operatives pulled his hands behind his back and shoved his wrists into too tight cuffs. Fuckers needed to have to take one of Tag's classes. These assholes had no idea how to properly bind a human.

His spine bowed when they shoved the rifle in. A sure sign they wanted him walking.

"Ian Taggart's not dead, you know." He shuffled along, not wanting to help them out by moving quickly. They forced him into the thicket of trees and shrubs they'd been hiding in, and he could see what he hadn't before. There was an SUV parked roughly a quarter of a mile away. They'd used the storm and cover of darkness to move into position. How had MSS found him so quickly?

"Keep moving," the Chinese operative ordered. "We have a plane to catch. I'll have you in Beijing and under my thumb before the day is through. Not that anyone will care. You've been disavowed. So sad for poor Mr. Smith. The Agency was all you had, and they let themselves be conned by a junior handler. I believe you know the man. You kept him out of active fieldwork. He was so easy to turn. Hate can do that to a man. When McDonald needed help getting rid of you, my man inside the Agency was more than willing to comply."

"Fucking Karriker." Scotty Karriker had been too weak for fieldwork, but he'd been right on the line testing wise, and Ten had been forced to make the call. He hadn't liked Karriker's psych reports, but the kid had friends on the inside, so Ten hadn't been able to remove him completely.

Someone was getting a visit from an old friend when Ten got back to the States.

"Get him in the vehicle," Lei ordered. "I think I'll let some of my agents have fun with you on the way home. Jiang? Would you like to slowly rip the American's balls off?"

Ten stopped, his whole being sparking with something very much like hope. Tag might have been the mighty warrior, able to take down man after man in battle, but Ten had been the chess player, and if there was one thing he did well, it was recruiting the right people for the right job. Every person who'd ever led a team knew that placing the right operative in the right place, at the right fucking time was essential.

A woman stepped up and she drew back her hood. Jiang Kun was a slight figure, her beauty obvious among the rough men she was surrounded by. She'd become one of China's most deadly operatives.

And her real name was Kayla Summers, daughter of Freddy Summers and Jim Gayle, who had adopted her after her mother had her smuggled out of the country. Kayla had been born a twin when China's birth rules allowed for only one child. Her sister, Kun, had stayed behind with their mother and eventually she'd become an MSS agent. When Ten discovered Jiang Kun's connection to a brilliant undergrad at Stanford, he'd recruited Kayla. When Kay had found her sister, she'd turned her, making arrangements to bring her back to the States.

And when Jiang Kun had been killed, Ten Smith had killed her assassin before he could verify the job and Kayla Summers had taken on her sister's life. She was the most brilliant double agent he'd ever had.

The last time he'd seen her in person had been from the top of a cliff in Goa, India. She'd been gathering information on the king of Loa Mali. Unfortunately, so had a rogue CIA agent Big Tag had been hunting. She'd helped them out then, too.

Her lips curled up in a cruel smile. "I think I would love to cut his balls off. Do you remember what you did to me back in Phuket?"

She'd been captured by the police and Ten had risked himself to get her out of there before she could be tortured. He'd offered to let her come home then, but she'd refused.

He'd bumped into her and slipped a gun into her bound hands. Shit. This was going down now.

"Yes, I remember. I remember every minute of it," Ten vowed. Sweet, sweet adrenaline started to pump through his veins. It was two against five, but they had the element of surprise in their favor.

She shoved him against the SUV, slamming him hard enough to rattle his teeth. It was also enough sound and motion to cover the fact that she pressed a small semi into his hands.

Too bad she couldn't have undone the damn cuffs, but a man worked with what he had.

"She's going to make you pay," Lei said.

Summers leaned, in whispering. "Two shots forty-five up and at your six."

The world slowed as his training took over. Calm was needed. The adrenaline was a rush, but if it wasn't accompanied with an almost Zen-like calm, then he was nothing more than an animal fighting for survival, and he wanted to be more.

He wasn't an animal. He was an artist.

The minute Summers moved back, he brought his hands up forty-five degrees from his spine and straight back. He didn't need to see to shoot. He pulled the trigger twice as the world around him exploded in gunfire.

Summers brought up her assault rifle, quickly taking out the two men in front of her.

Ten whirled around, kicking out and catching Lei with his mouth hanging wide. The operative brought his rifle up but stumbled back as Summers took him out.

The jungle was suddenly overbearingly silent.

"I want a fucking hot dog." Summers put a hand on her hip and her dark eyes narrowed. "I want a hot dog that I know is made of beef and not some weird found-it-in-the-street beef or someone's kitty cat. More than that, I want some freaking iced tea. Is that too much to ask? A little ice. A little sugar. And a taco. I miss tacos and goddamn margaritas."

Kayla Summers wanted to come home.

"I will throw you a coming home party you won't ever forget, Kay. I promise. I'll spring for some barbecue if you'll get these cuffs off me."

She frowned at him. "So you can go after that girl?"

"So I can go after my fiancée."

"Holy shit. Hang on. This asshole had the keys." She kicked Lei's corpse and said something in Cantonese that Ten thought was the equivalent of calling the man a limp dicked penis head who couldn't find a clitoris with a compass. But he was rusty. It could have been a very nice good-bye. Summers quickly had him out of the handcuffs and then was going through the dead man's wallet. "So you're getting married. That's awesome."

"What are you doing? We don't have time to loot."

She dumped the contents of the wallet on the grass, picking up a single key with a sigh. "We have time to loot this. This is everything Lei had on McDonald. His spirit animal might have been a castrated howler monkey, but the man knew how to dig up dirt. You taught me to keep a burn file. Lei had one, too. This is a key to a safe deposit box in a bank in London. I thought you might like to take a look. I think you'll find everything you need to burn that fucker Karriker and get your old job back."

He was so happy he'd hired her. "You are a goddess, but I'm not going back to the Agency. I have a new job."

"I'm also unemployed and will be needing a reference."

"Shit," a dark voice said. "Charlie's going to freak out if I put you on the payroll. I tried to explain to her that I slept with your twin sister, not you. I don't think she cares." Big Tag stepped into the clearing, Case, Erin, and Hutch at his back, and none looking worse for the wear. "Any chance you'll settle for the London office, Kun?"

"No way. I want American food and I want to be on the same continent as my dads. And the name's Summers. Kayla Summers." She gave Tag a smirk. "Got my text, huh, big guy? Do you have any idea how hard it was to find your phone number?"

Tag nodded. "I did indeed get your text and I salute your superior skills. I let Hutch explode the mine they left for us."

"It was cool," Hutch said with a grin. "I'm used to blowing things up in a virtual fashion. There's something to be said for real life explosives."

"Summers, how close is the plane to the compound?" He needed to start thinking about how to get Faith out of that house without her father putting a bullet in her or using her as a shield.

"We used a commercial airstrip, but we're supposed to swing by and pick up the two men we left behind. They set up the mine and we're supposed to meet at 1600 hours, which is very soon," Summers explained. "I can drive us in. If you look in the back, there's a nice weapons stash, including some C-4 and grenades if we need them. The person sitting next to me has to wear one of these jackets though. The girl could manage it. She's small enough to be one of our guys."

Erin started pulling a jacket off one of the dead men. "Hey, if it gets me close to McDonald, I'd wear a chicken suit."

Ten looked over at Tag, glad to not be alone. "Thanks for coming back for me."

"Always. And Case is keeping an eye on Erin. He won't let her do anything dangerous."

"Who's keeping an eye on Case?" Ten asked.

Tag shook his head. "Case is a good kid. He knows what his brother would want and that's for Erin to be safe. If she wasn't here, I might worry."

Ten looked back and Case was watching over Erin with a grim resolve.

"I've got Sean, Brody, and the Russian moving ahead on foot to the compound. They'll relay anything they see. This is your girl and your op. So do we move?"

Ten picked one of the assault rifles left by the fallen MSS agents and recovered his SIG from Lei. "We move."

One way or another, he was getting his girl back.

* * * *

Faith looked around the building she'd been sure was a storage facility for gardening equipment and wondered exactly how stupid she could possibly be. It was some kind of hospital/torture chamber, and she had to wonder what had been going on down here and for how long.

She shivered as she looked over and saw the blood-stained sheets poking out of the trash receptacle.

"Your sister does like to play," her father said as he entered the room.

She could barely look at him. When she was a kid, he'd been larger than life. He'd been that man who would come home from long times away, bringing her toys and candy. He'd left her and Hope with nannies and then placed them in boarding schools. Later in life, he'd been the man who wrote the checks and called her when he needed her to show up for some event.

She'd been a prop to him. She'd loved him in a distant way.

"How long has she been experimenting on the locals?" It made Faith want to puke.

Her dad crossed his arms over his chest and sighed. "I don't ask her about her experiments very often. For a while, I suppose. The nanny found her cutting up animals at the age of nine. She was a curious child. So very interested in the way things worked."

"She's psychotic."

"She's a visionary," her father insisted. "Do you even understand what she's managed to do?"

At least she could find out how far Hope's experiments had gone. "Time dilation. She's experimenting with screwing around with people's perception of time."

"She's not experimenting. She's making it happen. Imagine how it will reform prison systems. We won't have overcrowding problems anymore. And pesky things like human rights won't matter because the actual punishment is virtual. You can really teach a man a lesson he'll never forget and not truly harm an inch of his skin. Your sister made it possible for your little boyfriend to keep his cock on his body. Well, until the Chinese cut it off. I've been told they have plans to bronze it and put it on the head of MSS's desk."

"I'm sure Ten will look back on what seemed like weeks of torture kindly." She nodded to the bloody sheets. "Someone got the real thing."

Her father shrugged. "Sometimes your sister doesn't listen to sound advice. Anyway, she's off the island now and gone to greener pastures, as they say. She's got new toys to play with, but I have to stay here for a while and deal with you. You've been a very naughty girl, young lady."

"This isn't a joke."

"It's not. I've been remiss in bringing you in line, Faith. I made a mistake with your mother, and I'm not making the same one with you." He stopped in front of her. "You know I love you. You look just like her. Hope took after my side of the family in looks and demeanor. But you, oh, you are as sweet and kind as your mother was. I loved her, too. So much I haven't taken another woman since."

Yes, his monogamy was so valiant. "So much that you had her killed."

"I wasn't happy to do that. It was necessary, but I've lived with that guilt and pain ever since." He held up a needle and smiled her way. "Luckily, I don't have to make the same mistake with you, princess."

Faith took a step back. "What is that?"

"This? It's your sister's miracle. When coupled with the right therapy, she believes it can be used to reprogram a mind. I'm going to use it to erase all the bad memories. We're going to our place in Munich for a few months. We'll tell the press you've gone into rehab after that horrible incident at your clinic in Africa." He tsked, shaking his head. "Really, sweetheart. You were drinking so much you didn't recognize you gave those patients the wrong drugs and then tried to hide it. You'll lose you medical license, but it's all right. I'll make sure you have a job helping out your dear old dad."

"Why?" Her hands were shaking. How far away was Ten now? Had they already gotten him on a plane? How would she ever find him? He'd seemed certain Taggart and his crew were alive, but her father seemed awfully good at killing people. How many more people would die today? "Why would you take away my career?"

"You've left me with no option. They're asking too many questions, and Kronberg stock would take a hit if it was known they'd supplied those vaccines that made people sick. It's the media's fault. They make a big deal out of everything. They can't see the point of true innovation."

"Apparently it's drugging your child so she turns into some kind of lobotomized automaton."

"Now that's not at all true," her father corrected. "I love you the way you are, Faith. But you've seen too much. You'll be in therapy until the memories are wiped cleaned, and then you'll be on the drug for the rest of your life. Can't have those memories resurfacing, can we? No torture, princess. I promise. According to your sister, we can wipe your memories out and you'll get to start over. How many people get that kind of chance?"

He was insane. Completely insane. Or completely amoral. He clearly had no idea that what he was doing was evil. Not that it mattered. He had to be stopped. Her sister had to be stopped.

"So Hope's gone back to Kronberg headquarters like a good little psycho." She backed up again because he was still holding that needle.

"I believe your sister has gotten everything out of Kronberg that she can. After how close that Agency fucker came to outing us, they declined to fund her further experiments, but it's all right. I have plenty of money stashed all over the world and we'd planned for this. She'll join us in Munich when everything cools down. I need her to help retrain you."

"I'm not going to let you do this to me."

"Oh, princess, you don't have a choice." He started toward her but that was when she heard the explosion.

It was enough to make her father turn around, and she picked up the nearest object she could find—an IV pole—and clocked him with all her strength.

He cursed and the needle slipped from his hand, crashing to the floor.

"Faith, don't make me hurt you."

She tried to get around him, but he'd kept himself in decent shape. He put an arm out, curling it around her waist.

"Not going to happen," he whispered in her ear. "It's time we get out of here. Guards!"

She fought, but her father was quite strong. Within seconds, two guards had joined them and one handed her father a pistol, which he immediately put to her forehead.

"Very fatherly of you." She hated him. All that teenaged angst she'd had over an absentee father melted in comparison to the loathing she had for him now.

All the people he'd killed. All the lives he'd ruined. He'd done it all for money and power.

If he took her memories, she wouldn't have Ten. Even if they never saw each other again, she would have the memory of loving him, of being in his arms.

Her father wanted to take that away from her, too. She couldn't let him. She couldn't forget Tennessee.

"What the hell's happening?" Her father pushed her toward the stairs.

One of his hired guards got in front of her while the other brought up their rear.

"Apparently the Chinese didn't manage to take out Taggart," the guard in front explained. "I told you we should have handled it ourselves. Actually, I believe I told you we should have left the minute we figured out who the hell we killed the other night. Ian Taggart wasn't going to leave his brother behind, and he won't give a damn that his brother was shooting at us."

"I'm not going to let some bit of cannon fodder ex-soldier scare me off," her father said.

"He won't stop," the guard in the back explained as they moved up the stairs. "That's what the rumors are. They say once Taggart wants to kill you, he won't stop until the job's done. I didn't fucking know it was his brother. I didn't know."

Apparently, the guards were spooked about Ten's friend. She would use that to her favor if she could. "I don't think he's going to care. You should probably run. I'll tell him it was all my father's fault."

Her father forced her to move. "They won't run, Faith. I pay them too well and they both know what I would do to their families if they did. Now get up those stairs. We're going to make it to the car and get the hell out of here. Stan, be sure the plane is ready. Have the pilot start her up. It's time to leave."

She blinked as they walked out into the daylight. Up ahead, she could see the main house was on fire.

She wished she'd been able to tell Ian Taggart to go after Ten. Once MSS got into the air, there would be no way to save him until they figured out where he was being held in China. One of the wounds she'd found on his body was from where her sister had pulled his tracking device. If they'd gotten Ten off the island, he would disappear.

"I'll kill Taggart myself," her father swore. "How dare he. I'll ruin that man. I want a full work-up on him and his family and everyone who works for him. By the time I'm done, he's going to be ground into dirt along with everyone he cares about."

Faith dragged her heels as they made it to the lawn. She couldn't get into that car. If she did, her father would take everything from her. She wouldn't remember who she was. She would be his puppet and his pawn.

Stan got on his phone and asked about the plane. After a second he turned back, completely ashen. "They blew up the plane, sir."

Her father's arm tightened around her. "Looks like you might be the only card I have left, missy. Let's see if Taggart minds killing women."

He put the gun right to her head.

"Stop!"

She looked up and Ten was walking across the yard, his hands held up.

"Don't hurt her."

All those guns were suddenly trained on him.

"I won't if you tell Taggart to call off his dogs," her father growled.

"As soon as I can find him." Ten met her eyes. "Are you all right, Faith?"

She nodded. "But you have to go. He'll kill you."

"Not if he wants me to talk to Tag. He was right behind me. He'll be here in a minute and I'll talk him down. I'm the only one who can do it," Ten promised.

"How the hell did you get away from the Chinese?" Her father sounded flustered, his usual authority fleeing as they were inundated with the sounds of gunfire.

"You have your friends and I have mine," Ten stated enigmatically. "All that matters is the Chinese agents are all dead and MSS is going to have some recruiting to do. Why don't you let Faith go? I know you don't want to hurt her. I'll take her place."

"No," Faith insisted even as her father tightened his grip. She couldn't breathe.

Her father wasn't backing down. "I will hurt her, Smith. I'll kill her. I'll do it before I let you have her so you better get Taggart out here or I'll have my men kill you and we'll make our own way."

"I'm here." Ian Taggart came out of the shadows, his big body moving through the smoke. He carried a long rifle, the kind she'd seen soldiers use, and he didn't lower it as he moved in.

"Put the gun down, Taggart," her father commanded. "Or I'll kill my daughter."

"The way you killed my brother? Do you honestly think I would negotiate with you? I just needed time to get my team in place." Taggart touched his ear. "Erin, Nick, you have a go."

She heard the sound, pings through the air, and then she felt her father's body shudder, felt the warm spray of blood touch her skin. The two men guarding her father went down as well and Faith was left, the only survivor.

Ten had her in his arms before she could really look around. "I'm so sorry. I couldn't risk him getting away with you. I'm sorry we had to kill him."

She wrapped her arms around him, burying her face against his neck. "You saved me. I would have done the same to save you."

"You'll never have to. I promise."

She looked back at the wreckage of the house she'd once loved and then clung to him again. Nothing would ever be the same, but she wasn't alone.

CHAPTER TWENTY-ONE

Dallas, TX
Six Weeks Later

Ten stared at the computer screen, the headlines flashing like a big neon sign. Contacting his old bosses at the Agency and turning over the evidence that Karriker was a double agent had been simple. The man had disappeared a few hours later, but the business with the senator had taken a few weeks to play out. This morning, the *New York Times* had broken the story of the recently deceased Senator Hank McDonald and how he colluded with five named corporations to profit off wars around the globe. It came complete with pretty pictures of CEOs and board members being hauled out of their offices by the police.

Including the entire board of directors of Kronberg Pharmaceuticals. Unfortunately, Hope McDonald wasn't among them. She'd disappeared off the face of the earth, and that didn't sit well with Ten. Until he found Faith's sister, he wasn't sure she was safe. He kept a watchful eye on his wife. He had to because two weeks into her new life she was chafing and needed something to do. Luckily, Karina Mills ran a community outreach in one of Dallas's neediest neighborhoods. She provided counseling and services, and now she and Faith were planning a free clinic.

The world needed saving and his fiancée was determined to do her part.

A babbling sound caught his attention and he found himself smiling.

Ten was getting used to having babies invade his space. He glanced up and Adam Miles was holding his toddler's hand as he passed out the morning's agenda.

"Sorry. He wanted to make the rounds with me. He's been clingy lately. I think he's wondering where Theo went, you know."

Theo Taggart had left a massive hole in McKay-Taggart. Every single person felt his loss, even the kiddos. "It's not a problem. You're welcome here, buddy."

He didn't flinch when the toddler crawled up into his lap. Tristan Dean-Miles was a sweet kid with a penchant for climbing things he shouldn't. At least once a week, the women who ran the daycare had to call one of the taller men in to rescue Tristan.

"Thanks. I kind of thought you didn't like kids," Adam said.

"I'm getting used to them. Faith wants a couple." He put a hand on the toddler's head and the kid leaned into him. "I think I do, too. And hey, I'm sure I'll be an uncle soon the way my sister and Jesse go at it. Could you make an announcement at the meeting this morning to lock the doors? I didn't need to see that."

Adam chuckled. "I'll put it on the agenda. Tag wants to see you before the meeting. He's waiting in the front conference room."

Ten stood, picking up Tristan as he did. He looked down at the child in his arms. Yesterday, he'd walked in and found Case sitting in the middle of the nursery, letting every kid in the room use him as a jungle gym. Something about the little ones calmed Case, made it easier for him to move through the day without his brother.

He wished Erin would sit with the babies. She came to work and then went back home to the house she'd shared briefly with Theo. She claimed she needed to prep it for sale because she didn't need or want the space, but as far as he could tell, she hadn't packed a thing. She hadn't changed a thing. Theo's clothes were still in the closet, his coffee mug exactly where he'd left it. Erin was living in a shrine to her lost love.

Ten passed Tristan back to his father. "He's a good kid. Oh, he's going to get beat up for that name you gave him, but he's a good boy."

Adam's eyes rolled as Ten passed him. "Hey, it's a McKay-Taggart thing. We pick weird names. Carys? Yeah, like she's going to be able to teach people how to spell that. How about Cooper? The kid sounds like he walked out of a Western. I won't even go into Kala. Still trying to figure that one out."

Ten stepped out into the hallway. How had Adam—who claimed to be the smartest man in the building—not figured that one out? "Kick A Little Ass. What the hell else would Tag name his kid?"

Adam's jaw dropped. "Holy shit. You're right."

Ten turned toward the main conference room, leaving Adam behind. Tag was standing in the lobby. Up ahead, Ten could see someone was sitting in the conference room. It looked like a man. Ten would guess an older man, and he was with a younger guy. Likely his son. Were they new clients?

"Hey, Adam said you wanted to see me. Do you have any news?"

Tag sighed. Since they'd come back empty-handed from the island, Tag had tossed aside all other cases to follow leads on Theo's body. "We finally got a trace on his locator signal."

"I thought they threw it in the trash the way they did mine." He still had the scar from it.

"We got hits on both Des and Theo's signals before we lost them. It was a lucky thing. Hutch was actually playing around on the computer when we took a boat from one island to another."

"They dumped the bodies in the ocean."

Tag nodded. "I can send divers down, but the likelihood that we'll find anything is very low. There are currents in that part of the sea that flow out to the Atlantic."

"I'm so sorry." It was an ache in his gut that they couldn't even bury Theo. They'd held a funeral, but the casket had been empty. The London team had been forced to do the same for Des. "I swear the minute I find Hope, I'll let you know. She can at least tell us what happened after we retreated."

"Good. Are you sure you want to do this?" Tag asked. "It might be better for you to concentrate on the wedding and settling in."

"We're not really settling. Eventually Faith is going to want to go back to Africa. Right now, I want to ensure her safety by finding her sister. I'm not sure anyone is safe as long as she's out there doing whatever the hell it is she does." He was going to find her. He was going to question her. He would dig up every nasty secret Hope McDonald was hiding and bring it into the light.

"Despite the loss of Kronberg's funding, I think she's likely still working. Adam estimated she got away with roughly fifty million of her family's fortunes before the feds froze her father's accounts. She's a smart cookie. Completely insane, but smart. I have questions I want to ask her about Theo's body. I have no doubt she was there when they dumped him. I have to make sure. Find her, Ten."

"I will." It was the only gift he could give his brothers now.

"Ah, there she is." Tag managed a smile as the lobby door opened.

Ten managed a brilliant smile because his whole world was walking in. Faith waved to Grace and then made a beeline for him, her face practically glowing. She was wearing a nice hunk of diamond on her left ring finger, a promise he meant to keep.

Damn, but love felt good. He opened his arms and she walked right into them. He was marrying her in a few weeks. They would keep it simple, but he wanted his friends and family there.

Her face tilted up. "Hello."

This was the best part of his day. Any time he got to kiss her. He brushed his lips over hers. "Hello, darlin'."

"I'm going to vomit," Tag said under his breath, but his lips were still curled up. "All right, Tennessee Smith. Your fiancée wanted me to put together a present for you. Chelsea actually did all the legwork and it was quite impressive. I have to hand it to my sister-in-law. I didn't think she'd be able to do it with the little information she had, but it turns out she's better than I thought."

"What are you talking about?"

Tag glanced toward the conference room. "I'm talking about the fact that all Chelsea had to go on was a date and a place. Your birthdate and the café you were left at. When she couldn't find anyone in that particular town who could possibly have been your birth mother, she widened her search. She went to a small town twenty miles away where one Carrie Holmes lived. It had been a closely guarded secret that she was pregnant. Only her two closest friends knew, and Carrie claimed to have given up the baby for adoption but no records were found. She had a very strict religious upbringing. I think she was trying to hide the pregnancy from her parents. She was in high school at the time."

"What did you do?" He looked back at the conference room.

Faith tugged his hand into hers. "Ten, your birthmother is gone. She died of a drug overdose years ago, but Chelsea tracked down her high school boyfriend. She apparently dumped him after she found out she was pregnant. He never knew. Ten, that man in the conference room is your dad. His name is Bill Hartford and he owns a gaming store that specializes in puzzles and strategy games. I thought that was very telling. He has one son by his former wife. You have a brother. They're both eager to meet you."

Ten stared as the man stood and turned. Bill Hartford looked startled at first and Ten knew why. It was why he was startled, too. It was like looking into a mirror. He was looking at a slightly older version of himself.

Faith squeezed his hand. "He says he would have moved heaven and earth to find you if he'd known. He's scared you'll hate him, but he's here because he wants you to know that you were wanted. You were loved."

Tennessee Smith proved he'd been wrong about one thing. He could cry.

He tangled his fingers in hers and walked in to meet his past. He already had his future. She was right there in his hands.

* * * *

Kai Ferguson sat down, his head still reeling. "What the hell is going on in the conference room? I swear to god I think I saw Ten crying." His gut took a nosedive. "Please tell me we haven't lost someone else."

He wasn't sure how the team would recover from losing Theo. He'd been giving Erin and Case space, but he was at that point that he would have to talk to Tag because they needed sessions. They needed a place to talk, and he was the resident therapist.

Alex McKay sat behind his neatly appointed desk. "Nothing of the kind. It's a little family reunion Ten's fiancée organized. I'm glad to hear it's going well. Now, I'm sure you're wondering why I called you in."

"Especially since I'm not technically an employee." He owned his own place. Yes, it was the building next to Sanctum and he was very slowly paying it off, but it was his. He ran a treatment center specializing in soldiers returning from war and others suffering from PTSD. Big Tag had funded him for the first year, but he was planning on paying that back, too. Now he accepted funding from military charities and private individuals.

"Yes, I know, which is why I really need you to consider doing us a favor," Alex allowed.

Favors in the McKay-Taggart world often meant getting shot at. He was a sadist, not a masochist. A happy, happy sadist who needed to stop thinking about his assistant and her far too juicy ass. It just needed a spanking so very badly. Kori Williamson was the most tempting sub he'd ever met and the only one he couldn't have. Because she was afraid of him.

"What do you need?"

Alex slid a thick folder across the table. "The FBI came to us yesterday asking for help. Specifically, they asked for you."

He opened the file and grimaced. Dead girls. Shit. He really hated the bloody stuff. Fun, consensual torture was one thing. These girls hadn't asked for what was done to them. He ran through the police files. Five women. All Caucasian. All brunettes with blue eyes. All healthy girls. They had been curvy women. "They think they have a serial."

Serial killers tended to prefer one type of victim above all. This man obviously had a type.

"Yes," Alex replied. "The problem is the locations of the killings. They've connected five murders over the past three years. Potentially there's more, but the killer moves around a lot. We also believe he's killed women in Eastern Europe and Australia. There are victims in both places who fit the profile and timeline."

Kai shut the folder. "So he's some sort of businessman or he's in the travel industry. Alex, this is obviously an important case. Why aren't you handing it to Eve? She's the profiler. I can give you my assessment, but she's the expert in this area."

"She's already working on a profile," Alex stated. "We don't need you to profile the suspects."

"Suspects? The feds have suspects? Am I interviewing them? Again, I think Eve's your expert."

Alex leaned back. "Did you know that Serena sold the film rights to Soldiers and Doms?"

Kai bit back a laugh. Film rights? He'd read the first of those books. They were pretty hardcore. "That should be interesting."

"Apparently BDSM is the new big thing. After that *Fifty* movie, every studio in Hollywood wants a shot. They're filming *Love After Death* right here in Dallas."

Kai felt his eyes widen. He appreciated a good train wreck as much as anyone else. "Are you serious? Isn't that the one where the big bad Dom's dead spy wife returns and he has to deal with her Italian mafia family? Someone really should have told Serena to cover that shit up better than she did."

Alex laughed, the sound booming through the office. It was good to hear it again. The office had been too quiet lately. "Ian's never read it and Charlotte vowed vengeance on anyone who told him. I'm so buying a ticket to that film. I can't wait to see the moment when Ian realizes millions of women are madly in love with a character based on him. It's going to be beautiful."

"I'll be right beside you." He wouldn't miss that show for the world. "But I don't see how this plays into the case." And then he did. It fell into his head, a neat answer to the problems. "Film crew. The feds think the killer is a member of a film crew. Lots of movie companies film in Eastern Europe and Australia these days."

"Exactly," Alex agreed. "All of the murders occurred during major motion picture filming. One of the girls was killed in Canada near a television show's set."

He knew more about the film industry than he wanted to. Not that he would ever admit it or why he knew. He tried to keep that part of his life very secret.

Of course, McKay-Taggart was good at unburying secrets. "Why me? Cut the BS, Alex. Let's get down to what you really want."

"Jared Johns is playing the lead in *Love After Death* and we have reason to believe either he or someone in his entourage is the killer. The murders have occurred during times when Johns was filming. He always travels with the same group of guys. He has since he got his first major TV role. When he jumped to film, he took those guys with

348

him. He's looking for a mentor, someone who will train him on how to be a Dom for the film. Ian's already agreed to let him into Sanctum as part of the FBI investigation. I think putting you as his mentor would be perfect."

Kai shook his head. He could barely get the words out because horror swamped his every sense. "No. I don't think that would work at all."

"He's asked for you," Alex replied. "Do you really want to tell your brother you won't help him out?"

His brother. His international superstar, didn't have a brain in his gorgeous head brother.

Watch out for your brother, Kai. He needs you in his life.

His mother's dying wish. He'd promised her and then failed so very badly.

"I suppose I could offer my own services." Alex reached for the file.

Fuck. His brother was the idiot who would hire a damn serial killer to party with him. "My brother isn't a serial killer. It's not him, but I'll do it."

He'd run from his family for as long as he could. Like it or not, he had a job to do.

"As long as I don't have to watch any of his films." Saving his brother was one thing.

"Not at all," Alex replied with a grin.

After all, there was only so much a man would do for his family.

Kai, Kori, and the entire McKay-Taggart team will return in From Sanctum with Love. As for Theo...

An island off the coast of Argentina

Theo. His name was Theo. Sometimes, it was all he could remember.

He blinked at the bright lights. So white. Everything in his room was white, from the bed to the walls and ceiling, to the cuffs that held his arms and wrists down. Everything was a stark, brutal absence of color.

"Hey, how are you doing today?" The blonde walked in. He

remembered her. Yes, it was impossible to forget the woman who tortured him daily with a cocktail of drugs that made his head feel like it weighed fifty pounds, and then put him through some kind of weird therapy. He was forced to watch films. Nothing that made sense. Pictures and images and accompanying sounds, but somehow he knew he was losing himself to the combination of drugs and those films. Something was happening in his brain. A rewiring was occurring.

"You are looking so much better." She smiled.

He was pretty sure she thought she was being sexy, but he couldn't help but see the shark behind those perfectly made up lips.

A vision of a redhead floated across his brain. She turned her head and she wasn't wearing a stitch of makeup, but she was the most beautiful thing he'd ever seen. Her lips curved up. She was wearing a bikini, the sunshine on her face. She brushed back her hair and reached for him.

"Your vitals are all back to normal. You've fully recovered. I wouldn't have thought it would happen so quickly. After all, I did perform open-heart surgery on you in pretty horrible conditions. I'm kind of a rock star."

He'd woken up on a plane, his body horrifically scarred. He'd been sure he would die, and all he'd been able to think about was that red-haired girl.

He wished he could remember her name.

The doctor frowned at him. "Are you going to give me trouble today? You nearly killed the guard yesterday. I had to reset his leg and bring in another man. I adore you, but if you try that again, you'll have to be punished."

His eyes drifted over to the door. There were two guards there, both heavily armed, and despite what she said, he was still weak. He should have been able to take that guard easily, but it had been a fight.

"Don't worry about it. You're still my perfect guy, and once the training really kicks in, you'll know it. Once you give over, everything will be easier."

She measured out the dose and there was nothing he could do. He'd fought the few times he'd been out of the bindings, and the guards had started carrying dart guns filled with tranquilizers.

You are a Taggart and you will survive this.

There were times when he heard voices in his head. Strong, male voices that urged him to survive. They often reminded him that he was a Taggart. Theo Taggart. He tried to hold on as the drugs began to course through his veins.

After a few moments, all the voices drifted away until all he could hear was her. The blonde shark he'd been caught by.

She talked, telling him things that made no sense.

He closed his eyes and dreamed of a red-haired beauty.

AUTHOR'S NOTE

I'm often asked by generous readers how they can help get the word out about a book they enjoyed. There are so many ways to help an author you like. Leave a review. If your e-reader allows you to lend a book to a friend, please share it. Go to Goodreads and connect with others. Recommend the books you love because stories are meant to be shared. Thank you so much for reading this book and for supporting all the authors you love!

Sign up for Lexi Blake's newsletter
and be entered to win a $25 gift certificate
to the bookseller of your choice.

Join us for news, fun, and exclusive content
including free short stories.

There's a new contest every month!

Go to www.LexiBlake.net to subscribe.

*In the tradition of Masters and Mercenaries comes
the next great brotherhood...*

SCANDAL NEVER SLEEPS

The Perfect Gentlemen, Book 1
By Shayla Black and Lexi Blake
Coming August 18, 2015

They are the Perfect Gentlemen of Creighton Academy:
privileged, wealthy, powerful friends with a wild side. But a deadly
scandal is about to tear down their seemingly ideal lives...

Maddox Crawford's sudden death sends Gabriel Bond reeling.
Not only is he burying his best friend, he's cleaning up Mad's
messes, including his troubled company. Grieving and restless, Gabe
escapes his worries in the arms of a beautiful stranger. But his mind-
blowing one-night stand is about to come back to haunt him...

Mad groomed Everly Parker to be a rising star in the executive
world. Now that he's gone, she's sure her job will be the next thing
she mourns, especially after she ends up accidentally sleeping with
her new boss. If only their night together hadn't been so incendiary—
or Gabe like a fantasy come true...

As Gabe and Everly struggle to control the heated tension
between them, they discover evidence that Mad's death was no
accident. Now they must bank their smoldering passions to hunt
down a murderer—because Mad had secrets that someone was
willing to kill for, and Gabe or Everly could be the next target...

* * * *

"I want to see you."
Even in the low light, he noticed her breath hitch. "You want me
to turn on the lights?"
"That's not what I meant." He never took his burning gaze from
her. "I want to see you naked. Take off your dress. Show me your

breasts."

"I'll close the curtains." She started to turn to the windows.

He caught her elbow, gently restraining her. "Don't. We're high up. No one can see in. Take off your dress. Let me see you in the moonlight."

Her gaze tangled with his, and he could see a hint of her trepidation. A gentleman might have backed down. But he knew what he wanted. She must want him too or she wouldn't have agreed to spend the night with him. He wasn't giving Eve the easy way out.

Finally, she turned her back to him and lifted her arms, struggling to reach the metal tab. "There's a zipper down the back."

He moved closer. "Let me."

Gabe ran his hands up her spine before finding the zipper. She lifted her curls out of his way, exposing the graceful column of her neck. Her skin looked pale, almost incandescent in the low light. He couldn't help himself. He leaned over and kissed her nape, feeling her shiver under his touch.

Slowly, he eased the zipper down, his fingertips brushing her spine. Once he passed her neck, she let her hair fall free, the strawberry-blond mass tumbling well past her shoulders, gliding over her skin. Her tresses were soft, too. Not severely flat-ironed. Different, like the woman herself. Fuck, he could lose himself in Eve.

She shrugged, allowing the straps of her dress to fall past her shoulders and drop to her waist.

Her bra looked plain and white. He was used to delicate garments meant to entice a man, so he had no idea why the site of her utilitarian bra made his cock jerk. She hadn't been seeking a man this evening, much less intending to seduce a lover. When she'd dressed, it had been for comfort. But now, she was here with him, slowly peeling away her clothes.

With practiced ease, he unhooked her bra with a twist of his hand and slid his fingers under the straps to strip them off. He closed his eyes and allowed his hands to roam across the wealth of smooth skin he'd just exposed. He drew her back against his chest and grazed his way up her abdomen until he found her breasts. Full and real, he loved the weight of them in his palms. He drew his thumbs over the nubs of her nipples and Eve rewarded him with a long intake of breath.

"That feels so good." As she leaned back against him for support, she shuddered and thrust her breasts up like twin offerings.

He would absolutely take everything she had to give.

Gabe filled his hands with her flesh, cupping and rubbing and discovering every inch of her breasts before he grew impatient to have her totally bare and pushed the dress over the curve of her hips. It pooled on the floor at her feet.

Her underwear matched her bra. If she were his, he would buy her La Perla. He would dress her like a goddess in silk and lace and know that she wore the most come-hither lingerie for his eyes only. She could wear her ladylike dresses and cover herself with all appropriate modesty if she wanted—but only until they were alone.

As he stripped off her panties, a wild possessiveness blazed through his system. Gabe turned her to face him, well aware that he needed to slow down but utterly incapable of doing so. He took in the sight of her breasts. They looked every bit as perfect as they'd felt.

"You're beautiful."

"I don't feel that way." She tilted her face up to his, drinking him in with her stare. There was nothing coy about her expression. She looked at him with naked yearning. "Not most of the time. But you make me feel sexy."

"You are. I want to be very clear about how beautiful I think you are." He kissed her again, lifting her up and out of her dress, heading back to the bedroom while his mouth ate hungrily at hers.

She didn't fight him, didn't fidget to make him set her back on the ground. She simply wrapped her arms around his neck and let him carry her. Her fingers sank into his hair and she held tight while her tongue danced against his.

Luckily, he knew Plaza suites like the back of his hand. He maneuvered her toward the bed, his cock throbbing insistently.

He wouldn't last long. God, he couldn't believe he was even thinking that. Usually, he could go for hours, but Gabe knew the minute he got inside Eve, he was going to lose control. He needed to make it good for her now because he'd barely touched her and already he wanted to throw her against the wall and shove his way inside her.

As he approached the mattress, he stopped and eased her onto the luxurious comforter. She lay back on the elegant duvet, her hair fanned out and her legs spread. Wanton and yet so innocent. He pulled at his shirt, hearing a button or two pop off, but at the moment he didn't give a shit. The need to be skin to skin with her drove him to haste. He unbuckled his belt and shoved his pants down.

"Foreplay." Freaking hell. He was so ready to go, he'd forgotten about that. Women liked foreplay. It tended to be necessary for them.

She shook her head. "The kissing was foreplay. We're totally good."

Shit. He had to slow down. He wasn't exactly a small guy. She needed to be ready to take all of him.

Gabe took a deep breath. "Need you aroused. It's okay. Just give me a minute."

"Gabriel, I am as aroused as I have ever been in my life. I'm a little worried about what kind of stain I'm going to leave for the staff on this duvet. So really, can we get this train moving?"

He gripped her ankles and slid her down the bed, spreading her legs wider in the process. His cock twitched when he saw that she was right. Her pussy was wet. Juicy. He could see its slick gloss from above, even in the shadows. A little kissing, some groping, and she was ready to go. He'd never had a woman respond to him so readily. "Tell me again."

"I'm ready," she vowed. "I am really ready."

"No, tell me this isn't normal for you," he corrected. It was stupid. She was right there, able and willing to give him the pleasure he sought—but he craved more. He needed to know that tonight was special for her. "Tell me you want me and not just sex."

She gave him a sheepish smile. "This isn't at all normal. I guess I've gone a little crazy tonight, but I don't do one-night stands. I can count the men I've had sex with on one hand and I wouldn't need all my fingers. And I've never, never wanted anyone as much as I want you right now. Gabriel, I don't need foreplay, just you."

ADDICT
Hunter: A Thieves Novel, Book 2
By Lexi Blake
Coming September 22, 2015

When Kelsey Owens returns home to Dallas, she is a changed woman. After months of training with Marcus Vorenus, she has more control over her abilities. She's ready to start her new job, even if it means dealing with the King of All Vampire and his partner, Devinshea Quinn. Her first assignment, however, will force her to face her past. Grayson Sloane is in trouble and she has to find him.

With the help of Gray's brother, a full empath demon, Kelsey tracks her one-time lover down. Before she knows it, she's pulled into Gray's undercover operation in a demon sex club and sitting across from a Duke of Hell. Abbas Hiberna plans to use her city to test his new drug, Brimstone. It doesn't just give supernatural creatures a high. It also leaves them vulnerable to demonic persuasion.

When the king's own men begin to turn against him, even the royal family is in danger. Keeping them safe will put Kelsey in the duke's crosshairs and test her fledgling relationship with Marcus. With her new life crumbling around her, a dark secret about her former lover is revealed and Kelsey will have to choose between saving Gray Sloane and the revenge she's waited a lifetime for.

* * * *

I turned and there he was. He was sitting on a couch, his big body lounging negligently. He was wearing tight black jeans and a dark shirt he'd left open as though he'd walked out of the bedroom without bothering to button his shirt. It left his perfectly cut chest on full, mouth-watering display. The tattoo that covered the left half of his torso looked sexy as hell in the low glow of the room, and I wondered if it still vibrated on his body after I left. His face was a tribute to masculine perfection. Marcus was the perfect European male, all fine lines and aesthetic grace. Gray was an all-American hunk of masculinity. He screamed dominant male and for good reason. He was and made no apologies for it. He was the kinkiest man I'd ever met. He preferred to tie up his sexual partners and when I was that partner, I'd been happy to do it.

I was thinking about doing it right now.

His deep blue eyes glanced lazily around the room. He had a female at his feet, her head resting on his lap. He didn't seem terribly interested in her. He was talking to another man, whose face I couldn't see. He was smaller than Gray with almost white hair. Gray stopped midsentence when his eyes caught sight of me.

"You do seem able to catch my little brother's attention, don't you?" Matt said, satisfaction oozing from his pores.

Gray sat up, and I noticed that his hair was longer than it had been when we were engaged. He used to wear it in a strict, military-style cut. It was a little shaggy now, reaching to the tops of his ears. It was thick and wavy. I'd always wanted to run my fingers through it. I flushed under his gaze, unsure if it was just the outfit I was wearing or complete and abject shame that I had a man who cared about me and I couldn't help but think about someone else.

He was the ultimate bad boy. Grayson Sloane was a half demon who lied to me, used me, and had potentially tried to trick me into going to Hell with him. And I was shaking at the thought of his hands on me. I was also resolute. No matter how much I was attracted to the man, I was going to resist because I knew the score.

Marcus was good, and Gray was bad.

Gray was also observant. He stood up abruptly, his face going cold. He stalked across the room just as another big man moved to intercept me. He was shorter than Gray, though he still towered over me. He didn't have great control over his form. His eyes gave him away. They flashed between red and brown.

"New girl, huh?" the demon said. His shirt was off and he had a girl on a leash trailing behind him. She didn't look terribly upset to be on a leash. I wondered how much she was getting paid. I hoped it was a lot.

"This one is for my brother." Matt attempted to dismiss him with an imperious wave of his hand.

"Oh, it's you," the man said, bowing at the waist. "I didn't recognize you, My Lord. His Lordship has enough pretty brunettes, don't you think? This one looks practically angelic. That's really not his style."

"I'll decide what my style is, Kall," Gray snarled at the smaller demon. "Go away and don't look at her again or we'll have a problem. Do you understand?"

Kall bowed from his waist again, his head down as he murmured, "Yes, My Lord."

Kall slunk away, pulling his girl behind him. Gray turned to Matt, his face tight. "Explain yourself, brother. How dare you bring her here."

Matt looked perfectly innocent. "I thought you would be thrilled, brother. This is the woman who caused you such distress, is it not? Here she is. I didn't even have to threaten her. The moment she heard you were in trouble, she was scrambling to get here to you. There's no doubt she still cares for you. You know I can't stand to see lovers kept apart. I know the feeling too well myself."

"I'm not in trouble." Gray finally turned my way, his eyes starting past my knees and working their way up. I felt his gaze like a caress along my flesh.

The woman who had previously had her head in Gray's lap crawled across the room and attached herself to his leg.

"Don't leave, master," she begged prettily.

Gray looked down like he'd already forgotten she existed and wasn't pleased to be reminded. "Go. Now."

He pointed to the elevators and she crawled off, her head hung low.

It was a disgusting display, and I wondered if that wouldn't have been me had I stayed with him. "Well, if you're not in trouble, then I'll feel free to get on with my life, Sloane. Matt, where are my clothes?"

The demon with the upper-crust British accent waved his hand. "Probably in the incinerator by now."

"What?"

He gave a negligent half shrug. "Well, they didn't suit you, dear. It looks like some old man picked them out, perhaps trying to de-tart his 'much too young for him' girlfriend."

Matt apparently really didn't like my current lover. That was no

360

reason for him to leave me without pants. "You asshole. How am I supposed to get home in this?"

"That's your problem, dear. I've done my level best to help. You can't expect me to solve all of your problems." Matt's mouth turned up in a slow smile. "And now my date for the evening is here."

A thin young man with curly blonde hair and blue eyes was walking toward us. He kept his eyes downcast and sank to his knees when he reached us. "My Lord, how may I serve you this evening?"

Matt looked down on the young man, his lips thinning as he reached out to touch his hair. "I'll think of something, Tristan. And tell the colorist your hair should be a bit lighter to get it just right."

Tristan didn't look up, merely kept this head down. "Of course."

"Come along, now. I know public sex is all the rage here, but I prefer a bit of discretion. I'm going to take my sweet little puppy somewhere private to play our games." His face turned serious as he regarded Gray. "I'm making do tonight, brother, as I have every night for the last ten bloody years. The object of your affection is in your grasp. I suggest you don't let her go."

With that I was left alone with the man who had lied to me. I was left alone with the first man I ever loved. With the man I couldn't get out of my head.

"You're supposed to be in Italy." Gray made it sound a little like an accusation.

"I just got back yesterday." I really wished I had more clothes on. I noticed that the man Gray had been talking to was watching us now.

"So it only took you twenty-four hours to get into serious trouble," Gray complained.

It wasn't how I expected the reunion to go. I was the injured party. I was the one who had come to save him even though he'd treated me like crap. The least I expected was a little gratitude. "I'm on a case."

"That's your excuse for everything, sweetheart," Gray said flatly.

Tears welled in my eyes and I fucking hated that. Only Gray ever made me lose control. That mask was coming in handy. I should have been happy. He was making it easy on me. I could go home to Marcus and cuddle up and know that I was in the right place with the right man. The time I spent with Gray had been a huge mistake.

"Then it can be my excuse for leaving. I can see you have everything under control here, Sloane. I won't bother you again."

His hand wrapped around my upper arm and drew me close to his body. Every inch of my skin came to life the second he touched me. "You bother me every second of every day, Kelsey mine, and it's far too late for you to leave." He pulled me into the confines of his muscular arms. His mouth went straight to my ear and he whispered. "I'm undercover, sweetheart, and now you are, too. You know how to play this role. Keep your mouth closed and look submissive. Please don't fight me on this. I'm trying to keep you safe. You have no idea what you've gotten into. Play along with me and I'll explain everything in a while."

I nodded. I knew exactly what he wanted. I was capable of keeping my mouth shut when the occasion called for it. I'd been in the business long enough to know that listening was way more important than talking.

"You're a sight for sore eyes, gorgeous." His hands slid along the curve of my hip. "I missed you, Kelsey mine."

FROM SANCTUM WITH LOVE
Master and Mercenaries Book 10
By Lexi Blake

Psychologist Kai Ferguson has had his eye on Kori Williamson for a long time. His assistant is everything he's ever wanted in a partner—smart, caring, witty, and a bit of a masochist. More than a little, actually, but that's the problem. Kori won't admit her own desires. She's afraid of him and what he has to offer. Luckily for her, helping patients face their fears is one of his specialties.

Kori knows she wants Kai. Her boss is the most amazing man she's ever met. She's also smart enough to stay away from him. Having been down this road before, she knows it only leads to heartache. She's just found a place where she can belong. Another failed relationship is the last thing she needs. It's better to guard her heart and let Kai think she's frightened of his dark, dominant nature.

When Kai is recruited for an operation with McKay-Taggart, everything is turned upside down. Kai's brother, international superstar Jared Johns, is in town and Kai must juggle his family issues along with a desperate hunt for a serial killer. The investigation throws Kori and Kai together, and they quickly discover the chemistry between them is undeniable. But even if their newfound love can survive his secrets and her lies, it may not be enough to save them both from a killer's twisted obsession.

ABOUT LEXI BLAKE

Lexi Blake lives in North Texas with her husband, three kids, and the laziest rescue dog in the world. She began writing at a young age, concentrating on plays and journalism. It wasn't until she started writing romance that she found success. She likes to find humor in the strangest places. Lexi believes in happy endings no matter how odd the couple, threesome or foursome may seem. She also writes contemporary Western ménage as Sophie Oak.

Connect with Lexi online:

Facebook: Lexi Blake
Twitter: https://twitter.com/authorlexiblake
Website: www.LexiBlake.net

Sign up for Lexi's free newsletter at www.lexiblake.net.

CPSIA information can be obtained
www.ICGtesting.com
ted in the USA
01n2145231017

9 781937 608439